The Hive Construct

www.transworldbooks.co.uk

ABERDEEN
CITY LIBRARIES

www.aberdeencity.gov.uk/Library
Tel: 08456 080937 or 01506 420526

Cove Library
Tel : 245350

Return to...
or any other Aberdeen City Library

Please return/renew this item by the last date shown
Items may also be renewed by phone or online

2 0 OCT 2014

1 7 FEB 2015

1 4 APR 2015

WITHDRAWN

The Hive Construct

Alexander Maskill

Doubleday

LONDON · TORONTO · SYDNEY · AUCKLAND · JOHANNESBURG

TRANSWORLD PUBLISHERS
61–63 Uxbridge Road, London W5 5SA
A Random House Group Company
www.transworldbooks.co.uk

First published in Great Britain
in 2014 by Doubleday
an imprint of Transworld Publishers

A CIP catalogue record for this book
is available from the British Library.

ISBNs 9780857522214 (hb)
9780857522221 (tpb)

Addresses for Random House Group Ltd companies outside the UK
can be found at: www.randomhouse.co.uk
The Random House Group Ltd Reg. No. 954009

The Random House Group Limited supports the Forest Stewardship Council® (FSC®),
the leading international forest-certification organisation. Our books carrying
the FSC label are printed on FSC®-certified paper. FSC is the only
forest-certification scheme supported by the leading environmental
organisations, including Greenpeace. Our paper procurement
policy can be found at www.randomhouse.co.uk/environment

Typeset in 11/14pt Sabon by
Kestrel Data, Exeter, Devon.
Printed and bound by
CPI Group (UK) Ltd, Croydon, CR0 4YY.
2 4 6 8 10 9 7 5 3 1

To my parents, for their tireless support

Prologue

One of the few visible abnormalities upon a horizon lined with glistening sand, the massive red-brown obelisk could be seen for miles.

Even so, it was only from maybe half a mile away that a traveller would comprehend how large it was, growing larger with each step as if still rising from the desert. Closer still, and what at first appeared just streaks of grey and light brown – perhaps some old stain or sandstorm erosion – revealed itself to be a network of windows, concrete doors and walkways: the first signs of the small human settlement embedded within the colossal concrete tower. This was Waytower Seven. It was an outpost constructed for a purpose: to provide an intermediate step between the harsh, desolate Sahara stretching in front of it and the metropolis that lay in the immense crater behind.

This purpose required that most of the floor space and utility availability was given over to shops, services and hotels. As a result the permanent residential areas were cramped, dingy and worn. Tarou Wakahisa, the tower's head mechanic, preferred to spend his time in the garage, among vehicles that the desert terrain had buffeted and baked. It was dark and the concrete walls lined with tools and spare parts kept the heat out admirably. Tarou would read or play his old guitar as his computer ran diagnostics of the vehicles' engines and propulsion systems. He'd relax in climate-controlled peace and quiet, occasionally getting up to fix something or gaze out into the desert looking for the flow of approaching customers, which the outbreak of the virus and the impending quarantine in the city below had reduced to a trickle.

As the sun began to sink over the horizon, a rarer sight appeared.

Tarou put down his book and grabbed his binoculars. He stood up from his seat and walked over slowly to the open garage door. A heads-up display fed information back from the binoculars into his field of vision. Three hundred yards away, a person was emerging from behind a massive sand dune, trudging slowly but surely, straight towards him.

Save for a large reflective visor, the figure was entirely hidden beneath a heavy black shawl. The shapeless mass gave away the probable presence of the same kind of climate-proof equipment they sold in the Waytower's stores – reserves of water, a personal cooling system and a steady influx of food. It also made it impossible to tell whether the incomer was armed. The Waytower was several hours' walk from the nearest settlement, compared to a half-hour drive. This was someone determined to fly under the radar. It was not a sign of good things to come.

Tarou lowered his binoculars and ran over to his work-desk. In a heavy drawer underneath a rack of different-sized SVL converters lay a gleaming metal box, never opened before. Tarou lifted it out, snapped a seal on one side and pulled the lid open before reaching inside. He scooped up the gun, loaded it with a fresh cartridge and jammed it into the waist of his trousers, then moved over to the garage door, pressed his back to the frame and poked his head out. The figure was closer now, maybe a hundred, a hundred and fifty yards away. Whoever it was would be weary, Tarou decided, and wouldn't know he was armed. They wouldn't put up much of a fight. These thoughts almost comforted him. His hands shook slightly as he removed the pistol from his waistband and wrapped his fingers around its handle. It was heavier than he had expected.

The figure was getting closer. He could feel its gaze upon him. Something shifted under the shawl.

His portable terminal let out a shrill beeping sound. Someone was calling him.

Not taking his eyes off the stranger, he clicked the answer button with his thumb.

A voice he hadn't heard in a long time sputtered out of the speaker.

'Tarou, you dick, it's me.'

It took him a moment to place the voice and further time to process the surprise. He let out a sigh of relief. 'Damn, Zala, is that really you? I was worried there. I was thinking raiders, or a crash. Something like that.'

'I can see that. That was a pistol in your waistband, right?'

'Ugh,' Tarou grunted. She'd noticed the gun. So much for the element of surprise.

'I'll be there in a minute. Make sure the coast is clear, and maybe put that thing away.'

The call ended. Tarou slid down the wall and sat there, waiting for his heartbeat to slow down. He felt a sense of relief as he placed the pistol on the ground. Only now that he didn't have to use it did he realize how little he wanted to.

And Tarou Wakahisa watched as, a few minutes later, someone he'd never expected to see again entered through the door of the garage. Zala Ulora, after all, was an exile from the city below.

The cloaked figure plucked at the clips holding cooling systems together and took the shawl off. The eight years had made a complete stranger of Zala. He'd heard she was a junk salvager now, among other things, and it showed. The sun had brought a rich brown to her skin, and there was a wiry, defined musculature to her that had never been there before. She still held herself in a way which made her seem small, though. And she wasn't small; though Tarou was a large man, he did not dwarf her by any measure. She still wore her black hair fairly short, though not nearly so tightly cropped as it had been. Her clothes had changed little too: a blue undershirt and a dark, thin jacket with a large hood, black trousers and walking shoes, as well as a large backpack.

'So what're you doing here?' Tarou asked. 'I mean, it's good to see you and all, but I'd have stayed far away.'

'I heard about what happened to Chloe Kim. I came to pay my respects.'

Tarou shifted and looked away, uncomfortable. 'Yeah . . . terrible business, that. She was unlucky. You know how it happened, right?' Zala shook her head. 'Soucouyant virus,' Tarou said gently.

'I thought so. What, it shut down her pacemaker or something?'

'It shuts down everything. Neural implants, bionic organs, optical enhancements, any tech you've got in you. God knows who she caught it from.' Tarou shook his head. 'So many people have all those machine parts, those bio-augmentations now? They're still trying to figure out whether it's a computer virus or an actual disease.'

'You get anything put in?'

Tarou pulled up the right sleeve of his T-shirt. There was a heavy scar all around his biceps, dipping under his armpit, and a bar code imprinted just below it, along with a tiny tattooed logo that read *NDLT*. 'Artificial muscle, all regulated by a little chip in my shoulder. I've got to eat about three thousand calories a day, but lifting's a breeze. Of course, now I'm terrified of getting too near someone coming out of the city and having my arm die on me. What about you?'

Zala shook her head, with a slight shudder that surprised neither of them. Zala knew technology better than anyone Tarou had ever met, but she still had her old phobias. Tarou pulled his sleeve back down – to be honest, the join that proved his arm wasn't entirely his still creeped him out when he thought about it too hard. 'So how're you getting in? They'll still have your charges on record. You won't get past the biometric scanners. Security Force will scoop you right up.'

Zala had taken a seat on a large metal crate and was making typing motions in thin air. The portable terminal strapped to her wrist sent images of a projected keyboard and monitor to digitized contact lenses, forming a computer visible only to her. Her fingers moved at incredible speed. 'I've got a plan. The less you know, the better for you and everything. I mean, there's a pretty good chance of it not working.'

'So why go?'

Zala sighed, then looked up at him, the glow in her pupils dimming as the contact lenses went into standby. 'I've been away too long. I've been salvaging junk in the desert, thieving and hacking in Khartoum. Dad died in a shack in Addis Ababa. He's the one they wanted. I was just his skinny little nerd daughter they wanted to use for leverage.'

Tarou had heard about Zala's father dying – a positive identification on the body of a respected local engineer turned criminal had earned some short-lived attention from the New Cairo news outlets – but the dismissive tone in her voice unnerved him. 'You miss the city that much?' Tarou said. 'And what if you get caught?'

'If I get caught? It's been eight years, and the charges were fabricated, they know that.'

'Fucking hell, Zala, they said you killed three people.'

Zala's discomfort showed. There was a silence.

After a while, she said, 'Look, can we just go?'

Tarou softened, unable to maintain his annoyance. This was not just the first time he had seen her in years. It might also end up being the last. 'Sorry, it's just . . . I've worried about you ever since you left, and now you show up again heading out of the frying pan and into the fire you jumped into the frying pan to get out of, because *apparently you missed the fire*.'

Zala laughed guiltily, and Tarou continued, 'Anyway, you're just in time. Any day now the city's going to be in quarantine, so sooner is better. We'll get something to eat in the food court, and then you can head in.'

They wove between the chassis of various large vehicles, including huge, boxy Lerasha Karkadanns which brought supplies to the Waytower and a sleek Faltach K-series left by one of the tower's landlords for a service, which Tarou had spent the last few days fawning over. Through a security door on the far side of the garage bay, they emerged into a long, curved room, the far end lined with panels of glass all the way up to a high, arched ceiling. The walls were given over to gleaming, angular boutiques and places to get a quick meal, all designed to part those passing through from as much of their money as possible.

The two of them walked over to a café selling sandwiches – the meat of which was, at best, dubiously sourced – and took a seat to discuss the intervening years. How Tarou had quit the cybercrime game and studied engineering at university, before squandering his education as a mechanic at the Waytower. How Zala and her father had fled to Addis Ababa, where, their combined technological abilities similarly squandered, they worked as technicians or freelance software coders, staying under the radar and not using their real identities, or real qualifications. How, when Zala's father died, she almost attempted to move back into New Cairo, but lost her nerve and wound up in Khartoum, where she scraped out a living as a low-level hacker, using only the most basic of her abilities so as not to attract attention. How she'd heard of the virus sweeping her old city.

'So you're just here to go to Chloe's funeral?' Tarou asked. She didn't answer. 'Christ, Zala, you're walking into the lion's den as it is, you're planning on staying there?'

'You can't say you're not curious.'

Tarou didn't know what to make of that. 'Curious about what?'

'About the virus. Where did it come from? Did someone make it? Why did they make it?'

Of course, Tarou thought to himself bitterly. He'd hoped she'd just be here to grieve, but this was Zala Ulora, who used to spend weeks slowly working away at the most secure of New Cairo's computer systems until they revealed their secrets to her, then shut it all down and delete all the spoils without making any attempt to profit. It was never about that. Not even this, not even with a childhood friend among the thousands dead or maimed. 'Tell me . . . tell me that this dangerous, potentially deadly virus isn't just another one of your puzzles to you.'

'It's a puzzle that needs solving,' Zala said.

'Oh yeah, because only the great Zala Ulora, master cyber-criminal, can save the day?' he proclaimed theatrically. 'And, lest we forget, perhaps even redeeming yourself in the eyes of the city that turned against you?'

The next thing he knew, Zala's palm had caught his face. He grunted and leaned back, arms up to stop any more blows finding their mark. Her glare still caught him. 'Our friend is dead,' she hissed, 'and if, in dying, she brought me back, the person who might possibly be able to stop the deaths, she won't have died for nothing.'

'I just don't want to see anything bad happen to you. Can't you go somewhere else?'

He watched as Zala stood up from the table and swung her backpack over her shoulder. She strode over to the glass side of the Waytower and placed her hands on the rail, gazing out of the window. In front of her, just intersecting with the edge of the Waytower itself, was a vast bowl in the desert. A perfect circle, many miles across. The twenty other Waytowers positioned around the rest of the circumference seemed so small from where she stood. The stone drop swept down until it met the angular black surface below. Tens of thousands of huge sheets of obsidian solar panels moved slowly over the top of the city as they adjusted to take in as much of the desert sun as possible. A massive white complex in the side of the bowl brought in water from the great New Nile Sea to the northeast. Beneath the silently shifting sheets of black, an amorphous surface over the city like an unquiet ocean, a metropolis awaited.

'No I can't,' she said. 'This is still my city. It needs me. Hell, I need it.'

Tarou got up to join her. She brought her eyes away from the view, up to his. There was fear and there was sadness, but behind that, a small, almost imperceptible sparkle of excitement. The two of them walked across to a small glass staff elevator, open to the public since the huge shuttle elevator had been put out of commission to stop people below emigrating too quickly following the viral outbreak. The elevator itself was plastered with signs and warning labels. YOU WILL BE REQUIRED TO ACCEPT A BIOMETRIC SCAN. YOU WILL BE SUBJECT TO NEW CAIRO LAWS WHILE IN NEW CAIRO. GENISEC WELCOMES YOU TO NEW CAIRO. Zala paused halfway through the door and looked back at Tarou. 'It was great seeing you again,' she said.

'If you ever wind up coming back through here, come say hi, and maybe don't slap me so much next time,' Tarou said, both of them knowing this was probably their last meeting. She nodded anyway, out of courtesy, then stepped inside. The doors closed, and Tarou watched as his childhood friend disappeared down into the city below.

Chapter 1

The elevator flung itself downwards and, through the glass, Zala watched the pelagic surface of the solar panels rise up to meet her, the inky exterior gleaming. She caught a glimpse of the wildly thrashing array of mechanisms moving the vast panels, then the elevator dropped through to the other side and the city below unfurled. Zala's breath caught in her throat as she took in the sight. She'd forgotten how beautiful the city was from this high up.

The Sol Lamp, an arrangement of powerful lights meant to simulate the sun, had drawn low along its arching track and evening loomed. The huge spires of the three main corporate buildings, lit up a cold grey-white, jutted like trident prongs from the city centre. Whatever the often vicious rivalry between the corporations was like behind closed doors, they were on good enough terms that their towers shared height and aesthetic sensibilities to an extent that could only have been coordinated. Around them, skyscrapers from more modest companies were dwarfed. The New Cairo Democratic Council building stood next to the soaring corporate towers, as round as a small stadium. On the sides of the huge crater which contained the city lay massive power cables, with offshoots winding down to the neighbourhoods and businesses below or snaking up to the power plant above. Roads, illuminated by heavy streetlamps, seemed bright ribbons weaving through the mass of buildings. Lights burned through the night air, each pinprick marking a streetlamp, a window or, as Zala got closer to the ground, an individual car sweeping around. Elevator Station Seven sat in the affluent Alexandria district and even after dark the illumination lent the area an air of frenetic energy. New Cairo might be a diseased city, even a dying one, but its vitality had not been taken from it yet.

The elevator drew to a halt in the terminal. A government-owned building, it was a banausic concrete box devoted largely to a cordoned-off space for two snaking queues: one for visitors and new residents, one for returning citizens. At the far end were the security checks, either to create or to confirm biometric records for the purposes of identification. In spite of the viral outbreak, the building was full of weary travellers wanting to get into the city and the queues to get past security were long. No doubt more than a few had funerals to attend. That it would not be a short wait suited Zala's needs perfectly.

The timing of Zala's visit was not entirely decided by the death of her childhood friend Chloe Kim, or the presence of the virus that had killed her.

Three months ago Zala had salvaged from a junkyard a large, rusty GeniSec Kowloon 310 full-body biometric scanner which had become redundant when Khartoum upgraded to newer models. After some quick research, she'd found that this model was still in use in New Cairo. Having dragged it back to her residence, she had powered it up and run a hacked version of the program for it. She'd then scanned in her own biometrics: her picture, her fingerprints, her iris, even traces of her DNA from her hair, and saved them as individual files, in formats identical to those the security in New Cairo used.

Zala now slid in one of her contact lenses and switched on her portable terminal. Instantly, the lens's heads-up display turned on and the orange outline of a keyboard and a monitor sprang up in front of her. She closed the lensed eye, confirming that the image of the monitor was visible only to her, displaying in the lens and not projecting out in front of her. She then placed in the other lens. She had a large scar on her side from a previous mis-adventure, that served as a reminder of how important it was to check that her activities were private.

She typed in the address for the administrator's access page within the New Cairo network page, and inserted a chain of code into all of the search and login areas. This code bypassed the website and gave commands directly to the network's server itself. One of the search bars gave a response from the server – a vulnerability. She typed in different variations on the format of the same basic command: 'Give me the username and password of an administrator'.

The server quickly spat out the information for one Jalia Furlekh. Username 'JFurlekh9', password 'uQhRL9FX2'. Zala used these details to log in and then worked her way through a series of menus until she found what she was looking for. The biometric database of every registered person in New Cairo, of anyone who had ever come or gone.

Zala did love the feeling of a solved puzzle, even one as quick and easy as this.

She sent out a search throughout the database for a New Cairo citizen, currently out of town, clean criminal record, female, 26, 5 ft 7 in, black hair, brown eyes. Someone a close match to her. The portable terminal chugged through the millions of names until it found four potential candidates.

One was altogether no good – she'd had her skin pigments altered to make her skin much fairer than was naturally found in this day and age. This was popular among the more privileged of New Cairo's citizens, to change the colour of their skin to unusually light or unusually dark. Ostensibly it was to make protecting the person easier for security personnel by making them stand out in a crowd, but it became a status symbol almost immediately. Either way, this would draw too much suspicion at Zala's darker skin.

Of the remaining three, any of which would have worked,

one stood out. Selina Mullur had no bio-mechanics or bio-augmentations. This was a value Zala could change easily enough in any of the other girls' data, but Zala felt a curious sense of kinship towards Selina. She was like her.

Zala opened up Selina's entry in the database and set to work. Identification photograph, genetic structure, fingerprint and iris scans were all replaced, with Selina's original scans kept for later. Zala saved the entry, accessed administrative functions, deleted the record of Selina's entry being changed and logged out.

Satisfied, she switched off her portable terminal and looked up. The crowd was still thick, and she could barely see the security section. The queue moved forwards over the course of the next hour, until Zala was the next in line.

Installed in front of her, shiny and new, was a GeniSec Kowloon 410 full-body biometric scanner.

Run.

Zala felt a knot in her stomach tighten. She didn't know a lot about biometrics, or scanners thereof, but she knew that if the scans she'd input were different in any way from what this scanner expected – wrong resolution, wrong bit depth, even wrong format – she'd be handing herself over to the five bored-looking security personnel in front of her.

Run.

Sweat sprang from her brow. She focused on her breathing. She inhaled deeply, her stomach puffing out and her chest rising, and exhaled long. She crossed her fingers. And she hoped dearly that the developers of the Kowloon 410 had decided that the scan data was good enough the first time around.

Zala stepped forward, looking straight ahead.

Run.

An increasingly high-pitched whirring came from the scanner, followed by a sharp clicking sound. Zala stared blankly.

She kept her breathing deep and steady.

'Ms Mullur?'

Zala's eyes snapped to a tall, portly man in front of her, in a blue and grey Security Force uniform with black trousers.

18

Tall, fat and at least forty – probable joint issues. A heel to one of his knees might disable him.

Glasses. A punch could shatter them – that would bring with it blinding and pain.

Balding – no easily accessible hair to grab.

Nothing around his neck to use as a choke.

Weight advantage.

Height advantage.

And then there were the other four security guards, all in better shape than this guy.

His nametag said 'Fernando Vinter'.

RUN.

'Ms Mullur, you can come on through.'

The knot in Zala's stomach unravelled all at once. She kept her face straight and she walked through the security area, out into the main commercial street of Alexandria, the most prosperous of New Cairo's five districts.

Zala inhaled the night air and took in the scene around her. She'd never had a lot of business in the most affluent parts of the city, but she'd been here once or twice before. Just enough came back to her to drive home how much eight years had changed it. The old streetlamps, with their lazy orange glow, had been replaced with much brighter ones of a cold eggshell blue similar to the lights that illuminated the corporate buildings. This made sense to her, as enough GeniSec, New Delhi Lifestyle Technologies and Banach-Tarski Operations executives lived here that there would be a crossover in aesthetic tastes. The street was long, and branching off from it were palatial gardens in which grand houses stood. The houses took after the currently dominant architectural movement, which was mostly characterized by its reconciliation of nineteenth-century western imperial stateliness and modern adoption of geometric tidiness, preference for straight lines and fawning reverence of the right angle. They were broad and rectangular, made from concrete or breeze blocks and stuccoed to off-whites or pastel colours, so as to stand out without drawing accusation of vulgarity. Rain was not an issue, this city being as it was in the middle of the Sahara desert, but these houses all had gently sloping roofs as an aesthetic concession.

Zala opened her portable terminal, this time not needing to worry about her contact lenses. She ran down her contact list and found Polina Bousaid. A friend of both Zala and Chloe, Polina was, when Zala had last seen her anyway, a bookish student of history at the same college at which Zala studied. Even through her extended sabbatical from New Cairo, the two had kept in touch. Indeed, Polina was the only person who had known in advance that Zala would be coming; she'd made arrangements in the planning of the funeral on behalf of 'an old out-of-town friend who'd hopefully be able to make it'.

Zala typed out a message.

>I'm in the city. What's been set up on your end?

A few moments later, a reply popped up.

>Great! I never understood that computer stuff like you but you have got to tell me how you swung that. I'm putting you up, the funeral is tomorrow. I'm living downtown now. 5393 Tani, apartment 7. I'll meet you outside. See you soon!

Zala felt rather taken aback; first, by the lack of a certain funereal quality to the message and then by the fact that she didn't really know that building. She put her lenses in and set her terminal's GPS to the address. The lenses superimposed onto the ground before her a glowing yellow line, snaking off down the road and out of sight.

The suburbs of Alexandria began to give way to office buildings, shops and restaurants after about twenty minutes of walking. The central business district of New Cairo had barely changed. The skyscrapers evoked both a claustrophobic narrowness and an immeasurable, expansive scale. Although most of the city was hidden from view, the presence of it was thick in the air – a presence that would be oppressive were it not so exhilarating. Khartoum had nothing even close to this. New Cairo was, after all, the nervous system of the United African Democracies and, beyond that, one of the most vital cities in the world, on a par

20

with New York or London, Tokyo or Istanbul. Even at such a late hour, almost every light in every building was on, be they offices, studios, apartments or stores. The Soucouyant virus had emerged weeks earlier, but to Zala it seemed as though it had barely touched this part of town. The yellow line leading the way contrasted with the blue and green and purple lights on the buildings in a miasma of colour.

Eventually the line disappeared and a glowing computerized flag appeared outside an elegant, expensive-looking tower block called The Ozymandias. Polina stood waving outside the front entrance. Zala's initial reaction was that she had grown into adulthood spectacularly. Long, shiny black hair, a dazzling smile and deep blue eyes that Zala did not remember her having eight years ago. She wore a loosely knitted light brown cardigan, beneath which was a black vest top, and a short black skirt with an asymmetric hem. Her toned legs poured themselves into knee-high leather boots. Zala suddenly felt aware of how little her own wardrobe, or living situation for that matter, had changed since she was a teenager.

Polina strode over to Zala, arms outstretched, beaming, and drew her into a hug, which Zala awkwardly allowed. 'It's so good to see you,' Polina cooed into her ear. 'I just got back from the museum about two minutes ago, you picked the perfect time to arrive.' She let Zala in through the entrance and went up to the doorman, a courteously smiling man in a royal blue blazer that had the building's name monogrammed on it in silver.

'This is the friend I was telling you about, Dane. She'll be staying with me for a few days,' Polina said. He looked with an unmistakably affected politeness at Zala's appearance, and said, 'It's a pleasure to have you staying with us, Ms . . . ?'

'Selina Mullur.'

Zala noticed Polina's eyes dart towards her. The doorman pulled up Selina's altered records, compared Zala with the photograph that appeared, nodded and said, 'Selina and Polina, eh?'

Polina forced a laugh. 'Yeah, we were quite the double act back when we were kids.'

21

'Everything seems to be in order. Welcome, Ms Mullur.'

Zala turned and followed Polina to an elevator opposite the doorman's desk. The doors closed behind them and Polina burst out laughing. 'Selina Mullur? Who's that?'

'Some woman close enough to me that I can replace her biometrics and use her identity,' Zala replied.

'You mean *steal* her identity.'

'Hey, I'm gonna give it back. I've still got her files and everything.'

Polina sat back against the handrail of the elevator and looked at Zala, eyebrow raised. 'Oh, I see. So whatever she might try and get into the city to deal with, it's less important than you attending a funeral?' Polina broke into a wry smile as her lips curled around the end of the sentence.

Zala searched desperately for words that would justify her actions – anything except that she cared more about getting back into the city and finding out about this virus than she did about this other woman – but found none. 'That's her problem,' she said.

The elevator came to a halt and the doors opened into a lobby which, despite the size of the building, had only two apartment doors. Polina opened hers and led Zala through an elegant hallway to a large, luxuriously furnished room, where they sat down on the leather sofa that took up much of one wall. Only now did Zala realize how much her feet ached. She had been walking for hours.

'So what's your plan for while you're here?' Polina asked, turning herself to face Zala, her arms draped wide over the sofa's arm and back.

'I'm here for the funeral. You, me and Chloe, together again for the last time.'

'Will you be sticking around afterwards?'

Zala paused for a moment. 'I might, yeah. I'm thinking about it.'

'Why?'

'To be honest, I'm curious. I want to find out what this virus is.

I want to know if I can stop it somehow. I was planning on hanging around for a little while longer and seeing what I can dig up. Play detective a bit.'

'And what about your record?' As if no time had passed at all, the anxious, hesitant tone Polina's voice had always carried in Zala's memories came through.

'I don't care any more,' said Zala, shrugging. 'My dad tried to steal his own artificial intelligence project back from the biggest company on the continent, he got me smeared as bait, he got us kicked out of the city and he died in a shack. It's been eight years, no one's looking for me any more, the only problem is if . . . ?'

Polina sighed heavily. 'You're going to the funeral of the most loved ballerina in the United African Democracies. It's going to be full of people who'll probably recognize you from back in the day, not to mention all the press. You end up in the wrong photo, you could wind up in a jail cell. Now you're thinking you'll stay? What do you get out of this?'

Zala failed to find a convenient lie. 'Honestly? I want to find out as much as I can about this Soucouyant virus, figure out where it came from or how to stop it, and I want to march into the CEO of GeniSec's office and say, "Here, you get to be the saviour of the city, just get rid of the charges you made up. Let me go back to a normal life, where I can use my name without 'Wanted in New Cairo for multiple murders' getting dragged up. Let me live somewhere, get a real job, pay taxes, maybe find someone to settle down with." This tomboy rogue hacker shit is something my goofy teenage self came up with and now it's how I'm forced to live if I want to eat or put a roof over my head. I just don't want to have to be this person any more. I want to be able to settle down and grow up and have my own life. Tarou is the head mechanic up at Waytower Seven. You're deputy curator of one of the biggest museums in the United African Democracies. I hate that I could have had that. I could have had a chance at a life. But more than that, I just want to come back to New Cairo and not have to risk stealing someone else's identity.'

Zala found herself worn out. She had never said all that out loud before. Polina had a look on her face she'd seen on other people's mothers' faces, one of concerned annoyance.

'You shouldn't want to come back. Christ, Zala, things are bad enough here—' She stopped suddenly.

'What?'

Polina shifted, grimacing. 'I don't know how much you've heard on the outside, but things aren't good here. Not nice. Not safe.'

'The virus?' said Zala.

'It started with the virus. Outbreaks here and there. Not many. No one knowing what caused it. Then as the weeks have gone by, more and more problems have surfaced. Well-to-dos like Chloe have died every so often, but the poor are getting hit way worse. I mean, the rich generally have better health, with less need of life-or-death technology, and they – well, we – can afford to replace our bio-augmentations when they get shut down. So the poor have lost their lives and livelihoods disproportionately.'

'What does that have to do with things not being safe?'

'They tried leaving. Half the Naj-Pur district and a substantial chunk of the Surja district upped sticks and streamed towards the big shuttle elevators in their area. The Council shut down the main exits, started forbidding people from the worst-hit neighbourhoods to leave. They said they were from "high-infection areas", which in fairness they were, and presented a risk of spreading the virus to the outside world. They said that people were simply panicking and that things would be worse for them if they flooded en masse into the desert. So the workers got angry. There've been riots. Every night, there are fire-fights throughout the poor areas.'

Polina went on: 'Word began to spread of an organization behind it. Arrests of purported leaders began. Violence prompts oppressive measures, which prompt more violence, and so on. Things were getting so much better, you know?' She sighed. 'It really seemed like we were headed to a great place. People were happy. The economy was doing great, the government felt like a friend of the people, a tool for betterment. We thought we'd left something dark and heavy behind. Then the virus struck, and it's all gone backwards. The violence and the chaos are back and worse than ever.'

Polina walked over to the window and stared out at the city, the golden networks of vehicles streaking along the roads and the rows of monolithic skyscrapers. 'You know the riots came right past here? The landlords did an admirable job of hiding it, but a bunch of the lower rooms were completely burnt out and windows were smashed all the way up. Once the rioters couldn't reach with things they were throwing, they started shooting out the windows. Shooting right into people's apartments. I was at the museum, watching on the TV and wondering if I'd come back to find my home destroyed. This revolution is still growing and it's angry. I'm not sure you can figure out a way to stop the virus in time to defuse it.'

Zala stared. She'd heard that there was unrest, but nothing on this scale. 'Is the funeral going to go ahead?'

'I don't think they'd start anything at a funeral in the middle of Alexandria. Just . . . try and get out of here before the Council extend the quarantine.'

Something rattling away in the back of Zala's mind clicked. She opened her portable terminal and typed 'Selina Mullur' into a search engine. A contact directory service came up, listing the address of Zala's assumed identity.

'She lives at 537 Kaladi. Where's that?'

Polina looked aghast. 'It's right in the middle of Naj-Pur. They're not going to let you out. You're labelled high-risk for infection.'

Zala sank back into the sofa. 'Sorry, Polly, it looks like I'm sticking around to look into the virus. I guess it can't be helped.'

Polina strode back over to her. 'Zala, *promise* me that you'll stay out of anywhere where it seems like there could be trouble.'

'You know I'm not going to stick to that promise.'

Polina grabbed her shoulders and pulled her into a position where she was looking her straight in the eye. 'Zala, they're shooting people on both sides. The violence is escalating. There are parts of this city that simply aren't under the Council's control any more. I don't care what you think you can do with this virus. Right now, the Naj-Pur and Surja districts are the last places on earth you want to be.'

Chapter 2

Alice Amirmoez crouched with her two children in a dark alleyway in the Naj-Pur district and tried her best to hide the blood on her sleeve from them. Every so often, she checked around the corner, to confirm that they were still undetected, but for the most part she and her children simply hid behind an industrial bin, out of view of anyone walking past the alley. Her oldest, Ria, cradled her sleeping brother, Zeno, in her arms, but Alice was terrified that he'd wake up and start crying. The last thing they needed was attention drawn to them. All it would take was some thug with a gun. Although this area had its troublesome periods, following massive government and private investment it had been safe even after dark for a while. Then the virus broke out, and the riots happened, and the designation of Naj-Pur as a 'high-infection area' trapped hundreds of thousands of scared, angry people here to live, disempowered and gripped with the fear of death. If someone decided she looked too well fed, too well off . . . the thought made her sick with fear.

She hated that Kahleed had chosen this place as their meeting point. Of course, for him, as the leader of the New Cairo Liberation Corps, the group at the forefront of the fight against the government, anywhere considered not too dangerous for normal police patrols was somewhere he could get arrested, or worse. This in turn didn't change the fact that anywhere that *was* considered too dangerous for normal police patrols was probably too dangerous to be a meeting place.

Alice felt a crust of dried blood on her palm. She scratched it off with her other hand and tried hard not to think about whose blood it was.

Her portable terminal flashed. She raised her wrist and turned it on. The holographic screen popped up a message from Kahleed in the air in front of her, which simply read:

>Where are you?

Alice paused for a moment. She had known Kahleed ever since her husband, Jacob, had introduced them ten years ago. The two men had become partners when Kahleed's terminal-building business had adopted an early form of a business-targeted operating system Jacob had created, for a contract to outfit the New Cairo Democratic Council with custom terminals. This work relationship then became a close friendship, born from their shared roots growing up in the poorer parts of Naj-Pur, which in turn led to an advocacy group to help revitalize the most poverty-stricken parts of the city. They had even stuck together when the Soucouyant virus began to make itself known and the lobbying for aid and evacuation had turned into something more destructive. Her husband would have trusted Kahleed with his family's life in a heartbeat.

But her husband was gone.

>The alleyway between Talim's and that old clothing shop on Falja. We're hiding behind a big bin. Come quickly.

Moments later, Kahleed appeared. In his early forties, he was a powerfully built man, with strong, broad features, dark brown skin. His tightly curled black hair and beard were far less well kept now than they had been when he was just a business executive. His eyes were bloodshot, and his voice wavered as he said, 'Alice. I'm so sorry about—'

Alice forced a neutral tone and replied with a curt 'I can't discuss it right now. Just get me to the safe house and make sure my children are looked after. We need to get out of here.'

Ria looked up, still cradling the baby. She'd been so strong, Alice thought. She still couldn't bring herself to tell her daughter what had happened. Kahleed nodded, scooped up Zeno, and turned on his heel, murmuring 'Come.'

Alice followed him, clutching Ria's hand. She tried to set off at a brisk pace, but Kahleed lightly touched her on the shoulder as they walked and said, 'It's okay. You're in no hurry now. You're with me. That means something here.'

So they walked along narrow streets lined with a mix of brick houses and some boarded-up shops. Shards of glass in broken windows glinted in the lamplight. The curfew was imminent and people were hurrying along the streets trying to get home. Although eyes followed them intently in a way that made Alice uncomfortable, just as frequent were nods of recognition or mutterings of 'Good man . . .' One old woman called out to Kahleed and, when he stopped, said, 'You keep fighting for us, son,' and shook his hand.

Alice stared ahead, holding Ria close. She had spent the last few weeks watching news reports of violence, riots and shootings, all part of an uprising she wanted nothing to do with.

They're not the ones that gunned down Jacob, a small voice in the back of her mind said. Her mouth went dry.

The road they now walked down was lined with tall terraced buildings, all scarred grey concrete and dirty windows. Bursts of colour came from huge illuminated advertising screens attached to the frontages. As Alice passed a convenience store, on the screen above multicoloured streaks wrapped themselves around a silhouetted figure dancing, a colourfully packaged bottle in its hand. 'FEST,' it proclaimed, 'LIVE MORE.' Beneath it, a responsible-drinking warning and the FanaSoCo corporate logo flashed. The massive billboard was the only thing on the street not covered in graffiti.

Kahleed turned sharply down a long, dark driveway between two dilapidated terraces. At the end of the path was the back of an abandoned clothing factory. It wasn't so long ago that the Preserve Our Manual Jobs Act had passed through the Council, guaranteeing that if a union could successfully prove that human interaction or participation was necessary for a job, that job could not be automated and pay could not be reduced. Then, the people of Naj-Pur had cheered for the Council and this factory had been full of grateful workers. What machine replacement could not get rid of, the risk of getting the Soucouyant virus or, worse, transferring it to your loved ones, had. The factory had been closed for weeks.

Kahleed gently passed Zeno back to his mother, took a set of metal keys out of his pocket, unlocked a door and led them into a narrow, musty-smelling hallway. The unpainted concrete walls disappeared off into pitch darkness as what little light the terraces gave off faded. Alice felt Ria press herself up against her. Kahleed selected another key, opened a door in the wall and muttered, 'Home, sweet home.'

Through the door was a staircase that led down to a basement full of people. As Kahleed walked down, the talking and bustle of activity stopped and the basement's inhabitants turned towards him. 'I've brought Jacob's family with me. They're safe.' He looked over his shoulder to Alice and motioned for her to come in.

The space beneath the factory was huge, seeming to match the main floor above in size and lack of decoration. Most of the area was given over to a main room filled with rows and rows of bunk beds, in anticipation of more fugitives. This confined the primary operations of the NCLC to a smaller room filled with personnel, weapons and equipment, and makeshift living facilities. However, its modest size belied a base of operations entirely capable of punching above its weight.

In one corner of the room and spread out along its walls was an impromptu command centre made up of an array of computer terminals, their holographic monitors showing communications with outsiders, blueprints of buildings, or security camera feeds. These terminals monitored huge amounts of incoming data, all of which could be sent to the base's real powerhouse: a central command station, at the intersection of the two rows, capable of directing large-scale military-level combat operations. Flanked by skilled operators feeding in information, a leader could run a war from that terminal.

Crowded around the command station was a group of tired-looking men and women who were staring at a large hologram showing the entire city. A wrinkled, bearded man in a dark green hoodie approached the newcomers and said, 'I'm Maalik. Your husband was good to us.'

One by one, a few others from the weary group introduced themselves. Suman Chaudhri, a fat, pimply hacker and technician who sat at the command station. 'The twins', Anisa and Thana Yu, two tall, heavily scarred women. Hoshi Smolak, a small, rotund accountant with smudged glasses and a stammer, and Serhiy Panossian, who couldn't have been more than twenty. Kahleed's partner, Tal Surdar, needed no introduction, and nodded respectfully. The last to introduce herself was Nataliya Kaur, a muscular woman with cropped hair and a serious expression. Most, however, stayed busy at the terminals, engrossed in whatever plans the group had going, their eyes flicking between the main terminal screen and their own.

Alice turned to Kahleed. 'Can someone please help me find somewhere for my children to sleep?' she said.

Kahleed looked at Nataliya and motioned towards the children. She nodded, fixed a smile on her face, turned towards them, and whispered, 'Come with me, Ria, we're going to find you and Zeno a nice place to go to bed.' Alice watched as the young woman led them off. As they walked with Nataliya towards the bunks, she heard Ria ask, 'Can we make Zeno a cot out of the spare pillows?'

'That sounds like an excellent idea,' Nataliya replied, still smiling, and they set about doing so. Alice watched, aloof, as they piled pillows on top of one another, and stacked them high enough around Zeno to form walls.

'You look exhausted,' said Maalik.

'Two hours ago I found my husband's body. He'd been shot, by the police or the Security Force, because . . .'

31

She felt the words reverberate around her. The first time she had said it out loud.

'Because of his involvement with you.'

Maalik looked apologetically at her and continued, 'I could regale you with justifications, that he knew the risks and felt they were worth it, but I can't imagine you care about any of that right now. He was a great man. He risked his life to try and help those less fortunate to escape the disease and the Council. He lost that life as a result. But we owe it to Jacob to get you and your family out of the city. You're right. His blood is on our hands.'

The look on Maalik's wrinkled face was genuinely penitent.

Alice raised her forearm and showed the bottom of her shirt sleeve, mud-coloured with dried blood, and weakly replied, 'I figure I probably outdo you in that department.'

Kahleed gently pulled her arm back down to her side. She felt as though someone had hollowed out her gut.

Jacob was dead. Shot.

Tal came over, a steaming mug of coffee in hand, which he gave to her. Her hands were trembling slightly as she took it.

'Getting you and the children out of the city will be difficult and may take some time,' Kahleed told her. 'Go to them and try to sleep. We'll talk more in the morning.'

A woman who had been too busy at her terminal to introduce herself suddenly yelled out, 'We've got him!'

As Kahleed ran over to her she turned her head and looked up at him, the movement revealing a cable plugged into the iris of an artificial right eye, the cable head pointed in the same direction as her gaze. 'I'm still tracking them, but he's in the bag. He'll be here in a little while, assuming there's no one set up to intercept.'

'Is there any indication that they found our escape route?' Kahleed asked.

'No, sir. It's well hidden, and the people running it are plenty reliable,' the woman replied.

Kahleed gripped her shoulder. 'Today, Juri, we may have tipped the balance of power away from the Council and the corporations and back towards the people. It has been a terrible day, but we may just have secured our most valuable bargaining chip.'

Chapter 3

Throngs of people packed the hallways of the New Cairo Democratic Council building. Administrative staff and cabinet workers scurried between offices, eyes on their portable terminals, occasionally bumping into one another. Reporters swarmed towards every passing councillor, desperate for a quote on the day's debates. Councillor Ryan Granier watched through the small peephole in his door. He'd expected a crowd, but this was getting out of hand.

His office was a large room, with enough space for its regular ten researchers and campaign workers. Old campaign posters, photographs and frantically scribbled 'to-do' lists lined every piece of the walls. The only respite was the window, which provided an ample view of the Chamber Gardens and the mass of reporters filling that too. Terminal screens displayed voter databases, desktop publishing software and pages of text from library services. His staff sat around the office in varying levels of exhaustion. One or two were typing away at computer terminals, but most were staring at newscasts, taking in the coverage of the day's debates. They'd used good photographs of him, dating from his campaign, back when he was the foremost young upstart on the New Cairo political landscape. He stood behind a podium, tall, fit and proud, delivering a speech to a baying crowd of supporters. He was slightly offended that the pictures had been doctored to make his artificially darkened skin a more proletarian shade, but he appreciated the effect it gave. Scrolling text at the bottom read:

COUNCILLOR GRANIER MAKES VALIANT LAST STAND TO STOP QUARANTINE, NUMBERS AGAINST HIM.

The feel of the office was one of victory. It had been a hard fight, but the researchers and communications staffers were at last sure that tomorrow's final vote would dismiss the quarantine bill. Local councillors had been inundated with letters from constituents opposing the quarantine. The black marks against the names of those who voted for it would make them easy pickings for opponents in future elections. No amount of corporate campaign contributions could outweigh the knowledge in constituents' minds that their representatives kept them in a cage, like animals. Or so the logic went.

Ryan Granier knew different. The vote was already lost.

The elections weren't for three years and in that time, with the quarantine in place, the virus would be eradicated by hook or by crook, all emergency measures would then be lifted and the Council's decision would be vindicated. Without a quarantine, New Cairo would be abandoned and the virus would spread to the rest of the world. The charge of constraining New Cairo would not hurt the councillors as badly as the charge of destroying it. On top of this, the biggest players in the Council were all directly or indirectly linked to the major conglomerates that made their home in New Cairo, and the conglomerates' money mattered. Their money bought campaigns. Their money bought votes and those bought positions. More importantly, political loyalty to the Council heavyweights would be repaid in kind. It was all about picking the battles that mattered and Ryan knew that, to the High Councillor, this battle mattered enough to go to war over. The councillors who had promised Ryan this vote would not keep their word. He hadn't expected them to, nor had he exerted energy or resources towards making them. What was important was that his show of resistance did nothing to stop the bill passing.

But he kept this knowledge to himself.

The speaker implant in his cochlea beeped. He brought his wrist up and opened his portable terminal. The High Councillor wanted to see him in the now deserted main chamber of the building. What he intended to be a mutter came out as an exclamation of 'Oh shit.' Several of his staff stirred from their rest to find out what had happened, immediately fearful of even more work.

'What is it?' Zareen Charmchi, Ryan's head of staff, asked.

'The High Councillor wants to chew me out in the main hall.'

Her eyes lit up. 'He thinks you're going to beat the quarantine bill. This is *really* good news!'

Ryan forced himself to grin. 'I think if that were the case he'd be telling me to meet him in the alley out back, in front of the big men with guns.'

'You could take them. Go knock 'em dead, boss,' Zareen said, as Ryan opened the main door out of the office.

Immediately he was beset by reporters, screaming questions at him. His voice rang out. 'You get three questions today. Decide among you who'll ask the best ones.' He needed the publicity they had to offer far more than they needed him, but they didn't know that.

'Time's up, ladies and gentlemen, your first question please.'

One man stepped forward. He was thin and unsuccessfully hiding a bald head with a poor comb-over. 'What repercussions do you think the vote going in your favour will have on the city?'

That was a good question, or at least a tricky one for Ryan to answer in a way that would benefit him. Eventually he decided on something empty and said, 'I think – or at least I hope – we'll see a change in the political climate of these chambers. I think that the councillors who vote for the quarantine, if they get defeated, will gain a greater understanding of the power that comes with truly representing the people who voted for them, as opposed to representing the people who funded them. And I think I'll be in trouble with the senior councillors.'

A light sputter of laughter came from the gaggle of reporters, before their conference began again. A broad, toad-like man stepped forward this time, and said, 'Do you think it'll stop the violence that's been going on in Naj-Pur and the like?'

This was easier, requiring only the recitation of a prepared response he'd thought of in the shower the day before. 'I don't pretend to understand the motivations of domestic terrorists, but I understand why so many people feel the need for the extreme measures that they advocate. This is a city of ten million, of vast social and economic inequality and of stubbornly entrenched power structures. In the face of those things, it's understandable that extremist vitriol would sound rational. But the fact is that the violence isn't senseless. I don't believe the violence is an end in and of itself to them. I believe that they have a goal in mind. And I have a sneaking suspicion that when those big shuttle elevators start up again, and the cowardly, discriminatory legislation that was unfortunately passed last month is rescinded, there'll be no more shots fired. All that remains is for the democratic process to achieve what their barbarism could not.'

A stern-looking woman pushed her way through the group and asked the final question. 'If this violence is a means to have the emigration restrictions lifted and that goal is met, doesn't that vindicate their methods, or prove that terrorism can win out?'

Ryan turned his body at a slight angle to the camera behind the reporter. His posture relaxed into a commanding stance. He raised his head, looking the reporter straight in the eye. This was going to be the video playing on every newscast. 'The terrorists have already lost, because the votes that get cast tomorrow will be cast by a Council that will ignore those butchers. They want our attention; they're not going to get any more of it from me. I'm not voting against the bill because of the violence. I'm voting against it because I believe it's fundamentally wrong that a government should be able to confine an innocent, healthy person against their wishes. That's enough. The best thing we can do is show the people of New Cairo that these goals are achievable without bloodshed. The courage of your convictions can change the world without a single bullet being fired. Thank you, ladies and gentlemen.'

He let his words ring out. They were a little overwrought, he thought, but they'd do. He strode off towards the main entrance to the council chamber.

The chamber in which the New Cairo Democratic Council resided was vast. The seating only had to accommodate two hundred people: members of the executive; local and district councillors; representatives from the Waytowers up on the surface. The architects of the room had given each member their own considerable desk space, resulting in an isolated seating arrangement that, Ryan thought, had done much to lessen the efficacy of party politics in New Cairo. The ceiling soared far overhead, with the vertical space exploited as in a theatre – the speaker's podium was at the lowest level, in the view of everyone, and the senior councillors sat high up at the back, in a balcony overlooking the body of the chamber. The decor was a regal blue and gold, paired with the sculpted grey marble of the room itself. This colour scheme informed every carpet, every piece of upholstery, even the custom-made portable terminal on each councillor's wrist.

Sitting in the main auditorium, as Ryan entered, was the High Councillor himself.

Ryan approached him quietly and addressed him in a restrained, respectful tone. 'Your honour.'

The man looked him up and down, frowning. At sixty, he had more than twenty years over Ryan. Most of that time had been spent serving in this room. Even to councillors who hated him, his words carried weight.

'You've done an excellent job of making me look bad on this one, Councillor Granier.'

He got to his feet. He was not a tall man, but he did not require height to project his presence. He controlled the space around him utterly. In addition to leading the Council, he was also the current patriarch of the family that owned the GeniSec Corporation and was still both a major force on the board of directors and its majority shareholder. He had the power to turn the cogs that kept the city moving in a degree no other person could compete with. Ryan had always admired him, in an envious way, and at the same time had always appreciated the cost of earning his ire.

'It's all in place, Councillor. The votes will go my way and the quarantine will be put into force,' the High Councillor said. 'In the meantime, your very public display of defiance, as represented by your resilient vote against it, will give the people who hate the bill a lingering source of faith in the Council. But of course, all this will be for nothing if anyone finds out you've thrown the fight.'

He shifted position slowly and heavily, in much the same way as tectonic plates might.

'Which raises the question – did you let anyone know?'

'I'm not doing this out of loyalty,' Ryan replied. 'I know that this is the best course of action. It'll go ahead, lesser of two evils though it may be.'

The High Councillor laughed a quiet, low chuckle. 'You'll feel less lousy when the Soucouyant virus is isolated and cured, and when your man-of-the-people shtick wins you a seat as a senior councillor.'

'People might get a little more suspicious of a thirty-three-year-old senior councillor who just so happens to have a very similar skin shade to the High Councillor, your honour.'

The two of them had, in fact, had their skin pigment changed to the same anomalously dark brown colour, though this was done before Ryan had gone into politics.

Another chuckle. 'Councillor Granier,' the High Councillor said, 'the people will be glad that their guy, their champion, is playing with the big boys.'

Ryan grimaced. 'I'm not their champion.'

The High Councillor's deep brown eyes settled on his. 'You're voting against the quarantine tomorrow. The newscasts are saying it's because you think people shouldn't be told what they can or cannot do without exceptional circumstances. The fact that you've ensured enough people will support the quarantine means you can vote along that moral line without repercussion. However else you've ensured other people will be voting, your own vote is going to be the one you've promised everyone. Regardless of the external arrangements, the political gamesmanship, the theatre of it all . . . what of that is not true?'

'. . . none of it, your honour.' He was right. Regardless of the political strategy in play, he was at least able to rationalize that his own vote was no one else's, least of all the High Councillor's. It hurt, but Ryan knew it was what needed to be done.

'It is unfortunate. Go relieve your staff. You've got an important vote tomorrow.'

Ryan turned away and walked back through the door of the chamber. Zareen was waiting outside, alone. The press, apparently satisfied with the sound-bites they had been given, were thankfully bothering other councillors now.

'Did Daddy have a thing or two to say about the vote then?'

'Apparently I'm getting nothing but socks for my birthday this year,' Ryan replied.

Zareen mock-winced as they wound their way into the crowded central lobby. 'No offence, but he's a fascist one step away from putting in martial law. I can't say I envy your upbringing.'

Suddenly, a loud crack went off somewhere ahead. A chunk of marble close to Ryan's head shattered. The air was thick with screams and yells as people in the crowd ran in every direction. Before Ryan knew it, two huge security guards were next to him, flanking him. One of them yelled, 'Councillor Granier! We need to get you out of here! Try and head to the side exit!'

Ryan nodded and they sprinted, heads down, along the corridor away from the gunshot and the chaos of the central lobby. The crowd battered against them, afraid, confused and directionless, but they pushed through. Eventually, one of the security guards got to the side exit, slammed it open with his full weight, and pulled Ryan through. He vaguely thought to himself that he'd never seen these security guards before.

At that moment, he felt a tiny, sharp sensation at his neck. He fell, his vision blurry and fading, his limbs weak. He felt himself being lifted by his armpits and dragged into somewhere dark. There was yelling and the sound of something heavy being pulled along the ground.

He felt a pang of worry that he might not be there for the vote tomorrow. He needed to be there.

His father had told him to be there.

Chapter 4

Zala looked down at the coffin, as it was lowered into the deep hole it would rest in. Tears streaming down her face from deep, gulping sobs, she realized that she had no idea what to do or how to behave in a situation like this.

When her father died, it was simple. It had come out of nowhere: a harsh, colossal stroke while he was putting some salvaged machinery back together in the run-down shack in the garden of their house. A few hours later, after he didn't respond to her calls, she went in to check on him, and found him lying there, cold and still. She'd tried to wake him; cried over his body. She'd called an ambulance, and then packed her things and ran. She couldn't risk being caught by police, doctors or anyone else who might have a biometric scanner. She never returned. It was sudden, it was adrenalin-filled and it was over quickly.

Chloe's funeral was less a mourning ceremony than a high-society function. It was staged, calculated, crafted and posed, and drawn out for spectators, and Zala hated it. The crowd that gathered in the lush Alexandria cemetery was huge. It was composed largely of theatrically wailing culture buffs and news reporters, all come to see off the great dancer, Chloe Kim, laid to rest at much too young an age. The headline news, of course, would be the kidnapping of Councillor Ryan Granier, but this

42

would be as juicy a B-story as the press was likely to get. Most enthusiastic of all was NCN, an upmarket-aspiring tabloid owned by the GeniSec Corporation, which held up Chloe's death as headline-making proof that the Soucouyant virus was hitting the rich and poor alike. The gutter-press appeal of a celebrity death and the highbrow lilt of cultural news made the story no less salacious.

Zala and Chloe's other old friends stood somewhere near the back where they would be undisturbed by social opportunists squeezing their teary-eyed faces in front of every camera they could find, and mourned in near silence. The night before, even Polina's seemingly good spirits had begun to give way after a few glasses of some foul eastern European liquor she'd improbably developed a taste for, and she and Zala ended up reminiscing until the early hours of the morning. They talked about how Polina had seen Chloe's first ever public performance and cheered at the end of her segment so long and loud that she had been thrown out of the theatre. How the three of them as teenagers used to get drunk and bitch about their professors, often waking up in a hung-over pile in their living room. How Zala and Polina had visited hospital every day for hours when, aged sixteen, Chloe had a heart replacement installed following a massive heart attack. Zala talked about reading reviews of Chloe's ballet company in Addis Ababa. How much it hurt to not be able to contact her, in case someone found out she was in communication with a fugitive alleged murderer. Now, Polina sat and wept into a handkerchief, unable to look at the coffin.

At the funeral ceremony acquaintances had been reluctant to give Zala more than a distant nod. She trusted Polina's insistence that most of them had no doubt she was innocent, and there was no chance of her still being actively pursued, but still her presence seemed to bring about a great awkwardness. Zala was impressed that they even recognized her. It had been eight years, she was taller, more athletic, and the long black dress and cardigan Polina had lent her was not even close to anything they would have seen her in before. However, as far as they were concerned, it seemed, she was maybe mad, maybe bad, but definitely dangerous to know. The guest most emphatic in avoiding her was an immigrant from Tokyo named Matsuda Oba.

Matsuda had been a close and greatly beneficial friend to Zala before her exile. He was the one who had shown her how to take all the things her father had taught her about computers and use them to do whatever she wanted, be it legal or illegal. From him she had learned, in his words, 'all the things that you don't get taught in computer lessons'. According to Polina he had become a surgeon and devoted a great deal of his time to helping those afflicted by the Soucouyant virus. He now stood some distance from Zala, talking with others of their old friends.

Zala opened up her portable terminal and sent him a message:
>I need a word with you, when you're free.

He glanced up, looked her in the eye and scowled, shaking his head. Zala theatrically rolled her eyes, before messaging back.
>What's the matter?

Matsuda, visibly angry at this point, wrote back:
>Honestly? One, I'm at a friend's funeral. Two, you've got a grade-A criminal record and that makes you a leper. People looking into my past too hard would ruin me. I mean, I have a family now.

Zala frowned.
>You're right. It's inappropriate. You've got a new life now. It's probably an improvement, actually. The old Matsu would have been bugging me all night to find out how I got past the city's security measures during what were basically quarantine conditions.

The response was almost immediate.
> . . . Fine. Tell me how you did that and we're on. We'll meet up after we're done here. We'll go for coffee or something. Just don't come over now. We're burying our friend, for god's sake.

'I wanted to talk about the Soucouyant virus,' said Zala.

She and Matsuda were sitting at a table in the nearest branch of a chain of coffee houses. The coffee was awful and the decor was apparently put together by someone who didn't understand interior design, but had read a few magazines on the subject and presumed they knew what they were doing. It was, however, full, noisy and inconspicuous. At the very least, Matsuda assured her, no one he knew would happen upon them.

'It's a tricky subject,' said Matsuda, pausing to take a wince-inducing sip of coffee. 'The Soucouyant doesn't leave many clues. Once the virus has fully manifested, the only real sign of its presence is a bio-augmentation that's not working any more. The only thing that seems to stop the virus for certain is just not having any bio-augs whatsoever. For a while we assumed it was somehow destroying the read-only programming that the rest of the bio-augs' code is built upon, breaking the whole system at its foundations. But we can't find any proof of it.' Matsuda shifted in his chair. 'The read-only code *is* corrupted, but we can't prove it's the root cause. We've done some tests, put simulated bio-augs in contact with people who've almost certainly got the virus in them but haven't had any shutdowns, and the simulated bio-augs caught it off those unmanifested infectees. It looks like it doesn't destroy all the bio-augs that get exposed to it, but we can't find criteria for those whose bio-augs malfunction and those whose don't, except that there's about a one-in-five chance of it taking all the tech in your body.'

That was a lot of 'don't knows', Zala thought to herself. 'Do you know what it is or where it came from?'

'It's hard to pin down. There are really two possibilities, from what we can tell. One is that it's a computer virus. If it's transferring via the wireless LinkUp ports doctors use to get status reports from the bio-augs during check-ups, being in the same room would open you to potential exposure.'

Zala shuddered and looked around. It was early afternoon, and the café was full of people in office wear chatting over a hot drink or eating the last of a late lunch. Smiling. Talking nonchalantly. No trace of strain or anxiety. Matsuda was speaking more quietly than he had been. Zala's skin crawled as she leaned in closer to hear him.

'What's weird, though, is that LinkUp ports have been around for about forty years, and a lot of the older software versions are incompatible with the newer tech. The poorer folk often don't shell out for the upgrades in the software or the relevant hardware, so I have to have about four different readers, one from each major iteration of the software, in my check-up rooms. They're completely unable to speak to each other. But we've got what we're pretty sure are people with completely alien operating software who caught the virus off one another. Which means someone would have had to code something that works with total compatibility between these pretty incompatible devices.' He paused, a slight frown developing. 'This is feasible, if difficult, but I can't think of why anyone would release the code as a virus rather than selling to LinkUp or one of the bio-augmentations companies and making a fortune.'

'So what's the other possibility?'

'Well, one of the things that jumps out at me is that while I say there's a one-in-five chance of probable Soucouyant infection leading to shutdown, that's all the bio-augs for a person. If one goes, they all go, without fail. This is weird because bio-augs don't really coordinate with each other if they're not part of a larger system. An individual bio-aug is generally no more related to others within the same person than it is to bio-augs in other people. It's a mechanism that allows for bio-augs of different generations and operating software to run without clashing. So, given that lack of specific relation, if this is genuinely regular malicious software, the one-in-five rule should apply to individual bio-augs not people. Instead, it's all going. So it's not the bio-augs. It seems like something that involves the person in the system. Like a regular biological virus. Like a cold or something. Maybe even being transmitted like a normal sickness, though only a normal proportion reported any typical sickness or immune-related symptoms.'

Zala sat back in her chair and let out a slow breath. 'If it's biological, how's it combining tech and biological traits to this extent?'

A brief smile crossed Matsuda's face. 'You'll *love* this. My theory is, in part, that we've honestly reached the point where that'll start to happen. We've taken so many machine parts into ourselves that there really isn't an "us and them" at this point. We're becoming more and more computerized, and in the wake of the IntuitivAI system, computers are becoming eerily human. Maybe there's no longer any reason why disease shouldn't affect all our body parts just the same.'

Zala felt faintly sick, her usual visceral response to the thought of bio-augs and the human body. 'But they're *not* body parts,' she insisted, 'they're . . . things. They're outside things that people take inside them. They're not *you*.'

'So suppose you have a computer, a portable terminal or something. After a year, you switch out the memory for a larger hard disk. You upgrade the RAM. The next year, you get a new, faster graphics unit and processor. The year after, you get a new case and baseboard, something with a few new attachment ports. After those replacements, there's not a single part in it which was a part of your original portable terminal. Is it your portable terminal? Is it the same portable terminal? If you were asked how long you've had it for, would you hold it up and say "I bought this three years ago" or would you specify for each of the parts?'

Zala didn't really know how to answer this. Her silence lasted long enough that a nearby waitress took it as a cue to clear the cups from the table. Eventually Matsuda continued. 'At this point, we're not stuck with the physical body parts we were born with, but the new ones are still a part of us. They respond to our own internal systems. Pretty soon, we may have to go back to soul–body dualism. People used to think of consciousness itself as the essence of humanity, and the body as a separate, finite thing the soul operates. I don't really have a problem with that, but they still thought of their bodies, tools of the soul though they were, as their bodies. As time goes by, we're becoming less and less biological, turning our bodies into tools in truth, or even just switching them out for the latest ones. Maybe a body is already just a tool, an extension of the true self. Hell, natural bodies replace so much of themselves so often that even an unaltered body still isn't really all the same body for ever. Maybe diseases are adjusting. Maybe they're learning to see little difference between the tools we're born with and the tools we choose. Maybe they're ahead of the curve,' he said, pointedly.

Zala couldn't help grimacing at the thought. 'So you think it's a regular disease that's just crossed over into dealing with bio-augmentations?'

Matsuda smiled. 'Not quite. I think that the disease is making people's bodies reject the bio-augs. Viruses work by inhabiting cells and hijacking them, forcing them to take on and reproduce their own properties. What happens if a virus can disrupt your compatibility with a bio-aug?'

'I guess the body would try and get rid of it, like it does with unprocessed bio-augs that haven't been acclimatized to the host's body.'

Matsuda sat back and shrugged lightly. 'I think it's that simple. I think it's a disease that makes bodies reject the parts. The read-only memory corruption is a result of the bio-augs' internal programming not being written to expect sudden, catastrophic rejection out of nowhere – they're powering down before they have a chance to shut down normally.'

Zala leaned back in her seat and exhaled heavily. 'Look, I need some fresh air and we both need to get back. Let's go.'

They left the café and started to make their way back towards the cemetery.

'Do you have any new bio-augs yourself?' Zala asked.

He pointed just below his ribs. 'I got diagnosed with diabetes about three years back, so they put in a few artificial implants. They replaced the islets of Langerhans, to boost the hormone-secreting bits. Less importantly, I've got a few muscle implants and some corresponding implants in the movement parts of my brain. When I'm operating on someone, they keep my hand entirely steady, amazingly precise.' He tapped a few keys on his portable terminal and lifted his right arm out in front of him, fingers pointed forward towards Zala, the hand uncannily still. 'There's no such thing as an off performance now, which is good because I have a career that's really not great for those. Then there's the regular stuff – eye correction and display processors. I'm going to assume from your whole "They're not a part of us" thing that you still don't have any bio-augs?'

Zala laughed self-consciously. 'Nope. I've even still got those old contact lenses. These days I have to reprogram my operating systems just so that they'll work with them, they're so outdated.'

'Well yeah,' Matsuda said, 'they became obsolete the moment they invented eye display processors thirty years ago. Add back five years to allow for laggard users and you're still using tech that's almost as old as you are. I swear, the lengths you'll go to in order to accommodate your anxieties . . .' His tone was so patronizing Zala couldn't help but get annoyed at her old friend.

'Hey, if I can make it work, it doesn't matter, right?'

'Whatever,' said Matsuda. 'So how did you get back into the city?'

'I found a scanner in a dump. I got an admin account with code injection on some obscure government agency site. Replaced someone else's biometrics with my own. As far as the city knows, Selina Mullur returned home yesterday. It was embarrassingly easy.' Zala laughed.

'Christ, just like that? I guess they wouldn't have replaced the scanners in all the stations just yet. Makes me wonder how many holes there'll be in the quarantine of the high-infection areas if that has to go up.'

Quarantine of the high-infection areas. Something about that – maybe the dismissive tone, maybe something deeper – turned Zala's stomach, but she shook it off. 'Oh, this was a replaced one. I guess it uses the same protocols, it just counted the older scanner's readings.'

Matsuda paused for a moment contemplatively, before visibly dismissing whatever his train of thought was. 'If only fixing your criminal record was that easy, eh?'

'Honestly, it still makes me laugh that, with all the illegal shit we were getting up to back then, they nailed me with a fabricated charge as a trap for my dad. A brief scan of my home computer would have been more than enough.'

Matsuda chuckled. 'I guess so . . .' Then his face fell and his voice became softer. 'I miss it, you know? I've never felt as powerful as I did back then.'

Zala realized he looked genuinely sad. 'You save lives almost every day, yet you felt more powerful back when you were going through databases or messing with web pages?'

'I guess it is kind of silly. There's just something about disengaging from all that high technology that's left me feeling kind of disempowered. Every time I lose a patient on the table I remind myself of how, back in the day, I could change things halfway around the world, reach through walls and over oceans. There's a lot of power in it all that you never really think about. Soucouyant victims say the same thing.'

Zala leaned across and touched his arm. 'That's nostalgia talking. It's not that great. I mean, I'd do anything to have your life.'

'Thanks,' Matsuda replied. The two of them had arrived back outside the graveyard and they slowed. 'My car is over there. It was great to see you.'

'Yeah,' said Zala, 'it was great to see you too. Thanks for everything.'

She stood for a moment, watching him go, and then turned away and headed back towards the city centre.

Zala lay on the apartment couch in a tank top and shorts, trying her best to unwind. Her funeral clothes had been returned to a still weeping Polina and she now had her portable terminal's projected screen illuminated in front of her. She was working on some fragments of code her father had left before his death. Most of what she had found she'd had no trouble identifying, and had reconstructed entire programs: the remains of an unusually complex firewall here, a powerful network analysis tool there. Others had presented a challenge. One remained a mystery; unlike the other fragments of code, it was written in such alien language and syntax she had been unable to decipher it, and had only just enough structure for her to be sure it wasn't merely corrupted or encrypted with a cypher. But almost all the rest had made themselves useful in some way.

Eight years ago, Zala's father had been a project leader at the IT department of GeniSec, but had been forced to flee after being accused of corporate malfeasance. He'd never told her what it was, but she had always assumed that he had attempted to steal something from the project he was working on, something valuable enough to risk his and Zala's safety. Six months after they had fled, GeniSec released a number of very important computer programs, which fit Zala's theory closely enough that she'd taken it as confirmed. These included the revolutionary IntuitivAI protocol, a new generation of simulated artificial intelligence which ended up being used everywhere from navigational systems to enemy behavioural programming in video games. Of course, that would mean that Zala's father had been trying to steal something huge, but she was always unsure just how much credit to give the man. After all, his greed, his selfishness had landed her with three alleged murders to her charge and made her a fugitive in her own right, which had lowered her expectations of him.

The lines of code blurred and Zala realized her gaze had been focusing on the terminal itself, a small black unit strapped to her wrist. She thought about all the things Matsuda had said.

There really isn't an 'us and them' at this point.

Zala closed her eyes and imagined wires slithering out of the back of her terminal and into her arm, under her skin. The cables branched out like roots, spreading further and further up her arm like great swollen arteries. The skin around the terminal began to creep up the sides of the terminal itself, enveloping it into her arm.

Zala felt a huge, disgusted dry-retch coming, and held her hand over her mouth. As she brought it away, her eyes fell on the outlines of veins in her wrists. She couldn't help but imagine them as thick, dark wires.

Chapter 5

As if a fire were being lit in the darkness, Ryan Granier slowly returned to consciousness.

Thoughts filtered into his mind, a low, steady vibration, becoming louder and clearer. He became aware of a cold, hard, dusty floor beneath him and of a deep ache in his muscles from lying face down on it. Something was wound around his head – what felt like a blindfold. He tried to bring his hands round to pull it off, but found himself straining against tight plastic ties which resisted his attempts to break them. His wrists had been bound, he realized, as had his ankles. He tried rolling onto his side using his shoulders and knees, but failed. The blind thrashing disoriented him and for a moment he lay there, trying to re-establish which way up was. Then he twisted and pushed again, this time succeeding in balancing on his side. Now his weight no longer restricted his breathing, he let out a yell.

'Hey!'

Moments later, he heard a shuffling noise in front of him. A muffled voice said, 'Is he awake?'

A second voice replied, 'From the sound of things, yeah.'

Ryan lowered his head and rubbed it against the floor. The blindfold loosened. He pushed again, and it lowered just enough that one eye was exposed. He looked around. He was in what seemed to be a small office. The windows had been painted black, but a little light came through gaps and cracks in the paint. He appeared to be alone in this room, but someone was standing just outside it.

'Hey! Who's there?' he shouted, louder this time.

Almost immediately, the door's lock rattled and it opened. Standing in the doorway was a tall, worn-looking woman with a cigarette in her mouth, wearing what looked like old Security Force overalls.

'Good morning, Councillor,' she said, leaning on the door-frame.

Ryan shifted himself round to face her properly and said, 'Where am I?'

'You, Councillor, are in a safe house of the New Cairo Liberation Corps, where you'll be staying until further notice.'

So I'm a hostage.

The woman crossed the room, grabbed a chair and dragged it in front of Ryan. Before sitting down she took a deep drag from her cigarette and let the smoke leak out from the corners of her mouth.

'What do I call you?' Ryan said.

'Call me . . . Matron.' She snorted with gravelly laughter at her own joke. 'I'll be the one looking after you during your stay with us. I'll be seeing that you get fed, keep an eye on you to make sure you don't overstep any bounds and I'll be discouraging any ill-advised escape attempts.' She motioned to the pistol in a holster on her hip.

Ryan nodded. 'Okay, okay . . .' He gathered his thoughts. 'So . . . how long am I going to be here for?'

'Matron' brought up the holographic screen of her portable terminal and opened up a newscast. She rotated the screen so that Ryan could see it.

The headline read:

QUARANTINE VOTE STALLED, CLLR RYAN GRANIER TAKEN
HOSTAGE

The picture showed the outside of the Council building crawling with police, reporters and onlookers. The voice-over said '. . . captors released a series of demands earlier this morning, including the scrapping of the quarantine bill, the reactivation of the shuttle elevators in and out of the city and an end to the existing moratorium on the emigration of citizens from high-infection areas. The council has put its vote for the quarantine on hold for the moment, as Councillor Granier was considered a major force on one side of the debate. In the meantime, the High Councillor made a statement outside the Council building.'

The video feed switched to show Ryan's father on the podium, addressing the mob of reporters in front of him. 'Yesterday a beloved public servant was taken from this very building. He is being held hostage by a terrorist group who are intent on destroying this city. But we will not bow down to the will of these loathsome thugs. They have killed and butchered innocent people, they have started riots which threatened to tear this city in two, all for the sake of saving themselves while inflicting upon the world a virus which would cripple all of humanity. And now they have taken hostage a great man who has fought tirelessly for the very people these terrorists claim to represent. I can assure you all that these base criminals will be brought to justice.'

As the clip was replaced with a round-table of pundits ready to pick apart the speech, Matron turned off the screen. 'So, to answer your question, it all depends on whether or not your dad plays ball. And he can huff and puff all he likes, but so long as he's not pushing forward on the blanket quarantine, you're all right.'

'But I was going to vote against that. I was the leader of a push to stop that bill. Why do *I* get taken prisoner?'

'This isn't really about you, Councillor, though, for the record, you didn't have the amount of votes you thought you had. We've taken you as our guest because of your father's position as High Councillor, and for the pressure it puts on him.'

She strode over to the doorway and motioned to someone standing outside. A stocky, bald man walked in and grabbed

Ryan's legs. Matron moved behind him and picked him up around the waist, and the two of them carried him through the door, depositing him on a chair.

The room he was now in was larger, a central hall with many doors around the perimeter. Whatever sort of business this building had once housed, the barred windows and the two-layer arrangement of heavy doors over what looked like the entrance suggested he was in Naj-Pur. Ryan's heart sank. Naj-Pur had been a no-go area for the police since the riots had started and, depending where you were, even the Council's military police organization, the Security Force, seemed reluctant to enter. The windows in this room too had been painted over in black and the walls were bare, though mounting brackets suggested that computer terminals had been set up there until recently.

'I've got work to do. Try not to swallow your tongue or anything,' said Matron, as she sat at a desk near by. The bald man had walked off to Ryan's left, through a door that appeared to lead into a long passage.

For a while she typed and Ryan Granier sat in silence, thinking things through and trying to move his arms enough to keep circulation going. As a teenager, he'd received training on what to do in a hostage situation; his father had insisted on it. The thought of it had at the time seemed scary to Ryan. Back then, it was as if the concept of kidnapping children of business magnates had only just been created, and Ryan had found it hard not to resent his father for not letting him live in ignorance. Rule One, the first thing he'd been told, was to under no circumstances try to escape. Matron was armed, and the doors were locked, so that wasn't a possibility anyway. From then on, he'd been taught, the steps to surviving a hostage situation were all in the mind. He thought back to his training all those years ago and checked down the list of rules he'd committed to memory.

He'd been informed of the motive for his kidnapping already, and had gained a sense of time and location. For now, cooperation and civility were important, but beyond that, actively being sociable and empathetic towards the people holding you hostage was the most useful thing. When it was decreed that he'd undergo hostage training, he'd expected an ex-soldier or police officer, someone who would teach him to defend himself, but instead he'd been placed under the care of a smiling young woman who specialized in psychology. She'd taught him that the greatest danger to a hostage was the threat of dehumanization, where a captor's empathy is lessened to the point where abuse and violence becomes easier and easier. The ability to engage and form a bond with your captor was the surest way to ensure that you stayed alive. Rule Two, she'd told him, was to make them like you, respect you and make them care what happened to you. The idea was almost a reverse Stockholm Syndrome. In addition, conversation and mental stimulation were essential for keeping the mind active and stopping the onset of depression. Ryan realized that the silence surrounding him was doing him no favours on this front.

'I voted for you, you know. We all did round here,' said Matron, looking up from her monitor.

Ryan had not expected that. 'Thanks,' he replied.

'The fact is, Councillor, we have similar goals. There aren't many hostages who can say that.' Matron lit another cigarette. 'So we figure you'll be more cooperative. Might even get that quarantine bill scrapped. We want the same thing.'

'I just want to go, place my vote and try and stop the quarantine bill. You've taken me prisoner and are ransoming me off,' Ryan said. 'We do not want the same thing.'

'Of course we do. Our ultimate goal here is the reinstatement of freedoms we had six weeks ago. They took away the right of people from around here to leave the city. They took away the right to be out after nine at night. And they're coming for whatever other rights they can get their hands on.' She took another deep drag of the cigarette. 'You know why I voted for you? You look out for the little guy. I look at the Council and I see people who've only lived at the top and who think that the worst it gets, the people that need protecting, are somewhere around the middle. Or I see people from the bottom who'll climb on everyone from where they came from to get to the top, and then promptly forget us. They all pretend that the city was some utopia, that it was all fine until the virus came along. Hell, at this point I wouldn't be surprised if some of them genuinely believed it.' Matron shrugged. 'They don't know how bad we had it here in Naj-Pur, or over in Surja. All the inequalities that have been brought up to the light of day with the Soucouyant were always there. They're just being exposed now. But you seemed to get it. You have more of a silver spoon than anyone else in this city. You're the prince of New Cairo, the heir to both a great political dynasty and the city's most powerful conglomerate.' She paused, then snorted derisively. 'You don't really know what the hell you're talking about when you're addressing the privilege you were born with. But you want to know. You care more about the vulnerable people in this city than the rest of those other ones combined. It helps that you're the only one who butts heads with your father and leaves with a political career still intact.'

'I appreciate the approval. I've seen how bad it gets around here,' said Ryan, trying to treat the woman like she was just another constituent, 'and I'm glad that you think I'm doing a good job fighting for you.'

'Oh, I didn't say that. Your heart's in the right place, but right now you're of more use to us as a hostage than as a representative. It's those others, the rich who serve the rich. Against them, you don't stand much of a chance. So we're repurposing you into something that'll get things done more efficiently.'

Ryan didn't know what to say to that. As he mulled over responses in his head, a woman came through the doorway the bald man had disappeared down. With her was a young boy of about seven who hung around in the doorway, allowing Ryan another quick glance down a long corridor. He noted a number of doors to add to his mental map of the building.

'We need more medicine; Lya's fever is still as high as it was,' said the woman, who was visibly distressed.

'Calm down, Kanak,' Matron replied. 'The medicine won't even have kicked in yet. Give it some time.'

The woman looked as though she was about to say something more, but then she spotted Ryan. Glancing back at Matron without turning away from Ryan, she said, 'He's out of the room he was left in, I see.'

'Oh really, Kanak? I hadn't noticed,' said Matron, rolling her eyes. 'He's no threat, he's a bureaucrat. And he can barely move.'

The child had abandoned his post in the doorway, and had made his way over to Ryan, eyeing him up suspiciously. He looked to be the same age as Ryan's own youngest son. 'Who're you?' he asked, in an accusing tone.

Ryan turned to face the child and said, 'I'm Councillor Ryan Granier. I'm a guest here.'

'And why're your hands all tied up?'

'Because your mother's friends want me to keep being a guest here, and I don't.'

The boy looked confused. His mother, Kanak, came up behind him and said, 'We're looking after him so that the bad person won't close down the city.'

This didn't help the boy's bewilderment. 'Is he a bad person?'

Kanak hesitated. 'No, but he needs to be here. It's complicated.'

The acknowledgement that the situation was difficult to understand appeared to vindicate the boy's trouble doing so and he nodded. 'I'm Vikenti, and my friends call me Vik,' he proclaimed.

Kanak strode over and pulled him away from Ryan. 'Don't tell him that!'

'But Mum,' said the confused boy, 'you always say to tell people your name when they've told you theirs.'

Kanak sighed with frustration and strode back over to Matron's desk.

A heavy knock came at the huge main door into the building, across the room from where Ryan sat.

Matron pushed herself up from her chair and walked slowly and warily towards the heavily secured entrance, pistol drawn.

Another knock.

Matron looked through a spyhole in the wall and muttered 'Shit' under her breath. She pulled open the door and three people in dark clothes stumbled into the room. They carried a slumped fourth between them, arms draped over his comrades. Something was very wrong. They laid the man on the ground face up, and Ryan realized he was bleeding heavily from the left side of his stomach. Kanak covered Vik's eyes and led him out of the room, slamming the door to the passageway behind them. Ryan diverted his gaze, trying as hard as he could not to look at the dark red pumping from the man's abdomen.

Matron strode across the room, head turned to keep her gaze on the wounded man, and grabbed a large green polymer case. She opened it up, and pulled out a big pair of scissors.

'What the hell happened?' she yelled.

'A couple of SecForce troops came out of nowhere, command didn't even see them until it was too late. Yosef got hit. We only just made it out.'

'Command had better have a damn good explanation for this,' Matron growled, more to herself than to any of the others.

She cut his shirt upwards from the hem and pulled the soaked material aside to reveal a gaping red-black puncture wound sunk low into the man's ribcage, blood oozing out. One of the other black-clad newcomers peeled off the blood-soaked carapace of light body armour and pushed his whole weight over the wound, trying to stop the blood flow, but the wounded man groaned at the pressure.

'Is there an exit wound?' said Matron.

The man pressing down on the wound quickly leaned down and examined the rest of the wounded man's torso, rolling him onto his side to check his back. 'No, from what I can see the bullet's still in him. It was just a pistol shot. Small calibre, pretty sure regular patrols only carry nine-millimetre rounds.'

Matron nodded, and jabbed a small green-black pad onto the wounded man's skin, an inch or so above the gunshot wound. It deflated onto his skin, leaking a haemostatic gel into the area around the wound. The blood stopped flowing so heavily; the skin around the wound turned paler. She ran one hand across the man's neck and another over his mouth and nose. Seeming satisfied there was a pulse and the man was breathing, she then attached a small silver thread to a port in the side of her terminal, and inserted the other end into the wound. The terminal projected in front of her what appeared to be a video feed coming from the other end of the thread. 'I can't see any major ruptures, but I can't see the bullet either. His body armour must have taken a lot of the momentum out of the bullet; I'm mostly just seeing muscle damage. I can sew up the arteries it's nicked and take more of a look around in the med room here. Hear that, Yosef? You didn't screw up getting shot so badly.'

The man grunted in response. This seemed to satisfy Matron. 'Just lift him onto the table in there and give me a second to turn on my bio-augs.'

She looked again at her terminal and flicked through a few menus. From where he was sitting, Ryan could make out the words 'stabilizer' and 'precision'. The three newcomers carefully lifted the wounded, groaning man and carried him into an adjacent room – a makeshift medical room, he ascertained, with a red cross newly painted on the door. Matron then threw her equipment back into the case and followed them out.

And Ryan was alone.

He'd never seen anyone with a gunshot wound, or really anyone in a state of mortal injury, he realized. He'd fought to end the violence in these areas for years, working with business leaders and lobbyists – including some who would go on to become the founders of the New Cairo Liberation Corps – to lower crime in the area. They'd done a lot. But the violence itself was an abstraction, a word written in a pleasingly formal font in a newscast. He'd never seen that – a human body, ripped and punctured, failing and leaking like a punctured bag of liquid. He'd never smelt blood so strongly.

He felt a visceral sense of horror spread from his gut out through the rest of his body. It was as though he could sense his every vein and artery and organ, and he found himself instinctively pressing his bound hands against his back, as though the veins criss-crossing them were too perilously exposed and in need of protection.

The dark red smear on the concrete floor across the room seemed so unnaturally vibrant to him.

Chapter 6

Suman Chaudhri slammed his fists down on the desktop and screamed 'Dammit!' at the screen. The other operators around him were too focused on their tasks to pay attention, and Suman Chaudhri was left to stare alone at the monitor. He was seated at the central command station of the New Cairo Liberation Corps's main base, where he had spent the last hour directing an operation a few miles away. From a damaged, uncomfortable chair across the room, Alice Amirmoez leaned to the left and saw red words scrolling along the bottom of his holographic terminal screen.

USER Y. J. KLEIN VITAL SIGNS UNDETECTED.

The personnel monitoring system the NCLC were using was different in its layout from the equivalent she had used years ago, but that message had always come in the same shade of red. Instinctively, she leapt up from her seat and ran across the room towards the man slumped at the massive terminal.

'What happened?' she said urgently to Suman, who turned round in his chair and gawped at her. She grabbed him by the shoulders and pulled him up to look her in the eye. 'Suman, I can help you. I did this for years. But you have to tell me what went wrong.'

Suman's voice was low and hoarse with anxiety. 'One of the smaller armed units was doing a sweep of a building that seemed suspicious. The New Cairo Security Force have been setting up safe houses in civilian areas to support a bigger push into Naj-Pur and Surja, and we thought we might have found one. The building was empty, but a Security Force team caught them leaving. One of them got shot, and they ran, dragging him with them. His vitals have been erratic for a few minutes, but they just completely cut out as the group got to Safe House Two.'

'How did you not see the Security Force team coming?' Alice asked incredulously, without even thinking about it and with more force than was probably necessary.

'I don't know, I must have missed them! I thought I had all the security cameras in network, but something must have happened to one of them,' said Suman, half sobbing.

Juri Dajili, the heavily bio-auged operator sitting on Suman's left, unjacked the cable from her eye and turned towards the two of them. 'If there was a security camera that spotted them in network, I'd have seen them. There must have been a malfunction. It's not his fault, Alice.'

Staring into the smooth metal sphere in Juri's eye socket Alice couldn't help but lose her train of thought. She nodded and turned back to Suman. 'Don't fall apart on me. You don't know what happened. Maybe when he got shot, the vitals sensor got damaged. Hell, maybe it just fell off. You can track the location of the sensor, right? Where is it now?'

'Outside the safe house.'

'And the rest of the group?'

'They're in the safe house.'

Alice could feel him trembling. 'Then there's no way his squad mates left him out there,' she said. 'The sensor may not be responding because it's not attached to him any more. It's probably fine.'

'Either way, we need someone coordinating another sweep right now,' said Juri.

Alice nodded. 'Let me take over from you. You go have a break, I'll handle this next operation and then I'll let you know when there's word on the injured man.'

Suman looked momentarily confused. 'What do you mean, you'll take over?'

'Suman, you practised for this with, what, a week of virtual training? I worked a field patrol for the Detroit Security Force for half a decade and was a mission coordinator for the police here in New Cairo for eight years. I did this for a living, and I was good, and right now you're in no shape to be sitting at this monitor making life-or-death decisions. So when I say I'll take over, what I mean is that I can run the next mission so you have a chance to get your head straight. Now get up.'

After a few moments, Suman nodded and went over to the makeshift kitchen on the far side of the room. Alice took his place at the central command station in the middle of the huge array of terminals. She looked over her shoulder at the nearest operator. 'So what's happening, Juri?'

'A regular bug plant,' Juri replied, reinserting the cable from her terminal into her eye. 'We're pretty sure the Security Force is setting up camp all around the Naj-Pur area, so we send a few people in plain clothes and lightly armed to go do some scouting. You're directing them, telling them where to go and what to do, but they're experienced operatives – ex-military or police for the most part, just like you – so they're more than capable of taking initiative if need be. If they find something they're briefed to break in and install some malware, something that'll let us see what SecForce is doing.'

'Do we have a backup plan, in case our guys get compromised?'

'If necessary, we send a reserve unit, heavily armed and with all the gear we can load on them, to tail the scouts as backup.' Juri tapped the metallic eye. 'Meanwhile, I scan the security camera network we've hacked and reroute any pertinent information to you. That way, whatever decisions you make will be as well informed as they possibly can be. The others keep their eyes on police or civilian communications in the area, and again, send you anything you need to know.'

'And I take all that and tell our people where to go, what to do and so on.'

Juri nodded. 'That's right. Now, you'll be doing so from a big map with everyone's locations and video feeds superimposed, and specific details at the bottom. We've got a pretty simple short-hand if you need to yell something – our guys in the NCLC are "operatives" and the Security Force people are "SecForce" or just "troops". We'll know who you mean straight away if you use that.' Juri looked round at Alice again, the head of the cable jack pointing towards her. 'You say you worked with the police doing this same thing, right? Well this is similar. All these guys have optical implants, hand stabilizers, stuff like that. They're as capable as anyone we have at our disposal and they're kitted out well enough that you don't need to worry about being outgunned. Just tell them where to go and they'll go there.'

Alice settled down into her seat and looked up at the program spread out on the main monitor of the command terminal. Dominating the huge holographic screen in front of her was a simple map, outlining in white on a black background a bird's-eye image of the area. Augmenting this otherwise Spartan approach were small floating windows depicting video feeds from hijacked CCTV cameras and harness-mounted wireless cameras belonging to the NCLC operatives. The effect was a simultaneous stripped-down geographical abstraction and borderline-cubist presentation of huge quantities of information. She at once knew where everything was in an immediate sense and, if she wanted it, what everything looked like, precise positions, and other such information the video windows imparted to her. It felt natural to her, like coming home.

The map detailed a portion of the lower-west end of Naj-Pur: two main streets crossing towards the top of the screen at a tight acute angle, with a wedge of terraced houses between them. One road, Bajil, went from north to south along the right third of the screen, and the other, Freja, ran diagonally from near the bottom left to the top right. Alleyways ran between the two. Of the buildings in the wedge, the computer coloured several green, a few blue, and one in particular – 264 Bajil – was coloured red. This, Alice assumed, must be the target house.

She saw the NCLC operatives, represented as white teardrop shapes, advancing north along Bajil. The video feeds showed a small group of men and women in plain clothes and apparently unarmed. The curfew was less than an hour away.

A regular patrol of SecForce troops were moving up and down Freja, towards the top right. The video feed showed that they were equipped for business, clad in typical military-style armoured helmets and visors which completely obscured their faces, with heavy body armour over the top of standard overalls. They carried high-calibre rifles, though they were slung low. It was an intimidating sight, as it was meant to be, but they looked like a pacifying force, there to make a presence felt within a potentially volatile community. Alice couldn't remember seeing this area on the news during the riots or any of the subsequent fighting, but all it took was for her to look at the relaxed stance and easy gait of the SecForce troops to know that they weren't expecting any real activity. Maybe they would glance down Bajil before passing the crossroads and continuing up Freja. Attention from the major forces should be focused on the other side of the district, following the evening's earlier fire-fight.

She looked over at the NCLC unit list to the right of the screen. She had control of six operatives, all of whom had whatever instructions were sent their way fed into their optic implants, allowing them to be directed discreetly wherever necessary. They could be sent commands by text, voice or contextual waypoints selected on the map. They could be commanded as a group, individually, or assigned to smaller units, typically of two or three. As well as being less conspicuous than a large mob all moving around together, smaller groups were more versatile, while standing a better chance in a fight than individual soldiers. Alice split them into three units of two, assigning each group a letter and an individual number to each operative within those groups.

It all came back to her so quickly, muscle memory she thought she'd lost years before.

As the rebel operatives closed in on the target house, she selected

Group C and set a waypoint around the front, attaching a small text instruction for them to act casually. The other four were sent into an alley which ran along the side of the house between Bajil and Freja. There was a 70-degree bend in the middle of the alley, which kept them hidden them from the SecForce patrol.

On command, Groups A and B moved up to the large concrete wall separating the property itself from the alleyway. Alice watched as Group B boosted Group A over the wall. Group B then walked on and stood at the bend in the alley, giving them good views either way; they lit cigarettes and talked in low voices, trying not to appear as if they were doing anything out of the ordinary.

Alice focused on the windows relaying audio-visual feeds from the operatives now within the house. She turned on her cochlear implant and heard a voice come through, the screen in front of her indicating that it was Operative A-2. 'Okay, the downstairs I'm seeing looks like a regular family home. But it's strange. I'm probably being paranoid but it feels a little too normal, a little too conspicuously lived-in.'

'It's so unsuspicious it's making you suspicious?' said Alice.

The operative laughed. 'Yeah, something along those lines,' she said. 'Living room clear. Not seeing anything SecForce-issue. No unusual tech . . .' She trailed off. 'If you don't mind me asking, who is this?'

'Alice Amirmoez. Suman's taking some rest.'

'Amirmoez . . .' Operative A-2 repeated. Alice wondered if she'd ever known Jacob or had just recognized the name.

Alice watched as the video feed swept along the downstairs. The camera was clipped to the operative's shoulder and the feed streaming back to the main screen was bumpy, over-compressed and only showed bits at a time, but a deflated feeling set in as she became increasingly convinced that all she was seeing was the normal downstairs of a normal house.

'All right, guys, check upstairs.'

Alice sat back in her chair and tried to release the tension in her shoulders. It was as if no time had passed at all. When she was first assigned her mission coordinator role in the New Cairo police, she'd resented no longer being in the field. But the timing worked for her – the better pay and far greater safety suited a mother – and after a while, she grew into it. She came to appreciate that while in the field there was the satisfaction to be had from concrete, assigned objectives, being a coordinator presented more of an intellectual challenge. It involved strategy and deduction, an understanding of the bigger picture and an ability to lead. And there was a power to it. When Alice ran an operation, she played it like a chess game against whoever, if anyone, was coordinating the other side. And she not only won, she dominated. She toyed with and then punished her enemies. She manipulated and tricked. No one under her command would have wanted to ignore her instructions. They knew that the reward for obedience was victory. In the field, a soldier's tool is their gun. Alice's tool was the soldiers themselves.

Now the opponents were the military police force and she was on the side of the criminals. For years, the police had been protectors of her family's safety, now they were what she was hiding from. It was a mental quandary she wasn't quite ready to resolve yet.

'Ma'am?'

Alice snapped to attention. Operative A-2 was calling to her. 'Talk to me.'

'We're upstairs, on the landing. We've got something. There are two rooms. The one next to the bathroom has a heavy bolted metal door with biometric locks,' the operative whispered, 'This is not normal bedroom security, this is not within a Naj-Pur budget and this is definitely not civilian tech.'

Alice's heart leapt. 'Is there anyone in there?'

'No idea. Can't tell from this side of the door.'

Alice thought for a moment. There was no other way.

'Take cover in the bathroom and try to stay out of sight of anyone coming through. I'm not sure what'll happen next, but I need you guys to be in place to do whatever I say needs doing when I say it. Get ready for my signal.'

The team had thirty minutes before the curfew started.

While Group A waited in the bathroom for further instructions, Alice ordered Group C to move from their lookout position around the front of the house and regroup with Group B in the alleyway. Like trained performers, the operatives in Group B quickly got into position and boosted Group C into the back garden. Operative B-1 then took up his old position in the bend of the alley while Alice sent Operative B-2 out front, with instructions to knock on the neighbours' door and ask about whether the noise from the recent refurbishments had bothered them.

In the meantime, it was the turn of Group C to get to work. Nodding to his companion, Operative C-1 cupped his hands low, providing a foothold, and C-2 stepped onto them, leaning against the building for balance. Reaching up to the first-floor window, he knocked twice, firm raps that shook the glass. No response from within.

C-1 widened his stance as C-2 stepped up onto his shoulders. Both were tall men, and with their combined height:

'I can see through the window,' came C-2's voice from the terminal. Alice leaned forward in her chair, trying to see into the window through C-2's mounted camera. 'It's a regular master bedroom, but something's wrong. Either their architect is M. C. Escher or the floor plan Group A scanned is wrong, because these walls aren't lining up with the walls they're seeing on this end, and there's no big heavy door or anything either.'

Alice paused and tried to make sense of this. Juri took the opportunity to send over a security camera feed, showing the SecForce patrol too far off to see or hear any commotion. Alice looked round at her and nodded in acknowledgement, then turned back to her terminal.

'C-2, can you open the window or break the glass?' she asked.

'Neither without attracting attention.'

A message from Operative B-2 came through.

'The neighbours are apparently used to lots of noise from this house as of late. There have been a whole load of renovations, and they've not met the occupants, so they're all pretty suspicious already. Don't make too much noise but some is fine.'

C-2 got out a thin stiletto knife from a pocket inside his jacket, and slid the point under the window, before pulling down on the handle. C-1 braced and prepared to catch his colleague if need be.

The window lifted up.

Alice heard laughter.

'What's up?' she said.

'It's a membrane monitor. There's a big flexible physical monitor over the window, so anyone looking in from adjacent houses will just see a regular bedroom.'

'Group A isn't reporting any activity on their end. I guess it's empty,' said Alice. 'Now get back over that wall and out of there. We need you ready for action if we're going to get this finished before the curfew.'

She turned her attention back to Group A, who she could see had moved out of the bathroom and were positioned in front of the reinforced bedroom door. 'How long will it take you to hack the door?'

'The code itself will be encrypted, but it's only a few days since we got the last lot of encryption codes from a compromised SecForce account. Assuming they haven't changed them, it shouldn't be long. Once we're in, it's a different story. Bugs, network info, drive copying, tracking software, and then deleting all the logs telling them what we did? That might take a while.'

'Do it. We're pretty sure it's empty in there.'

Alice watched as, within thirty seconds, Group A were through the door and Groups B and C were back in their original positions. Alice kept tracking Group A's video feeds on the screen, completely engrossed. The operatives' cameras revealed a large room – banks of computers and a cache of weapons and body armour, and the windows with the huge membrane monitors draped over them, displaying the image of the master bedroom out into the world. Alice momentarily regretted that they couldn't steal or at least sabotage the guns, but this was potentially a gold-mine of valuable data and intelligence, not to mention a precious network they had easy access to. Restraint was advisable here.

'Ma'am, this looks to us like an unmanned safe house. No regular inhabitants. Any SecForce personnel under heavy fire could hide in here, or just refuel.'

'And what do we say to that, A-1?'

The operative laughed darkly. 'We say that there's nowhere they can hide from us, ma'am. In times of war you can't give your enemy any quarter.'

And with that they set to work, installing malicious software and cloning contents of hard drives.

'Alice, we've got a problem,' a small voice came from behind her.

Alice swivelled her chair to face Juri, whose silver socket-eye was still uncovered. 'What's up?'

'Up the end of Freja, at the crossroads? I'm seeing a large group of kids, maybe forty or fifty, pelting the security patrol with stones, trying to send them running back down Freja. I don't know who put them up to it, but I'd be looking for a safe house right about now if I were those soldiers.'

Alice felt a chill go through her.

She took a deep breath, holding it for a moment, before exhaling heavily. She turned back to the terminal, and the huge map monitor. In the lower part of the screen, pertinent security camera feeds and communication feeds were sent in. The words RETREAT TO BASE NO.52 were repeating over and over again.

'How're you doing, Group A?'

'This is going to take maybe another fifteen minutes. What's more – fuck – this door can't open for another ten. The entire thing shuts down for fifteen minutes after it closes, inoperable from either side. Just clams up.'

'Why the hell does it do that?' exclaimed Alice. The curfew was in twenty-five minutes, and it'd take them five minutes to reach a neighbourhood SecForce considered unsafe to patrol. If the SecForce troops couldn't get the aggressive crowd under control before then, they'd be forced back towards the house prematurely and the entire mission could be compromised.

'It's a security measure against hackers,' Operative A-2 replied sheepishly.

A low-resolution security camera image showed four SecForce troops aiming their weapons above the heads of the children as they backed off. They couldn't shoot at them, and the kids knew it, pressing the troops back down Freja with thrown stones and bottles.

Alice saw her opportunity. They'd be coming down the alley-way rather than straight through the front door.

'Group C, the SecForce patrol is coming your way fast. They're being chased by a mob of kids throwing rocks and bottles. Hold them up and buy some time, but make it look unintended. Group B, get across the road and keep an eye out for the backup.'

Alice then typed and sent the attached reserve combat unit a simple message: ALLEY OUTSIDE 264 BAJIL. SUPPRESSIVE FIRE ONLY. LEAD AWAY, KEEP EXITS OPEN. DELAY FOR 10 MINS, 15 IF POSSIBLE.

It would take them two minutes to find a good position, and the SecForce troops about that to emerge from the alleyway. Alice enlarged Group C's hidden camera feeds and watched the chaos unfold on the screen in front of her.

The four SecForce troops were shuffling fast down the alley-way, at this point batting stones and chunks of brick away with the butts of their rifles. As they neared the Group C operatives, now sitting casually in the alley and blocking the way, the lead SecForce trooper roared, 'Move!'

The two men looked surprised but feigned intoxication and delayed getting up just long enough that one of the troopers stumbled and fell over them. The others dragged their fallen comrade upright, then, with the angry crowd still advancing on them, pulled the NCLC pair to their feet and shoved them ahead down the alleyway. The Group C operatives protested the whole way, screaming about 'police brutality' and digging in their heels, while debris and rubbish bounced off the troops' body armour in an increasingly percussive fashion. Eventually, the troops gave up and pushed past the operatives. The crowd of children, uninterested in civilians, began to barge past too, but the operatives stood in their path, yelling, 'Stay back, they're gonna start shooting!' Faced with bellowed orders from two tall, powerfully built men, the youths lost their bravado and obeyed, continuing to throw their missiles from a distance.

From the alleyways across the road, Group B saw men in long coats begin to appear seemingly out of nowhere, hiding behind dumpsters, cars and low walls. The leader of the heavily armed combat unit, Maalik Moushian, gave Group B the signal to hide, and seconds later the four Security Force troops spilled out of the alley. Maalik's backup squad opened fire on them, bullets burying themselves into the thick walls of the mass-produced Naj-Pur houses and ricocheting off the pavement – hitting everything but the troops themselves, until the magazines ran dry. The backup squad then turned tail and ran, and the SecForce troops, at last faced with an enemy they could shoot at, gave pursuit.

'They'll be in for some fun. Maalik and his boys know this area like the backs of their hands,' said Juri, before muttering under her breath, 'Oh, Maalik's taking them *that* way? I'd have never thought of that . . .'

The map lit up with Maalik's men surging up the backstreets, alleyways and maze-like through paths – just slowly enough for the SecForce troops to keep up, but fast enough to confuse and disorient them. More than once they led them in circles, with the troops seeming more lost the second time than the first.

A rough voice filled Alice's ear implant. 'It's Maalik here. Sorry, but I'm going to have to disobey an order. Two of these guys are good shots. They're making things too risky for my team.'

Through the high-grade security camera feed, Alice watched Maalik stop for a moment and fire twice. Two of the four troops' heads flew back, dark red spurting against the heavy impact of the bullets, and they slumped to the ground. 'There,' said Maalik, 'hopefully that'll make things easier.'

Alice watched in horror as every gut-wrenching memory of officers under her command getting hurt came rushing back into her head.

'What the fuck was that for?' she screamed into her headset.

'They were problems. The problems have been removed. I've got people shooting at me, trying to kill us. Why would I not shoot back?'

Alice shook in her seat, trying to form some semblance of a response Maalik would respect. She couldn't think straight. Loud, sharp images in her mind twisted and distorted every fragment of thought, a darker, fresher horror reviving beneath it. The blood, the slumped, wrecked body. Smell of iron in the air. Red stain on her sleeve.

She did her best to push away the intruding memories and focus on Maalik. He'd been kind before, but if she didn't have an undeniable reason for the moratorium on killing active, deadly threats, he'd laugh in her face. She was new, she wasn't formally a member of the NCLC, she'd wanted no part in the movement until Jacob's death. He might not even be willing to take orders from her.

She straightened up in her chair and spoke into the headset microphone as calmly as she could.

'You're trying to keep them away from that safe house, not panicking and running home, and you shot their best people. Is having a few less bullets flying your way worth getting the operatives in the house killed?'

There was silence.

'All right, fine, but if this doesn't work and one of my people gets hurt, you'd better believe I'm coming to you about it. What do you want from us now?'

'Yell for retreat. Loud enough that the Security Force can hear.'

When she was coordinating missions for the police, she'd only ever sent a kill order out against armed, dangerous criminals. That had been easier to rationalize. They were an immediate threat, to the police and to those around them. Many were already murderers. The dead SecForce troops had been a danger to her people, a threat to the mission, but they were men and women doing a job, trying to make the city secure for their families and friends.

Alice thought of Ria, and of Zeno.

Those troops were the other side, but they were men and women who were running from a mob, in a part of the city which hated them for reasons they had little control over. Had they been scared?

And there was a part of her, deeper down, that was appalled that someone had disobeyed her direct order for suppressive fire only, that they had disregarded her authority. But that was the part of her she kept to herself, and buried deep in the back of her mind.

'Ma'am, if you're not too busy, we're done here.' Operative A-1's voice crackled in Alice's ear. 'Can we go?'

Alice snapped to, and gave them the call to leave. They ran downstairs and out of the back door, where Group C helped them clamber over the wall. The backup operatives were given the signal to lose the remaining two troopers and retreat, and as quickly as they arrived, they had disappeared off into the city. The six plain-clothes operatives met in front of the house and ran back the way they had originally come, with just enough time to get to a safe area before the curfew started.

Alice slumped down in her chair, breathing deeply. She felt calm. She felt strong. For the first time since she'd discovered Jacob's body, she felt like she was in control. Spinning her chair round, she saw that the command room was now full of people, all of whom had their eyes on her. Suman looked at the screen with a mix of envy and nausea in his eyes, aware that he wouldn't have been able to do anything close to what Alice had accomplished. Tal and Nataliya beamed at her. Kahleed simply smiled, nodding.

'Ladies and gentlemen,' he said. 'No deaths, all the intelligence we could want and few signs we were ever there. I think a round of applause for Mrs Amirmoez is in order.'

The room rang with applause and cheering. Alice heard it, but as if it were somewhere far away.

No deaths, he'd said.

The two bodies going limp replayed over and over and over in Alice's head. Her hands tightened into fists.

Chapter 7

Zala woke to the shrill sound of her terminal's message alert. Shaking herself awake, she half fell out of the fold-out sofa bed in Polina's apartment and blindly reached around on the floor for her terminal, weakly opening her sleep-knotted eyelids to gaze at the small holographic screen. It was a message from Matsuda, his first since the funeral three days before.

>I put together a collection of the memory dumps we've managed to salvage off shut-down bio-augs. We're analysing a bunch of it, but the more hands at work the better. Plus, we only have access to legal methods of analysis, hint hint. Let us know if you get anything.

What followed was a link to a download containing several thousand memory dumps – emergency records of their working memory prior to crashing, made up of communication logs and process logs for the most part – almost all of which were corrupted.

Zala pulled herself up onto the bed, sat back and opened up the virtual operating system she used to carry out her illicit activities, and ran the logs through a scanning program. Piece by piece, it scanned for similarly sequenced segments, formulating possible lines of code from the matches it found. Of course, chance similarities in the strings of useless characters thrown up by the corruption caused a lot of false results, but occasionally strands of code that actually made contextual sense came up.

In particular, as Zala scrolled through the results, she kept noticing a connection log that appeared over and over again. The readout from the program told her that, of the 2,379 memory banks, 594 had uncorrupted logs of a file 'gssmr.auge' being transferred to it at some point. Another 1,006 had fragments of code that the program decided could well be other gssmr logs. The time between the file arriving and the termination of the bio-augmentations varied wildly but its presence was a common factor.

The program spat out a list of all the bio-augs with the gssmr file and the Extended Internet Protocol addresses which detailed the rough location of the device from which it had been downloaded. Zala then fed these results into one of those less-than-legal programs Matsuda had hinted at. It was adapted from a network analysis program her dad had been working on. Ostensibly that was to help companies track where malicious software on their networks had come from, but Zala figured it was actually a mechanism he'd designed so that he could steal even more from his former employers at GeniSec. So she'd taken something created by her father for stealing more, and turned it inside out. She fitted it with automated hacking scripts and upped its ambition from local networks to international ones. The program looked at the EIP addresses and sent probes to check them out. These would then map every connection in every log, millions an hour, using automated hacking scripts to get access to the addresses. Eventually, most of them would find their way to a central address, which with any luck would be the virus's origin point. This process, however, would take an hour or so, even on the standard of terminal set-up Zala used. She checked the time, set the program running, and messaged Matsuda.

>Found a link. A file a load of them had in their memories. gssmr. auge. I don't know the file type off the top of my head. I'm running an EIP trace on the confirmed ones at the moment. I'm going to find out where this is coming from. Still keeping an eye out for other leads though.

A percentage point on the tracing program's progress bar later, and she got a response.

>Damn, you work fast. Great find. How many EIPs are you tracing?

Zala checked her notes.

>About 600, with 1,006 possible EIPs I can also run.

Matsuda's response came much faster this time.

>Wow. 600 simultaneously? That's . . . okay, I can't ask you any more because I am out of that scene and I don't know who can read this but . . . that is eyebrow-raising. I'll let you get back to that. Keep me abreast.

Behind the pop-up with the progress bar, the terminal's monitor showed a network of connections threading together like a great big cobweb. The program passed to and from EIP addresses belonging to bio-augs. The thicker a thread was, the more common the connection. As the bar ticked along, the web grew in complexity, as though a spider was weaving it in real time, filling in the gaps, out of strands of gssmr. The mesh of gold against the black background reminded Zala very much of the view of the city from above when she was in the elevator coming down a few days ago.

Slowly but surely, as Zala showered, got dressed and made herself some toast, the probing software found its way to fifty or so people who didn't appear to have received the gssmr.auge file from any other infectee – the patient zeroes. Zala noted down their bio-augmentations' EIP addresses. However, the path didn't stop there. It continued forward, showing Zala that the virus had transferred to the bio-augs of those patient zeroes after they had interfaced with infected medical scanners. Without a directory there was no way to tell if the medical scanners were located in a doctor's office or with one of the groups that had appropriated the technology for information smuggling or the like. But the trail kept going, past those, into the computers the scanners fed into, and, through a complex network, eventually joining the one big stream of the internet.

The trace travelled on through a number of seemingly random servers, computers and other networked devices, until to Zala's surprise it reached a sticking point, being redirected over and over between eight servers which formed an endless loop it couldn't get past.

Zala tried to find some client-side vulnerability through which she could feed the probe, but from where she was it seemed airtight. From the look of the set-up, the servers worked on a one-way system; there were a large number of servers, of which almost all could only be accessed via one remaining 'gateway' server. Coming in from the other side, any attempt at interaction would result in being batted from one server to the next, like being caught in a revolving door with one entrance locked from the outside. The data the servers contained was only accessible via the gateway server.

The catch, of course, was that Zala couldn't get the probe past those eight servers to locate the correct entry point. The only individuals who could access that were those who knew about it in the first place, and who could successfully connect to it without having to go via the loop servers that the criminal traffic was directed through. Cursing, Zala realized she would need to go to the server itself.

The servers were, from what she could tell, all in the same geographical location: a New Delhi Lifestyle Technologies server farm located on their campus downtown. This was a huge complex full of computer servers, which operated everything from internal databases to NDLT web pages. And of course, from time to time, there were stories of IT techs ordering in more servers than they needed and renting them out to cybercrime syndicates and other such enterprising individuals.

There were ways to get around this impasse, but Zala knew it wasn't going to be easy.

Polina came in behind her, still in her pyjamas and squinting, red-eyed, at the morning light. 'What're you up to then?' she said blearily.

Zala turned her head towards her. 'I've got to find a way to get access to a bunch of computer servers in the heavily fortified NDLT server farm, that are, in all probability, being used by a cybercriminal far more talented and way meaner than me, in order to figure out where a horrific, deadly virus came from.'

Polina screwed up her face and rested her head in her hand as though she had a headache. 'Okay, I get the whole misplaced guilt thing over this virus, and while what you're doing is merely ill-advised and criminal you know I'll be there cheering from the sidelines. But Zala, those things are more fortified than your average military base. Is it even possible for you to get in?'

Zala shrugged. 'If it is, I'll manage it.' She grinned.

The server farm itself was located in the basement of the city's main New Delhi Lifestyle Technologies complex, a stylishly designed campus located at the point where New Cairo's Alexandria district and the Downtown area where Polina lived met. NDLT had always separated itself from its main competitor, GeniSec, by appearing more modern and upmarket – the fact that New Delhi, their eponymous base, was the greatest cultural and artistic hub within 3,000 miles of New Cairo certainly helped with this image – and their corporate territory went out of its way to reflect this. At the heart of the campus were the NDLT Five Prongs: five broad, interconnected glass spires, branching off a flat plaza to create a gigantic, meticulously engineered hand, fingers reaching up as if to grasp at the sky. The complex contained most of the city's NDLT workshops and office space, a number of floors of high-end apartments, several hotels, a large multi-screen cinema, nightclubs, a three-floor mall packed with NDLT's various brands' flagship stores. Then there were underground levels with still more facilities: several small-scale factories and a number of laboratories as well as the very large server farm. The main entrances to the lower levels were locked at all times. Entry required a handprint and voice scan as well as a passcode that changed each week. Even most of the corporation's employees didn't have access; to those who worked in the tower offices, the lower levels were as much a mystery as they were to anyone outside the company. The only people who were allowed in were those directly employed down there, plus the security and maintenance crews; the latter were the only ones with access to more than one floor.

Zala had never seen the Five Prongs plaza this empty. Normally, it was somewhere between bustling and so full one had to fight through the crowds to get anywhere. It was essentially the only place with anything to do in Alexandria, and most of New Cairo's rich and privileged young people met there every day. At the very least it was usually a fool's mission to attempt to count the people in sight on the floor below, from her current vantage point on the second floor. But today when she tried, they numbered only around thirty. They seemed aloof, giving one another a wide berth and glaring suspiciously. No one knew over what distance the Soucouyant could be transmitted. Two people, looking elsewhere, almost walked into one another and upon realizing they scrambled backwards in panic. It would have been a funny sight, Zala thought, if the fear were not so thick in the air.

Supposedly, the plaza had changed a great deal since the Soucouyant virus had taken hold. On one hand, during the day it was this sparsely inhabited – limiting one's exposure to the outside world reduced the chances of catching the Soucouyant. During the night, however, escape took a different form, and throngs of people packed the nightclubs and bars. Alcohol sales had shot through the roof, victims of drug overdoses were clogging emergency wards, and more than one social commentator had speculated that nine months down the line a significant baby boom would be in full swing.

Zala's portable terminal told her that she only had a little while before the young, rich and self-destructive packed the plaza and her plan would begin.

The good thing about the Five Prongs being this empty was that it was very easy to keep tabs on the black-uniformed maintenance workers.

NDLT maintenance teams, especially the ones from the Five Prongs, were famous. A crew of almost two hundred, most were fully qualified engineers, and supposedly did everything from changing light-bulbs and cleaning toilets to fixing and calibrating machinery so advanced that the scientists using it barely understood it. They were an enigma; they rarely spoke to anyone other than their colleagues and they moved around by concealed passages and walkways that no one else could access. Zala had heard they were compensated handsomely for their expertise and their silence. Engineering was a difficult business; the industry had evolved to the point where people tended to be hyper-specialized freelancers who would be hired for a project on their own individual reputation. Most young people who qualified to be engineers but had no buzz behind them came out of university fighting for the few internships that were available, and if one of them missed an opportunity or simply made a few mistakes, they had no way into project teams or any other kind of regular employment as engineers. Many became mechanics, as Tarou had done up in Waystation Seven, but others were employed to maintain the premises of NDLT or its corporate competitors.

If Zala was going to find a way into the server farm, it would be through one of these uniformed workers.

From her position on the second floor of the plaza, she watched as one of the maintenance crew walked up to a panel of the wall, placed his gloved fingertips to the surface, and pushed it in to reveal a passageway into which he disappeared. She typed a few quick notes onto a document on her portable terminal and looked around for another crew member.

She'd been meticulously taking notes and testing theories about the maintenance crews all day. They were a strange group to study – one of them might be leaning against a wall, eating her lunch, then would turn round, place her hand over the same spot of wall she'd been leaning on, and disappear in. Another might suddenly rise up through a trapdoor in the floor. The Five Prongs had made such good use of well-hidden space in the layout of the building that more than once Zala had seen one of the crew emerge from a passageway that seemed geometrically impossible.

Zala closed down her terminal. She had enough notes for now.

Across the plaza, on the lower floor, was a bar called Ohm. Late afternoon not being a prime period for bars, it looked mostly empty, but in a few hours there would be lines around the plaza for its main attraction, a superclub called Amp. There would be thousands of people around, all drunk or high or otherwise indisposed, causing chaos. It was exactly the cover she needed.

Zala ducked into a nearby café, ordered a drink and sat down in a booth, ready to kill some time.

'Half an hour until closing time,' yelled the barista. Zala checked the clock on her terminal – not far off eleven – picked up her backpack, and walked across the room into the bathroom. Once she was safely inside a locked cubicle, she hung up her rucksack and opened it. Inside was make-up and a small, revealing dress belonging to Polina, which she had borrowed without asking. Zala took off her own clothes and put on the dress. She clipped a golden necklace around her neck and hooked a pair of earrings into her earlobes, all of which had cost her less than a sandwich and were nothing but gaudily decorated tin. She kept her walking shoes on, having been unable to convince Polina to part with a pair of her heels, and stuffed her own clothes into the rucksack along with the rest of the gear she had brought with her.

The sight of herself in the mirror made her pause for a moment. Zala never dressed this way, never had reason. She wished she'd found more excuses to do so. She'd not realized before that she could look like this.

She double-checked and triple-checked every piece of information she'd gathered, then she opened the cubicle door and walked out. She spent a few minutes applying light make-up in the bathroom mirror, and then she left.

The queue for Amp exceeded her expectations. It seemed like everyone in the city south of fifty years old was lined up and ready to release whatever tension the Soucouyant virus had inspired. Zala walked past all of them, up to the bouncer, and said, 'Selina Mullur, I'm on the guest list.'

The bouncer looked her up and down, then consulted his list to make sure the name was there. Zala had spent the hours in the coffee shop breaking into their network to ensure that it was, and so the bouncer nodded and waved her inside. She checked her backpack in at the cloakroom and headed upstairs.

Amp was full to capacity. The music was deafening. A band Zala had heard on the radio before was playing on the stage, light streaming from behind the five musicians into the otherwise dark room until they seemed like silhouettes. While four used analogue-style instruments, the fifth member manipulated the signals in real time on a terminal, crushing, modulating and distorting the music into one great ever-shifting sea of complex sonic flourishes on top of a thick, heavy rhythmic throb from the drums and bass guitar. The crowd danced as one great mass, already drunk and sweaty. Zala threw herself into the mob and within minutes smelt suitably of sweat and alcohol. Satisfied that she now looked and smelt just like anyone else in the nightclub, she went back downstairs.

She retrieved her rucksack, made her way into one of Amp's bathrooms and, once two women talking loudly about a man they had evidently each been dating without the other realizing had left to go and hunt him down, she walked into a cubicle. She took from her bag a can of expanding watertight foam that was normally used to seal leaking cracks in ceilings. Zala pulled a large handful of toilet paper from the dispenser, sprayed some of the foam onto the centre sheet and wrapped the rest around it, then quickly flushed the whole bundle. Almost immediately the toilet bowl started to overflow. Zala then moved into another cubicle and waited.

Barely a minute had passed before a section of the wall slid away and one of the black-clad maintenance workers emerged, cursing lightly under his breath.

Zala listened carefully as he walked over to the cubicle and groaned at the sight of her handiwork. She took a deep breath, then opened the door and stumbled out, laughing, until she steadied herself on a sink. The man looked round, and his eyes met hers.

'Oh!' she slurred, 'I caught you! You're not allowed to laugh or something, right?'

The maintenance man rolled his eyes and turned his attention back to unblocking the toilet.

'Hey!' said Zala, making a show of staggering over behind him. This caught his attention.

He twisted round, and patiently said, 'Ma'am, if you could leave me in peace, I'm just trying to do my—'

Zala grabbed the sides of the cubicle doorway and brought a foot up, before pulling forward and kicking. The maintenance man's head flew back and smacked into the tiled wall, cracking it. He slumped with a splash to the side of the toilet.

A few minutes, a locked bathroom door and some duct tape later, he was stripped to his underwear, bound and gagged, and still unconscious. Zala changed back into dark trousers and shirt, threw on her hoodie, and wrapped a black scarf around her face. Over this, she pulled on the man's overalls, meaning that if worst came to worst she could claim to be a maintenance engineer. Finally she donned the maintenance man's gloves and shut the cubicle door on him. Whatever technology was in the gloves began throwing images up onto Zala's contact lenses. A bright rectangular doorway of light appeared superimposed on the wall, and beyond it was the outline of a corridor. 'Very cool,' she muttered to herself, grinning.

She reached out and touched the middle of the doorway of light, and it slid open to reveal the corridor.

The passage was cramped and lit by a weak bulb that tinged everything a harsh green-yellow. The walls were lined with pipes and thick cables. The undulating bass from the nightclub overhead echoed down through the ceiling. Zala followed the corridor until she found herself at a concrete spiral staircase. She went down it, further and further, constantly listening out for anyone approaching, her eyes straining in the gloom.

Four floors down from where she had entered, she reached the bottom of the staircase. She followed a long, wide corridor until she came to another door. Pressing her ear to it, she could hear the muffled hum of massive fans coming from behind it. She reached forward with her gloved hand and touched the door. Slowly, it slid aside, revealing a metal walkway which branched off above an L-shaped room the size of an athletics field, lined from wall to wall with racks of servers. Zala couldn't help but smile.

Server Room D of the NDLT server farm.

Zala had worked with server farms before, but this was an operation of an entirely different magnitude. Every bookshelf-sized rack was filled with large NDLT-branded server units, all steel ventilation and rapidly blinking LEDs. The cooling system seemed to her as loud as the music upstairs.

Zala made her way along the walkway and down a set of steel steps to the floor below. In front of her was a small terminal with a single option: DIRECTORY. She accessed it and a list of server blocks came up. While she eyed 'NDLT Mainframe' and 'Rendering Neuroprocessors' with longing, she eventually found her target: a section entitled 'Private Use/Misc.' and a list of EIP addresses for each server. She opened her portable terminal and compared the EIP addresses in the directory with the ones that were blocking the probe trail.

There they were. The eight servers her probe had been unable to pass, in their own rack with one other – almost certainly the gateway server. The directory even singled them out on a mini-map, indicating that they were on the far side of the room.

Zala moved quickly down rows of computer equipment, pulse racing. Past the first ten rows, left at the end, then second right and sixth left.

There they were. Zala stopped in front of them and grinned. Nine gleaming NDLT MBL5000T computer servers, twice as big as the rest of the servers in this room and surely more powerful than any other in the building. Whoever rented this set-up had some money behind them. Each one had its EIP address laser-printed on its front, corresponding to the EIP addresses of the servers that had made up the loop, except for the one at the top. Flicking open her own terminal, Zala set up a connection with the new server. A login screen opened – no endless loop. She ran a simple profile scraper program and within a few minutes a user-name and password appeared. Clearly the server's user was so confident in their external security that they felt no need to have any more than a simple, scrape-vulnerable password on the other side – though it might also be so that they could feign enough ignorance of computer security to be perceived as incapable of any cybercrime. She typed in the details. The servers yielded, and she disabled the loop. The IP trace still running back at Polina's apartment would be able to get through to find the source of the gssmr.auge file.

A message beeped at her terminal.

From: ANANSI (EIP: ----.-.------.-------.---.-----.----.------)
>I see you.

Zala felt a chill run down her spine.

She closed the message, disconnecting from the server and the NDLT local network, and shut down her portable terminal. For a moment she was tempted to claw the terminal from her wrist and smash it, but she calmed herself.

The words echoed in her mind. Had someone spotted her? Someone on the security team, or was someone tracing her? Were they going to alert security? Or was there something else going on? The dashes that littered the EIP address were something she hadn't seen in a long time. She had gigabytes of programs constantly running to ensure that no technique she knew of could hide a person's EIP from her. The person who created the server loop her trace had got stuck in couldn't hide their EIP from her. She hid her own EIP using programs no one but her used or understood, using protocols she had written and never, ever shared. It would take a supercomputer to get around them.

'I see you', it had said.

The roaring ventilation system suddenly seemed too quiet and she found herself listening intently for something. She glanced around wildly.

The sound of footsteps grew louder and clearer as their sources grew closer.

Zala lightly crept two rows of servers to the right. Crouching down, she peered through a small space in a server rack, to see four armed guards round the corner and stare at the servers she'd accessed. Her eyes widened.

Suddenly, icy focus took hold. She reopened her terminal and scanned for communication networks. One popped up on her browser, revealing the EIPs of both the computer sending the guards instructions and the guards' portable terminals. She needed a way to get around the guards without alerting them to her presence. Her plan in the club was to make it seem as though the only notable thing that had happened this evening was a drunken clubber attacking and stripping a maintenance man. Given the increased prominence of domestic terrorism as of late, even Zala in her normal clothes attacking the man would provoke the authorities. She couldn't risk attracting any more attention to herself.

Zala scanned the data being sent to the guards – maps, routes, visual instructions and audio. For now, the squad of four were heading away from her, but they stood between her and the closest exit. She looked back at the intercepted map. She was two rows of server racks from the back of the room now, and there were sixteen rows and five columns of—

Holy shit, there're over twenty thousand servers in this room alone and it's not even the biggest room they have in this facility!

—five columns of server racks between her and where she needed to be. In addition, the walls of racks were long, leaving little opportunity to hide if someone came past. And, of course, the security team were armed. Zala figured she had three advantages. One, the cooling system the servers used made finding her with thermal vision nearly impossible. Two, she had their information feed right in front of her. Three, she knew how much of a threat she was, and they did not.

She moved to the edge of a block of server racks. There was a two-foot aisle between her and the next block of servers along. If a guard was looking the right way she'd essentially be throwing herself into their field of vision. Going by the intercepted data, while there was indeed a guard walking down the gap between these two columns of servers, he should be facing the other way seven rows down. Unless he wasn't. Or he heard her. Or he just had a bad feeling and turned round.

Zala closed her eyes, and thought quiet thoughts.

She crossed the gap so lightly she could have been floating.

A sigh of relief and a satisfied grin. Her eyes on her wrist terminal, she watched as the security guard kept walking in the other direction. She straightened up and reoriented herself. She needed to move down another six rows before she could work towards the door. There were two guards in front of her and to her right and one in front of her to her left, as well as one behind her and to her left.

Wait, she thought, *there's one behind me?*

Panicked, she looked around. She'd lost track. There were only two rows of server racks behind her, and she was in the furthest left column of this part of the room. While the guard had not seen her the first time, there was no way he'd miss her a second.

Zala could hear his footsteps drawing closer. She had seconds.

She looked up, at the steel-grate fronts of the row of servers to one side of her and the tangle of cables and cooling hardware that formed the rear of the row on the other, disappearing into the ceiling. She pulled her rucksack off her shoulders.

The footsteps came closer.

The guard ambled past the row of server racks, his gaze sweeping over the gap between them. He lingered for a moment. It could have been anything, but to Zala it looked as though he might have heard something. Then, he continued on.

She slid down off the top of the rack using the cables as handholds, unable to believe her luck. The map showed the guard walking along a bank of servers ahead of her. The gap between the columns she needed was free. She padded along, down the side of the wall and out into the wider section of the room. Three columns and ten rows away was the exit, if she could just—

'Hold it!'

Zala jumped, and looked round to see a guard she hadn't spotted. He was about three yards away, a tall, well-built man with a shaven head and a wary, gaunt face, and he had a handgun trained at her head. She raised her hands.

'What are you doing in here?' His voice seemed to grate its way up out of his throat, quiet enough that the others wouldn't hear unless he raised it further.

'I was going to ask you the same thing,' she replied. She had one chance, being as she was still in the maintenance uniform. 'If we're going to fix this coolant leak, the last thing I need is security waving guns around, shooting up even more holes.'

She turned on her heel, away from the tall man pointing a gun at her, and opened her portable terminal. She typed quickly, inserting instructions of her own into the connection between the security coordinator's terminal and the security guards. Twenty seconds. 'It's around here somewhere.'

'Ma'am, I'm going to need you to present ID.' His voice was growing more insistent. He lowered the pistol slightly.

'I don't have time, you idiot, if we let it rupture any further for all we know we could have liquid nitrogen spraying out of the cooling system. I don't even want to think what that would do to the servers, let alone—'

'I need backup!' he yelled, raising his gun and levelling it again at Zala's head. 'Nice try, ma'am, but this cooling system uses freon gas.'

Another guard appeared behind him, weapon raised. Five seconds.

'Radio ahead and tell the folks upstairs we just caught a member of the New Cairo Liberation Army,' the gaunt-faced man told his colleague.

What, the terrorists? Zala felt faintly insulted.

The countdown reached zero. The signal from the security computer centre spiked. Cochlear implants played a deafening high-pitched tone, optical implants let out a sheet of blinding white light. The guards screamed, though they were unable to hear themselves do so. The tall man, doubling over with his hands over his ears, squeezed the trigger of his gun in pain, and a bullet whizzed high over Zala's head, sinking into a thick mass of cables behind her. She ran, pulling out the power cables from random servers as she went, her blind, deaf, agony-ridden would-be pursuers now writhing on the floor. Alarms sounded. Zala clambered up the steel staircase, taking the steps two at a time, all the way up to the maintenance walkway. A loud crack rang out somewhere below and Zala felt a burst of dust and concrete fragments explode just behind her head. She bolted down the final section of walkway amid flurries of shattering wall and dented, sparking metal. Her outstretched hand got her back through the concealed door. It snapped shut behind her.

People are trying to kill me.

The words seemed so insurmountably big in her head. She ignored them and focused on her breathing. She inhaled deeply, her chest rising, and exhaled long.

Run.

Zala sprinted forward, stumbling as she made her way back through the long, thin, low-lit corridors. The thick, snaking cables along the wall seemed to push in against her. She hissed her destination at her terminal, which managed to work out her hurried demands – the outside of the Five Prongs. Her terminal ran through the maps it had downloaded from the security connection. A golden trail unfurled before her, up winding stairs and round tight corners, showing her the way out. She ran so fast the display for the guide trail had trouble keeping ahead of her.

Finally, it brought her to a tall ladder. Zala placed her foot on it, and as she pulled herself up a shot rang out, ricocheting off the wall next to her. They'd kept up with her this whole time. She pulled herself up the ladder with her arms, her legs kicking off the rungs below as she leapt to reach higher and higher. She placed a gloved hand on the glowing door at the top. The trapdoor slid open to reveal the outside courtyard of the NLDT campus. Zala heaved herself up and waved the door closed. She quickly opened up a brute-force passcode cracker and trained it on the door. In a fraction of a second, the program fed enough random, incorrect guesses into the door's lock that it shut down as a default security measure. Zala could hear yells and hammering on the other side, but they weren't getting through.

She bent over, sucking in great lungfuls of the cool night air. Her exit had the good fortune to be on the opposite side of the campus from the main public entrance, and there was nobody around to see her – at least, not until a security team or maintenance workers came to follow up on the information from her pursuers. She set off briskly down the side of a neighbouring building. Finding a quiet corner, she took off her rucksack and shed the overalls so that she was back in her street clothes. She crammed the overalls into her rucksack, then strode purposefully across the courtyard and disappeared into a Downtown back alley.

Chapter 8

'I'm telling you, Kahleed, it wasn't any one of us!'

Matron looked ready to break her portable terminal in half. On the larger home terminal screen on the wall, a New Cairo Network newscast had headlines emblazoned all over it. 'Terrorist attack on the Five Prongs'. Across the screen, talking heads discussed the five people in hospital, one with a broken jaw and concussion, and the other four deafened. The message sent was clear – the previous night, the conflict in the Naj-Pur and Surja districts had boiled over into the rest of the city.

'I don't know. It doesn't look like much of anything actually happened,' Matron said into her terminal. 'I mean, I'm not seeing any convincing physical damage in the footage. I dunno, I'll talk to our people on the inside.'

She powered down her portable terminal and turned to look over at Ryan Granier, who was seated in a corner. 'What's your take on this, rich boy?'

Ryan shifted uncomfortably in his chair. Three days since he'd woken up in that office and the restraints which had bound his hands were off. He'd managed to gain his captors' trust up to a point, but on more than one occasion he had said something that inadvertently earned Matron's rancour. He could do without her 'forgetting' to feed him today.

'You guys have the support of most of the population in Naj-Pur and Surja. That's a good, what, six million? If the Council's outreach people don't consolidate the support of the upper and middle classes, they're not going to offer much of a fight. The Council's media relations teams are making a mountain out of a molehill. If there's an armed uprising and the Council need to suppress it with violent means, genuine fear of the people they're suppressing will keep the more liberal voices in the middle and upper classes silent. Plus, this news network is wholly owned by GeniSec, and this break-in is pretty embarrassing to NDLT from a security perspective. If NDLT can't keep their server farms secure, what else might get compromised? It might be worth checking today's financial news.'

Matron raised an eyebrow. 'That figures. I'm amazed GeniSec and the Council can manipulate the press like that.'

'People are asked to bury or push stories all the time out of corporate interest. It used to be that the profits of revealing a scandalous story were enough to cover expenses, but news isn't the business it was.' Ryan shrugged. 'A lot of institutions have a hard time keeping up with the pace of the demand for information; it's an expensive business, so they've got to cater to the moneymen.'

Matron cast a sideward glare at the screen. 'Bastards.'

'Can you blame them? Like I say, media budgets are getting slashed and the media companies have employees to pay, and those people have families to feed and clothe. They're just trying to do the best they can in those circumstances, but a roof over their children's heads will make all those corporate demands seem much more reasonable.'

'That's all very well,' said Matron, a look of disdain on her face, 'but those corporate demands are for the media to demonize the poorest, most vulnerable people in this city as diseased, violent or both. They portray us as being less worth keeping alive. I mean, Christ, the Council put a major piece of legislation on hold to keep you alive. They wouldn't even fund my cousin's replacement pancreatic implants. If it weren't for our funding here, he'd have died.'

Ryan had no idea where to go from there. Defending or playing devil's advocate for the people who would have let her cousin die, or, worse, enquiring about where this 'funding' was coming from, could have dire consequences.

Rule Three was to never antagonize your captors regarding religion or politics, especially when those beliefs were the reason they'd taken you in the first place.

So instead, he just nodded and said, 'Yeah, it's horrible.'

Satisfied that she had won the argument, Matron turned away. 'You've got sandwiches for lunch. Ration-grade, of course. Think shuttle food, only a little drier. Don't look at it while you eat it and you should be fine.'

And with that she stood and walked off, leaving the newscast to flicker away.

With her gone, Ryan stretched in his chair and gazed around the large, bare room. From here, the only other room he could see into was a bathroom on the other side of the hall, because, aside from the office he had woken up in and now slept in, it was the only other room he was allowed into. The medical bay and the rest of the complex seemed to be behind large, locked doors that opened only to certain people. In the event of a raid the police had tools at their disposal that would make short work of the locks, but they looked tough enough that they'd give the NCLC time to get their people out of the building.

His captors weren't being especially cruel to him, he'd realized as he watched their comings and goings. He had been granted access to the bathroom, was allowed to wash in the small shower cubicle, and was given food three times a day, although it had been made clear to him any of these privileges could be taken from him if he misbehaved. The biggest problem was boredom. The compound had almost two dozen people living in it that he knew of, with the accommodation area being located somewhere further down the long corridor towards the back. Almost everyone residing in the complex regarded him with nothing more than distant curiosity. It was now late morning, and the place felt empty, its inhabitants off carrying out whatever their duties were as part of the uprising. Hours of bored eavesdropping on the conversations between Matron and the others had told Ryan that they were mostly support staff to the active operatives within the NCLC, and so worked fairly long hours.

The children were all looked after by various members of the NCLC's core team. Today, they had gone off with an older, worn-looking man called Maalik who spent most days working at some other base. The kids seemed to like him, because he taught them how to fire guns and how to fight hand-to-hand. It all reminded Ryan of ancient photographs he'd seen in history books of old-world children, who were given drugs and made to fight and die for causes they couldn't possibly have understood. He thought of hungry-looking kids in over-large sportswear posing with assault rifles, or white-skinned fourteen-year-olds in trenches, the promises of adventure and glory no longer keeping them warm.

He couldn't know for certain, but his imagining of what Maalik might be preparing the children for was one of the many things that reminded Ryan that the NCLC, however reasonable they seemed, were terrorists.

A metallic clank resonated through the steel door that led to the main complex. It opened and a large man in a wheelchair that could barely contain his muscular frame pushed through. He glared at Ryan as he said, 'Where's the nurse?'

Ryan pointed to the medical bay. The man wheeled himself over to the door, raised a fist, and pounded on it. 'Ava! Where the hell are you? My patch needs changing!'

The medical bay door opened and Matron – Ava – stood there, staring down at the man in the wheelchair. 'Go wait, Yosef. I've got prep to do, and your patch still has hours of meds in it.'

'You're going to leave me out there with the prisoner?' Yosef said incredulously. 'I get shot furthering the cause and you're going to leave me to rot in the company of this filth?'

'Yeah, I am, and you're going to wait there, with the prisoner, until I'm done here,' Ava said testily. 'Then I'm going to bring you in here and I'm going to use my years of medical experience to magically fix your broken, battered body. Wait, and be fuckin' grateful.'

And with that, she closed the door, leaving a fuming Yosef to his own devices. He turned in his wheelchair and his eyes met Ryan's.

'It's nice to see you in a more collected state, Councillor,' he said in a mock-civil voice. 'Your family ravages our people, I get shot in the line of duty, and you're the one in better nick? If I were in charge I'd have you chained up in some windowless cell sitting in a pile of your own excrement. That'd teach you.'

Ryan didn't ask exactly what it would teach him.

'But I'll tell you the worst, the fucking gall of you people,' Yosef spat. 'You try and sabotage your competition over at the Five Prongs, and you blame it on us. Like we'd have the fucking ineptitude to yank a few cords out of some servers and scarper.'

The colour rose in Ryan's face. Quietly, he said, 'Are you quite finished?'

'I'll tell you when I'm fucking finished, you arrogant, pampered little squirt of shit. It's people like you, who think you run the fucking world and that the rest of us are ants, who are killing the poor folk of this city. You and your quarantines and your shutting down the shuttle station and your—'

Steel locks whirred, and the main door into the room opened. The old man Maalik came in, with a gang of children trailing close behind him. 'Is something wrong here, lads?' he said, in a jovial voice.

'No, Maalik, the councillor and I were just discussing some social issues,' Yosef growled. Maalik laughed.

The medical bay door swung aside, and Ava came out. She smiled at Maalik, then at the kids. 'Did you guys have fun with Mr Maalik?'

The children nodded and replied almost in unison, 'Yeeeeessssss.'

Vik, the child Ryan recognized from before, piped up near the back, 'He took us to the range and I hit in the red zone.'

The smile faded from Ava's face for a moment, then returned. 'Oh, really? Well done you! I bet pretty soon, if Mr Maalik keeps taking you guys shooting, you'll get them all inside the red zone!'

The smile was strained. Ryan wondered if she felt as uneasy as he did over the question of why the children were being taught to shoot. She said nothing more, but turned and took Yosef inside the medical bay to re-dress his gunshot wound, and most of the children followed Maalik back down the main corridor to the rest of the complex. Only Vik remained behind.

'Hey, Ryan,' he said, coming closer.

'Hey, Vik. They took you shooting today, did they?'

'Yeah!' Vik exclaimed. 'Maalik showed us how to use a hand-gun.'

'Oh? Were you any good?'

Vik looked dejected. 'I got my first shot inside the red zone but I missed most of the others. I must have just been lucky with the good shot.'

'Aw, that sucks,' said Ryan. 'But you know, that's not always a bad thing. When they're shooting at other people, most people instinctively aim wide anyway. They don't want to shoot someone. So it's not such a bad thing you missed the target.'

'I'm not shooting someone though,' Vik replied, 'I'm just trying to hit a target. It's just a goal. I'm aiming for it, but I can't hit it.'

Ryan stopped for a second, and conceded that Vik had a point. 'Fair enough. So when's the next shooting session?'

'A few days from now . . .' Vik looked up at the large monitor, suddenly noticing the frenetic newscast. 'What happened? Did we do something?'

'Someone broke into the Five Prongs and messed with their computer systems. Ava doesn't seem to think that it was any of you guys.'

Vik nodded, and the door from the main complex opened once again. Kanak walked through. As she spotted her son, she broke into a smile.

'There you are!'

'Look, Mum,' he said, pointing towards the monitor. 'Someone broke the computers at the Five Prongs. Was that one of us? Was that Dad?'

Kanak froze for a second.

Then the smile bloomed again. 'No, sweetie, I told you. Daddy's undercover with the secret unit,' she said.

Though obviously not so secret that she can't bring it up in front of a hostage whose father signs the Security Force's pay-cheques.

Vik grinned with pride at this. Kanak took his hand and led him from the room, back towards the main complex. Ryan watched them go, wondering what had happened to the boy's father.

It had become hard for Ryan to begrudge most of the NCLC members their hiding place from the Security Force; they were either terrified children or parents trying to keep their families safe. This was, after all, a safe house and by its very nature was defensive. But this father . . . he was an NCLC man and, judging from Kanak's response, he was almost certainly under arrest or dead. Perhaps the 'secret undercover mission' explanation was the NCLC equivalent of telling a child their dog had gone to live on a farm out of town. Maybe he'd been shot, as Yosef had been the night Ryan had awoken to find himself captive. Maybe he was rotting in a prison cell in the Security Force building. And maybe whatever it was had happened to Vik's father and his colleagues while they were hurting or killing someone else. The more he thought about it, the more Ryan was becoming certain that something had happened to the man to tear him away from his family, and it wasn't likely that he was simply hunkering down in a safe house.

And some small part of Ryan's psyche over which he had no control thought:

Good.

He sat there, horrified at himself for being glad that little Vik, who didn't even understand what his father was doing, might grow up without a father. Yet on further examination, he found that gut reaction less appalling. The NCLC killed or maimed people, and not always defensively. They started riots that killed innocents. The entire point of a governed state with a monopoly on legitimate use of force was to protect the general populace from people like that. Was it wrong that they fell victim to the mechanisms put in place by the Council to maintain that protection?

Not to mention, they kidnapped me.

The justifying arguments were now pushing to the forefront.

These people are using violence and destruction to force their political desires upon the society around them. Of course that society is going to fight back. If their assertion of their agenda is violent, the rejection of that agenda has to match that violence right back. Order needs to be restored.

Even as he thought it, Ryan knew this was nonsense. Aside from the fact that in this situation civility and survival went hand in hand, he consciously did not want that sort of mindset. These were people, and the ideal scenario was that nobody would get hurt. In a more abstract sense, he even recognized that the first act of injustice was the quarantine and curfew imposed on the high-infection areas. The NCLC's aggressive approach was a response to the violent ways in which those policies were often enforced – an escalation, but within a cycle of violence which didn't start with them.

He understood this, on an intellectual level.

But it seemed like so long since he had last seen his children or kissed his wife, and it was these people who were stopping him. Resentment ground in the pit of his gut.

Vik poked his head around the door again, interrupting Ryan's soul-searching. He was carrying a plate of sandwiches. 'Hey, Ryan, I've got your lunch.'

For a moment so brief that he could almost pretend it never happened, as Vik walked through the door, Ryan saw only Vik's father, a terrorist, probably a killer, and wanted, on a cruel, animal level, to knock the sandwiches from that terrorist's son's hands, to hurt him, just out of spite.

Ryan was disgusted with himself. He thanked the boy, took the plate, and felt a great unburdening when Vik turned and left him alone. As he ate, he thought about his family, and tried to bury the dark, visceral urges as deep down as he could.

Chapter 9

A lice Amirmoez swivelled round in her chair to face her examiners. Behind her, the command terminal she'd run a mission at three days ago flashed 'Simulation objective complete' up onto its monitor. Kahleed Banks and Tal Surdar looked impressed, Tal even nodding to himself slightly. Following the success of the mission she'd stepped in to coordinate, they'd spent hours trying to persuade her to participate in a rebellion she'd made clear she hated. Eventually, attrition had won and they had talked her into demonstrating her skills on one of their training simulations.

'Very good, Alice,' said Kahleed. 'I'd have thought you'd be rustier than this. It's been how long since you left the police?'

'I quit being a coordinator two years ago. Before that, I was a field agent. But yeah, I did this for a long, long time.'

'From what I could see,' said Tal, 'the only mistakes you made were the result of either your having to get used to the system, or the constraints of the program. By the end you'd even adjusted to that. I mean, I'm pretty sure that in real life that shopfront thing would have worked.'

Kahleed straightened up. 'Of course, this does rather skip around the question. You're going to be here, waiting for us to get all the pieces in order to smuggle you and the children out of the city. It seems like a waste to not use talents of your calibre. Can we at least discuss you coordinating our missions for us while you're here?'

Alice sat back in her chair and asked herself the same question. She didn't care about the NCLC in any real sense. She hadn't been able to sleep the last two nights and she was beginning to feel the effects. She'd hated the fact that she had been the subject of conversations she herself was not privy to. Mostly she hated that she was being drawn into someone else's battle.

She thought of her children. Ria had spent the last few days being more bored than she had ever been in her life. Alice's time being taken up by simulated operations meant that Ria only had Zeno for company. There was no one for her to play or socialize with. After all, this was meant to be a temporary, transitional shelter. The other children being sheltered by the NCLC were at larger bases with their parents, and Ria's friends' parents couldn't be trusted not to turn Alice in. And then, of course, she had yet to tell Ria what had happened to her father.

Still awaiting a response, Kahleed continued, trying to fill the silence '. . . and of course, we understand that your first responsibility is to your children—'

Alice looked up at him, eyes cold and piercing. 'I don't need to be reminded of my responsibility to my children.'

Kahleed's eyes widened. Tal stepped in, hands raised. 'We never meant to imply that you did—'

'Look,' she continued, leaning forward and cutting him off, 'you seem like you've got a well-meaning cause going here. I've known you two for years. You're good people. But you got my husband killed not five days ago. I could have been arrested. My children could have been taken from me. This organization threw my life into chaos.' She paused. 'I'm grateful that you're helping my family escape this place, but I never agreed with Jacob about this. I stepped in the other day because Suman Chaudhri was in no state to be leading an operation. He was liable to get people hurt. But right now I don't want to be the one ordering the deaths of people I don't have a problem with.'

She sat back in her chair, her arms crossed and her face stony. 'That's what you're up against. Now sell me on your rebellion.'

Kahleed nodded. 'Jacob always mentioned your distaste for his "game of cops-and-robbers". Now, of course I can't speak for him, but I can explain why *I'm* doing this.'

He wheeled over one of the operators' chairs and sat facing Alice, looking her in the eye.

'I grew up maybe three blocks from here. Gang territory. Most of the rows of houses I lived in were labs for making Poly or Flush. Not much actual violence – we were too deep in one gang's territory for corner disputes – but the threat, the fear hung in the air like smog. Naj-Pur was conceived as a manufacturing district, a source of good jobs that people could rely upon, and for about a decade after New Cairo's completion it did just that. Enough for a community to grow up on the promise that the work would always be there. Then, work moved elsewhere. Parents left to follow the jobs, and all the kids who didn't have the brains, money, luck or work ethic to move into middle-class careers watched on hopelessly as the industries failed. It cost less just to ship in materials that had been manufactured in Khartoum and Addis Ababa, so that's what everyone went for. This entire district of the city was betrayed by the breaking of the promise it was founded on. The only industry that didn't leave was the drugs. There was always money in sitting on a corner. You could buy decent clothes, better gadgets. Kids were raised thinking that was what people like us were meant to aspire to; it was the only place where we saw people like us doing well for themselves.'

Kahleed's eyes were unfocused, as if he was staring at something in the distance. Tal looked down at him, brow furrowed – he was a middle-class Falkur kid, like Alice. She wondered if he'd ever heard this story before.

'Thanks to dumb luck, I got out,' Kahleed continued. 'I worked myself half to death, studied business at university and got a grant to start my own company, manufacturing terminals. I got a contract to create custom terminals for the Council and all of a sudden our bank statements were in the black. But more than that, the government tie gave us the power and connections to change things. So I kept working with Jacob, the other Naj-Pur boy who'd done good. We got a petition of almost five hundred thousand signatures stating that the signatories would buy products made in New Cairo to the exclusion of any competitors. Manufacturing savings don't mean anything if no one's buying your product. We built up the oversight infrastructure, and we went to the corporate headquarters of the four big companies. The head of NDLT refused to even get on a video call with us. Banach-Tarski had a bug in their message system and sent us the same rejection twice. That was a blow to the ego. FanaSoCo said, with all the earnestness in the world, that they would come on board if they had the money to fund the redevelopment of the factories, but they trailed the other three companies too much to risk it.'

Kahleed chuckled to himself. Behind him, a terminal monitor was showing a newscast discussing Councillor Ryan Granier's kidnapping and the subsequent legislative delay.

'It was GeniSec who took us up on it in the end. Tau Granier heard us out and shook our hands. Within six months they'd re-outfitted a third of the old foreclosed factories and employed tens of thousands. A month after that, they were running at seven million dollars of additional production expenses against fifty million dollars of additional profit. The people of Naj-Pur were buying their New Cairo-made products. The people of Surja were buying. Hell, the people of Alexandria, the city centre and Falkur were all buying, figuring that a regeneration of their city could only benefit them. GeniSec went from third place to the biggest corporate body in the United African Democracies, and stayed there.

'Jobs came flooding back. Not only was every old factory refurbished and opened, they had to make new ones. Young men and women had work that gave them back their dignity and pride. Not to mention it gave them an estimated life span above thirty, which is a perk the gangs certainly couldn't provide. Parents stayed in the city because the jobs were there, and the influence of the gangs began to diminish. Violent crime rates plummeted, and the lessening impact of the drugs trade meant that money was staying off the black market and going back into the local economy. Jacob and I checked the warehouses, assigned the "Made in New Cairo" status to products which earned it. We directed the entire consumer body. And we formed the New Cairo Labour Commission – the first NCLC.'

Alice nodded. 'Yeah, I know this part, Kahleed, I was there for it. Jacob was actually more my husband than he was yours, all things considered.'

'You're a middle-class Falkur girl, Alice. You were around. You weren't there for it, not like the people from round here.'

Oh you pompous ass, Alice thought to herself, *like I've never met a poor kid who made something of themselves before.*

Kahleed continued. 'So Naj-Pur was getting better, Surja was getting better, the economy was booming and the NCLC were effecting real change on an institutional level. Industrial work brings problems – combined with the Preserve Our Manual Jobs Act, it guaranteed jobs, but it meant that injuries became more common than they had been. The tax revenue the Council brought in meant they could afford to make the essential bio-aug installations free at point of use, but a mechanized generation grew up, dependent on and glad of our bionic implants. People started getting them put in just to help with their jobs or improve their lifestyle. Most, whether they'd admit it or not, got extensive bio-augmentation just because they knew on some level that it was about empowerment. They'd been dealt a bad hand at first. Bio-augmentation looked like a reshuffle to them.

'And then, a few weeks ago, these implants begin to shut down out of nowhere. Maybe an arm here, eyes there, maybe a faulty knee or so. But then bio-aug lungs, hearts, kidneys. People who'd had their lives given back to them, thanks to this miracle of science, started dropping down dead. I've never seen people so scared. Around here, everyone has those machine parts.'

Kahleed worked through a few menus on his portable terminal, then leaned forward towards Alice. He raised his right hand, index finger pointing upwards. The skin parted in a vertical line up the middle, and folded back on thin plates to reveal the small metal frame, vents and grilles of the finger of an artificial hand.

'Wanna know why I got this? I broke my finger. The doctor told me that either they could set it in a cast, but it was too fragmented to heal straight, or they could replace the entire hand. The skin's real, grown in a lab from my own skin cells. The muscle in there is all carbon nanotubes – strong, fast, all regulated in my hand. I didn't know at the time that I'd be pulling triggers as much as I am now, but I can type like a motherfucker too. Before this whole thing started up I was honestly saving my money to get some elective replacements. I mean, there's a pride in it, in a way. I like them, or at least I used to. But now, I and several million others are trapped in here, knowing that any day could be the one where our arm, or our eye implant, or our heart stops working, like that ballerina we all heard about.'

He exhaled and shook his head. 'We tried to get out. The people of Naj-Pur and Surja are the most vulnerable people in the city, the ones who've been most punished, and now we're the first people they stopped letting out. All we have left to do is wait in our homes for our bio-augs to fail. They lock us in a cage and they tell us it's for our own good. And you know what? People aren't working. The gangs are starting up again. The drugs are starting up again. And I for one have no intention of standing idly by while this place goes back to how it used to be. We're trying to get people out, and we're trying to do so by fighting back against a police state. And if there's one thing I've learned in my life, it's that taking matters into my own hands is the only course that's changed anything for the better.'

Kahleed straightened up, an exhausted look on his face. 'That's why I'm doing this, anyway. And it's why Jacob did what he did.'

Alice nodded slowly. That last sentence hurt. She'd heard all this before. She understood why they felt that it was important. There was no need to bring up his name. She was tired and she was angry, and somewhere deep down, in a way which concerned her, she was scared. She had known stability all her life and it had been taken from her. It was as though the ground beneath her had given way, leaving her to plummet into darkness. And she had to admit that something about coordinating the mission three days before had offered her a solid hold to grab to break her fall.

She knew mission coordination. She was good at it.

A part of her had found relief from the chaos when she was sitting at the command terminal. This terrified the rest of her.

The question was whether she could do more good than harm, and whether by the end that would remain a priority.

It was not a question she could answer there and then.

'How long will it take for the arrangements to get my family out of here to be in place?' she asked.

'Another week. Got a lot of favours to call in.'

Alice swung her chair back round, resting her hands on the terminal keys. 'Until then, I'll do it. I'll coordinate your operations. I'll incriminate myself in your rebellion. But hear me: this is for Jacob and Jacob alone. He cared about this cause, and I'll see that out. This isn't my fight. It's just one he left too early.'

She heard Kahleed's footsteps recede behind her. 'That works for me.'

Chapter 10

Lines of EIP addresses ran across the width of Zala's field of vision. Each one carried its own branches and paths and processes to and from a myriad of other locations, all following the elusive threads the gssmr file left as it wove its way through cyberspace. Eventually, though, every trail converged on a single location.

Zala's stomach sank.

The threads which followed the trail of the Soucouyant virus met at an EIP matching a terminal in a software development laboratory owned by GeniSec.

This was the conglomerate whose gratitude Zala had been relying upon for her freedom, and all signs pointed to them being in some way responsible for the virus. It came right from their labs. They'd even routed it through one of their competitors' server farms.

Zala strained to remember what Matsuda had said.

'The poorer folk often don't shell out for the upgrades in the software or the relevant hardware.'

Perhaps it was some kind of forced obsolescence scheme, foisted upon the most vulnerable, in a manner that was killing people? Zala felt sick with anger at the thought of it. Maybe the push in the Council to quarantine the city was just politicians whose campaigns were paid for by GeniSec working with them, maximizing the number of infected. Maybe they hoped it'd drive up adoption of new bio-augs, or, worse, maybe they'd 'miraculously' develop some cure and license it to the government for hundreds of millions.

She felt confined, claustrophobic. She found herself staring out of the window of Polina's apartment down a long adjacent road, lined on both sides with skyscrapers. She was certain that some-one must be watching her, someone knew she was there.

'*I see you*', it had said.

She nodded to herself, and began to wonder how best to hurt GeniSec.

Within an hour, she had all the information she'd managed to gather compiled and packaged into a single compressed folder, ready to be transferred if necessary. There were the memory records from the bio-augs which Matsuda had sent her, along with the information she'd gleaned from them – in particular, the recurrence of the vital gssmr.auge file. There was a record of the trace which had tracked down the origin of the gssmr.auge file, with the EIP addresses and relevant connection logs of every bio-aug, terminal and server through which it had spread. Directories which contained the locations of the EIPs, identifying the trace's terminating point at GeniSec's development labs. A complete record of her investigation.

This information could potentially bring down the most powerful corporation, run by the most powerful family, in the United African Democracies, and that made it the most powerful weapon on the continent.

She couldn't do it alone. She needed to find someone in this city who could help her.

Of course, potential allies who might use these data were few and far between. There were the crazed pundits who made up the conspiracy theorist circuit in New Cairo, who ranted and raved about this sort of thing all the time. They had an audience who would be receptive, and would probably take the information without wasting time vetting Zala. But they wouldn't know what to do with actual proof if they had it; after all, these pundits thought they had proof already, and they thought the best thing to do in response was to blurt out hundreds of podcasts' worth of stream-of-consciousness rants. Amongst the people who mattered, their testimony was worth less than nothing.

Then there were the main media bodies in the city. The big corporate-owned news sources would be ideal given their audience size. They'd also probably jump at the chance to discredit a competitor conglomerate and steal viewers away from GeniSec's NCN network at the same time. Similarly, if there was a worthy independent news agency down there in the city somewhere, this could put them on the map. GeniSec's involvement in the Soucouyant virus was the kind of story journalists dreamed of breaking, the kind that established legacies. But then, of course, there were the legal ramifications of releasing the information. This had 'potential libel proceedings' written all over it at the very least. There'd be police investigations at the highest possible levels, not to mention the potential for reprisals. GeniSec had influence in every layer of the city's political establishment, be it through campaign financing or the high standing of the Granier family. If they felt the need for revenge, they had plenty of options. Zala was careful, but probably not completely untraceable if someone were actively looking for her. There were the other dangers too. The press was nobody's friend, after all, and though the continent's largest conglomerate spreading a deadly virus to an unsuspecting population would be the headline news, a sidebar on the 'hacker and alleged killer who infiltrated the city to have revenge' would make for an excellent B-story that Zala could absolutely not allow to run. The last thing she needed was the attention of someone who might be able to track her down and publicize her involvement.

The presence of that ANANSI person was still weighing on the back of her mind.

The real issue, Zala decided, was that GeniSec needed to be brought to justice. But more than that, imprisoning or bankrupting all the people who had ordered this seemed insufficient. This was a chance to punish GeniSec. For the virus, for the conflict and destruction which had claimed lives and crippled people, for Chloe, for her father—

She didn't want bankruptcy or arrests. She wanted blood.

And now she knew who to get in touch with.

She opened up a custom-built, nigh-untraceable web browser and punched in the EIP address of an old military server, somewhere out in Uganda. This patched into an equally ancient telecommunications network, and then to a number of discarded internal computer servers that had been hijacked long ago by a community with alternative uses for them. Crude web pages opened up, offering shipments of drugs or automatic weapons. Chat rooms buzzed with activity, hosting gunrunners, drug cartels and terrorist groups, as well as mischief-makers, mid-level hackers and the unadvisedly curious. This was the dark internet, a hidden, anonymous enclave of the net inaccessible through conventional means.

The first time Zala had accessed dark internet pages, she'd felt there was something Lovecraftian about it – something old and vast, lurking below the surface of the everyday, something that you weren't supposed to see. It felt like living in a village with a river running through it, and for generations never leaving your section of the river, then, one day, walking downstream for a few minutes and discovering the ocean. Vast, untapped, free, but with an unfathomable depth which could hide any number of dangers. After a while, it all became pedestrian – just more water – and it rather lost its forbidden allure. Of course, it retained its usefulness; when Zala had been hiding out in the middle of the Khartoum region, coordinating gun and drug deliveries for local gangs was a valuable and lucrative way to get by. What she needed now, however, was the right chat room.

She scrolled down a long list of IRC channels, each full of people. Many had ostentatious, theatrically evil-sounding names which were doubtless the creations of thirteen-year-old wannabe hackers showing off their criminal chic. The scary ones were the channels which were titled with a string of incomprehensible characters. If someone was concerned with anonymity even here, they were someone to be avoided.

Zala went into each chat room in turn, running the IRC channels through her EIP tracing program to search for those with large numbers of people located in New Cairo, or better, in Naj-Pur. With luck she'd walk right into the New Cairo Liberation Corps.

>IRC: S4IH9R454445G

>27 OF 30 LOCATED IN NAJ-PUR AREA

Zala opened a page and logged in using a new account, calling herself Maat8025. In front of her, chat logs at the very least suggested association with the NCLC. This was it.

>Maat8025: I need someone who can get me access to the NCLC.

Immediately, the chat buzzed with braggadocio, as every participant claimed that they had connections. One boasted that he was the one who sabotaged the NDLT server farm, and the chat lit up with disputes that no, *they* were the one that did it. Zala grinned, but stopped and leaned forward.

>Suchan: If you were the real thing, if you were from where we come from, you'd know how to get in touch with us. What do you have to offer?

>Maat8025: I know who sabotaged the Five Prongs server farm, and I know what they got from it.

>Maat8025: and it's something the New Cairo Liberation Corps will find very interesting.

>Suchan: I want proof. Upload it to an anonymous cyber-locker. If it's the real thing, I've got higher ups in the NCLC right across the room from me.

The IRC channel was still. The others seemed to have grasped that this was the grown-ups talking now, and wisely stayed out of it. Zala searched through her terminal's saved files for the records of the security guards' feed she'd hacked into that night at the Five Prongs. It was low-risk, it didn't incriminate her especially, and it was compelling, if not indisputable. She sent it to Suchan.

Almost immediately, she received a reply.

>Suchan: Oh wow, okay, this is the real deal. I'll organize a channel to discuss this all further.

The details of a private IRC channel appeared in Zala's inbox. She wrapped a scarf around her face, leaving just her eyes uncovered, turned on a voice scrambler in her communications client and opened a video call. The person on the other end picked up; Suchan, it turned out, was an overweight man wearing a balaclava, in a room which appeared to be lit mostly by a monitor. Zala didn't know if this was normal for revolutionaries, but it looked very similar to what was normal for basement dwellers trying to appear tough on the internet.

'I've verified that I'm the real thing,' said Zala. 'Now I need you to.'

'Just a second,' said Suchan. He closed down the video call on his end, leaving Zala looking at a blank screen. After five minutes, she began searching chat rooms again, convinced she'd struck up conversation with someone trying to seem more important than he was. As she made her way through a new IRC channel, trying to find a new lead, Suchan called her again.

'First of all, I'm going to need to see your face and know your name,' he said.

'Oh fuck you,' she snorted, 'how entry-level do you think I am?'

There was another pause.

'Type out an eight-digit number.'

Zala smirked, and entered in some random digits. A minute later, she was sent a link to a site on the dark internet, without any upload source. It was a single video: a tall, muscular, bearded man, looking into the camera.

'This is for Maat Eight-Oh-Two-Five. Seven-nine-nine-four-oh-two-one-six.'

Zala recognized him from the news. It was the purported leader of the New Cairo Liberation Corps, Kahleed Banks.

Zala turned back to the video call. This guy certainly appeared to be for real. She turned off the voice scrambler and said, 'Okay, you seem like the ones I need. I'm not going to take off my mask, but my name is Selina Mullur.'

'Take off the mask. We need to run a check.'

She hesitated and then pulled off the scarf. Suchan stared intently off camera at his monitor, then said, 'She checked out!' to someone.

Another man appeared behind him, looking down at the screen. He was wearing a helmet which obscured his face. Upon confirming the check, he pulled the helmet off. It was Kahleed Banks.

'Hi,' said Zala. 'I'm the one who broke into the Five Prongs server farm.'

'We saw that on the news,' said Kahleed, in a gruff voice. 'You really gave those power cords hell.'

Zala felt herself blush, and hoped it didn't show up on the video call feed. 'That wasn't why I was there, that was something that happened when I was running away from the security team that got called in.'

'Okay, so what do you have?'

'I've been investigating the provenance of the Soucouyant virus,' said Zala. 'I think I've found something. The trail was run through a security trap in some privately rented servers, so I had to break in and unlock it. But now I think I've found the source.'

Kahleed looked down at his companion. 'Is she for real?'

'Sir, you've seen me break into government and corporate cyber-security without a hitch,' said Suchan. 'Right now, I'm completely unable to find this woman's location. I can't find her EIP. In the meantime, I'm pretty sure that when we were in the dark chat room, she knew all our EIPs immediately, which is how she stumbled into our chat. I don't know any program which does that this well, especially not on the dark net, which means she probably made it herself. If she's sane, she's a prodigious hacker. If she's crazy, she's crazy and also a prodigious hacker. I'm coming down on the side of checking this out.'

Kahleed Banks was looking Zala straight in the eyes throughout. If he was good enough to understand the extent of her skill, she thought, he was good enough to know what to do with the information she had.

'All right,' said Kahleed. 'Make the arrangements. I want to hear what this one has to say.'

Surja was an area somewhere between the Soucouyant-ridden poverty of Naj-Pur and the modestly middle-class Falkur, but whereas Naj-Pur had experienced a substantial revitalization in recent years, Surja had been this poor for decades. The district was unique among the areas of the city in that it was built upon three massive tiers almost like a wedding cake. These colossal platforms protruded, one above the other, out from the side of the crater in which New Cairo lay.

Each level had a separate street plan, converging on the massive columns which supported the tiers and spreading out around residential blocks, squares and road layouts all of its own, so that Surja appeared for all the world as three different city districts floating over one another. In reality these tiers were hundreds of feet apart, each with the profile of a city skyline; taking all three together, the district became a great wall of buildings at least a quarter of a mile high. The architects' vision had been to cram as many people into the area as possible, and this aim covered more than just the tiered arrangement; almost every building was a tower block.

This extraordinarily dense population meant that, while not nearly as large in area as Naj-Pur, Surja was home to almost the same number of inhabitants, and what local economy it had was not big enough to support them. Most residents took public transport downtown to work menial jobs that they hoped would evolve into full-blown careers. For many, however, Surja was a service district, specializing in the few salacious services that a poor area could provide as well as a rich one. Zala had never liked being in the red-light district. It was a good location for clandestine meetings due to the large number of people, the amount of noise and the lack of police, and had been so even before the area became widely supportive of the New Cairo Liberation Corps. During her teen years she'd often come to this area to meet up with other hackers. But she was never comfortable. The voluptuous women and slender, muscular men whose time was for sale gave her an overwhelming sense of alienation, as though she had failed to understand a joke everyone else was laughing at.

She rounded a corner, went past a group of women in what looked depressingly like poodle costumes and into the bar where she had agreed to meet Suchan. It was a run-down establishment, where every surface was sticky with congealed smears of old drink, and the patronage seemed exclusively made up of the dishevelled, the lousy and those whose drink of choice and future cause of death would be the same thing. This was a bar for people who hated their lives. Zala had heard too many stories about Surja's backstreet taverns making their liquor in old salvaged bathtubs that were never washed out, and while she couldn't be sure this wasn't simply societal demonization, she wasn't willing to drink it and find out personally. Instead, she asked for a bottle of beer and, after insisting that she open it herself, sat at a table in the corner and surveyed the room.

She lit on a table at the back with two large men and one very fat one, notable amongst the clientele by their lack of obvious lice. Kahleed apparently deemed the news important enough that he had come himself; Zala knew that Surja was almost as solidly on the side of the NCLC as Naj-Pur, but this was none the less a bold move. They spotted her, and after a while the three of them walked over to her table.

'You must be Selina,' Kahleed said.

Zala motioned towards the empty chairs and they took their seats.

'I'm Kahleed Banks. I'm involved in the NCLC. This is Tal Surdar, and you've met Suman. I understand you've got something to tell us.'

As Zala explained the information she'd acquired and what it meant, the demeanour of the group changed visibly. Kahleed's face grew stony, and his breathing became deep and laboured. Suman simply fidgeted and poorly fought to keep back his fascination, especially at the prospect of computer code bridging the gap between digital and biological virus. Tal looked more worried than anything, and kept glancing aside to the ever more enraged Kahleed. After she was finished explaining, she sent the compiled data to Suman, who went off to analyse it, leaving Zala with an agitated Kahleed and a cautiously assuaging Tal.

'They're killing us,' Kahleed growled, shaking his head.

Tal placed a hand on his arm, but Kahleed pushed him off and looked at Zala. 'Why? Why did they do it?'

Zala tensed her legs, prepared to kick herself backwards and run if the large, muscular man decided he didn't like her answer. 'I just got the data today. I don't know any of the circumstances. Just that this program, which seems to be related to the Soucouyant virus, seems to go back to there.'

'Where?'

'It's a research lab owned by a GeniSec subsidiary, dealing in computer programming. They work under the same team who designed IntuitivAI back in the day.'

Kahleed's face softened. 'So, why is it that you're coming to us with this?'

'I have a long-standing family issue with the GeniSec con-glomerate, one that's still causing me problems. So I came back here to try and set things right with them by solving the Soucouyant problem, hoping that they cared more about being the heroes who saved the world from the virus than they did about continuing to screw me over. Now that's not possible, I just want to hurt them as much as possible however I can.'

'Oh, there will be pain for them,' Kahleed assured her.

Tal intervened. 'Kahleed, we need to expose them, to pressure them into releasing a cure. It's not about anyone else getting hurt.'

Kahleed's hands tightened into fists. 'But maybe that's exactly what this should be about. Maybe I should have a few words with Maalik.'

For a moment, a look of genuine fear seemed to cross Tal's face. 'Don't use Maalik for this, not right away. This doesn't need escalating.'

'He's a capable soldier and an intelligent man, and I want his input. Maybe we should go send a message with our guest.'

Zala wondered if they were referring to Councillor Granier – there had been plenty of speculation on the news, and it seemed the most fitting solution. Tal looked exasperated. 'We'll discuss this back at base with the others,' he said, then turned to Zala. 'So what now for you? You want in with the NCLC?'

Zala thought about this for a minute. If nothing else, she could use shelter, and there was maybe a half chance that the NCLC could provide that. Of course, they could lead the authorities right to her, so it went both ways . . .

'Thanks, truly, but I'm going to pass. It's really not my fight, and I have my own affairs to deal with. All I want is that you use the information in that folder to damage GeniSec as much as possible.'

Kahleed nodded and thanked her for the data. Then he and Tal stood up from the table and left the bar.

As soon as Zala was alone, she slumped down, head on arms, and relaxed for a minute. It hadn't sunk in quite how tense she had been during that whole exchange until they'd gone.

So those are the terrorists.

By the time Zala got back to The Ozymandias, Polina was sprawled out on the sofa in her front room, watching an evening newscast on the large monitor mounted on the wall. More scenes of the Five Prongs played across the screen, along with commentators discussing the condition of the guards in the hospital. Zala felt a twinge of guilt at the news that two of them would be deafened permanently. She slumped down onto the couch next to Polina and they made small talk over the claims that the break-in was 'not worrying for its immediate results. It's worrying because it was a demonstration that NCLC terrorists in this city can get past our security measures with relative ease.'

Then the screen flashed to police sketches of the suspect: an athletic young woman in a revealing dress; another of a figure in black maintenance overalls with an oversized hood and a scarf wrapped around the lower part of the face, hiding its identity.

'Hey, I have a dress just like that which I haven't worn since university,' Polina murmured.

Then, she sat bolt upright and wheeled around to look at Zala, her face aghast. 'Holy shit, that was the server farm you were breaking into?'

'You didn't make that connection?' Zala asked.

'No! I assumed you were breaking into some little computer lab in Falkur or at the university. I didn't know you were the fucking terrorist hacker that broke into the Five Prongs!' Her eyes widened. 'Zala, tell me you're not affiliated with the New Cairo Liberation Corps.'

'I've got nothing to do with the NCLC,' she lied, 'and the police've got nothing on me. That sketch looks nothing like me. I'm a foot shorter than that and significantly skinnier; they've drawn me like a bodybuilder. My hair's not that cropped and they've got basically nothing on my face. It looks nothing like me. We're fine.'

Polina began rocking backwards and forwards, trembling. 'Oh my god, if you get caught, they'll shoot you. They'll execute you. And Christ knows what'll happen to me. I could lose my job, I could get thrown in prison! All the old lot who were at the funeral, one of them has to figure it out, right?'

'You only figured it out because you knew I was breaking into a server farm and because you recognized clothes you haven't worn in half a decade,' said Zala, not quite believing it herself. 'There's ten million people in this city and there's no way there aren't a few thousand who look more like that picture than I do, even to people who know I'm here.'

'BREAKING NEWS' suddenly swept across the screen and a shocked-looking newsreader appeared.

'Breaking news tonight as Security Force troops rush to the scene of a hostage situation developing at a GeniSec office block as a result of action by the New Cairo Liberation Corps. Two people are confirmed to have been shot, their condition unknown. We are going straight over to Ryuji Calgren, live at the scene.'

'Thanks, Marjani.' A smartly dressed young man appeared

on screen. 'Details are still sketchy but witnesses from the street report three armed figures in the building, two of which appear to be heavily scarred women. This could be the two women who were reported to have killed seven Security Force troops last week. The power to the floor that the hostages are thought to be on has been cut, so we can't see much in there. Police are already at the scene, and the Security Force are on their way. I'd wager they're not going to be taking prisoners on this one.'

Polina couldn't stop shaking.

Chapter 11

'They're coming!' said Juri. 'Intercept in thirty seconds.'

'I see them,' replied Alice. The twins, Anisa and Thana Yu, and their young colleague Serhiy Panossian had made plenty of noise and news crews had so many cameras pointed at the GeniSec Regional Administration building with hasty, loosely encrypted connections back to the newsrooms that the various operators around her had twice as much information to send as they usually did. Alice could see that outside the building, from behind a cordoned-off area, thousands were gathered to watch the stand-off unfolding. The CCTV intel Juri had sent through to her monitor showed six SecForce troops preparing to storm in through the rear fire exit of the office block and up the long flights of stairs. Alice's fingers flew across the holographic keyboard. The three NCLC operatives were in a large office on the seventh floor of the eight-floor building, waiting for the signal to stop the diversion and meanwhile pacing between the desks, guns pointed at the forty-one bound and gagged hostages on the floor. The twins' grotesque reputations preceded them to the point where the terrified hostages had practically rounded themselves up, but when one person fought back, it was Serhiy who'd shot her in the arm, bringing her protest to a halt. As useful a decision as this was, Alice couldn't help but be disturbed at his readiness to do so and the frank brutality of it. The nineteen-year-old was Maalik's protégé, and Alice felt justified in not trusting him completely. This wasn't meant to be a bloodbath. If the countermeasures worked, it wouldn't have to be.

The video feeds now took up much of the map space, most of which had been accessed and fed through to her by Juri, whose web of manipulated security cameras had expanded in both scope and capability. It was a sight to behold; every poorly secured camera in the city was accessible to her, and her bio-aug eye allowed her to see a large number of feeds all at once. When something pertinent came up, she sent it through to the main screen for Alice to take care of. On top of this, each camera had 'blank' footage available, showing nothing in particular happening, which Juri could insert on command, meaning that the identities and entry points of the NCLC operatives could be hidden from the view of the security camera's owner. Alice had found herself using Suman less and less as Juri came into her own.

Alice quickly checked on the second team, who were working feverishly on the floor above. Led by Nataliya Kaur, the five operatives had managed to get into the building earlier in the day simply by putting on business wear and behaving as if they belonged there. They had kept a low enough profile that none of the employees now held hostage had even noticed them enter. With eyes off them, the operatives were hard at work accessing as much GeniSec data as they could.

Most importantly, they were awaiting the signal.

'Ten seconds,' said Juri.

'All right, guys, brace yourselves,' Alice said into the microphone.

Tal, Maalik and Kahleed stood behind her, watching intently. She had never seen Kahleed anywhere near this angry before. Tal was trying to calm him, but his soothing words were apparently doing nothing.

'What're the ratings like for news channels right now?' said Alice.

Somewhere behind her, Suman yelled, 'NCN's getting two

million, Empire News is getting one and a half million, VBN is getting half a million, and there's about half a million watching other news sources.'

They'd picked their moment perfectly.

Two.

One.

Right on cue, the SecForce troops came up the flight of stairs onto the seventh floor and rounded into the lobby, heading towards the room where the twins and Serhiy were with their hostages.

The power was still down, and they didn't see the tripwire strung tightly across the floor at ankle height.

The explosion was loud and bright. From the grainy feed coming from the camera on Serhiy's jacket, Alice saw all six soldiers on the floor, either writhing in pain or unconscious. Nataliya had vouched repeatedly for the efficacy of her 'raspberry grenades' – a brutal but non-lethal combination of disorienting stun grenades and 'sting grenades' full of rubber balls designed to beat anyone in the vicinity to a pulp. It appeared she hadn't been exaggerating.

Suman piped up. 'Okay, talk of a bomb going off has hit the web and it's spreading fast. I'm seeing fifty thousand – no, a hundred thousand extra tuning into the news and it's rising fast. If the backup team's all sorted, now's the time to go.'

Alice turned and looked for Kahleed's signal. He nodded.

'All right, Nat, hit it.'

An old portable terminal that Alice had picked up in a salvaged junk store buzzed, along with thousands of other portable terminals across the city, throughout the government, the media and various whistle-blowing network sites. Alice picked it up in a gloved hand and switched it on. Inside was a message.

Subject: Our ill-gotten gains
>Sorry for all the mess. We promise we've yet to kill anyone, and if all goes according to plan, we won't need to. Enclosed is a dump of as many GeniSec documents as we could get our hands on, and a cache of compelling evidence which suggests that the

Soucouyant virus originated at a GeniSec tech lab. Hopefully it should be good for a story or two.

And remember: these people are responsible for hundreds of deaths, and their former CEO and main shareholder is the head of the executive and the head of the legislature in this city, responsible for the push for quarantine, locking us all in with the disease they helped create.

Here's to us doing your jobs for you,

The New Cairo Liberation Corps.

'It's out, you guys,' Alice said.

All eyes turned to the bank of monitors already tuned to different newscasts. One by one, shocked news anchors announced to their millions-strong audiences that the NCLC had sent them documents alleging that GeniSec created the Soucouyant virus.

Alice grinned and turned her attention back to the operation at hand. 'All right, guys, get home as soon as you have the opportunity.'

Thana Yu gave an acknowledging grunt as the three operatives on the seventh floor ran out of the office and into the corridor. They met with Nataliya and her four squad mates coming down from upstairs. They needed to be quick – any moment and the security drones and helicopters would be there. Nataliya brought up a menu on her portable terminal and pressed a big red button on her keyboard.

Across the road, in another large office building, there was another loud, bright detonation, spraying glass just short of the crowd outside. Even to Alice and the others hearing it through the news teams' microphones, the volley of noise was deafening. Most of the spectators in the courtyard turned round. Then, another blast. It was closer to the near side of the building, right next to the press, civilians, police, and Security Force troops. The crowd erupted, afraid for their lives and getting in everyone else's way in their attempts to run from the source of the noise. They streamed every which way, shoving and trampling obstacles and completely ignoring the cordoned-off space the police and Security Force troops had set up. The police themselves were caught in the middle, as the mass of people closest to the explosions attempted to push past the thousands that had gathered behind them to gawp.

The explosions had also disguised the sound of another, smaller detonation in the basement of the GeniSec building. A hole large enough for a man to get through had breached the brick wall separating this block from its neighbour, and the operatives scrambled across it. Their fatigues stripped off to reveal street wear underneath, they ran past the ingredient store of the restaurant above, up the stairs into a large, shining kitchen, where food had been abandoned mid-preparation. At the back of the kitchen was a side door out into the street. Thana Yu cracked it open and checked her camera feed; it took in nothing but wave upon wave of fleeing civilians. In the distance, yet another bomb went off, loud enough to be heard from where they were. The operatives pushed open the door and ran out into the crowd, each in a different direction, until they were dispersed in the mob.

Alice pulled off her headset and smiled. It wouldn't take the Security Force long to realize that the hostages were unguarded, and only a short time more for roadblocks to be established, but every one of those operatives knew how to capitalize on that window of opportunity. For her, there was for now only the afterglow: the visceral rush that came from humiliating people who really deserved it. They'd exposed GeniSec and made fools of the Security Force. They'd attracted the entire city's attention and still made it out unnoticed. What's more, it was said the SecForce had begun to make use of the IntuitivAI protocol to coordinate their operations. An artificial intelligence equivalent to several people with genius-level IQs and linear thinking power beyond the capacity of any human, and somehow she had managed to beat it. Victory felt good.

Around her, people were cheering: the technicians and co-ordinators, Maalik's backup crew who were simply glad they didn't have to go out and get into a fight, and the younger, newer members who were being trained up. In all the commotion, it took Alice a while to realize that the door to the sleeping quarters was open and her daughter had wandered out, rubbing her eyes. She got up from her chair, rushed over, and crouched down to look Ria in the eye.

'Hey, sweetie, did we wake you up?'

'Wazzgoinon?' a groggy Ria murmured.

Alice grinned and hugged her daughter to her. 'We just made some very bad people get in trouble for the very bad things they were doing, and we're celebrating. The good guys have won, sweetie!' And she hugged her daughter tighter. Maybe it was the sleep deprivation talking but today seemed like a good day.

'Does that mean Dad can come home now?' said Ria.

Alice paused.

Not yet. Not tonight, please not tonight.

Maalik's voice came from behind Alice. 'Ria, your dad's doing a different mission right now. It's a big, dangerous mission that only the bravest and strongest can do, so he was the person we wanted for the job. And he's going to be away for a little while. It's hard for him too, but it needs to be done, okay?'

Alice could have kissed Maalik right then.

'Can we go home then?'

Alice responded this time. 'That's still a bit too tricky, sweetie. But Mum's trying to make sure everything's all right, okay?'

Ria yawned wide and nodded. 'I'm gonna go back to bed now, Mum.'

Guilt gripped Alice tight, but she put on a smile for her daughter's sake. 'Okay, sweetie, I'll come and tuck you in.'

Then, from above the factory, in the street outside, there was the sound of roaring engines and gunfire.

Everyone jumped. Alice instinctively pulled Ria to her chest and looked around for the source of the gunfire. Before she even had time to ask, she was having details yelled at her. There were two SecForce vehicles in the street above. They were grabbing civilians, beating them and demanding to know where the NCLC was based. Juri, seated at her workstation and watching the commotion through her network of compromised security cameras, described with horror a boy, aged fourteen at most, being beaten with rifle butts while he screamed that he didn't know anything. Alice looked back to her monitor. She counted twelve SecForce troops, all with mid-range weaponry and body armour.

Maalik spoke up first. 'Kahleed, me and my boys can be ready to go in two minutes. We may need you two as well.'

Tal rounded on him. 'Listen, they don't know that we're even here, and neither does anyone else who isn't one of us. We don't need to go up there. They're not going to find us.'

'That's what you think this is about?' Maalik growled back. 'They're beating the shit out of random people in the street to get to us. They're beating the crap out of random people because they think they can just waltz into Naj-Pur and knock the trash about when they're angry. Christ, Tal, I thought this was why you and Nat quit the police in the first place.'

Tal looked ready to explode. 'You don't know shit about why I left the police, old man. Right now, our long-term goals mean that we need this place. We're not wasting it to go after the first people to rough up some civilians.'

'They're violent people, Tal!' roared Maalik. 'They only understand violence! They're like wild animals. They need to be shown that they're not in charge here any more, that they can't keep making victims of us. We need to thrash it into them!'

Alice couldn't do anything but stare in shock. Ria huddled close to her, shivering.

'Just, for five seconds,' said Tal, frustration in his voice, gesticulating wildly, 'stop trying to make this more violent than it needs to be! You don't know anything about these people!'

Maalik fumed. 'No, Tal, *you* don't know anything about these people. You don't know what it's like growing up afraid of every cop who walks down the road, not being able to go to the police when your child has been assaulted because they'll just assume he's a gang member. You have no idea what privileges you've enjoyed that some of us have had to go without. And your experiences don't mean anything arou—'

Kahleed yelled for them to shut up. They both wheeled round, shocked. Kahleed was breathing hard, his anger breaking out again. 'GeniSec, the Security Force, they're all puppets of Tau Granier. Let's show him we're the new power in this city. Get everyone available up in two.'

Tal stepped forward. 'Kahleed, they'll—'

'I don't care if they find us. I don't care if we have to move to one of the other safe houses. I just want my people, the people I grew up with, to be safe. If they're not safe, what's the point of all this?'

Tal looked like he wanted to start yelling again, but contained himself and nodded.

'I'll get my crew ready,' said Maalik, his voice returning to its normal pitch. 'Tal, you're a capable fighter. I know you're opposed to it, but it would help greatly if you and Kahleed would take the trainees up and provide a diversion. My people will loop round and come from the other side so they won't know we were right here. We can at least scare them off.'

Tal agreed miserably and he and Maalik walked towards the armoury to equip themselves. Kahleed turned to Alice. 'Put Ria back to bed, and get ready to coordinate our response.'

Alice nodded and looked down at Ria. 'Come on, the grown-ups have got work to do.' Ria took her hand and the two of them walked back to the sleeping area.

Alice had pushed two bunk beds together to make a double bed in which she and Ria slept. Zeno was right next to where Alice slept, in his pillow cot. He still slept most of the time and when he was awake, Alice knew she could rely on Ria to look after him. If she was bored or he was too much of a hassle, the accountant, Hoshi Smolak, was always willing to keep an eye on him. He'd had three children of his own, and his days were mostly spent waiting for hours on end for fund-transfer chains and money-laundering algorithms to complete. Hoshi had probably seen more of Zeno than she had, she realized.

Alice tucked Ria in, then stopped for a second, and said, 'Ria, sweetie? There might be more noise coming from outside, so I'm going to turn down your cochlear implant like I do with Zeno so you don't have to hear anything loud, okay?'

Ria looked up at her. 'I thought you were going to do that anyway?'

Alice's breath caught in her throat. She'd been unable to get more than a few hours' sleep each night since she and her children had been here. From time to time she'd mute Ria's ear implants while she slept so she wouldn't be disturbed by Alice's pillow-muffled sobs.

'And you're okay with that, me controlling your implants while you're asleep?'

'Sure. You've got the controls anyway,' Ria said, smiling up at her mother. 'Night night.'

'Night night, Ria.' Alice opened the controls on her portable terminal, found the volume for Ria's auditory implants, and turned it right down. There'd be noise – total, utter silence does strange things to a person – but nothing to wake her. Certainly, the volume throttle would mute anything loud near by.

Like gunshots or explosions.

Alice shivered. She kissed Ria and Zeno on the forehead, and then headed back into the main room, closing the door behind her. Already, it was full of people in combat gear – body armour, roomy civilian clothes over the top and balaclavas. Maalik and the six soldiers in his backup unit looked completely at home, self-assured and prepared. By comparison, the four new recruits who stood with Tal and Kahleed looked out of place, even as the body armour moulded to their body shapes. They were all former factory workers, and with only a few days' training under their belts, they really weren't ready for this. But they were enthusiastic and angry, and that was worth something. Alice walked past them and sat once more in front of her terminal.

Maalik stood in the middle of the room, addressing the group. 'All right, everyone, the cameras put them right next to us, on the street just west of here. We're going down the alleyway, looping around two blocks. Kahleed, your team will be Squad One. You attack from the north at the junction; my team circles round and attacks their left flank through the back street. They'll think there's loads of us, it'll be great. We'll cut their communications channel. Let them run if you can.'

Armed and armoured, thirteen people who hadn't thought they'd be fighting that day filed up the stairs to the factory corridor and out down the driveway.

Alice watched on the main terminal monitor as they turned the corner and circled the block. They were in luck; an angry crowd had formed around the SecForce troops, blocking them from view as Squad One took position and Squad Two disappeared round a corner. A few warning shots and some errant rifle butt swings from the troops soon dispersed much of the crowd. Squad One leaned out from their points of cover and raised their guns. Tal fired two warning shots into the tarmac in front of the troops.

'This area is under the protection of the New Cairo Liberation Corps! Leave now!'

In response, the SecForce troops spread out and raised their rifles, as one of them in front yelled, 'Drop your weapons and get on your knees with your hands behind your heads!'

'Not going to happen! You're going to leave here now before this goes any further!'

'On your knees, hands behind your heads!' the SecForce trooper yelled, moving forward, eye to his rifle's scope.

The first gunshot went off. It hit the lead SecForce officer high in the chest and he fell backwards, breaking his fall with the rifle. A stream of smoke rose from the barrel of the gun held by one of the new recruits.

The street erupted. The NCLC operatives were already in cover, but the SecForce troops had intensive training, expensive equipment and were bio-augmented to the nines, with astonishing stability and accuracy. The NCLC operatives were rarely able to squeeze off a single shot between the volleys of gunfire. The SecForce troops fanned out, finding their way behind cars or small walls, keeping up their barrage.

Maalik's voice came through Alice's headset. 'Alice, get them firing now! They need to be holding the SecForce troops' attention!'

Alice nodded, and entered a command into the console. Clusters of chemical pads embedded in the new recruits' body armour released a cocktail of adrenalin and dopamine subcutaneously and directly into their bloodstreams. Within seconds, they were shooting from over their cover as if the SecForce troops were firing paper balls. The sudden offensive caught the SecForce troops off-guard. One fell, hit in the chin. Alice watched the chaos through the tiny video feeds from the NCLC guns' scopes and cameras on their equipment harnesses. The remaining troops moved back, attempting some suppressive fire in any gap in the NCLC fusillade.

There came a sudden lull in the crossfire.

'Drop your weapons, gather your wounded and leave now!' Tal yelled over the concrete barrier he was crouched behind. Alice was surprised. Was he that scared of what Maalik would do?

One of the SecForce troops dropped his rifle, flipped up his armoured visor to reveal his face, then, with hands raised above his head, walked out from cover, forward towards the first injured man. Slowly, his eyes on the NCLC operatives at all times, he knelt down, looped his arms under the wounded man's shoulders and began dragging him back to where the rest of them stood. One by one, the other SecForce troops began to slowly lower their rifles to the ground and step backwards towards the truck they'd come in.

Somewhere in the next street along, where Maalik's group was waiting, a completely different storm of gunfire started up. Startled, the SecForce troops grabbed their rifles again. One of the new NCLC recruits let out a scream, his torso spattered with assault rifle fire, and collapsed backwards. The armour stopped the bullets that hit his head and chest, but his right shoulder was shredded, two shots forming one gaping exit wound.

The screen in front of Alice showed that Maalik's group had come across another, smaller squad of SecForce troops who had evidently taken exception to the armed men sneaking towards their comrades. With Maalik's team occupied, Kahleed and Tal's group were at a two-to-one disadvantage against opponents with far more training than they had.

Kahleed fired from underneath the car he was hiding behind, hitting a SecForce trooper in the shin and foot. The man fell to the ground and, with another few bullets fired into his body, stopped moving. One of the new recruits sprayed an entire magazine of bullets at two exposed soldiers, hitting them both through sheer law of averages, before being knocked off his feet by a volley of return fire. Another recruit was hit through the meat of his thigh and slumped down against cover, screaming with pain.

Kahleed and Tal were pinned down on opposite sides of the street. Alice quickly mapped a sequence of instructions to a single key on the keyboard, and the reverse sequence onto its neighbouring key. Tal leaned forward from behind cover, then fell back immediately as gunfire pounded the concrete barrier protecting him. With enemy attention focused on his partner, Kahleed quickly let off a burst of shots at an exposed SecForce trooper, which in turn drew their fire and gave Tal an opening.

Alice was reminded of going ten-pin bowling as a young girl and the difficulty of a seven-ten split.

Kahleed leaned out again and almost immediately ducked back behind cover. The remaining six SecForce soldiers were now covering both sides, giving neither the chance to counter, and began to move forward, gaining on the pinned-down NCLC operatives.

Two shadows appeared behind the SecForce troops, disappearing around the corner of a nearby alleyway.

Alice scrolled frantically through the video feeds she had available to try to identify these interlopers, but they were not in the field of vision of any of the networked cameras Juri had gained access to. Maalik's group were struggling to finish off the last two of their combatants, but all seven of his team were still accounted for.

The SecForce troops edged forward, guns trained on the corners Tal and Kahleed were behind. They weren't far away now.

A rapid salvo of gunfire came over their shoulders. Within seconds, all the SecForce troopers were dead. Behind them stood Anisa and Thana Yu, each holding a sub-machine gun. Nataliya and the rest of her group appeared at the end of the street. On the next street along, Serhiy Panossian opened fire on the two remaining soldiers facing Maalik's squad.

Alice let out a great sigh of relief. Her sense of ease soured quickly, though, as the euphoria of deflecting a threat to her family gave way to the realization of how she had achieved it.

The street was now littered with corpses, and the gutters ran red with blood.

She had indirectly facilitated a massacre.

Had it been worth it?

Moreover, it had been carried out by people who were around her children every day, sometimes looked after them. This was somehow much easier to accept when the action was further away. Kahleed and Tal and Maalik, the people she spent time with, slept in the same room as and, in the case of the former two, had known for years, were in a strange way divorced from Kahleed and Tal and Maalik, the abstract figures she commanded on a computer screen. Something about the fight being adjacent to the very building she was in seemed to muddy this separation. She began to wonder exactly why she had surrounded her children with terrorists and killers.

This was apparently the price she was willing to pay for safety.

The sounds of gun chambers being emptied rang through the wall as the NCLC operatives finished off any SecForce trooper still clinging to life. Kahleed, Tal, the new arrivals and the remaining new recruit then picked up their dead or wounded compatriots and began to carry them towards the safe house. The members of the NCLC were heading home to see what would happen next.

Chapter 12

A harsh blunt pain in his side woke Ryan Granier with a start. The room was dark, but he could make out the outlines and sounds of at least three other people in front of him. He sucked in air painfully. Another strike came, this time to his stomach, winding him. The pain was intense. He tried to bring his arms up and curl into a ball, but two of his assailants prised his arms away from him and picked him up in such a way as to restrain him.

The light came on, blinding him for a moment. In front of Ryan, still in his wheelchair, was Yosef Klein. Surrounding him and holding Ryan up were the other members of Yosef's unit.

'Good morning, Councillor,' said Yosef. 'I hope you're ready to go about your day.'

Ryan struggled to breathe as Yosef continued, 'I wonder if you saw the news last night?'

Ryan shook his head, still gasping, almost unable to keep his chin off his chest.

'Ahhh,' said Yosef, a sick grin on his face. 'Well, it turns out – and I was just as shocked as anyone else to hear this, in spite of my low opinion of you and yours – it turns out that the Soucouyant virus originated in a computer programming facility. And that computer programming facility was owned as a subsidiary of . . . what major New Cairo-based conglomerate was it again, Suhayl?'

The man holding up Ryan by his left arm said, 'That'd be the GeniSec Corporation, Yosef.'

Yosef pointed at him. 'How right you are, my friend. How right you are. The problem is, Councillor, we feel as though the misery brought upon us, and upon our friends and families, and really upon this whole city, is your fault by proxy. You got rich and powerful off the back of the exploitation of the downtrodden and the unfortunate. It's because of you that the people of this city are suffering.'

Yosef reached up, crooked a finger under Ryan's chin, and brought it up until he was looking him straight in the eyes.

'We're suffering, Councillor. We're in pain, and we feel that it's time that we share that pain with you.'

Ryan attempted to wrestle free from the grip of the man Yosef had called Suhayl, but a stabbing sensation flared where he had first been stomped, and he let out a whimper of pain.

Yosef did a half-turn in his wheelchair and said to the others, 'Come on. Let's take him downstairs.'

'Please, don't!' Ryan gasped.

Yosef looked back over his shoulder, a glint in his eye. 'It's not my call, Councillor. It comes from higher up.'

The two NCLC operatives carrying him followed Yosef through the large steel door into the corridor leading towards the main complex of the safe house, Ryan slung between them. Whatever the building had been used for in the past, it was large and secure. Small letterbox windows were set all along the top of the ceiling, and most had been covered in black tape.

Suhayl clasped a hand over Ryan's mouth as they entered a large room filled with mattresses, on which dozens of people appeared to be sleeping, though it was too dark to identify them.

'Make a sound, and everything that's going to happen to you happens much, much slower,' Suhayl hissed into Ryan's ear.

Moving between the mattresses, the group crossed to a door in the other side of the room, then went down several flights of concrete stairs. The wheels of Yosef's chair warped as they descended, the tyres and spokes shifting, clinging to the steps and allowing him to roll down the stairs smoothly. Ryan was not so lucky. Every step the people carrying him went down caused a jolt of pain to run through his side. The stabbing sensation was becoming more and more intense. Ryan realized that he must have at least one broken rib. As his grunts became more and more audible, the jolt became harsher with each step and the resulting pain became worse.

Eventually they arrived at the bottom of the stairwell, facing into a long corridor. On the right side were four doors, each one looking heavy and tightly locked. Yosef spun round again to face Ryan.

'This building used to be a bank, Councillor. I won't tell you which one, because you not knowing where you are is rather important. But these are the vaults in which the safety deposit boxes are kept. They're large, they're impenetrable and they're sound-proof. As suited as they were to their old job, we've decided to appropriate them for our own uses.'

'Is the white room finished yet?' asked one of the NCLC operatives, a scowling woman a head taller than the rest of the group. The others looked at her, surprised.

'No, it's still under construction,' said Yosef, taken aback, 'and besides, we're saving that for his father.' He faced Ryan again. 'We've got a far more immediate method of treatment for you, Councillor.'

He turned to the nearest door and tapped on the keyboard projected from his portable terminal. The door opened inwards, revealing a large room, its walls lined with metal drawers. In the centre was a single steel chair with handcuffs attached. The only light came from a large lamp which pointed at the chair and glinted off a steel tray on a stand near by. The operatives dragged Ryan inside, dumped him unceremoniously onto the chair, and clasped the handcuffs round his arms and legs.

'Where's Ava?' Ryan yelled into the darkness behind the blinding light now trained on his face.

'Oh, she won't be up and about for another two hours or so. More than enough time to be done here and get you back.'

Ryan looked at the metal tray to his right. Lying on it, each on its own paper towel, were what were mostly either very old surgical tools or very old woodworking tools. His eyes widened. 'What are you going to do to me?'

Yosef rolled into his field of vision, into the light from the lamp. 'Oh, I'm not going to do anything to you. I'm in a wheelchair, you see.' He motioned down facetiously. 'And if I'm being entirely honest, I'm not sure that I could, even in an able state. But we've got a guy for this. Normally he does it for information, or he used to at least. Passwords to networks, plans for secret events. It's amazing what he can make people do.'

There was a knocking sound. A coarse, deep voice rang out. 'You didn't start without me, did you?'

Yosef quickly turned himself around. 'No, sir.'

'Good. Let's have this ready for the morning news. I want this setting the Council's agenda for today. We might even have a response by lunch.'

Only the figure's shoes showed in the lamplight. They were expensive-looking leather loafers, quite at odds with the clothes he'd seen on the other rebels. The metal door behind the shadowy figure closed with a heavy percussive *clank*.

The figure walked towards Ryan. 'You, in the chair. What is your name?'

Ryan looked up. 'What?'

A large gloved hand reached out and wrapped around the back of Ryan's head, pulling it forward. At the same time, a hard elbow swung inwards, colliding with Ryan's left cheekbone with extraordinary force. He felt himself falling backwards, in too much pain to realize precisely what had happened. He landed hard, his arms trapped under the back of the chair. He let out a scream of pain, and frantically twisted his body, trying to turn the chair onto its side and free his crushed arms. This just aggravated his broken ribs, resulting in an impotent flopping motion. Powerful hands pulled him back up, held him in place and sank a punch into his stomach. Again, the wind was knocked out of him and he doubled over, tears in his eyes.

A slight darkness encroached around the edges of his vision for a second and receded.

'STOP!' he yelled. 'My . . . my name is Ryan Granier.'

The gloved hands clasped his jaw and scalp and roughly held his head forward. 'Say it again, with your title.'

'My name is Councillor Ryan Granier.'

'And who is your father?'

'My father is High Councillor Tau Granier.'

'The majority shareholder and former CEO of which conglomerate?'

'The Genesis Security and Technology Corporation. GeniSec.'

Ryan felt the hands on his face loosen slightly, pinching less. He realized he was bleeding from a split cheek. Drops of blood spattered his already filthy shirt.

'And how many days has it been since you were first taken?'

Ryan had to think for a moment. This was apparently a moment too long. The hands pulled him forwards again, and with his arms and legs still tied to the chair he was unable to stop the chair tipping forwards all the way, crashing with all of his weight onto his knees and face. He felt more blood well up, this time on his brow, and the rest of his face throbbed with pain. The chair was pulled back up, and him with it, and the hands grasped his head again. 'How many days has it been, maggot?'

'N-n-nine days, nine days,' he said, his already swelling face tightening.

'Good. Here's today's newspaper, to confirm that this isn't staged.'

The figure behind him drew out a newspaper, but pointed it in the opposite direction, so he couldn't see the headline or the date.

Who is he talking to?

'As you can see, Councillor Granier is still alive.' His tone was forceful and deliberate, as though he were formally addressing someone. 'You graciously put your plans for total quarantine on hold for now. However, in light of recent developments, we've decided to push for something a little more ambitious.'

Ryan saw in front of him, in the darkness, a tiny little red light. They were filming this.

'We, the people of New Cairo, want to see the ban on people from "high-infection" areas getting in and out of the city lifted, seeing as how being poor and scared is not in fact a sickness. Furthermore, we want to see the resignation of the High Councillor for having overseen the greatest massacre this city has ever known. We want an investigation into who created the virus and, more pertinently, under whose orders. We want whomsoever this investigation turns up, at whatever level of the government or corporate ladder, to be tried and, if found guilty, executed for crimes against humanity.'

The figure, still masked by shadow, gestured towards Ryan.

'You have a week to comply with these demands, or we will kill your son, Tau Granier. Of course, we expect that you will require extra proof that this really is the councillor. He's not shaved in over a week and he's not currently in the best physical condition, after all. With this tape, you'll find a viable DNA sample. You won't be able to miss it. *Hold him.*'

Four masked operatives rushed forward and held Ryan in such a way as to stop him moving anything other than his neck. He thrashed and struggled all he could, but the people holding him were too strong.

The man who had been tormenting him walked round to his right and reached for an object on the tray. It was a thin handle of what looked almost like a craft knife. A gloved thumb flicked a switch on the handle. A steel blade protruded from the top, about an inch in length, which quickly began to glow red.

Ryan's breath caught in his throat. He yelled, horrified, and struggled even harder against his captors, disregarding the pain in his ribs or his face. He thrashed his head around, trying to bite or head-butt, and desperately attempted to move his limbs. It was no use.

The figure leaned forward into the light. It was the old man who had taken care of the children, whom Ryan had not trusted. Ryan searched for the name. Maalik. Expertly, the bearded old man sliced at the material of Ryan's left trouser leg, the edges burnt black, opening a small window and exposing the skin of his thigh.

'If you'll notice, the skin on the enclosed sample is artificially darkened, as is Councillor Granier's, and also High Councillor Granier's, as a matter of fact,' Maalik said into the camera. 'As status symbols go, it's certainly the only one of his that still endures now. So we feel that it's useful for our purposes.'

The blade grazed Ryan's skin. The heat was extraordinary, more than Ryan could have imagined. He let out a scream and recoiled, attempting to get away from the pain, but his captors held him tight. An angry red burn sprang up.

The stroke completed, Maalik reversed the blade and brought it back. It slid into Ryan's skin as easily as into butter, the skin melting and charring where the blade came into contact with it. Ryan screamed again, louder this time, and struggled still harder against his restraints, disregarding every injury but the one being inflicted upon him, but the NCLC operatives were much stronger than he was. The blade completed its stroke, and a wafer-thin slice of skin fell to the ground. Ryan sobbed and muttered whatever pleas he could string together, but his captors continued regardless.

'As you can see, Councillor Ryan, a small piece of flesh gets burnt too easily. The greatest boon of this particular tool is the instant cauterization. Which allows us to do this.'

He plunged the blade into Ryan's thigh, and pulled it down. Ryan howled, every thought and sense blocked out by one great message of pain, pain, pain.

A second stab and pull yielded a wedge of flesh, which Maalik tugged from Ryan's leg. There was only a small amount of blood. As Maalik had said, the wound had been cauterized immediately, leaving a gaping wound and a smell sickeningly reminiscent of steak. Ryan twisted and vomited from the pain, spraying one of the operatives standing next to him. He heard a storm of expletives, as though they were somewhere far away, and receding. His vision grew dark.

A few trace sensations lingered, and then stopped.

*

For the second time that day, Councillor Ryan Granier awoke in pain. There appeared to be a mask over his face, blindfolding him. He tried to reach up and pull it off, but was stopped by the extraordinary pain in his arms.

'I wouldn't. You have a number of fractures, plus that mask's all that's keeping the cuts and swelling where we want them.' He recognized the voice. It was Ava. 'I don't know what happened, and I don't want to know. I'm assuming this came from higher up the food chain from me. As far as I'm concerned you have a hell of a bad sleeping position. But I'm going to do what I can to help you.'

Ryan attempted to muster a response, but all that came out was a groan.

'You're welcome.'

There was a small, cold pressure on the back of his neck. The pain began to melt away, leaving him with a detached floating sensation.

'Now, that nerve block should help the pain. You've cracked your seventh rib through ninth on your right side. I've done what I can with calcium scaffolding there, which should stop anything really bad happening. You're lucky you don't have flail chest. As for your leg, congratulations, you've got a wedge of your thigh missing, which I'd imagine you can feel. Now, you should be haemo-dynamically stable, but I can't get in there and rebuild anything because, I'll be honest, if I use medical supplies that are meant to help people who get shot fighting I'm going to get in a lot of trouble. Your left forearm's fractured, but calcium scaffolding is already making good progress; I've relocated your right shoulder dislocation and the mask is reducing the facial bruising and swelling. You're in for a boring day of waiting around for different treatments to work, but it's all just going to get better from here.'

'Is the video on the news?' asked Ryan, his voice raw from screaming and vomit, and muffled by the mask.

'Headline. It feeds nicely into the overarching "GeniSec is

public enemy number one" narrative, and it's antagonizing both GeniSec and the Council at once.'

Something damp and cooling slid into the dent in his leg.

'There,' said Ava, exhaling with relief. 'That's as much as I can do with biological medical solutions. As for mechanical, if there's still a GeniSec left after all this is over, I'd imagine you can swing whatever bio-augs will help.' For a moment, Ryan lay there, enjoying the relief from the crippling pain in his leg.

'So do you think your father's company really did make the Soucouyant?'

Ryan hadn't had time to consider the question properly, so he thought out loud. 'I don't know. I mean, we basically know nothing about the virus, except for what it does, so that's really all I can judge. But I don't understand why it was to their advantage to do this. Last time I checked, GeniSec was doing great. I get why people might think that it's forced obsolescence for the bio-augs, but there's honestly no need. There was no new generation of bio-augs coming for at least another half a decade. The research and development money is all going into more AI development right now.' He paused, letting the pain in his raw throat subside. 'The risk is pointless. If it could be proved, GeniSec would be destroyed overnight, and most of the people who wouldn't get the upgrades don't have the money to replace dead augmentations anyway. I don't know how it got there, but I don't think GeniSec ever knew it was coming from them.'

Ava peeled the mask from Ryan's face. 'Don't try and sit up yourself.' He was lying on an elevated bed in the middle of the office used as a makeshift operating room. Ava grabbed his still bound ankles and swung his legs round so they were dangling over the edge of the bed. Taking hold of his shoulders, she pulled him into a sitting position, and it was only then that he realized he was wearing a medical gown and a pair of shorts as opposed to the suit he'd spent most of the previous week in.

'Can I stand?'

Ava let out a snort of laughter. 'Councillor, they took a chunk out of your leg that'd feed a family of five. The flesh binder will heal a lot of it within a few days, but for now, you're going to have to use these. The calcium scaffolding on your ribs and shoulder should keep it from hurting too much.'

She handed him two crutches, and he placed them under his arms, balancing on his good leg.

'Hey, Ava . . . thanks.'

After a pause, Ava replied, 'I didn't sign up for this. It's all getting out of hand. At one of the other safe houses, a dozen Security Force officers were killed last night.' Her composure left her and she looked sick with anxiety. 'There's something good and righteous at the heart of this organization, something about fighting for the right thing. But there's so much anger, and it's growing worse. They didn't have to do this to you.'

'Why did you join?'

'Because I hated the Council. I hated the fact that people like me or my cousin, the most vulnerable kinds of people in this city, were considered necessary sacrifices, rather than people with a right to decide what to do for ourselves. So, between my shifts at work, I started volunteering with the old NCLC, back when it was an advocacy group. Even after it changed into a paramilitary operation, there were people like Kahleed and Jacob, who were just trying to make a bad situation better. But then Maalik came along, with his dead son and his military experience, and I'm here thinking, does he want a war? Jacob got killed and now it's all just about striking back. Honestly, I hate this whole thing. This isn't what I wanted.'

'What did you want?'

Ava contemplated this for a while.

'I wanted safety. I wanted to feel safe.'

Ryan remembered back to the meeting he'd had right before being taken. How he had just finished selling out the safety of the people of Naj-Pur and of Surja just as much as the rest of them. He was suddenly deeply glad about the postponement of the vote.

Then, Ava looked him straight in the eye. 'If we can organize it so that no one gets hurt, I can get you out of here. I can get you out, and you can get me out in return. I want to be done here. Out of this place, out of this city. You must have the connections to make that happen. Can you get me out of here safely?'

Ryan thought for a moment, about the risk, about how this could be a trap.

He thought about his wife and his children.

He nodded.

Chapter 13

The newscasts unfurling across the screen in front of Zala showed GeniSec coming under fire from all angles. She had mortally wounded her foe, but now she had to watch as it cried and begged and slowly succumbed.

Its own news network, NCN, seemed to contort itself schizophrenically between pretending nothing had happened and viciously discrediting anyone who said GeniSec's name in the same sentence as 'Soucouyant'. Meanwhile, the competitor channels gleefully took their rival apart, with half their airtime devoted to reports on GeniSec and the allegations. The news anchors on Empire News and VBN claimed that 'Some are asking, what if GeniSec created and unleashed the virus as a way to make people get new bio-augs?', doing their best to plant the idea in the public consciousness. Share prices dropped, protests were being organized, and interviews with teary-eyed relatives of Soucouyant victims were all over the news channels. They finally had a real black-and-white story with a villain to go after.

There was satisfaction in having exposed GeniSec's connection with the Soucouyant virus, Zala decided. She was glad to be hurting them, after all they'd done. But she'd needed GeniSec on her side to win back her freedom. She always knew it was a long shot and that she might fail to clear her name. But she hadn't failed. That was the most frustrating part. She hadn't failed to find a common element in the virus's victims, or trace it back to its source. The source was the exact group she had needed on her side, needed to exonerate her. Every battle had been a rousing success, but the war was doomed.

What was to come next was another matter altogether. She couldn't stay in this city. She'd aided terrorists and, in doing so, had pissed off the most powerful force in New Cairo. Her name could plausibly get out, or at least Selina Mullur's, and they'd be able to trace her back to this building, back to Polina. At the same time, she couldn't leave. Her assumed identity had the Naj-Pur address, so she couldn't get out using that. On top of this, security fears following the kidnapping of Councillor Granier had resulted in all emigrating people's profiles being checked for consistency with older backups. With luck, they were backups from after she stole Selina Mullur's identity, so Zala wouldn't be exposed during any random checks, but it was far too late to try the same thing with anyone else. Every precaution was being taken by the authorities to ensure that the NCLC didn't leave the city with Granier.

Her musings were interrupted by the news. A sombre-looking anchor appeared on screen. 'Now, breaking news, Empire has just received a video from the NCLC, showing Councillor Granier, injured but alive, along with their demands for the GeniSec Corporation. This arrives less than a day after they exposed GeniSec's connection to the Soucouyant virus. We warn you, while we have redacted the most disturbing elements of this video, we advise young children or those of a nervous disposition to leave the room.'

The tape played.

Zala's first reaction was one of deep, resonant nausea. Not just because she had worked with these people, but because she was directly responsible for the horrific acts unfolding on-screen. The way the Councillor had trembled as he recovered from one of the blows, the stammer in his voice, the barely audible sizzle when the knife went in that, once heard, could not be forgotten. His wild, desperate stares, searching for a faint trace of compassion and finding none.

She'd thought she wanted blood. She'd thought she wanted petty, vindictive, personal revenge, and so she'd made all this happen.

Her second reaction, emerging from somewhere beneath her disgust, was the realization that there was information that was far more valuable than where the Soucouyant virus originated.

The identity of the person who made it.

A thrill ran through her, evaporating the nausea in an instant.

If it was someone in GeniSec – or better, if there was proof that it was created at the command of someone higher up the corporate ladder – the Council would jump at the opportunity to wash their hands of the increasingly toxic High Councillor Tau Granier. If it wasn't someone in GeniSec, their exoneration was critical to them. An opportunity to clear their name and redeem themselves could yield any number of possible rewards. She owed that to a man she'd just caused to be tortured.

Zala opened the simulated operating system in her portable terminal and scanned through the cache of incriminating data she'd given the NCLC. The directory to which she'd matched the final EIP address claimed that it was at GeniSec Development Falkur. She checked where this was on a map of the city.

In the middle of Falkur, a middle-class district often jokingly called 'Diet Alexandria' for its status as distant second-best to the more upmarket district, was a familiar cluster of buildings. The last time she had been aware of it, GeniSec Development Falkur had gone by a different name. It had been the LC Headquarters, the main site of the Logic Collective, a successful software development collective with whom she had interned just a few months before she had to flee. She'd loved it. Her father had offered to get her a position at his GeniSec development lab, but she had instead opted to go for the hip, independent development company over the corporate one. Whenever she thought of what her exile and fugitive status had cost her, she imagined herself working there.

So much for that.

She'd had two of the best weeks of her life there. She knew the location, she knew the opening and closing times, and she had at least a vague idea of the physical security. Unfortunately, they also knew her and presumably, if they remembered her at all, they'd remember that apparently she'd turned out to be a murderer. Maybe some of them still told the story now.

Zala got to work, poring over maps, blueprints and all the public information she could find. Going by a testimonial their director had left on a security firm's website, they'd just recently had an upgrade, revolving around an Elkab TS803 entrance system. Further snooping told her that this, essentially, was a very secure door and doorframe. Thick steel 'bones' anchored the doorframe into the wall and ground, and the door was reportedly almost impenetrable. The only way to gain access was to put in an individually assigned twelve-character passcode. This kept out the incognito invaders that the barbed wire and tyre spikes hadn't blocked.

And then she noticed a detail that could potentially help her.

She checked the clock. It was 9:07 a.m. This was achievable if she got to work immediately.

Zala stood next to the buzzer, outside the gate of GeniSec Development Falkur. She was dressed as a generic professional, in a white shirt and black skirt that could very well have been the dress code for some nondescript security firm. She pressed the button on the gate to ring reception and get buzzed in. At the very least, she hoped the person on the other end of the security cameras trusted her authenticity.

The Falkur district had, as its main characteristic, the safe predictability of an area built to be as marketable to the average family as possible. Here, the professionals and white-collar workers of New Cairo retired from living in the Downtown area and enjoyed a less frenetic pace, good schools and attractive, spacious homes. Falkur was the aspiration point for the everyday person, the worthy goal within reasonable reach. It was cosy middle-class normality. The Alexandria district was for the lucky few and Falkur was for the hard-working many, or so the narrative went.

This was, for the most part, a fiction. What happened more often was that the children of Falkur families moved to Downtown, and then right back to Falkur once they'd grown older and wearied of the city life. The denizens of Surja and Naj-Pur rarely trickled in. Landlords were apprehensive of letting to people who came from poorer areas, for whom up-front instalments on rent had a tendency to accrue extra charges all of a sudden. And as for their buying property, discriminatory practices were easy to enforce if the potential buyers didn't have extra capital. The prevailing attitude in the poorer districts, where existence was often hand-to-mouth, was that excess money had an expiry date. Going from 'If I don't spend it soon, it'll be gone anyway' to 'I've got enough money coming in, I can afford to accrue savings' was a difficult transition. Consequently, Falkur had become a solipsistic suburban sanctum for those who mistakenly assumed that the median income was also the mode.

It was also home to an array of technology firms, especially programming laboratories. Many such institutions had begun life in back rooms of homes, where a lone founder or two had coded something that had made them money, and had expanded to occupy actual commercial premises. Some, such as the Logic Collective, had set up full-scale offices on the site of what had once been their houses. The newly christened GeniSec Development Falkur presented the odd spectacle of a large, modern, three-floor office building surrounded by residential property, its sizeable gates preventing any street-level snooping. It was at these gates that Zala stood.

The buzzer clicked, and a tinny staccato voice grated through the speaker. 'State your business.'

'Hi, who am I talking to?' she said.

'Dima Dua from reception.'

Oh, thank god, the receptionist. The one person in the building who doesn't necessarily know about computers. I won't even have to come up with a good lie.

'Hi, Dima, my name is Narges Shadiya, I'm from Elkab Security. I'm here to perform a firmware update on the door?'

The brittle tone from the speaker took on an apologetic lilt. 'I'm sorry, ma'am, I can't let you into the building myself. Do you have a code to get in?'

'I don't need to,' said Zala, 'the door has limited connection ports on the outside for this exact reason. Just buzz me through the gate and I can get it done.'

The gate opened to a shallow driveway full of cars. The heavy alloy door on the front of the building was an incongruous new addition. Zala took a new, cheap portable terminal out of her pocket and installed a small memory chip with her clandestine operating system on it. She plugged it into the small concealed ports in the door and activated a key-logger. Pressing a few keys on the door's input pad, she watched as they also came up on the key-logger. Zala then loaded a fake timed progress bar with an eight-hour window, giving the key-logger time to gather results. On the outside of the terminal she placed a big sticker with the Elkab logo on it and large text saying 'FIRMWARE UPDATING, DO NOT TAMPER'. In smaller font below, it read. 'Elkab Security takes no responsibility for safety or security issues caused by customer interference with updating process.' Finally, she turned on the failsafe. This program locked the terminal, leaving only the current programs running, and would systematically destroy every piece of data on the terminal if the correct passcode was not entered.

Zala tucked the terminal round the side of the step leading up to the door and walked back out of the gate. She stopped, rang the bell again and said, 'Dima, it's Narges here. I've left the terminal plugged into the gate's door. It's a backup terminal and it's pretty slow, so if you can just tell anyone who asks to leave it there and continue on as normal, that would be great. I'll come pick it up later.'

'Sure. I'll let them know.'

Zala crossed the road to a café on the other side. She ordered a hot chocolate and sat by the window, watching the gates. From where she was sitting, she could just about make out where the terminal was tucked away. She unstrapped the portable terminal from her wrist and placed it on the table, where it projected its screen like a home terminal, and she set to work gathering information. She looked up message addresses on business networking sites, cross-referencing them with others on leaked security databases. Slowly but surely, she built up a list of possible profile details, and, most importantly, possible passwords.

Every so often she looked up and checked across the street. The cables still led off around the side of the step. Technical computer talent made up only a small part of the cybercriminal's skill set and only really came into its own at high levels. Often, the weakest link in the cybersecurity chain was the people who already had access and this made aptitude with manipulation important. For instance, while the fact this was an IT company evened the odds somewhat, most people, upon seeing a computer with a large ominous sticker on the front that looked like it was supposed to be there, would leave that computer alone.

So Zala spent hours sitting in the café, searching for information and killing time. Every so often she ordered some food or drink, which seemed to satisfy the woman behind the counter. Suchan – the NCLC's Suman Chaudhri – had taken to emailing her with IT questions and ranting about some woman who had taken his job as NCLC mission coordinator and was showing him up. She gave curt, functional answers which she hoped would encourage similar brevity in return.

Eventually it grew dark, and Zala saw people beginning to leave the GeniSec Development Falkur building. She looked down at her terminal's clock and was surprised to see that it was almost ten o'clock. The eight hours she had set her terminal for was over, and only now were they going home. To be leaving so late, they must have been coming up to a deadline. She closed her portable terminal, put it back on her wrist, and went into the café bathroom. She changed into her dark hooded top and trousers, and wrapped a black scarf around her neck, stuffing the discarded clothes into her backpack. She left the café. The last few developers were disappearing down the road. Zala walked up to the exterior gate and prised the front cover from the passcode box she had used earlier in the day. She plugged in her portable terminal and ran a brute-force code-breaking program. The code here was simple: four digits or a pass-card. The program gave up the four digits almost immediately, and the gate opened. She disconnected the portable terminal and replaced the front cover. Now she just had the massive Elkab door to get past.

The terminal she had left down the side of the steps was still powering along. She typed in the code to disable the failsafe and closed off the key-logger. It had logged 559 keystrokes; all were in sets of twelve random figures and a click of 'enter'. She picked one at random and entered it into the keypad on the door with a gloved hand. The door swung open. Zala grinned to herself.

She made her way towards the nearest set of stairs and began to climb. The person she'd managed to find the most information for was the CEO of the company, a Mrs Kishori Ueno, and if nothing had changed in the intervening eight years since Zala's internship, the CEO's office was on the first floor. At the top of the set of stairs, Zala put in her contact lenses and turned on the low-light option.

The large open room that made up this floor's main workspace was divided into rows of cubicles. Around the sides of the room were executive offices, the largest of which was Mrs Ueno's. There was a numerical lock on the door but another quick application of the brute-force code cracker had it open almost immediately. The room itself was lavishly furnished and stylishly decorated, complete with an adjacent bedroom which, thankfully, appeared unoccupied. A terminal sat on a large glass desk which looked out of a floor-to-ceiling window over an adjacent park. She switched the terminal on, also opening up her own.

To Zala's surprise, the computer took a very long time to load. She hoped for this company's sake that Mrs Ueno was very good at the business end of its operations because clearly IT wasn't a priority with her. Eventually a login box popped onto the screen, requesting a password. Zala ran through the list she'd gathered earlier, entering them one by one. The fifth one down prompted a happy trill of music and the desktop opened up. It revealed connections to several different networks. The first was the local area network, which gave her administrator-level access to just about every file on every computer in the building. Supporting this were connections to the files on the main storage servers. She went down the EIP addresses of the computer terminals in the network, comparing them with the one at which the gssmr.auge file's trail stopped, in the hope that she could locate the specific terminal on which it had been created.

She found it.

Opening up the user details, she realized that the terminal wasn't assigned to a programmer; it belonged to someone who worked in accounting, a Hiroshi Amon. She brought up his record in the registry on the main server. He had no programming qualifications or background that indicated he would be capable of creating such a complex, skill-intensive program.

Zala's trace of the gssmr file had dated the first transfer at six weeks and four days ago. She opened up the directory's list of assigned passcodes for the main door downstairs and found Hiroshi Amon's. There were hundreds of input codes that day registered on the door's entry log to get into the building – and Hiroshi Amon's wasn't among them. In fact, she could see he'd left the day before and returned four days later.

Zala then opened up a file detailing the login times of the various computer terminals, and looked for his. The file showed that, while Hiroshi's computer had been turned on – it appeared that all the terminals in the building were turned on every morning by one big switch – no one had logged in on it all day. It was as though the gssmr.auge file had come out of nowhere. And GeniSec suddenly seemed like a less credible potential culprit.

Zala was so caught up in trying to find a further origin point that it was several minutes before she realized that she had received a message on her own terminal. She opened it up.

From: ANANSI (EIP: ----.-.------.-------.---.-----.----.-------)
>Someone's looking where they're not supposed to.

Something sick and horrified gathered in her stomach. She swung round and stared into the darkness, looking for someone watching her. Suddenly her light-amplifying contact lenses seemed ineffectual. She logged out of the network and shut down her portable terminal. Her lenses dimmed and switched off.

Zala had apparently attracted someone's attention again.

She moved slowly and quietly out of the office, crouching behind cubicles as she groped her way back to the stairwell in the dark. Without her contact lenses she felt oddly disorientated in a way that didn't seem to have anything to do with the darkness.

Zala kept moving towards the stairs. Someone knew where she was. Every footstep was slower and quieter than the last.

Somewhere downstairs, glass shattered. Someone else was in the building.

Apparently these intruders were less concerned about making a mess than Zala was. She crept down the top few steps of the staircase and slowly peered over the side. A beam of torchlight cut through the darkness of the floor below, sweeping along the far wall. She ducked back. Instinctively, she tried to open her portable terminal and take a look at any outgoing connections the new arrivals were jacked into. She suddenly realized what she was doing and hurriedly turned it off; if this ANANSI character could track her, then it wasn't to her advantage to give him something with which to pinpoint her location. Instead, she steadied herself and strained to listen.

'. . . upstairs, and try to get into the GeniSec representative's office. Grab the terminal and we'll get out of here,' came a man's voice below. *Thieves*, she thought. *Affiliated with some other organization or just opportunistic thugs?*

One of them was coming. They appeared not to know that Zala was here, or at least they were here for something other than her. That suited her fine. She slipped behind a cubicle and watched as light flooded the partition in front of her. It then spun towards Kishori Ueno's office. Footsteps clomped against the ground, softer and softer as the figure moved away from Zala. This sound was quickly eclipsed by a loud crash coming from the floor below.

Great metallic clatters followed by the rattling of small loosened parts. They were destroying machinery. With the figure on her own level preoccupied, Zala moved from her hiding place down to the half-landing. There seemed to be three others, each focused on the destruction of the office equipment. Heavy crowbars and pipes rained huge swings down upon the terminals and peripherals in front of them. Errant torchlight gave away angular bulges under their shirts that suggested pistols tucked into their waistbands.

Zala waited for a moment in which all three had simultaneously found a new object to trash, and crept down the remaining stairs, crouching behind a cubicle at the bottom. She stole a glance over the top. These intruders had broken through a large floor-to-ceiling window ahead and to her left. Having started there, they were now moving away to other areas in search of more potential carnage, clearing a path for her. Zala began to sneak across to the broken window.

'Hey! There's someone else here!'

Torchlight washed over her. The one from upstairs reappeared behind her. She'd forgotten about him. She threw herself to the left. A burst of light and sound overwhelmed her momentarily. She clambered to her feet and began to run.

Another gunshot rang out. A harsh, heavy impact ran up her right arm. Intense pain. She gritted her teeth and ran. Adrenalin dulled the agony to the point where she could concentrate. She spotted the broken window.

'Gotcha!' a man growled to her right. She turned and instinctively raised her wounded arm. A small, skinny figure with a patchy beard brought down a crowbar onto it. There was a damp snapping sound, like a large branch breaking. More pain, greater this time. The gunshot wound had torn through the muscle, taking plenty of meat with it, but compared to this new agony, it was nothing. Zala felt her bone contort, each movement sending shockwaves through her musculature. She screamed and kicked hard. Her foot drove into her assailant's stomach and he doubled over, groaning.

155

Zala pushed herself up and sprinted, holding her maimed arm against her body. Every excruciating step sent a new paroxysm through her body, but she kept moving. Out of the building's courtyard, into the street . . .

Another gunshot. This time, the blow struck just below her right shoulder blade. Ribs splintered, lung and back muscle tore. She tried to suck in air to scream, but her ribcage felt as though something was crushing it, compressing it inwards. She couldn't breathe.

Zala collapsed against the window of the café and slid down onto the pavement.

Chapter 14

For all the talk of Naj-Pur being NCLC territory, it didn't take
the Security Force long at all to make their presence felt after
the fire-fight. During the battle, the SecForce troops' communications network had been taken down, but word got back anyway.
Within half an hour of the last shot being fired, the entire street in
which the battle had taken place was crawling with investigators.
Dozens of armed, angry police and SecForce troops combed the
street for clues or informants.

The people in the NCLC main base hid in the windowless sleeping area until the police went home. They were, after all, right
next to the crime scene and attracting any attention to themselves
whatsoever could have been disastrous. For two days after the in-
cident, they locked their doors, shut their windows, closed down
their networks and lay low. Only Maalik left the building, in the
dead of night, and only for stretches of a few hours.

By the time the authorities decided they had spent enough
time in Naj-Pur, it was three in the morning on the third day.
The inhabitants of the NCLC main base began to pack. Home
terminals were detached from their stations, clothes and personal
effects were put into bags and new plans were made. The two
dozen people at the base would split into two groups; Alice, Ria,
Zeno and nine others would go with Maalik to a base in an

abandoned bank two or three miles to the east; while Kahleed and Tal would go with the rest of the group to another safe house in an old tenement building that lay within walking distance.

There was something demoralizing about stripping down the base. Alice had her desk, her bed and her routine. They weren't good or bad, but they were hers. That had been comforting. That was what she feared: the distraction and the comfort which had allowed her to function being taken away from her. The illusion of stability, after everything that had happened to her, was something she had grown to depend upon. That fear was added to the long list of reasons she had to hate the tyrant Tau Granier.

It took a while to convince Juri to disassemble her camera network. She argued for a long time that it was the only reason they'd won so successfully, but the fact was that she didn't want to see her work taken apart. Eventually, she agreed, permanently corrupting every security camera she had access to and giving her allies the cover of darkness. Once they were packed, three hours had passed and it was time to go.

Alice used her terminal to turn off the limiter on Ria and Zeno's cochlear implants and went over to her daughter's bed to shake her awake. For a moment, she hesitated. Ria looked so peaceful, and there were so many terrible things for her to wake up to again.

Alice remembered two weeks before, when Jacob had told her that he and his associates had engineered the riots. She had spent the day huddled up with Ria and Zeno, watching the riot coverage on the TV, terrified that the mob would course up their street, smash in the windows of their house. Jacob was out there somewhere, with his advocacy group, working overtime to try to find an end to the carnage. That was what he'd told her, at any rate. As the sun began to sink and the police and Security Force troops had begun employing harsher and harsher repressive measures, the crowd dissipated, leaving images of a shattered, burning Downtown area. Safe in the knowledge that the riots were over for the moment, Alice had sent Ria off to bed and carried Zeno up to his cot. As she came back downstairs, she'd heard a noise coming from somewhere below.

She had crept downstairs, trying to locate the person who'd broken in, and walked into the hallway. In the kitchen, washing a cut on his head, she had found a filthy, grinning Jacob.

He was a handsome man, even with his face bloodied, but there was something jarring about the smile on his face and his dishevelled appearance that Alice hadn't noticed at the time. Her immediate response had been one of panicked concern.

'Are you all right? What happened? Are you hurt?' She grabbed his arm, turning him to examine him properly.

He shook her away, no longer smiling. 'I'm fine. But I've got something to tell you, and I need you to hear me out.'

He pressed a wet washcloth against the cut and strode into the living room. Alice followed. There, they sat down on the couch and Jacob turned to face her.

'I was there at the protests today,' he said.

Alice had been dreading that sentence ever since she saw him. 'What the hell were you doing at the riots?'

'*Protests*,' he said, 'and I was helping to coordinate the protestors, and keep them safe from the SecForce.'

'People were shooting at the SecForce.'

His face had appeared strangely calm. 'The protestors were safer once the SecForce knew they couldn't just be bullied.'

There was a bulge under his jacket. Alice lifted the jacket to reveal an empty holster.

They sat there for a while, not speaking.

'I want you out,' said Alice.

Jacob seemed to have expected that. He nodded and got up to leave. Alice hated him for that. She had so much more to say. She wanted to tell him that she couldn't believe that he'd get involved with something like this, and endanger his own life when he had a family who needed him. That she couldn't believe he'd run the risk of getting her or the children involved in his nonsense. That she felt shocked, sickened that he had the capacity for that kind of behaviour in him. And that she was hurt, deeply hurt, that he made no attempt to promise her that it would never happen again, that he was done, that this was a one-off. He made no attempt to hide that, right then, what he did at those riots and what he intended to continue to do up until his death was more important to him than his family. She let him leave without saying another word.

The next morning she'd had to tell the children that Daddy would be gone for a while. Now, in this cold, damp factory basement she had to wake them and tell them they must go because they were in danger.

And then there was that bigger secret, but that was for some other day.

Ria's eyes opened and Alice told her it was time to get dressed. The two of them packed their possessions and went into the main room. Alice thought of her children being uprooted from a safe place again. Her fists clenched.

The escape plan had been discussed many times. Everyone knew where they were going and the best routes to get there. Of course, there was now no security camera network, no top-down map and none of the wealth of information and intelligence the NCLC had become so adept at gathering. They were going in blind.

Kahleed and Tal's group would be leaving first. They'd exit, in groups of two or three, taking different routes to their destination, hopefully avoiding suspicion. Kahleed was, of course, already a major target but his massive, bushy beard and wild hair stopped him looking anything like the clean-cut business magnate he had once been, so as long as no one scanned him, he'd be fine.

As his group picked up their luggage and prepared to move, Kahleed pulled Alice aside. 'I just want to say, thank you for everything. I know you're reluctant about this whole thing, but you're incredibly talented and it's been a real blessing to us.'

Alice blushed. 'Thanks, I guess . . . I just found that after a while, keeping myself busy helped push the bad things away.'

Kahleed nodded. 'You're one of our best people, and if you'd be up for it I'd like you and Maalik to take over command of the other safe house. I've been giving them orders from here but it's not really as good as having some trusted people running the show.'

'I'll do it.' Alice surprised herself with how quickly she made the decision. It seemed like what Jacob would do. Kahleed nodded and walked back over to the huddled team he would be leading to their new home. He and Tal led their group up the set of stairs to the main factory and out of sight.

'Give it a quarter of an hour,' said a voice behind her. She turned round to see Maalik standing there, several large bags over his shoulder. 'If there's a trap we need to know whether or not they've fallen into it before we make a move.'

Alice nodded. The group she had been assigned to was a capable one. The safe house they were moving to had originally been a shelter and hiding place for families of NCLC operatives, and was now the prison for Councillor Ryan Granier. Kahleed had decided that greater armament and more direct organization was required for it. So, as well as Alice, Ria and Zeno, the group was made up of Maalik, his protégé Serhiy Panossian, Nataliya Kaur, Juri Dajili, Suman Chaudhri and the twins, Thana and Anisa Yu, plus three other operatives. All were armed with small arms hidden on their person; most had pistols, though the twins had sewn their favoured sub-machine guns into the inside of their jacket linings, ready to be torn away in an instant. Alice was having a harder time; though Maalik had given her a pistol, she was going to be holding Zeno in her arms, making a gun hardly practical. She trusted most of the people she was with, but dreaded any opportunity Maalik might be offered to escalate things.

They checked their gear to make sure they hadn't left anything behind and prepared the basement for their departure. The twins covered themselves in niqabs to hide their now infamous scarred faces. Most ushered themselves outside, leaving Nataliya to torch the place. It would of course attract attention when the authorities got there, but by then they'd be far away, and they couldn't afford to leave DNA evidence.

It was half past six in the morning and if they were lucky the

SecForce presence which followed the shoot-out would not be out in any great numbers for another hour or so. The group hurried down the long, thin driveway on the other side of the factory from the street where the battle had been. At every corner they paused, one scouting ahead and signalling to the others when it was clear. As they moved further and further away from the factory, they began to relax slightly, moving as one large group and talking amongst themselves. Maalik in particular seemed eager to raise spirits, conversing and joking with the rest. It did help; after a while, all but the eternally grave Yu twins had calmed.

They had rounded a corner into an alley less than a mile from the safe house when Thana Yu raised a hand, signalling them to stop. They quickly stepped to the side, pressing themselves up against the alleyway wall, and Maalik whispered to Thana, 'Did you see something?'

Thana pointed ahead and rasped, 'I think I saw a shadow disappearing around the corner. I don't know for certain, but I don't like the idea of walking into a trap.'

Alice at once became more aware of the space around them. The alleyway was long and narrow, with tall brick walls on either side.

'Let's head back and take another way round,' said Maalik. The alley felt as though it was shrinking.

They turned and hurried back the way they'd come. Alice kept glancing over her shoulder, holding Zeno tight to her. Ria was close behind, murmuring, 'Mum, what's going on?'

'That way's blocked off, sweetie, we're going to go around it,' said Alice, unable to stop her voice quivering.

Suddenly, in the distance, there was the approach of a roaring engine. Maalik looked back at Alice, eyes wide. 'We need to go, now.'

Serhiy scooped Ria up into his arms and the group broke into a sprint, back up the alleyway and then in the opposite direction from the growl piercing the morning silence. They turned left down another street. A SecForce car sped round the corner and screeched to a halt in front of them. The doors opened. Three helmeted SecForce officers leapt out, holding pistols with both hands.

'Names and business!' shouted one.

Maalik stepped forward. 'My daughter just went into labour. We're heading to the hospital to make sure it's all going okay.'

The officer who'd yelled looked across at one of his colleagues, who shrugged. He turned back. 'We're looking for terrorists around this area. We're going to need the women to lower their niqabs so we can see their faces.'

Anisa brought her hand to her chest in feigned outrage. 'Do you have any idea how disrespectful that is?'

The trooper raised his gun again. 'Lower your niqabs now!'

'It's because of things like this that you lot can't maintain a patrol around here!' said Maalik, stepping in front of the man's gun and playing up his indignation.

'Lower your niqabs, last warning!'

Thana and Anisa looked at one another.

'Do you want us to be the terrorists?'

Everyone looked round. It was Serhiy who had spoken up. The guns turned and were trained on him.

'I mean, if we are the terrorists you're looking for,' he continued, 'we outnumber you nearly four to one, and god only knows what we're capable of. If we're not the terrorists, then you have no reason to detain us and should send us on our way, without anything bad happening to anyone.'

He turned to the Yu twins. 'I mean, these women could be two of the few still observing the old religion. They could be harmless, kind and deferential. Or, they could be those very bad women with the scars on their faces, "The Wailing Sister" and "The Roaring Sister", I believe they've been nicknamed. It's not outside the realms of possibility, and if they have the decency to try and take a subtle approach where nobody gets hurt, I for one wouldn't push them to start hurting people. Just my opinion.'

He turned to Alice and Zeno. 'And then, of course, there are the children. If we were the terrorists, you'd be forced to either arrest or shoot us. And I imagine that, if pressed, their mother might do something very hasty to stop herself getting arrested and her children being hurt. It's quite a conundrum. So I suppose the question is, why don't you try a little less hard to prove that we are the terrorists?'

The three SecForce soldiers were looking at one another now, hoping one of the others would make a decision. While the tinted visors on their helmets gave nothing of their faces away, their body language told the entire apprehensive story. The leader spoke first. 'The one holding the baby's the mother, right?'

Serhiy didn't move or say anything, but the trooper's confidence in his deduction grew. 'She and the kids can get out of the way and go. The rest of you will stay where you are.'

Maalik looked back and nodded to Alice. She began to step away. But Serhiy wouldn't let Ria go. He was holding her even tighter in front of him, blocking the line of fire to his body and most of his face. Ria was crying, but the young man was strong and she couldn't struggle from his grip.

'Get your hands off her now!' yelled Maalik.

Serhiy shook his head. 'Let us go,' he said.

'This is your last chance! The children and their mother can go, the rest of you stay!' said the SecForce trooper. All eyes were on Serhiy and Ria. No one noticed the Yu sisters fidgeting under their niqabs, or a faint sound of material ripping.

Serhiy slowly released Ria, crouching behind her. As his grip loosened she ran over to Alice, who held her close and began to walk slowly across the road away from the group. Alice set the noise gate for Ria and Zeno's cochlear bio-augs and braced herself.

There was yelling behind her. The Yu sisters' sub-machine guns of choice were a bizarre shape, with almost all of the firing mechanism and stock located behind the trigger and handle. They were fast-firing, easy to conceal and deadly at close range. The nearest SecForce officer fell under a blaze of bullets. The other two took shelter behind the squad car. One of them fired blind at where the cacophony of gunfire was coming from. He hit Thana Yu high in the chest. The other opened up his portable terminal.

He's going to radio for backup, thought Alice. *They're going to catch and kill us.*

The call would go through shortly and the message would be brief. Every moment was vital. Alice passed Zeno to Ria, and then reached behind her back and drew her concealed pistol from her waistband. She aimed. The troopers didn't notice her – they were too occupied by the sub-machine-gun-wielding twins.

Her hand shook.

These people had let her and her children go. None of them wanted to hurt her. She knew this on an intellectual level. She also knew what Jacob would have done. Jacob, who had thought of this cause as important enough to risk his family.

Jacob, who had been gunned down by SecForce troops just like these.

Jacob, who was gone.

He wouldn't have hesitated.

Her hands steadied. Her knuckles whitened as her grip grew tight. She wanted to do it.

'Ria, sweetie, cover your eyes now.'

She fired quick bursts of two shots.

The SecForce officers crumpled, blood dripping from under their visors. Not seeing their faces had made it all so much easier. From the far side of the squad car, the other NCLC members looked on in shock. She felt calm, focused. The others were around her now, pulling on her arm and yelling that they needed to go, but it was as if she couldn't hear them.

It had been a long time.

165

Chapter 15

Councillor Ryan Granier had concluded that he could feel the individual hairs of his beard growing from his face. It had been almost two weeks since he had last shaved, the longest he had ever gone without doing so, and the tight black bristles rubbed irritatingly against the parts of his face that had swollen up. The painkillers and the lack of sleep, not to mention the delirious, shell-shocked haze which Maalik had left him in, only exacerbated the sensation. He sat in the room he had first woken up in, feeling the weight and tightness of the distended flesh of his face and trying to figure out what of the great bureaucratic machinery he had access to would be the best route to get him and Ava out of here.

Ryan turned his head to the right and saw light coming through the cracked black paint over the windows. It was morning. He pushed himself up onto his good leg and grabbed his crutches. The putty Ava had put in the wound in his thigh had stopped the pain completely and was slowly rebuilding his flesh, but it was still heavy to lift and unstable to balance on, factoring in the missing muscle tissue that was no longer pulling weight. His leg would heal with time. It wasn't the cataclysmic mutilation he had believed it to be in *that* room, under all that fear and adrenalin.

In the meantime, it was another frustrating factor to be accounted for in the escape plan.

The sound of the huge reinforced doors opening in the next room shook the windows. Ryan hopped over to the door, using his crutches to balance; he still had not mastered walking with them. He pulled open the door and poked his head out. There was a group of people standing in the main room, all carrying large bags and pieces of equipment, one cradling a baby and another holding the hand of a young girl. A tall woman with several disfiguring facial scars held a red rag to her shoulder – though from the looks of the edges of the rag it had once been white. All of them seemed exhausted, as if they had been running. Ava came out from the long corridor on Ryan's right, holding her medicine bag. She fought her way through the crowd and began work on the scarred woman's shoulder. A red wound revealed itself.

A burning hot knife against flesh.

Ryan looked away. His heart was pounding.

As he looked back, he saw the woman who'd been holding the baby step forward. She had light brown skin, reminiscent of someone born in one of the North or Central American cities, and long dark hair tied in a low ponytail. Of everyone in the group, she seemed the calmest, and where the others were gasping for air she seemed like she'd just strolled through the door. 'Are you Ava Ferreira?' she asked.

Ava looked at her and said, 'Yeah, that's me. You must be Mrs Amirmoez.'

'We got ambushed by the SecForce. They knew we were coming. I need to use your communication channel to check that Kahleed's group are okay.'

Ryan watched as Ava took her over to the desk and Mrs Amirmoez sat down, typing rapidly on the terminal. After a while she let out a deep sigh of relief, looked back up at the group and said, 'They're fine.'

Everyone in the large crowd seemed to relax somewhat. Ava came forward again. 'It's good to meet you, Mrs Amirmoez.'

'Call me Alice. Kahleed sent me to run operations out of here.'

Ava nodded. 'He told us, but this has been a shelter for non-combatants and support staff so far, plus our prisoner, so you'll have to set it all up yourself. We don't have anything in place, although we do have an encrypted data line, some decent terminals in the back, and room for more if you've got 'em.'

'Where is the prisoner right now?'

Ava looked over at Ryan, and Alice followed her gaze. She frowned. 'You're letting him listen in and you leave his door open?'

Ava shrugged. 'If the police get him back, they'll already know more than he's overheard, and he's on crutches so he's not really in any condition to mount a daring escape.'

The frown remained on Alice's face. 'What happened to him that made him need crutches?'

'You haven't seen the video?'

'I haven't seen anything, we've had a communication shutdown for days.'

'Well then, your man Maalik can bring you up to speed.' There was a bitterness in Ava's voice.

A dark, familiar voice came from the back of the group. 'I'll explain later.'

Ryan felt his heart begin to race again. There was a faint smell of cooked meat. He took a few deep breaths and shut the door. He closed his eyes for a moment. The ache in his leg deepened. The cuts on his wrists and ankles stung as though the plastic binds still tied him to the chair. Somewhere far away, he felt as though he were falling, but the knife was hot and his skull rattled and he didn't really notice.

Then he was back in the real world, being lifted off the floor and into the next room. Strong arms laid him on a sofa. Ava leaned over him and placed a hand on his forehead. 'It's not an infection then . . . You all right? You collapsed in your room. It made a hell of a thud.'

It took Ryan a few moments to grasp what was happening. 'I'm fine, I just lost my balance.'

Ava helped him to his feet. She gave him an uncertain look as if she knew he had bigger problems than being prone to falling. The other newcomers had gone, leaving just Ryan, Ava, and the apparent new leader, Alice Amirmoez.

Alice looked him up and down, and said, 'When this is all over, Councillor, and if you make it out alive, you're going to want to see a shrink.'

Ryan nodded, his face flushed red.

'Whatever happened to you, it appears to have given you Post-Traumatic Stress Disorder. I have a few old work colleagues who got it after bad injuries and the like, and it looks like your case is pretty damn bad. I'm guessing you haven't been sleeping?'

Ryan shook his head. Out of the corner of his eye, he saw Ava looking taken aback. 'I thought that was just the painkillers . . .'

'Dose him up and get him some sleep, or we'll be handing him back to Tau Granier in a straitjacket,' she said to Ava.

Ava nodded, hesitated a moment, then said, 'Ma'am? I'd like to request that Maalik receive some kind of formal admonishment. He did far more than he needed to here.'

Alice raised an eyebrow. 'But this man is the reason that every male over the age of fourteen in this district is liable to be killed as an enemy combatant. This man is why the Security Force is beating civilians in the street. This man is the crown prince of New Cairo, emblematic of the people who have oppressed the most vulnerable in this city for generations, and he hasn't felt a fraction of the pain that his existence has inflicted on us.'

Despite her venomous words, her composure never faltered for even a second.

Ava struggled to find words that wouldn't anger her new superior. 'Except he's not any of those things. He's not an archetype for you to pin your resentments to. He's not a symbol for a greater system. He's a person and he doesn't deserve to get used as a way for us to thrash out our political frustrations. I'd appreciate it if you'd remind Maalik of this.'

Alice nodded, but the disdain never left her face. She turned on her heel and left.

'Don't worry, she's leaving in a few days with her kids. She shouldn't be a problem,' said Ava.

'Yeah . . . and that scarred woman, the wounded one, that's one of those two twins who've been terrorizing the Security Force in Naj-Pur, right?'

'That's her,' said Ava. 'And the one in the niqab is the other twin. We've got some of the biggest guns in the NCLC in this safe house and we're trying to get out without a fuss.'

Ryan nodded, still groggy with lack of sleep. 'Listen, if you can stop me dreaming so I can just pass out somewhere for a while, I will honestly do my level best to get a street named after you when we get out of here.'

He thought he remembered another of the rules he'd been taught all those years ago. It was to keep reminding your captor that you exist and have a life outside of the kidnap situation, though considering that Ava was helping him break out she probably didn't need to be sold on him quite so much any more.

Ava looked round at him. 'All right,' she deadpanned, 'but it had better not be one of those little five-address closes. I want the real deal.'

The two of them made their way over to the medical room, Ryan hobbling inelegantly on his crutches. When they got there they found the scarred woman, the Yu twin, inside, examining herself. 'Sorry about that, ma'am,' said Ava. 'This one had passed out.'

The scarred woman raised her disfigured face, her gaze peering out from jagged, cracked flesh. 'That's how you treat such high-class guests, is it?' she said, in a surprisingly high voice. 'He looks almost as bad as me.'

Ryan had no idea how to respond to that. This was one of the Yu twins. The newscasts had always reported on them as if they were vengeful spirits sweeping down upon patrols and Security Force missions, leaving only dread in their wake. To see one of them up close, vulnerable and making self-deprecating remarks, rather went against that image, simplistic as it was.

'I haven't seen a mirror in days. How swollen up am I?' he asked.

'It's pretty bad,' said the disfigured woman. 'It's going to be a hard sell at election time if it stays like that.'

'You don't think I'd get the sympathy vote?'

The shards of skin that made up her face shifted into what might once have been a smile. 'I'd say your best bet is to focus on policy and don't rely on your looks so much at the next election.'

It was just like talking to any other constituent. Make them sympathize, exchange small talk, convince them to think of you as on their side. It was all about personality. *This is how a politician gets elected and how a hostage stays alive*, he thought to himself.

Ryan moved over to one of the makeshift hospital beds in the corner, and lay down on top of the sheet. Ava stood beside him, peeling the film off a medication patch. 'This'll get into your system nice and quickly; you can get right off to sleep without reliving the experience. And I'll try and find something for your face, to stop any more swelling.'

Ryan nodded. Off to his right, the Yu twin said, 'Count your lucky stars, Councillor, that your father's military police didn't bludgeon your face half off like they did me and my sister. Some contracting mask will sort you right out.'

She's still thinking of me as my father's son, thought Ryan, frustrated. Ava placed the patch on his arm and it began to deflate as the serum was absorbed through his skin.

'Right,' said Ava. 'Give it a minute or two and you're all right to try and get some sleep.'

Ryan lay on his back, without the energy to move. He thought of his family, and he thought of what lay ahead of him. The light above him turned off and for the first time since fainting in the cell downstairs, he drifted off to sleep.

Chapter 16

New Cairo First Hospital, located on the border of Falkur and Alexandria, was remarkable among hospitals in the city of New Cairo in only two respects. It was the city's very first operational hospital and, despite there being newer, larger and better-funded hospitals out there, it ran the finest Emergency department that New Cairo had to offer. This was credited largely to the successful direction and management of Dima Farida who, after a long career as an exemplary nurse, had made her way up the ladder to become the department's Primary Administrator. New Cairo's citizens used to joke that people with heart attack victims in their vehicles used to drive right past other hospitals on the way. So when the owner of a small business sent out a message to the city's emergency services that a bloodied and battered young woman had just slumped against his front window, they patched him through to the First.

The two paramedics who loaded her onto a stretcher and into the back of the ambulance were the first people to get a good look at her and were also the first people to realize that she had been shot. They placed a tube down the woman's throat to make sure her airways were unobstructed and checked immediately for any bio-augs that could give a vital sign report. To their surprise they found none. They took her pulse and confirmed her shallow, laboured breathing. They continued their initial trauma survey, trying to establish the extent of her injuries. This was when they discovered the wound in her back. Covering it with a plastic dressing, they then began to stem the blood loss. Her heartbeat stammered out a quick, irregular beat as it attempted to keep her blood pressure up, before settling as her one uninjured lung began to get uninterrupted oxygen via the tube.

A scan of her biometric data revealed a name. Selina Mullur. No bio-augs, so the state would cover costs if they were necessary. She was also from Naj-Pur. Her kind always took bio-augs if it was an option, so the go-ahead would probably be given even if she didn't wake up and give consent herself. The issue was, of course, the overbearing shadow of the Soucouyant virus that was making surgeons less willing to use bio-augs unless absolutely necessary.

The ambulance pulled up and the paramedics wheeled out the stretcher, into the arms of waiting Emergency staff. They pulled her inside, straight into a vacant operating theatre, and made their assessment. Calcium scaffolding would keep the ribs in place while they healed, but she'd need some Vaxibone to fill in gaps. Operating machines, powered by the IntuitivAI protocols, performed expertly, with a degree of precision well beyond that of a human surgeon. The muscle could be reset with artificial tissue which would be fully integrated within hours. The lung was a different story. It was full of blood, and there was a gaping exit wound where the bullet had pushed out through the right lung. There was additional damage where the bullet had ricocheted off one of the front ribs and torn away at some more of the lung. It was a miracle that the young woman had not bled out or asphyxiated. Her right arm was also a mess. The heavy slug had gone right through, shattering bone and pulverizing muscle, and it was close enough to the elbow joint that the arm would never work properly again. Beyond that, the bones of the right forearm were completely shattered.

Two months earlier, the surgeon realized, there wouldn't have even been a question. She needed a bio-aug lung and arm. Hell, he thought, if she were awake, people like her never turned down any tech that they could justify having put into them. They needed extra funding for traditional surgery, but the chaos in the Council's budgeting meetings following the disappearance of Councillor Granier had put paid to any chance of that. All the hospital had was a store room full of gleaming new bio-augs.

There was no reason not to give this woman a new arm and lung except that at any moment they could shut down.

Zala awoke slowly, sluggishly, as if being lifted from immersion in a great sea, to a high staccato beeping. She had heard things like it a million times in videocasts, but upon forcing her eyes open, she saw that she was indeed attached to a heart monitor. She had no idea where she was, or why she couldn't move anything except her head and the very tips of her fingers. Everything else was heavy, too heavy. Zala looked down. In her hand was a remote with a large physical button marked 'CALL'. She pressed it.

A few minutes later, a woman came through the door. She was wearing a purple and gold hijab under a long white coat, and looked to be in her fifties. She smiled when she saw Zala.

'Ms Mullur, it's good to see that you're awake. I'm Doctor Lawahiz Chipo. You're at the New Cairo First Hospital; you were brought in two days ago. We've been taking good care of you.'

For a moment, Zala could not figure out quite why she was calling her 'Mullur', but then it clicked and she nodded. 'What happened?'

'You got shot. The police think it was because you saw a break-in occurring at a GeniSec subsidiary. They're going to want to ask you about it when your condition has improved, but you've got a few days to recover.'

The terrible pain in her back. Short, painful breaths. A warm liquid, what must have been blood, making its way up her throat, choking her. Unimaginable pain in her arm. Then she was back in the hospital room, with only the ghosts of her injuries.

'Why can't I move?'

Dr Chipo looked down at her. 'There will be some effects of sedation. I can dial them back. You should be fine to move.'

'But I was shot through the chest and arm . . .' she said, still not quite present.

'We gave you a new arm and lung and they've taken fine, so you should be okay to get using them pretty soon. Good job you didn't have any other bio-augs, or they might have been damaged. Either way, you're going to be here for a few days still while we continue to ply you with antibiotics.'

Zala's brain whirred away. Dr Chipo had said something strange, something . . .

'. . . new arm and lung?'

'Oh, they were beyond saving, so we gave you bio-augs. It has all the latest security, so it's as safe as you're going to get in this climate.'

Zala realized she was shaking her head and as she did so, the rest of her body began to shiver. She didn't want bio-augs, she didn't want bio-augs, she hated bio-augs, she didn't want—

'Ms Mullur, calm down,' Dr Chipo said firmly, spotting Zala's building horror.

'No, no, no, no no no you *took my arm*,' Zala screamed.

'Get a hold of yourself. Your arm's right there, at the end of your shoulder.'

Zala looked at her right arm, horrified. They'd taken the whole arm? They'd replaced her entire arm with one of those . . . things? For a moment, she found herself unable to do anything but panic.

'We had no choice,' Dr Chipo said firmly. 'You were unconscious, in no state to consent, and I've never in all my years seen someone from Naj-Pur turn down a bio-aug.'

Zala was breathing quick, shallow breaths now, her heart pounding. On some level, she was convinced she could feel the artificial sac in her chest, and as her breath rate increased it was as though the foreign organ was breaking free from her control, tearing itself loose, sucking in air in such great quantity as to burst her torso and crack open her ribcage. Ribs shattering and

175

snapping like dry twigs, skin ripping, organs slopping obscenely from the chest cavity—

'If you want, I can book you in for some therapy. Difficulty in emotional readjustment is very common after what you've been through, but it's something you can overcome.'

Her arm. Her chest. There was something inside her, something alien and wrong and she wanted it out, she wanted it out of her.

That or drugs. Drugs will do.

'Ms Mullur, calm down or I'm going to have to sedate you again.'

'*Please* . . . yes . . . do that . . . sounds great,' Zala managed.

Dr Chipo looked at her, then pulled out a small chemical patch from her pocket, unwrapped it, and pressed it against the back of Zala's hand. Her panic melted away as chemicals coursed through her veins. For the next hour or so, she lay there, staring up at the blank white ceiling, her anxiety for the time being suppressed.

She couldn't look down at her body, so she tried to make sense of what had been done to her. Any way she thought of it, she could not rationally begrudge the augmentations that were keeping her alive and able, but the disgust at what had been done to her pervaded any other consideration she attempted.

As the sedation wore off, she began flexing and unflexing her fingers. Though at first the small details of the motion seemed off to her, clashing with her muscle memory, the new hand seemed adequate so long as she did not think of what lurked under the new skin. She bent and straightened her elbow. There was nothing unfamiliar about its arc. She rotated her shoulder next; there was even a slight improvement in flexibility, but this was enough to bring up a deep sense of nausea within her. When her stomach had settled she rolled her arm around a few more times, acclimatizing herself to the feel of it. The limb had never been the sum of its components to her before, she thought. It had only ever been her arm, an abstract grouping of properties and functions, not an extension of bone and muscle. Did the difference in components, which had never mattered before, matter now?

Zala opened her hands flat and placed the two sets of fingers together. They matched perfectly. She then set her palms on the mattress beneath her, turned herself around and pushed herself off the bed.

Her room was rectangular, with a door on the wall opposite the foot of her bed leading off into the hospital corridor, and another near the head of her bed opening into a small bathroom. She walked slowly into the bathroom, stood in front of the large mirror over the sink and removed the mint green pyjama top she had woken up in. The first thing she noticed was that, save for small wounds around her arm and the trace of an incision in her armpit which dipped down under her breast, she was comparatively unmarked. When she turned round and looked over her shoulder, there was a scar on her back where new skin had been placed over the bullet hole and was slowly replacing the damaged cells. The new arm was odd – it felt fibrous and although there was no give to the bones as there supposedly was with cheaper bio-augs, compared even with her muscular left forearm there was an inorganic firmness to it that felt alien.

Zala turned to the doorframe and reached up to grasp the lintel. Slowly, painfully, she pulled herself up. She then dropped down and reached up with her new right arm. The hand took hold of the frame with an unerring grip, tight and controlled. Zala pulled up. The ease was extraordinary, far greater than with her natural arm. She dropped down again and looked at her new arm with a dread fascination. This was once again replaced with a wave of disgust and she quickly found herself on her knees, retching over the toilet bowl.

She stood up, put her pyjama top back on and returned to the bedroom. She found her portable terminal in the drawer of the bedside locker, lying on top of some clothes in clear plastic bags. She turned it on. The time was 17:14. As the screen projected out in front of her, it brought up the last message she'd received. It was the message – the warning, the threat, whatever it was – from ANANSI, which she'd received before she was shot. This person had found their way past her security – custom protocols, which she had written herself and believed to be watertight – and managed to track her down and interfere with her work at the Five Prongs server farm and at GeniSec Development Falkur. For all Zala's ability with computers and technology, ANANSI completely outclassed her, and that left her exposed. They'd found their way through her defences and that placed her at their mercy, vulnerable to whatever they might decide to do to her. She shuddered.

This must be what it felt like for the various people I've screwed over in my time.

She opened up a reply window. There had to be a way to placate ANANSI; indeed, they surpassed her own abilities to the extent that it was the only option left to her. With any luck, they were currently monitoring all her outgoing connections, reading any message she might send. Even if she sent a message off to the blank EIP, surely ANANSI would intercept it anyway. That could be the way to contact them, to reason with them.

What do I want to say to ANANSI?

Zala typed out a message. A simple, focused question, just enough to start a dialogue, but not to concede any further ground.

>What do you want?

There had to be a thread for her to start from. Anything else was a puzzle to be solved.

She pressed the Send button. With ANANSI's EIP address hidden, the message whizzed off to nowhere in particular.

A new message came up almost immediately. Zala's hunch was confirmed. ANANSI was watching.

From: ANANSI (EIP: ----.-.-----.------.---.-----.----.-------)
>Now that's a complex question, Ms Ulora.

Zala felt another pang of dread. They knew her name, a trump card she hadn't realized they were aware of. They were, however, apparently open to talking.

>Let me simplify it; what do you want, and why does that involve me?

From: ANANSI (EIP: ----.-.-----.------.---.-----.----.-------)
>I want you to cease your prying.

>No can do, I'm afraid, she replied, her mechanized fingers

working faster against the keyboard than her flesh-and-blood digits ever had. Unless you can give me a good reason to, that is.

From: ANANSI (EIP: ----.-.------.-------.---.-----.----.------)

>The good reason is that I will destroy you in order to stop you, Ms Ulora. I will destroy everything I can until you get the message. You know I can. So I would advise again that you cease your prying. Hopefully that is a sufficient reason?

Zala stopped for a moment. This person had her real name and potentially any amount of unknown information besides. She worded her response carefully.

>My prying can end, if it stops you taking any more action against me.

From: ANANSI (EIP: ----.-.------.-------.---.-----.----.------)

>Or it could end with you in prison, unable to pry any longer. And what would happen if New Cairo First Hospital knew that they had, in their care, the murderer Zala Ulora?

Zala froze for a moment, staring at the screen. ANANSI had no intention of bargaining. They were simply setting her up for imprisonment, or worse, and it was coming soon. She needed to get out of here.

She closed the messaging system, ran over to the locker and pulled the clothes out of the plastic bags. Inside was an outfit similar to the one she had been wearing on the night she had been shot: black trousers, a blue T-shirt and a grey jacket. The hospital must have replaced her tattered, bloodied garments. She threw them on, picked up what few possessions of hers she could find in the drawer. She fished out her contact lens case and carefully inserted a lens in each eye. Her portable terminal found a floor plan of the hospital and brought it up, weaving a trail through the building to the exit. Zala followed it out of the room.

She looked around. To her left, a number of hospital staff were crowded around the nurses' station. Hoping that they weren't staring at an alert with her face attached, Zala slipped right. As she rounded the nearest corner, down a short corridor which led to a set of stairs, Zala heard a yell. 'I can't see her!' came a rough female voice. Doubling back, Zala peeked around the corner. A group of three of the hospital's security staff and a tall SecForce officer were entering her hospital room, the buzz of electrified stun batons following them. A nurse trailed behind, protesting vigorously at the prospect of a patient under her care being beaten and electrocuted, but they weren't listening. Either they'd figured out that Zala had been inside GeniSec Development Falkur, or ANANSI had followed up their threat. Zala turned and followed the trail down the staircase and out onto the ground floor with a new-found briskness.

'Ms Mullur?'

She ignored the voice and kept going.

'Ms Mullur?' the voice said again, more insistently this time.

Zala kept going. A crackling, accompanied by a low hum, sparked to life behind her.

'Ms Ulora, come with us now.'

Zala's heart sank.

They know.

She looked over her shoulder to see two Security Force officers standing behind her. They were both tall, formidable-looking men, even without the heavy armour plating patrolling officers wore, and the buzzing stun batons were raised in front of them. Distinctive tattoo patterns on their brows suggested armour-plated skulls and probably more modifications besides. These were military police, highly trained and, from what she had heard, not subject to many moderating codes of conduct. She turned back to see a third officer blocking off her path, who smirked as their eyes met.

Zala's gaze whipped back and forward, trying to keep track of all three of her assailants at once. Not taking his eyes off her, the officer who had called out to her felt around his belt with his free hand for his handcuffs. Zala turned and stepped towards him, pushed his baton hand away. Her right arm punched upwards beneath his chin with the speed and power of a firing piston. His legs gave out beneath him and his baton fell away, clattering against the ground. As Zala moved to reach for it, the smirking man who had stood in her path rushed forward, baton raised like a hammer. Zala stepped inside the arc of his downward swing, blocked his right arm with her left, and reached up behind it with her new right arm, grasping his wrist. She pulled down. His arm twisted against her shoulder and snapped. He screamed and stepped away, but Zala grabbed the back of his neck and twisted him round, tipping him off balance and hurling him into the third officer. The whole thing had taken mere seconds. As the men fell over one another, Zala saw the group of security guards from her room barrel into the corridor behind. With a path cleared in front of her, Zala ran.

The hospital walls were a blur, seeming to swirl around the digital line her portable terminal mapped out for her, and the racket of screaming hospital staff and yelling assailants disoriented her. Sprinting all the way, she weaved between shocked staff and visitors. She took a right turn and reached the crowded main atrium, and beyond it the big glass doors that led out of the hospital. Outside she could see a large Security Force van. Almost certainly more SecForce officers. Instead, Zala ran through a nearby set of doors labelled 'Cafeteria'. She wheeled round and, spotting a small switchbox in the doorframe, pulled down a lever marked 'Off'. The doors snapped shut and clicked as they locked.

Diners rose in confusion, which turned to consternation as they heard the crashes of the SecForce officers outside charging shoulder-first into the doors. The metal foundations crunched and strained against the frame. Zala pushed her way through a crowd that slowly began to grow resistant and towards a door which her terminal told her led to the kitchens. A cafeteria worker let out a screech of 'You can't go back there!' and attempted to get between Zala and the door, but Zala shoved her aside and sprinted into the kitchen.

The heat hit her first; everywhere seemed to be billowing with steam or giving off the roar of commercial-sized ovens. The ruckus outside had drawn the attention of the kitchen staff, and they took a wary step back as Zala ran through, eyes roving for an exit. Behind her, she heard the heavy metallic scraping of the cafeteria doors giving in. They would be right on top of her soon. She whirled around, catching sight of a huge steel trolley full of trays. She pulled it behind her, blocking her path, and wedged it sideways between a wall and the counter. Satisfied, she spotted an exit door to her right, dashed over to it and slipped out into a back alley.

Zala ran up the alleyway. The exit out into the street was blocked by a wide, tall gate, bound tight with an old, rusty lock. She was trapped. There was an almighty crash behind her, a crash very much like the noise she imagined several large SecForce officers knocking over and tripping against a very big, very heavy steel serving trolley would make. In frustration, Zala growled and shook the gate. The rusty lock warped under the mechanical force of her new arm and shattered. Startled by her own strength, Zala pushed the gate open and walked briskly through, to mingle with the early evening rush of city workers making their way home. She turned off her portable terminal and looked about her, trying to orientate herself. She'd known every street in this district once, but that had been eight years ago and the place seemed unfamiliar. Once round the nearest corner she ran again as hard as she could manage, choosing her direction at random whenever she reached an intersection. She didn't look back or think about whether or not anyone was behind her.

Slowly, the ache of overworked muscles began to set in, and Zala slowed her pace. She found herself in the area where Falkur began to degrade into the dingy outer districts of Surja and, upon realizing that she was no longer being chased, she stopped altogether, doubled over and sucked in gulps of air, too exhausted to feel relief setting in. She'd run further than she would have been able to before. She knew where this new-found endurance had come from, but couldn't think about it now; the last thing she needed was another bout of nausea. Near by, among boarded-up shops and dirty-looking apartment blocks, was a franchise of a local bar chain. No one would turn Zala in to the police or the SecForce in Surja, not while the locals were so invested in the NCLC's efforts, but that wasn't to say they wouldn't find reason to stab her anyway. Bars around this area were, first and foremost, for those who wanted to drink until they couldn't feel their knuckles fracturing against another person's skull. Hopefully the franchise was the least likely venue for that sort of behaviour. Looking around for pursuers, Zala ducked inside.

Chapter 17

The lights turned on with a faint hum, revealing the floor space of what had once been a huge industrial cold-storage unit. Although the fans and ducts which had once brought the temperature in the unit to around minus fifteen degrees Celsius were no longer functioning, the stained concrete walls and sharp white lighting gave the place a strange chill independent of actual temperature. The room was located in the back of one of the largest meat-processing facilities in the city. It was soundproof, secure and easily accessible. Against one wall, piled high, were bags filled with sand, each of which had a paper target stapled to it. Along another wall were around two dozen Franz Geller Kaufer Mark 25 combat rifles and several crates of ammunition. When Maalik was deciding where to train potential New Cairo Liberation Corps personnel, this had been the logical choice.

Alice got the distinct impression that Maalik was very proud of this place as he led her to it for the first time. They had brought thirteen new recruits, all eager to become involved in the revolution. News coverage of NCLC rebels taking over a tower block, emptying its data banks and leaving undetected through crowds of civilians and SecForce officers had made the group legendary and had greatly increased their allure to many young people. Almost all the thirteen newcomers were students, excited

184

by the NCLC's social agenda. They lined up in front of Maalik and Alice, shaven-headed and in ill-fitting combat fatigues, to begin their training. Maalik ran them through their paces.

Their enthusiasm was short-lived. Maalik's training methods were harsh: they were made to run until they collapsed; they paired off and were taught hand to hand combat in full-contact sparring; and they fired seemingly endless rounds into the targets stapled to the sandbags against the wall. Every time they under-performed, Maalik would scream tirades of abuse at them; even at his nicest he referred to them all as 'maggots', 'filth', or 'scum' and kept calling them 'worthless' or 'disgusting'. If they talked to one another at all, they were hit. If they attempted to help one another, they were hit harder. This kind of deliberate, systematic dehumanization was not something Alice had ever gone through as a police officer – it resembled the socialization techniques of the military. Soldiers needed to have their regular social norms broken down, then reformatted around unit cohesiveness, obedi-ence and a willingness to hurt or kill when told to.

It lasted for hours without break. Alice's portable terminal was the only time-keeping device available in the building and with no windows to the outside world the room was divorced from the regular pattern of the day. Despite their having started at five in the morning, it was almost three in the afternoon before stomachs began to growl. At that point Maalik set the trainees a deal. He brought out new paper targets, each printed with the image of a gun-wielding Security Force officer. The recruits were to pick up their rifles and set them to three-shot burst. If, having exhausted a magazine, a recruit had at least two dozen shots within the targets' kill zones, he or she could have a small piece of meat.

Maalik then brought out cut-out targets of a teary-eyed child. He set the same goal of two dozen shots within the kill zones of this new target, the reward in this case being a sandwich and a drink.

Upon hearing this, many of the recruits looked at him as though he was insane, their eyes flicking backwards and forwards between the target and Maalik. It made sense, Alice realized. The instinct not to kill had once been paramount, especially not to kill or even harm children. But Maalik and the NCLC needed a new instinct to take precedence: the instinct to not care about doing terrible things. If they did what they were told to do, the recruits would get food. If it was good enough to get a rat through a maze, it was good enough for them.

The first few took the option of shooting at the adult target. Those who did well were rewarded with a single piece of cold chicken, or a quarter of a beefburger, and those who didn't got nothing. Maalik ruled that they couldn't try again until everyone had shot, so they grew hungrier and hungrier.

A young woman stood up next to shoot, shaven-headed and stony-faced. She raised her rifle to eye level, lining up the sights. She was aiming for the child. At first her hands shook, but they steadied with a few deep breaths. She squeezed the trigger, and three shots landed in the kill zone.

'Again,' said Maalik.

Three more shots tore at the cut-out, leaving great gashes in the paper. The recruit fired her magazine into the child's form. Twenty-eight of thirty-six shots had landed within kill zones. Maalik smiled and threw her a packaged sandwich and a bottle of soft drink, then brought out a fresh cut-out to replace the old one. 'Enjoy,' he told the woman. 'You earned it.' She tore the packaging apart and wolfed the sandwich down.

The tension broken, the rest of the recruits without exception lined up to fire at the cut-out of the little boy.

Within thirty minutes, all the trainees had shredded a cut-out of a crying child and were sitting on the ground hunched over sandwiches and drinks, plus extra food Maalik provided once they had all gone through with their trial. He and Alice watched from the other side of the room as they ate.

'I'm very impressed,' said Alice. 'They really seem to be taking to this. I had no idea they'd come this far so quickly.'

'They'd better; I've only got today to get them through this,' he replied stiffly.

Alice's jaw dropped. 'They only get one day of training?'

Maalik shrugged. 'It's all the time we can spare. We're ramping up for a new series of riots. We need manpower and we need it with minimal resources. It's not great, sure, but it's good enough.'

'How on earth did the Yu twins or your backup unit get to where they are on a day of training?'

'Most of the heavy hitters in our organization are ex-police or ex-military. I can only speak for myself, but I spent forty years trying to make sure that this city was stable and that the vulnerable people were safe. That was something that mattered to me, it's what got me out of bed in the morning, or got me to sleep when I had to hurt someone. And I think that's why other people did it.'

'And Serhiy?'

'He's . . . difficult, but I'm working with him.'

Alice turned towards him. 'He used my child as a human shield, Maalik.'

Maalik nodded. 'Hence the difficulty. There's a good kid in there somewhere, he's just angry, like the rest of us.'

Alice couldn't bring herself to agree. 'So it's either police training or one day's worth?'

Maalik shifted in his seat and looked down at the ground. 'Well, these guys are only getting training because they're in good physical shape and they have potential to be useful in operations. If they do well, they'll get more training down the line, but until then – like I say, we're making up numbers with people who are young and fit. We've got about four hundred people this well trained and this well armed. Apart from that, there are the technical people, like Suman or Juri, who didn't get any training at all: they got in because they had skill with computers and were sympathetic to our cause. Then there's people who want in but aren't suited to being full-time operatives. We just give them small arms and ammo and let them know when we want something done. We've got about a thousand people willing to kill for us, but only our four hundred ready to die for us.'

Alice thought for a moment. 'When do the next riots start?'

'Six days from now, if nothing forces our hand.'

'Then these guys need to get at least another two days of train-ing. Have them running drills, get them more conditioning. They need to be able to do damage. You're not going to be able to rely on my skills when the big day comes. You'll need to sharpen up any way you can.'

Maalik raised an eyebrow. 'So it's not that you want them to be safer?'

Alice thought for a second. 'What I meant to say was that I wanted them to be safer so that they could be more effective.'

A sly grin crossed Maalik's face. 'I heard a story a long time ago, from back in the Age of Nations. Back when this was all called Egypt, they worshipped a whole pantheon of animal gods and there was one called Hathor. She was the cow-horned goddess of happiness, motherhood and music. She was one of the most important gods the ancient Egyptians had, beloved by all.' Maalik leaned in closer, a glint in his eye. His voice quietened. 'Yet they say that, when war came, she turned into something quite different. She became Sekhmet, the bloodthirsty lion-headed goddess of war, a side to her no one had seen coming. She laid waste to their enemies. The urge to slaughter was so great that, even after all her enemies had been destroyed, she kept on killing. At that point, it was no longer about the cause, or the original grievance. It was about the killing itself, and the thrill of sating her rage. She even drank the blood of her enemies.'

Alice nodded. 'And it's that side of these people that you're trying to bring out, is it?'

Maalik paused for a second, then nodded and said, 'Exactly, that's precisely what I mean to say. But Sekhmet wasn't a bad person. She was a mythic representation of the pharaoh's armies, who regained a part of the country which had rebelled. For the people who wrote the story, her violence, joyous and manic as it was, had a good cause behind it. That violence was the only way to achieve what they felt needed to be done. It was the best tool for the job.'

'And once she'd killed sufficiently, how did the other gods stop Sekhmet?'

Maalik's grin widened. 'They replaced the blood she drank with alcohol and they drank her under the table.'

It was coming up to ten at night. The training was over until five the next morning. Alice was seated at a table with Juri, Anisa Yu, Maalik and Suman and they all had open bottles of beer in front of them. They talked and laughed, and Maalik told them about the looks on the new recruits' faces when he'd informed them that, for the first time in weeks, their day of training was to be just one of many. This made a rather drunk Juri squirt a mouthful of beer out through her nose, though even that didn't stop her giggling. In front of them, some old comedy vidcast was playing on the wall, though none of them were really paying attention. They were simply enjoying one another's company, while they still could.

The comedy show ended and, absent-mindedly, Alice flicked over to a newscast. The headline ran across the bottom of the monitor, below a picture of a young woman's face.

MURDEROUS HACKER ZALA ULORA FOUND BACK IN CITY, it read.

Suman sat bolt upright. 'Oh my god, Selina!'

Everyone else turned to look at him. 'I read about this story before but I hadn't seen a picture. That woman, Selina Mullur – or Zala Ulora, I guess – was the hacker who got us the intelligence that linked the Soucouyant virus back to GeniSec.' He waved his hand, still clutching a bottle, at the screen for emphasis. 'Then, on what I thought was an unrelated note, a couple of days later some of our freelancers were breaking into the lab where the virus came from to find evidence, based on her intel. They found someone else sneaking around the place, so they shot her. She ends up in hospital, and somehow the administrators find out who they've got in their care, so she runs off. Apparently they're the same person!' He slumped back in his chair. 'That really sucks, I quite liked her. Now I find out she killed a bunch of people.'

'I bet you liked her, she's cute!' slurred Maalik, nudging Suman with his elbow. 'And a hacker! I bet you thought all your dreams had come true.'

Alice looked uneasily at the screen.

'Any chance we could help her?' said Anisa, her scratchy voice unaffected by the four beers she'd downed. 'A new hacker is always welcome, especially if she's good. She could be an asset.'

Maalik nodded at Alice. 'I defer to the lioness.'

Alice had already made her mind up. 'Look, I'm going to be out of here in a few days. This doesn't affect me. But we're doing fine for hackers as we are. If she's a fugitive wanted for murder—'

'We're all wanted for or in connection with murders. Murders of police and military, no less,' Anisa interrupted.

'Bullshit. We're fighting a civil war, not hurting innocent people. Not like this Zala woman. She's clearly dangerous; she's attracted police attention. If she's unstable and she knows things about us and the information we're working with, she could be a liability. We don't know what she'll do if she's backed into a corner. Sell us out? Cooperate with the Council?' Alice turned towards Suman. 'See what you can dig up on her. Get back in touch. If at all possible we need to get to her before the police do.'

Suman's face dropped. 'But I can't—'

'I'm just saying, see what you can find out. She's a loose end. She presents a danger. What we're doing here matters too much. If we get the chance to take her out of the picture, we should. If nothing else, we can't afford to have someone in this city who knows more about hacking than you, can we?'

Suman and Juri shared a brief look, which Alice caught. 'What?'

Juri sobered. 'There's more than one major hacker in this city. A large portion of our intelligence has been coming from a benefactor who can pretty much only be getting the intel they're providing by using really advanced hacking abilities and utilities. Whoever it is, they're certainly above my technical level – I don't know about Suman.'

Alice shook her head. 'So who is this, and what do they want?'

'I don't know motives, I don't know location. They hide themselves exceptionally,' said Juri. 'And they use a weird name. It's one of the old mythological figures from way back, a trickster god. Fitting for a high-level hacker. They're called Anansi.'

It was around midnight and the others had gone to bed, but Alice was still up. Juri had made her something quite extraordinary for her portable terminal: a low-powered version of her coordination software. If she so desired, she could control an entire operation from the front lines, with all the usual feeds coming straight to her over a heavily encrypted channel. She was increasingly tempted to try out this capability in practice. It had been so long since she'd gone out on patrol. Some other side to her, the side that came out when she was off-duty, disliked knowing what she was going to do, but during a patrol or a combat situation, there was a comfort and a thrill to be found. It had been so long that the other side of her had quite forgotten the rush.

The previous head of the safe house, an exhausted Ava Ferreira, appeared next to her. 'You seem rather the worse for wear.'

Alice laughed and pulled the collar of her shirt up to her nose. 'I don't stink of booze or anything, do I?'

'It's not you, it's pretty much this whole place. From what I saw, the girl with the eye aug got more beer on the table than in her mouth.'

'I'm glad they could unwind,' said Alice. 'It's been pretty intense. Everyone trying to take this movement in their own direction. Things have been really hard to keep together. I feel like I'm holding this whole thing together on my own, and I never even wanted to be involved in this. It was Jacob's big cause. I haven't even told the kids about what has happened to him yet.'

'I hear a lot of that going around. We've got another woman right here. Her husband died defending civilians in a curfew dispute. It was after a mission, his team was heading back to a safe house. A fight broke out with SecForce troops. His son still doesn't know. He thinks his dad's off in an undercover unit or something.' Ava pulled a tin from her pocket. She took out a cigarette, brought it up to her lips and lit it. 'If Suman had been watching the coordination software, he could have kept them on track, but he thought the mission was over, you know how it is. He blamed himself for ages.'

Alice nodded. 'We had that happen once back when I was working in SecForce. Someone stopped paying attention to the environmental interface, thought they were done. A guy got shot. After that, we never took our eyes off our guys' surroundings until they were back through the door.'

'Well, most of us are still largely amateurs at this,' said Ava.

Alice sighed. 'It's horrible that you guys had to learn the hard way too.'

'I guess that pretty soon none of this will be your problem though, right?'

Alice's brow furrowed. 'What do you mean?'

'The reason I came to find you. Message just came through from Kahleed. You and the kids are good to go. You're getting out of here.'

It took a moment for Alice to grasp what Ava was saying. She squinted at her, slowly computing what she'd heard. It was time to go. She had forgotten about that.

'It's . . . when?'

Ava shrugged. 'The plan is to get you over to Kahleed's people at about ten tomorrow. We can set off for the main base now, or in the morning. Whenever works for you is fine.'

Alice didn't know what to say.

She had wanted out of this city, somewhere her children could be safe, away from the violence and the terror and the death and the revolution, the revolution she had wanted no part in. The revolution she'd been a tremendous help in, that had put her once-proud skills to good use and made her feel powerful and stable. The revolution that would get them all killed for the sake of a dying city. A city she had loved. A city that had turned on her, inhabited by the institutions she'd worked for and believed in, which had killed Jacob and threatened her freedom and the freedom of her children. And the family of people who had supported and protected her in the face of these injustices.

She could get away from all that, to a safe new life. A life she didn't know and didn't have any real control over, where she would have to live knowing she had abandoned the cause Jacob died for.

However she considered these absurd, contradictory, maddening thoughts, they led to just one conclusion. 'Forget it.'

'What do you mean?' said Ava.

'I have a job to do here and I want to see it through.'

Ava looked at her as though she had just announced that she would be challenging Tau Granier to a fist fight personally. 'So you want me to tell Kahleed you're sticking around?'

Alice nodded. 'I can't leave now. Too many people need me. I feel like I have something to give and this is what I need to be giving it to.'

A strange look passed over Ava's face which Alice couldn't quite figure out, and then it was gone. 'I'll let him know.'

She turned and left Alice alone with her thoughts.

Chapter 18

Minutes, hours, days. Maybe weeks, though that was probably stretching it. The men down in the vaults below had
said they were going to kill him after a week when he was being
tortured, but the organization seemed to have fallen into disarray
since then, and neither Ryan nor Ava knew whether that order
was still valid.

Ryan had given Ava a list of trustworthy names, where they
worked, who they worked under, who to play them off against.
The plan for his escape needed to be quick, and it needed to be as
clean as possible.

He was going home.

They'd decided that he was not allowed to know the plan. He'd
been tortured before. If he could have told them something to
make it stop, he would have. So instead he waited, and in doing
so he felt as though time was going by more slowly than he had
ever known it to before.

The worst part was the absence of anything to occupy himself
with. He remembered back to sitting alone at school as a child.
His father's shadow loomed over him, long and pitch dark, and
intimidated even the other children. He was something apart from
them. So he kept an old coin his grandfather had given him in his
pocket and he would practise performing tricks with it. A point-

less activity in hindsight, flipping and palming a metal disc that had served no practical purpose for generations. But he gleaned some small measure of satisfaction from the act.

It had been years since he lost the coin. His father had been so angry. It was rare that he hit Ryan – it would be politically damaging were it discovered – but he had hit him then. Only later would Ryan realize that the beating was only partly about his losing the coin. It was an antique and one of the few things belonging to his grandfather that he had left, though he had always suspected that his grandfather wouldn't have minded him losing it; after all, why else would he have bestowed his coin on a child?

What wouldn't Ryan have given for a coin at that moment.

To his right, the door leading to the corridor opened and Vik walked through. Close behind him was an older girl, aged maybe eleven or twelve, holding a baby. Instinctively, Ryan tried to look down the corridor before the door closed, trying to flesh out his understanding of the building, but then he realized that it really didn't matter; he was getting out either way. So instead he waved at Vik.

He recognized the other two children. They had accompanied the unwounded Yu twin the previous day. While he didn't know who they were for sure, the girl was the spitting image of the Alice woman who seemed to have taken the reins of the organization.

'Heya, Ryan,' said Vik, beaming, 'I have a new friend.' He turned towards the girl. 'This is Cancer Ryan Granner. He's hiding out here, like the rest of us.'

'It's Councillor Ryan Granier actually,' said Ryan, smiling and nodding in acknowledgement of the girl.

Vik blushed. 'Oh, I'm really sorry! This is Ria Amirmoez, and the baby is Zeno. They're staying here for a little while and then they're going away to meet up with their dad.'

'We're not really,' said Ria. Vik spun round and looked at her, confused. 'We're leaving the city soon, but we're not meeting up with our dad. Either they've got him captured, or they killed him. If they'd captured him, he'd have been on the news like those others were.'

The girl's eyes had a weariness to them that disturbed Ryan, but she was clearly sharp. 'That all seems like rather a leap,' he said.

She shrugged. 'My mum spends hours every night crying. She leaves me to take care of my little brother all day while she's off working with the others. When she is around, which doesn't happen much any more, she keeps treating me like I'm four, which happened a whole lot when my granddad died. I know something bad has happened.'

'What did you say your surname was again?'

'I didn't, he did,' she said, pointing to a put-out-looking Vik over her shoulder with her thumb. 'I'm Ria Amirmoez.'

Amirmoez. The name was familiar. He'd not quite picked up on it when their mother introduced herself to Ava. He'd seen it a long time ago. Suddenly it came to him. He was reminded of news footage from right when it had come out that the riots had been orchestrated. Jacob Amirmoez was one of the founders of the NCLC. Ryan was taken aback; for some reason he'd never thought of the man having a family. What was stranger was the incongruity between this information and his previous impressions of Alice Amirmoez. She had an authority about her which had made him assume she was in charge of the base, rather than someone trying to leave the city.

Ryan made a mental note to check with Ava that this wouldn't affect their plan in any significant way.

'Are you all right? You seem kind of . . . unfazed by what you're saying?' he asked Ria. The girl's jaded demeanour still troubled him.

'I've been terrified for days and exhausted from looking after Zeno. I've been trying to be good for my mum so that she can cope with whatever's happened to Dad, and trying to keep out of the way. There's something big and scary out there that wants to get me, and I can't do anything about that, and I'm just tired of it. Do you know what that's like?'

Ryan nodded. Ria looked down at his leg. His trousers were still torn, revealing bandages underneath.

'Anyway, I'm going to go and show Ria the rest of the building,' said Vik. He waved goodbye, and dragged the girl towards the door. She glanced back at Ryan, over her shoulder. He supposed that, in the state he was currently in, he must have looked rather odd. He had been wearing the same clothes for two weeks and while he kept trying to wash them in the sink of the bathroom, the only difference it made for the most part was that his clothes were wet and filthy as opposed to just filthy. There was no mirror in the bathroom, but he could feel that he had grown a short beard, and his hair was probably getting longer than he'd worn it in a long time.

As the children neared the door, it opened and a surprised-looking Ava nearly walked into them. They dashed past her and up the hallway.

'They bothering you?' she asked, motioning towards them.

Ryan smiled. 'I'm so bored in here that it's a welcome distraction.'

'If you get too bored we can always have Maalik carve you up some more.'

A faint smell of cooked meat. 'Shut up, Ava,' he hissed.

Her eyes widened. Ryan tried to settle himself. 'I'm sorry. It's just . . . having him in the same building is . . . It's really getting to me.'

Ava winced apologetically. 'If it's any consolation, it won't be long now.'

'Without getting into specifics, can you tell me anything?'

'It'll be quick and your contacts have given me a guarantee that any non-combatants they find won't be abused. I got the impression they're afraid you've got Stockholm Syndrome and will open up a world of hurt if they mess with anyone. As for anyone who's got a gun, it'll be harder. Luckily, I've planned it to coincide with a big training push that got ordered.' She exhaled heavily and gave him an anxious look. 'Everyone's getting additional training, which I don't like the sound of. If the NCLC keeps escalating the violence that could be dangerous for anyone who's present here.'

'I don't want anyone to get hurt if they don't have to be.'

Ava shrugged, her brow furrowed. 'And, fingers crossed, neither do the people with guns and batons whose opinion on that matter is the one that counts. They want heads, something to show that they can hit the rebels where they live, maybe send a message to some of the participants on the periphery who don't really understand the reality of what they're getting involved in. At least everyone here has played a part in something big. They knew what they were getting involved in.'

'You didn't.'

Ava looked at him, surprised. 'Now's really not the time to introduce doubt into this plan, Councillor.'

'I'm just . . . I get these people wanting to keep their kids safe. I can't begrudge them that, and yet we're going to ruin it. We're going to turn their parents in to the police and I have no idea what'll happen to them.'

'Right now they're in the most dangerous part of the city in the near-constant company of terrorists and under sustained threat of the building being attacked. Anything that happens to them will only be an improvement,' said Ava. Ryan still felt as though he was going to throw up. He knew how much it hurt, fearing that he'd never see his children again. He'd felt it in this very building. If he had a choice he wouldn't wish it upon anyone. Ava's features softened. 'I know it's horrible, Councillor, but it's the best of a bad situation. With luck, it'll all be pretty painless.'

Ryan slumped back in his chair and stared up at the ceiling. The price for his freedom was that these eight children would be torn away from their parents. Those parents might be imprisoned or, worse, executed. Those children would probably end up in the care system and have a relationship with their family only during visiting hours, if at all. He thought of watching his children being taken away from him, knowing that he had failed to protect them.

His children.

Suddenly his concern vanished. It didn't matter. What mattered was that he would be out of here soon. He'd hold his wife and children. He'd get back to work, slip into his routine like an old slipper. This room would, over time, become just another room to him, in a part of town he rarely went to and in a building he had no business being in.

That was what he looked forward to most. Never seeing this room again.

Chapter 19

The newscast played over and over. Whenever it reached the end of the segment, Zala skipped back to the beginning and watched again. The screen of her portable terminal showed a teary-eyed Polina being taken from her home at The Ozymandias in handcuffs and bundled into the back of a police van. Below, the running headline was 'Deputy Curator Shelters Anti-Aug Hacker-Killer'.

Zala couldn't help but reach with her finger towards the image of her friend, arrested and humiliated because of her. Just to try to touch her. The finger passed through the holographic screen instantly. Polina was gone, and Zala was alone.

Zala had managed to get to the boundary between Naj-Pur and Surja and had located a small abandoned flat. She had hacked the central registry again, using the same credentials as before, and looked for families which had left following the outbreak of the Soucouyant virus. Assuming she hadn't lost her talents for breaking and entering, the list was as good as a hotel directory. She had found one and made short work of the household's home security. Her hunch paid off – the family had obviously left quickly and not only was most of the packaged food still good to eat, but they had kept a fully stocked drinks cabinet. Zala had indulged herself and the previous night's intoxication had given way to a thunderous headache and further pain added to her already fragile emotional state. She missed the drunkenness none the less. Her face was everywhere, more prominent in recent public service announcements than that of Kahleed Banks or Maalik Moushian. She couldn't blame them; when she'd replaced Selina Mullur's records with her own she'd given them a photograph. Her alleged three murders, all blamed on 'virulent anti-augmentation sentiments', had all been dragged back up. The media, the newscasts, they all but openly accused her of creating the Soucouyant virus. It wasn't an illogical conclusion, wrong as it was. She was probably one of the few people in the city who knew the virus well enough to know how far above her own coding ability it was. But the Council's records showed that eight years ago the murder of three bio-augmented gang members was attributed to a young woman who'd fled the city, who reportedly hated bio-augmentations; and that her reappearance had coincided with the outbreak of the virus which was ravaging the bio-augmented citizens of New Cairo. It made total sense.

For that, Polina was being imprisoned.

Zala reached over the edge of the bed, trying to figure out whether any of the bottles she had stolen the previous night still had any alcohol left in them. She hit upon one that felt half full, but upon pulling it up and taking a swig, she found that it had already been drained and refilled with water. She didn't recall doing that and chalked it up to her drunken self apparently having more sense than she did sober.

The tiny projected image of Polina being thrown into the back of the police van replayed for the umpteenth time. Zala told herself that Polina had known the risks, that she had been prepared for this. She'd told herself this before. It had worked when it came to the victims of the criminal organizations Zala had armed or acquired drugs for; the people she had stolen from; the people she had physically hurt; the people whose trust she had betrayed; the people she had deceived and exploited. Zala had always slept fine. They were an obstacle, nothing more.

But Polina looked so scared.

Zala drank the last of the water, then closed the video window on her portable terminal. She ran every system analysis, every probe, every measure she had to check that she wasn't being watched. Then, deciding that anyone who could evade those checks had kind of earned the right to find her, she loaded up her shell operating system. She found Suman Chaudhri, and opened up a chat window before he could go offline.

>Suman, I need your help.

It took a while for a reply to arrive.

>Zala – that's your real name, right? Look, I can't help you. I'm part of an organization that routinely attacks policemen and yet you're still too toxic for us. Right now, half my superiors think that you represent a loose end that needs to be tied up and the other half think you're the one who wrote the virus in the first place. You can't be anywhere near here.

Zala stared at the screen. Apparently she had united the city's police and leading terrorist group in their desire to see her destroyed.

>Is there any way you can help me at all?

>Even if I thought I could do it, I'd still be obliged to track you and pass on your location. You don't want my help.

Exhausted, Zala slumped back onto the bed. She thought for a moment.

>Do you know anything about a hacker called ANANSI?

There was a long pause, and for a moment Zala assumed that Suman had blocked her.

>How do you know that name? he replied.

>They've been in touch. No idea who they are though. I was hoping you could clue me in.

>I've heard a few things. Every so often their name will come up in a chat, if you've got the right people around. I didn't even think they existed.

>That's not good enough, Suman. What do you know?

>I know the name ANANSI is taken from an old spider god from the Nations days. A trickster god at the centre of the web sounds pretty appropriate. The name was knocking around after it was referred

to in a leaked internal GeniSec document from about a decade ago. Just referred to once, very mysterious, but it gained traction on the conspiracy theory forums. I know that, for years now, if there was ever a big hacking job that no one took credit for, it was attributed to ANANSI. I know that they have access to a tremendous amount of information that suggests very high-level technical ability. That said, I'm still not entirely convinced. There's so little proof that it wouldn't surprise me if they're a cover for another hacker – or a number of other hackers – who're shifting the blame for the stuff that would get them into the most trouble.

>Is that all you've got? asked a disappointed Zala.

>What're you even asking about them for?

Zala's fingers hammered away at the holographic keyboard in front of her.

>I'm running an investigation. Not only is ANANSI the only lead I've got in this mess, they're trying to turn me off the trail every chance they get, which means I must be going in the right direction.

>What, are you talking about the same investigation you were on this whole time? It was GeniSec. You're the one who found the evidence for that!

Zala thought back to that evening, in GeniSec Development Falkur.

>I did some more checking but I can't find a source at all. The trail stops there, sure, but I still don't know who created it, so we can't pin it on them yet.

Suman didn't reply for a moment.

>How much of this is just that you want to believe there's more you can do?

Zala had no answer to that. Suman waited for her response, and then, when she didn't reply, he logged out. Alone again, she went back over the events of the night she had been shot. That the other break-in at GeniSec Development Falkur was simultaneous with the arrival of ANANSI's message was probably not a coincidence. Was ANANSI warning her? Did they direct the guys in the building? She looked back over the message she had been sent on the evening she'd been maimed.

From: ANANSI (EIP: ----.-.------.-------.---.-----.----.------)
>Someone's looking where they're not supposed to.

ANANSI definitely didn't want her looking into the Soucouyant virus, that much was certain. But could that message have
been a warning? Was it even a reference to her assailants? Could
the message in the hospital have been a warning that the hospital
knew, and not a threat? Would she have escaped either of those
situations if she wasn't already alerted to danger?

But that was just conjecture. There was something more, something she was forgetting. There was a potential link she'd missed,
somewhere along the way.

She looked back up at Suman's chat log. I know that they have
access to a tremendous amount of information that suggests very
high-level technical ability, it said. Oddly specific and with no explanation. He'd claimed not to know much, but he was curiously
aware of ANANSI's ability to get information. At the very least,
there was something he wasn't telling Zala. He knew more about
ANANSI than he was letting on, she was sure of it.

Her thoughts turned to Suman's own activities: a major player
in the city's cybercrime scene, now a senior member of a massive
terrorist organization. It made sense that he and ANANSI would
have crossed paths.

Then it came to her. That day, in the café, waiting for the
key-logger to collect its data – while waiting, she'd been sending
messages, in a comparatively open security state, to Suman. This
could mean anything or it could mean nothing. Zala took a
few deep breaths to calm herself. Perhaps ANANSI was simply
monitoring her. Perhaps Suman had sent ANANSI information
about her. Or perhaps—

Hacker. Political streak. Insight into Zala's location and activities.

She felt the colour drain from her face.

Zala sat very still and very quiet for a long time. Polina was in
police custody, and Suman Chaudhri was potentially the hacker
who had been opposing her all along, or at the very least in league

with him. She was exhausting her allies and in the meantime the videocasts were making her the enemy of the entire city.

Zala had never felt so lost before, so without hope.

She needed to distract herself and so, as she did in every spare moment, she toyed with the code her father had left her: those few fallow lines, sitting in their own folder. Nothing new was revealed to her. It was in a coding language she'd never seen before, and the syntax was bizarre but seemed to conform roughly to the structure of code meant to end a number of specific processes for use in a unique program. This essentially made it useless: it was far too specifically coded to be used unaltered and new terminating code was so easy to write that it wouldn't be worth converting it for use with a new program. It was only capable of stopping one program in existence, and that was clearly not a program Zala had ever encountered before. With everything else in the massive stores of data her father had left, there was a use, an obvious, practical purpose. The rest of his work was written in coding languages she understood, which left this one piece of essentially useless code as an outlier. She kept it none the less. It was a memento.

So Zala worked instead on a few programs she had in progress, switching to a new one each time she grew bored. Hours passed. As she coded, she turned the newscasts back on to make sure that, at the very least, there were no camera-crew vans pulling up outside the flat.

She killed time and she waited. And then she sent a single message off to the same non-address she had used for the other messages to ANANSI.

>I want to talk.

Chapter 20

Six shots punched through the paper target and into the sand-bags behind. Maalik pulled the target from its heavy industrial staples and surveyed it. Even from where Alice stood, she could see that most of the shots were in tight groups and all within kill zones. The shooter, Pratima Rachana, grinned shyly as Nataliya Kaur patted her on the back. She had been the first of the recruits the day before to shoot the child target, which had been a more morbid achievement; the switch back to adult-sized targets had possibly restored her enthusiasm. Pratima turned to the three other recruits waiting behind her and whooped. They were quick to congratulate her. Maalik stapled a new target to the sandbags and the next shooter stepped up. Behind them, Anisa Yu and Serhiy Panossian sparred, demonstrating unarmed close combat techniques to eight other partnered trainees. One from the day before had not returned; Maalik was pleased – it was a lower than expected dropout rate – and joked that he had been especially harsh to them before.

The effects of his mind games had taken hold quickly. Already the new recruits were taking pleasure from hitting targets or successfully executing some grapple, laughing over their potential to snap arms or shatter ribs. More importantly, the drive to fulfil an order as successfully as possible was starting to grip them; everything else was just muscle memory.

At this point, Serhiy and the 'Roaring Sister' Anisa Yu, both participants in the hostage situation at the GeniSec Regional Administration building, had been all over newscasts and public service broadcasts. They had gained a level of notoriety which had bought with it an ironic celebrity. When it transpired that they would be helping with training, some of the good spirits the recruits had first arrived in had returned. Today, Maalik did nothing to quash this enthusiasm.

Behind them, Alice and Juri looked on. Alice's decision to put a priority on training had been vindicated. One more day like this and these new recruits would be useful combatants when the riots started up again. They'd probably never be genuinely good soldiers; the time necessary to truly make warriors of them was far in excess of the time available to them. The Council would either crush the NCLC, raise the restrictions they'd put in place, or create a cure for the Soucouyant virus, but in any of these scenarios there was probably less than a month remaining in the conflict. The question then became whether the new trainees would live to see the end of it.

A message rang out from her terminal. The tone carried further than she'd have expected, and she realized that the other NCLC members had also received messages. She turned on her screen. It was from Suman.

>raid

She turned instantly to Maalik, eyes wide. Looking up from his own terminal, he met her gaze and nodded, before switching his attention to the rest of the room. 'Everyone, your training is over. It's time to go to work. Grab your guns.'

Anisa and Serhiy began herding the recruits out. Those not already holding weapons gathered some up from the stack in the corner of the room. They quickly filed out of the cold-storage area and through the factory. Alice tried to break into a run, but Maalik held her back. 'Don't run and draw attention to us. This could be an ambush.'

The group threw on coats or other outer wear to hide the fact that they were all in military garb and body armour. They folded up their rifles and hid them under their coats or in bags. They then walked out into the street. The shutdown of most of the businesses in Naj-Pur meant that the streets were full of people trying to find something to do. The group blended quickly into the crowd, drawing little comment, though Anisa's niqab stood out as ever. As they moved, Alice hissed back at the group, 'There's been a raid on our safe house. That's all the details we have, but if it's the Security Force, we're going to take a look at their numbers and if it seems like we have good odds, we need to try and stop our people getting arrested.'

Pratima turned her head. 'Is there anyone at the safe house who's a priority to keep safe if it comes to that?'

'Councillor Ryan Granier,' said Alice. 'He's probably the reason the safe house is getting raided. He's our bargaining chip. We can't lose him.'

There was murmuring behind her. Anisa quickly caught up. 'Alice, it's okay if you want some of us to make a beeline for your kids.'

A sudden, resonant sense of terror ran through Alice. Her children were in there. Some part of her had failed to grasp that they were in danger. She murmured, 'Oh god . . .' then hung back until Serhiy came level with her, and grabbed his arm. 'Serhiy! If you want to get back into my good books, get my kids out of there!'

'I'll see what I can do,' came a gruff reply.

They turned a corner into the road where the safe house was situated. Almost immediately, they ran into a tightly packed crowd of people, all straining to see something ahead of them. Over their heads, Alice could see the tops of a convoy of heavily armoured SecForce and New Cairo police vehicles. Her breath caught in her throat. She clambered up onto a nearby car to see what was happening.

Further down the road, beyond the crowd, she could see that the door of the bank, which had served as an NCLC base and housed Ryan Granier, was wide open. Men, women and children

– the fugitives who had been hiding inside – were being led out at gunpoint by SecForce special forces troops and thrust into the backs of two armoured vans parked on the far side of the area. The rest of the perimeter was lined with the armoured personnel carriers SecForce used for taking troops into heavy combat zones. They'd come in full force; the NCLC were outnumbered and outgunned. It was already over.

Occasionally the procession was interrupted by Security Force officers carrying out stretchers on which lay bodies covered with sheets.

And there they were. A SecForce officer was leading Ria to the furthest van, the young girl carrying Zeno in her arms. The van's heavy steel doors shut behind her. Alice stared, unable to take it in. Before she could process what was happening, she realized she was fumbling under her coat for her rifle.

Strong hands reached up from below and wrestled it away. Maalik was there, her rifle in his hands, hissing, 'Don't you *dare* make orphans of those children!'

Suddenly deflated, she climbed down off the car. Her hands were shaking. There was nothing they could do. She began to sob. 'They've got my children, Maalik.'

Anisa Yu drew her into a hug. There was something so comforting about the huge woman's arms enveloping her. Anisa rasped, 'We didn't get any intel, our sources never turned anything up. There was nothing you could have done to stop this.'

For a moment Alice let herself believe her.

Then, a voice from somewhere behind Anisa asked, 'Where's Serhiy?'

This was followed almost immediately by a loud cracking sound – gunfire – and a volley of screams. Snapping back to attention, Alice looked around. The noise had come from near the vans, but there were too many people in the way for her to see what had caused it. She pulled away from Anisa and began pushing through the crowd.

The mass of people had become startled by the sound, and a nervous energy began to build throughout as everyone strained to see what was going on. By the time Alice made it close enough to the police barrier that she could see, they seemed to collectively be on the verge of bolting. The safe house was to her right, with the armoured personnel carriers parked in the road to the left and the vans loaded with rebels ahead of her. The space outside the front of the building was full of SecForce and police, all scanning around the crowd frantically. Two SecForce troopers were on the ground, bleeding heavily and writhing in pain.

The troops began yelling at the crowd to give up whoever had shot at them. They were so preoccupied in hectoring the crowd that no one noticed a young man, who couldn't have yet been twenty, creeping around the side of one of the armoured personnel carriers towards a SecForce officer. He grabbed the man tightly from behind, pulling him off balance, and pressed a handgun to his cheek. 'Back up!' he screamed to the man's comrades as he dragged the trooper backwards, further and further towards the rear doors of the van containing Ria and Zeno.

The other troopers raised their guns, but inched backwards. 'Drop your weapon and let the man go, son!' called one.

'I can't do that, sir,' Serhiy shouted back. 'I made a promise.'

The SecForce troops seemed to sense an opportunity to de-escalate. One by one, their weapons lowered, ever so slightly. 'What do you want?' yelled the one who was apparently in charge.

'There are some children in the back of this truck right here,' Serhiy motioned behind him with a jerk of the head, 'and I've got to get them back to their mother. So you're going to let me climb into the front of this van and drive off.'

'I'm sorry, son, but I can't let you do that,' said the SecForce officer. Around him, armed, uniformed SecForce troops began to move forwards again, guns raised, slowly flanking him. Serhiy would be surrounded before he ever made it to the van's cab.

Serhiy nodded, then pulled the hostage's head back and fired. There was a flash of red and a thunderous crack, followed by screams of panic from the crowd and a tattoo of returning gunfire. Anyone in the crowd who was second-guessing the decision to flee no longer had a choice in the matter, and they began to

210

scatter. Alice ran with them, caught up in the chaos. Behind her, gunshots rattled off, cracking against concrete or APC plating.

Finding shelter behind a car, Alice turned and looked back at what was happening. Serhiy lay on the ground, blood soaking his shirt and pooling out from underneath him. The SecForce officer stood over him, rifle pointing down. There were two gaping wounds in the young man's back. Both bullets had torn right through his bulletproof vest. Serhiy looked up, his gaze rising to the approaching SecForce troopers and then past them, meeting Alice's horrified stare. In the moment before he disappeared from view, Alice could have sworn he looked as though he were ashamed.

With nowhere else to go, the rebel group reconvened and made their way back to the cold-storage unit. Alice had to be dragged there. Everything felt strangely distant, as though she was outside herself, looking on. As soon as they were through the door, Alice wiped the tears from her face.

'I–I–I have to call Kahleed. We have to make sure they didn't get him too.'

'I'll do it,' said Maalik, who was visibly shaken himself. 'You're in no shape to do anything.'

'You think this is the first time I've done something like this?' Alice found herself yelling. 'I saw people *die* on my command in the Security Force, Maalik. I need to handle this. Just . . .' She took a deep breath. 'I saw my children get taken from me and a comrade die, and there was nothing I could do. Give me control over something.'

Maalik looked at her as though he was confused, then nodded and went to sit down against the wall opposite. Alice brought up Kahleed's name on her terminal. A dozen agonizing rings sounded before he finally responded. 'Is everything okay on your end?' said Alice.

'Yeah, everything's fine. Has something happened?'

'There was a raid at the safe house. Granier's gone. They're all gone. Someone's dead, don't know who. They carried them out on a stretcher, wrapped up in a blanket. And Serhiy.' Alice took a deep, shuddering breath. 'Serhiy's dead. A bunch of us are still safe, but we're hiding in the training factory.'

'Who's still with you?'

Alice took another deep breath. 'Maalik, Anisa, Nataliya, Juri, and a dozen of the new recruits we were training.'

'Everyone else is gone?'

'Yeah.'

'Fucking hell,' said Kahleed. 'Where are the children?'

Alice tried desperately to keep her voice from wavering. 'They got everyone who wasn't involved in the training exercise.'

'All right . . . You should all get yourselves over here as soon as possible. Bring what gear you can. Do you know how much of your equipment they got?'

'I have no idea, I haven't gone in to check. They've probably got everything. Our equipment, my things, the things my children brought with them . . .'

Alice trailed off. Kahleed was silent for a moment. 'Go ask Maalik about the failsafe.' He hung up.

Alice turned to survey the assembled room. The new recruits looked awkward and unsure of what to do, while the more established NCLC members sat talking quietly among themselves, trying to take in what had just happened. Maalik was hunched over, staring at the ground. Alice walked over to him.

'Was there anything I could have done to stop him?' rasped Maalik.

'Nothing. There was nothing you could have done. Serhiy got it into his head that he needed to make things up to me. That was my fault. You couldn't have stopped it.'

Maalik nodded to himself, still not taking his eyes off the floor in front of him. 'You're right, I couldn't have stopped it. He was his own man. Thank you.'

Alice reached out and touched his arm. 'You were right, in the end. He was a good kid.'

Maalik shuddered slightly, then looked up at her. 'We're going to get your children back, Alice.'

'We don't have shit on them. Granier's gone. We don't have any leverage.'

Maalik stood up and walked past Alice towards the main door out of the storage area. 'Come with me. I want to show you something.'

Mystified, Alice followed.

The two of them walked through Naj-Pur and up to the city boundary. It wasn't too far; they were near the edge anyway. The NCLC wasn't needed in the city centre. Here, the high-density tower-block housing was at its worst; nestled in among it was Elevator Station Sixteen. No one who was from the wealthier parts of New Cairo, and thus cleared to leave the city, would have braved this desperate, dangerous neighbourhood to get to Elevator Station Sixteen, so it had been unused since the crackdown on emigration from 'high-infection areas'. Next to it was a huge concrete building, above which was a long cluster of cables that snaked down the side of the city crater from the main power lines out of the solar membrane. Beside that building was an old, deserted restaurant, its wooden sign rotted and its boarded windows covered in dirt, diminutive next to the massive towers and industrial buildings around it. Maalik walked up to the front door, where the lock was long broken, and led Alice inside.

The inside walls were covered in graffiti and the premises smelt strongly of stale sweat and piss and whatever else whoever had been squatting there had produced. Maalik took her behind the old counter and down a flight of stairs, at the bottom of which was a large steel door. It was noticeably newer than anything else in the building and had not yet been vandalized. Maalik fished out an old-fashioned metal key from his pocket, inserted it into a lock and turned it. The door swung open to reveal a bank of inactive computer terminals, wired into an old, beaten-up looking computer. It took a while to place, but Alice had seen something like it before.

'Is . . . Maalik, is that an In-Network Explosive Device terminal?'

Maalik nodded. 'We've got about seventy networked explosives wired up around the city, and an additional thirty wired up to the solar membrane above us, all of which feed into here. It's our last resort, if everything else fails. It's time for you to know where it is and how to use it.'

'What do you think it's worth as an ultimatum? As something to bargain with?' said a stunned Alice.

'It's worth getting your kids back. Our people released. The elevators turned back on. It's worth whatever we decide it's worth, if we play our cards right. It'll kill our public approval, but it might just get the job done. And if needs be, we'll destroy the city and the system which infests it and start over with something better.'

Seemingly unconcerned by the gravity of his words, Maalik switched on the monitors and began to run the operating system, beckoning Alice closer.

Chapter 21

Grey walls. Grey carpet, a grey which not only showed up every piece of dirt and stain but would always in itself look dirty. Almost but not quite the same cinereous shade as the floor in the former bank, except of course for the rust-coloured stains. Grey drawers and cupboards. Councillor Ryan Granier examined his new surroundings with a manic energy.

'Councillor?'

Ryan snapped back to attention. He found himself staring into the eyes of the rotund woman sitting in front of him.

'Are you back with us, Councillor Granier?'

Ryan nodded, looked away and tried not to meet her gaze. The grey room was in fact the medical bay in the New Cairo Police Department building.

The woman in front of him was Dr Tasnim Albrecktsson, a psychiatrist under contract with the police force. She was a dowdy-looking middle-aged woman with a gruff personality that Ryan would never have placed on a shrink, and at that moment her voice seemed to resonate at the exact frequency ideally suited to annoy him.

'What is it?' he muttered.

'Ah. Right, now that you're present, let's try and get through the basics. Have you been sleeping well?'

He hadn't been sleeping well, no. Ava had been giving him help for that. Ava, who—

'I've been sleeping fine.'

Dr Albrecktsson looked him up and down for a moment, then typed the response into her terminal. 'Have you experienced mood swings or erratic emotional states since your kidnapping?'

There were his panic attacks, his sudden turns to anger. Sometimes, when he had been left alone with nothing to occupy himself with, he'd felt depressed. He'd told Ava . . .

'No.'

Again, Dr Albrecktsson scanned him, and said only a curt, 'If you say so.'

Ryan looked up. 'What have you written about me?'

'Your demeanour has swung back and forward about five times since you entered this office, Councillor. You took about two minutes each time to answer those questions, and I'm pretty sure you weren't fully aware of our surroundings for most of that period. I've noted that you're suffering from Acute Stress Disorder, and probably the seeds of Post-Traumatic Stress Disorder. I saw your medical report; anyone who'd been in your situation would have similar diagnoses. We can take some scans, some blood work to confirm.'

'So my answers were . . . ?'

She shrugged. 'I wanted to see if you were being cooperative or not. A warning to myself, or to whoever else you may see in the future.'

Ryan stopped for a second. 'Uncooperative? I thought you said I wasn't aware for the big pauses?'

'Lying. It's fine, it's a symptom of your condition, but it's unhelpful for us and it's potentially damaging for you. Internalizing your trauma makes it harder to stop reliving it.'

'So what do you want me to do?'

'I want you, starting from the beginning, to tell me what happened from the moment when you were kidnapped. Or backwards from today. Whichever you find easier.'

A faint smell of burnt meat.

'I can't.'

Dr Albrecktsson leaned forward, a look of concern on her face. 'Is it too traumatic, or are you having problems remembering?'

'It's . . .'

Ryan stopped. The burnt meat smell grew more and more intense.

With nothing better to do, Ryan practised his walking. The newly arrived operatives had all disappeared, leaving the base emptier than it had been in days. Even when they didn't engage with him at all, they were something, *a distraction, colourful and energetic, a whole new network of people and interpersonal relationships to watch. For two days, they had been something new and stimulating. At the very least, unlike the safe house's regular inhabitants, they spent most of their time camped out in the large foyer he had access to. It was the closest he had been to social engagement outside of the conversations he'd wrangled out of Ava, Vik or Kanak. Without this to occupy him, physio seemed like the thing to do. Still confined to crutches, he fine-tuned his balance, experimented with different gaits. His confidence built and he began to speed up his pace.*

After a while, his expedition was interrupted by the intrusion of two of the newer non-combat personnel: Hoshi Smolak, a bespectacled accountant in his forties, and a stout, pockmarked computer genius named Suman Chaudhri.

'Is there a reason you're pacing?' asked Suman.

'Boredom.'

'I can imagine that, yeah,' said Hoshi, nodding. 'You never really think of being someone's hostage as getting quite dull after a bit, but I guess you really don't have anything to do here.'

'I get tortured every so often, that livens things up,' said Ryan, suddenly bristling. Hoshi looked uncomfortable.

'Did you hear the latest news then?' said Suman, breaking the tension. 'Your father's lot think they've identified someone they're pretty sure is the person who created the Soucouyant virus.'

'*They've got what?*' *They had Ryan's attention now.*

'*A hacker who apparently killed a bunch of bio-augmented people a few years back. It's weird. She actually helped us out a bit with regard to bringing down your father's company, using a stolen identity.*'

'*What's her name?*'

'*Zala Ulora.*'

That rang a bell. Something from a long, long time ago.

'*I think I remember her father,*' *said Ryan.* '*Dr Kweku Ulora. He was the project lead on the IntuitivAI development; I remember meeting him. There was some issue there, he got charged with corporate espionage. It was pretty big; he ended up escaping the city before the police could track him down.*'

Hoshi looked over at Suman. '*Did she mention any of that to you?*'

'*Not a word of it,*' *Suman replied.* '*Check it out.*'

Hoshi entered the name into his portable terminal's network browser. A series of news articles from eight years ago appeared. Most of them revolved around Dr Ulora's daughter, Zala, escaping the city – she'd been accused of three counts of murder, and he fled with her. It appeared that it was only after Dr Ulora had left that the allegations of corporate espionage came out.

'*Computer expertise, a hatred of bio-augmentation – it doesn't sounds implausible,*' *said Ryan.*

'*I'm pretty sceptical that she'd be behind the Soucouyant virus,*' *said Suman.* '*She's good, but she's not nearly as good as whoever coded it, unless she had one arm tied behind her back whenever I've seen her work. But it wouldn't surprise me if she knows something. Maybe her old dad isn't really dead, and he created it out of revenge.*'

'*You know,*' *Hoshi said to Ryan,* '*if your father's people wind up finding her, and a cure is released, it'll get you off the hook. You might be out of here sooner than you think.*'

'*Maybe,*' *said Ryan, trying to remain non-committal.*

*

Babirye Granier was already in tears by the time she walked into the room, and the moment Ryan saw his wife, he began to cry too. Babirye ran to the side of the hospital bed, stumbling around a doctor and throwing herself onto Ryan. He embraced her until his muscles ached. It was the first time he had held her since the morning he had been taken. From behind her, Hafiz and Dalin, his boys, came into view and joined the embrace.

'I'm amazed you guys recognize me, I look terrible,' said Ryan, unable to stop smiling.

'You look pretty scruffy, yeah,' replied a beaming Hafiz. He reached up and brushed his hand against Ryan's two weeks' beard growth.

'Are you back for good?' asked Dalin.

'I'm not going to be going anywhere for a while.'

'Not for want of this leg: it's been put back together pretty well,' said the doctor, examining the large scar. She seemed to be both fascinated and surprised. 'It's expensive stuff they used, a proper high-grade flesh binder. They did what they did for the video, then patched you right up. Your face, too. It's not great, but they used proper contracting masks on you.'

'Still hurt at the time.'

Babirye looked down at the ugly gash on his leg, and covered her mouth in horror. 'It's fine, Babs, it's not as bad as it looks,' said Ryan, though the look of concern on her face did not diminish. 'Did you have to come from work?'

'I've been on leave since you were taken, you idiot,' said Babirye, sitting on the edge of his hospital bed. 'I tried to keep busy, but they sent me home. Everyone in New Cairo's been holding their breath for you.'

The boys climbed up onto the bed. Dalin crawled right into the doctor's line of sight and over onto Ryan's lap, hugging his father tightly. Hafiz stayed distant, less sure of what to do. Ryan realized it must have been a terrifying two weeks for those on the outside. He reached out to his son, and slowly Hafiz allowed himself to be drawn into his father's embrace with his brother. Ryan hoped desperately that they hadn't seen the tape of him being mutilated on the news. Eyes squeezed shut as he clutched his sons to his chest, he didn't notice the Secret Service agents gathering outside.

'So what is your father really like?'

Ryan looked up at Hoshi, unsure how to reply. 'Why do you ask?'

'I worked in the accounts department of FanaSoCo for fourteen years, then I came here as part of a movement to fight against him. You get a very skewed impression of a person when he's the adversary of every group in which you've worked for the better part of a decade and a half.'

'He's . . .' Ryan stammered, unsure as to why on earth he would want to have this conversation but complying none the less, 'he's very much like how he comes across, I think. I mean, when I hear people talking about him, it sounds a lot like how I used to think of him.' Ryan chose his words carefully. His father was distant, yes, but distance was different from negligence, a difference which felt important to him. 'There wasn't really a "High Councillor Granier" and a "Daddy". I think that when you're in a position like his, which requires such a specific, formidable type of person to do it, there isn't really space in there for another kind of mindset.'

Hoshi nodded. 'That . . . definitely makes sense. I mean, his home life has been in the papers for years. Yours too. He never seemed to let up on the High Councillor persona. Detached, disinterested, that kind of thing.'

Ryan thought back to weeks before, when his father had tried to explain to him why he wanted to stop people leaving the city. He had spent hours talking economics, voter strategy, demographics, slowly exhausting every logical reason Ryan put forward for voting against it; not one had swayed him. As the debate went on into the early hours, his father had looked him in the eye and told Ryan that he would not be the person to allow the plague they faced in New Cairo to be unleashed upon the rest of the world. Whatever the price the people of the city paid, it would be worth *the time it bought the surrounding cities and settlements, the rest of the continent and other continents beyond. It was an unholy burden, and High Councillor Tau Granier would not ask anyone else to shoulder it while he was still able to.*

Ryan's eyes clouded. 'Those aren't the words I'd use.'

For the first time in Ryan's life, he didn't realize that his father had entered the room. It was the sound of his bodyguards escorting him which attracted Ryan's attention and when he looked up his gaze fell upon a hunched, weary man. He walked slowly over to the side of the hospital bed, standing next to Babirye.

'You're safe,' he stated.

Ryan stared at his father.

An awkward moment of silence passed between the two of them.

'Do you know when you'll be able to resume work?' his father said, with a veneer of affected peppiness that didn't suit him. 'We need to get the votes taken on some of these bills.'

Babirye leapt to her feet and glared at Tau Granier. 'Tau, they tortured him! He will be back at work when he is good and ready!'

'There is . . . we have important things that need to be done!' the older man stammered, suddenly on the back foot.

'Oh please,' huffed Babirye. 'You know he's going to lose the quarantine vote, just do it without him and let him recover!'

'No, I need to be there for that,' said Ryan, trying to pull Babirye back, but she ignored him and continued to round on Tau. Behind him, the bodyguards seemed unsure of what to do.

'Only you – only you! – the *king* of New Cairo – would walk into your own son's hospital room, stand by his bed as he recovers from imprisonment and torture and make it about you!'

Never before had Ryan seen his father shrink back. He met his gaze for a moment. His father's expression made him seem lost and, for the first time that Ryan could remember, strangely powerless. Tau Granier turned and wordlessly left the room, his entourage close behind him. Ryan watched as he disappeared down the hospital corridor and out of sight. He wanted to say something, but the exchange had left him speechless. Babirye fumed next to him; Hafiz and Dalin clung tightly to his chest, both alarmed at their mother's outburst.

'So who was it who fixed you up?'

The doctor was leaning back over his scarred leg, admiring the work. Ryan realized his fists were clenched. 'Their medic. The others left me as I was. She patched me up. She helped me a lot.'

The doctor smiled. 'I guess even terrorist cells can't keep a consistent level of evil across the board.'

After a while, Suman and Hoshi went to resume their duties and Ryan was left to sit in the main room of the base, alone with his thoughts once more. In the time since he had been kidnapped, the possible creator, or at least the possible distributor of the Soucouyant virus had come to light. The virus had appeared so suddenly; perhaps there was a way to make it go away again. Ruined limbs and organs come back to life. An end to the fear and anger in Naj-Pur. It would be hard to let this Zala woman avoid being executed if she was guilty, but perhaps they could coax a way to stop or reverse the virus out of her, or at least a way to protect against it if they were able to appeal to her better nature.

Lost in his thoughts, he didn't notice Ava until she was standing over him, prodding his arm. 'I unlocked the front door. We need to go into the other room, now.'

He spun round in his seat and looked up at her. She nodded. Ryan pushed himself up from the chair, compensating for the still weak muscles in his left leg, and placed his crutches under his arms. Hobbling into the side room where he'd first awoken, he sat down in a chair across from the open door, looked out into the main floor space of what was once a bank, and waited.

For several minutes, there was nothing. Ryan leaned over towards the blacked-out window, and thought he saw shadows moving outside. He felt a curious nervousness, almost like stage fright.

Through the doorway, he saw the front door of the building open slightly.
Showtime.

'So what happened to get you back here so quickly?'

Dr Albrecktsson sat patiently behind her desk. He was back in the medical office; until he was assigned a proper psychiatrist, he had her number. Her stare still made Ryan uncomfortable. He'd delivered public addresses to crowds of thousands. This was different. He was vulnerable here. He could be hurt.

'I lost my temper at a doctor who was examining my leg at the hospital yesterday. I practically screamed the hospital down.'

The doctor leaned forward. 'I'd have thought that you'd be good at containing your emotions, considering your professional life.'

'I've had to contain my emotions at gunpoint for two weeks. I guess I unloaded some of that.'

'Tell me about it.'

'She . . .' Ryan licked his lips. 'She was mocking the medic they had at the safe house, the one who patched me up and helped me escape.'

'Okay,' she nodded encouragingly. 'Was there anything else that might have contributed towards the outburst?'

'There was a . . . a pretty tense situation between my wife and my father just before. Could that have been it?'

'Increased agitation is a symptom of your PTSD, Councillor.'

'I know, I know. But it's more than that. I . . . you've seen the news reports of what happened in that safe house, right?'

'I've not seen the news, but I got the report from the investigative unit about an hour ago. It was worse than it needed to be.'

'It went wrong and I caused it. It's my fault.'

'Oh?' said Dr Albrecktsson. 'It wasn't their fault, for kidnapping you, or allying with a dangerous cause? It wasn't the Security Force personnel's fault for not pursuing non-violent options?'

Ryan shook his head. 'It was my fault because I get it. I get the

NCLC's point. I feel like their cause was right and I feel like I punished them for doing what they believed in.'

'You think that they were right to kidnap you?'

'It did a whole lot more to keep them alive than my meaningless Council vote will.' Ryan leaned forward on the desk, staring down at the floor as he spoke. 'And now, people who were scared of being imprisoned and torn from their families have watched as their worst fears became real.'

'*You* were imprisoned and torn away from your family,' she replied tersely. 'Look, come with me.'

Ryan followed her out of the office and down the hallway of the New Cairo Police Department. They walked into a large, nondescript room with one wall taken up by a monitor. On it were two groups of pictures: a large one higher up, with dozens of smiling headshots, each in dress uniform, and a smaller one below, made up of faces including Maalik, Kahleed Banks, the Yu twins, and a number of others who had been with Alice Amirmoez's group. Ryan noticed that Alice herself was not on there, but said nothing.

'You'll recognize the group on the bottom. They were your hosts for the last fortnight. The people above are the police and Security Force personnel they've killed. Some would say that the NCLC are murderers, not heroes. They crossed a line, and as a result, yes, they'll be imprisoned, and yes, some of them may be killed. They became a paramilitary organization, a terrorist organization. That's why they're locked up right now. It's not because of their cause, it's because they picked up guns and shot at public servants. Do they really deserve your sympathy, or are they just as much a problem as the Soucouyant?'

'Those aren't the only two options—' said Ryan, before falling into uncertain silence. He wanted to believe her. When she talked, it was as if the dark little voice in the back of his head, the one he tried so hard not to indulge, was saying the same thing. 'What's happening to the children?'

Dr Albrecktsson shrugged. 'We'll look for non-combatant relatives willing to take them in. If that doesn't work, we'll start looking at foster homes.'

'Okay,' said Ryan, motioning for the holographic keyboard to move towards him and typing out the names of Vik, Ria and Zeno onto the doctor's terminal. 'If you don't find anyone for these children, I can look after them at least until their parents' trials. I've got the space and the money.'

Dr Albrecktsson seemed taken aback by this. 'Erm . . . Fine, once we've finished here. But first there's all manner of forms to sign off on and we can really only do that once we've figured out the best treatment plan for you.'

A lone shape slunk into the main room adjoining the office where Ryan and Ava were hiding, and disappeared behind a desk, hidden from his view. Slowly, it re-emerged, moving around the perimeter, and was followed by a second and third skulking figure. Security Force special operations troops. They spotted Ryan immediately through the open doorway and signalled for him to stay where he was and not make a sound. Ava remained hidden from their view, standing further back, out of the doorway.

All three now trained their guns on the door which led down the corridor to the rest of the building. The point man stepped silently over to the door and swung it open. Almost immediately, he moved back to crouch behind an old desk. Seconds later, a wheezing Suman hurled his full mass into the room, desperately scrambling for the door.

The Security Force troops revealed themselves from behind their cover and aimed at him. 'Police! Get down on the ground now!' yelled the point man.

Suman's eyes widened in wild, gibbering fear. For a moment he didn't move, instead coughing and sucking in air. With a scream, he sprinted for the door, disappearing from view. Gunshots rang out, tearing through the air with punishing amplitude. Ryan flinched and clapped his hands over his ears. He wanted to yell for them to stop but the noise felt like it was tearing through his eardrums.

The rescue team were ignoring Ryan's clear orders that no one be harmed.

Ava grabbed Ryan's arm and pulled him over to a chair further into the room, out of sight of the Security Force troops. 'What are you doing?' he hissed. Then he saw her face. In the two weeks he'd known her, he had never seen Ava scared. At that moment, she was terrified.

'You know, I have read all the case files,' said Dr Albrecktsson, pacing the length of the office. 'It's okay if you want to talk about what happened.'

Ryan felt trapped.

'I don't,' came his immediate reply. Attempting to soften his bluntness, he elaborated. 'It was just yesterday, doctor. I'm still processing it.'

'Did you think people wouldn't get hurt? Kidnap is a dangerous business.'

'I specifically told them not to hurt anybody. I deliberately tried to make sure that the right people would hear, that they'd understand.' Ryan's head sank. 'It was my responsibility, to make sure no one got hurt. I promised my . . . accomplice . . . I'd do that.'

'You mean Ava Ferreira?' said Dr Albrecktsson, opening up her dossier, and rotated the holographic monitor so that Ryan could see. Ava's weary scowl was apparently not a new feature, adorning a picture from a two-year-old medical licence. Forty-eight. Married twice, divorced twice. No children. An address in one of the safer areas of Surja. A bulletin for her to be arrested on charges of terrorism, which had been recently cancelled. *'Mistaken for enemy combatant, killed in action'*. Ryan felt sick.

She had been weary.

Footsteps clattered on the other side of the wall, and one of the Security Force troops barrelled into the room. From behind the dark visor, he spotted Ryan. He spotted Ava behind him. In a split second, the man's gun was raised.

*

She had wanted all this to stop.

'Wait!' yelled Ryan, reaching a hand out towards the man.

She had wanted to be away from the violence.

A crack of gunfire, even more deafening than the last.

'It was my responsibility to make sure she was safe.'

Ryan felt something hot and wet spatter against his neck and back.

Ryan's head sank. 'It was my responsibility, and I failed her.'

The Security Force trooper called out, 'Are you okay, Councillor?' Ryan tried to respond, or scream, tried to let loose the words clawing at the inside of his throat, but none came out. He sat there, staring forward, shocked, the gunshot echoing in his ears, lingering on the edge of his senses. This wasn't how it was supposed to be.

Dr Albrecktsson reached across the desk and grasped his hand. It didn't help in the slightest.

Chapter 22

It took more than twenty-four hours for ANANSI to reply to Zala. Why was never elaborated upon, but Zala never doubted for a second that the wait was exactly as long as ANANSI wanted it to be. If it was Suman, it was smart of him to hold off. Whether it was logical or not, ANANSI suddenly becoming talkative from the moment Zala approached Suman for information would have felt suspicious.

When the message finally came, it was two words.

From: ANANSI (EIP: ----.-.------.-------.---.-----.----.------)

>I'm listening.

Zala smiled. Surrounding the message window on the holographic monitor were a day's worth of notes, all arriving at a simple opening message.

>I give in, she said.

The response came quickly.

From: ANANSI (EIP: ----.-.------.-------.---.-----.----.------)

>Wise move. It's a shame you didn't make it sooner.

>Please tell me there's nothing more coming. I'm on my last legs here.

From: ANANSI (EIP: ----.-.------.-------.---.-----.----.------)

>If you're not creating a problem, there's no need to create any problems for you.

>So, ANANSI, one professional to another: why have you been doing all this? What's in it for you?

The response didn't come. Zala waited for a while. Eyes trained on the space on her monitor where the cheery 'New Message!' pop-up would appear, she stood up without looking. Her heel stomped on a wayward drink container, which rolled under her weight, sending her stumbling forwards. Her right arm reached out with an uncanny speed, grabbed the handle of a wardrobe and steadied the rest of her. She looked at it, at the unfamiliar muscular bulges and white-firm grip, feeling not at home in a way the unfamiliar apartment was not responsible for. A shudder ran up her spine.

New Message!

Zala shook the unease – which had begun to coalesce into the familiar nightmare image of the portable terminal burrowing under her skin – from her mind and looked down at the terminal window.

From: ANANSI (EIP: ----.-.------.-------.---.-----.----.------)

>Are you familiar with the concept of emergence?

Zala decided to play dumb.

>I'm guessing it has something to do with something coming out of something else.

Aberrantly quickly – even exceeding speeds possible with a high-end bio-aug – the reply came.

From: ANANSI (EIP: ----.-.------.-------.---.-----.----.------)

>Emergence is the idea that complex systems are created from the interaction of small, simple constituent parts. By coordinating and feeding back information between each other, large numbers of small actors following simple local rules can create a complexity which no one of those actors could reproduce, even with all the time and resources in the world. An ant could never create a colony on its own – it interacts with the chemical trails of other ants, in turn creating its own chemical trail to be followed. A single neuron could not spew forth the Iliad or the Vedas. Economies emerge from the interaction of financial institutions and individual consumers, their behaviour altering the behaviour

of all the other entities. Cultures bloom from the swarming mass of individual ideas, none of which has the capacity to create that same culture without those interactions. Even much of human behaviour emerges from the effect of outside stimulation on two interacting impulses: the drive to succeed, at the expense of others if necessary, and the drive to live in a community where people do not simply try to succeed at the expense of others. It is the process of something being more than the sum of its parts and it is at the core of all life, of all mass interactions.

Zala struggled to keep up with the pace of the text flooding the screen in front of her.

>Right now, I have a great deal of stake in the unfolding events of this city. I have assembled the single greatest information network in human history. I know the agents, I know their patterns of behaviour, and I know the interactions which will lead the situation to evolve. Where others see a sprawl of chaos, I see a massive body politic growing and maturing. I know where I want it to go, and I know how to make it go there.

And then you entered the city, unaccounted for, a mystery for the last eight years. What I do relies on me knowing where every-thing was, and where it is, so that I can ascertain where it's going. And you ruin that.

Zala paused a moment to take all that in, then typed:

>So what, you just don't want me messing up a sequence of events you've got lined up to go your way?

From: ANANSI (EIP: ----.-.------.-------.---.-----.----.------)

>Glad you understand.

>All right then, Zala responded, but what am I meant to do in the meantime? I'll be fucking torn apart out there before the cops can even get to me. The NCLC are after my head, as are the police and SecForce, and the people in this city think I developed the virus that's tearing it apart.

From: ANANSI (EIP: ----.-.------.-------.---.-----.----.------)

>Your fate doesn't matter to me in the slightest.

Zala gaped at the screen. She typed as quickly as her hand would allow.

>So you're telling me that despite my already having hit rock bottom here, your only threat is things getting worse? Bad move, kid. Right now, you've pretty much done your worst. My best friend is in prison for giving me a couch to sleep on. My face is plastered in the ad-space of half the network as a killer and terrorist. I've not got a whole lot more to lose and that makes it my turn. Unless you can come up with a better motivator, you've made yourself a bitch of an enemy. You know I'm a threat and you've played your hand.

There was a pause.

From: ANANSI (EIP: ----.-.------.-------.---.-----.----.------)

>Ask yourself: with all that, what can I do to make it better again? You returned to a city where you were wanted for murder, you hacked and trespassed and assaulted. And then you got caught, because sometimes that happens. So what? What am I supposed to do now?

>Can you get me out of this city? she replied.

For ten minutes, Zala waited for a response, her head buzzing with different scenarios. She thought about skipping off into the desert from whence she came while Polina rotted in prison, and felt ashamed, but the reality was that either Polina was in prison or they both were. Barring a minor courtroom miracle, Polina would be imprisoned for sheltering someone the vast majority of New Cairo thought had something to do with the creation of the Soucouyant virus. With any luck, Zala's name now carried such weight that finding an impartial jury would be ruled impossible and Polina would be freed. The slightly more realistic expectation was that the government would find a way round having to hold a trial at all.

As Zala stewed in her own regrets, her terminal beeped. She opened it up and read the message.

From: ANANSI (EIP: ----.-.------.-------.---.-----.----.------)

>There is a way to make this happen. A smuggling operation intended for a family involved with the NCLC. They opted out of it. You may be in luck.

>That is the payment you will accept for the cessation of your interference?

231

Zala grinned. So ANANSI just happens to have connections with the infrastructure that the NCLC uses? Suman was either taking refuge in audacity or very bad at avoiding suspicion.

>If you can get me out of here, you'll never even have to think of me again. I'll cease to exist for all you'll care. You're better connected here than I am, and I'm a thorn that doesn't need to be in your side. Just make what arrangements you can.

ANANSI didn't respond, leaving Zala sitting staring at the monitor. Looking down at her arms, she became aware that she was shaking vigorously. Her heart felt as though it was trying to burst through her chest. There was a way out, an escape.

After several minutes of silence, Zala's portable terminal flashed up a new message.

From: ANANSI (EIP: ----.-.------.-------.---.-----.----.-------)

>Kafut Processing Facility. It's being held up, but this is your last chance. Be quick.

If she hadn't barely had any sleep since leaving the hospital, and if doing so wouldn't have sent her scarf slipping dangerously low off her face, Zala would have sprinted. The Kafut Processing Facility was near by. The facility petrified exports and unpetrified imports of any goods which had to go through desert transport. It was a huge building that had expanded even more since Zala had last lived in New Cairo, but according to newscasts Zala had been following it was now almost completely inactive. Even though the mechanisms that brought supplies down from the surface were unmanned and there was no chance of transmission of the virus to the outside, it appeared that businesses weren't producing anything or ordering supplies. The rumours were that business owners didn't believe New Cairo would last long enough for them to sell their wares.

As Zala neared it, her portable terminal beeped. A message popped up in the corner of her contact lens.

From: ANANSI (EIP: ----.-.------.-------.---.-----.----.-------)

>Go in through the side entrance. I've just given your terminal the authorization codes. Once you're in there, look for this man.

An image popped up: an identification photo of a balding,

pale man with an oddly bulging face.

From: ANANSI (EIP: ----.-.------.-------.---.-----.----.------)

>Tell him 'We need to get a move on, the others aren't coming.' He will know what to do. You will be put inside one of the containers that take the petrified goods up to the surface, and you will go up in the tube. There will be someone at the top to get you out of the container. You will be near Waytower Sixteen, and you will be given some climate gear. From there, just walk away. Never come back here again.

Zala grinned. She had a way out. Staying in the city would bring only arrest, maybe even execution if she got convicted for coding the Soucouyant virus. Instead, she had a chance to slip away. It would be as if she had never been there.

She would avoid imprisonment, unlike Polina.

Zala shook the doubt from her head and walked up to the side door of the processing plant.

She would avoid abuse and torture, unlike Councillor Granier.

The door hissed open and she walked inside.

She would avoid having to watch the city fall apart, unlike all the people who didn't have permission to leave or the means by which to do so. Unlike people she cared about. She'd get to avoid the consequences of her actions. Those were other people's problems now.

She stood in a brightly lit hallway with frosted glass doors on either side leading to, she presumed, offices. Only a few had their lights on, and inside she could see solitary figures hunched over terminals. Zala wondered if she should start knocking on doors. She needed to be out of here before anyone recognized her from the news.

If someone knew who she was, she'd end up in prison.

Like Polina.

I can't leave.

The thought seemed so obvious once it took full form. Zala had made herself want to leave, want to escape. It was the objective she had given herself. It had never occurred to her to ask – was it what she really wanted to do?

The more she thought about it, the more she realized the answer was no.

Having made that decision, she didn't know what the next step was – turn herself in and try to get herself and Polina acquitted of as much as possible? Offer to trade information to the Security Force? But she had harmed or brought harm to a lot of people, more than she had ever done before. People she cared about, and complete strangers. It was her fault, and she had to make up for what she had done. She couldn't abandon them.

Zala turned to leave the processing plant the same way she'd come. ANANSI would have to put up with her being in the city for a little while longer now. She had—

Something was wrong. Something in the back of her mind, raising the hairs on her neck. Zala glanced around, looking for the source of her discomfort or for an escape route. There didn't seem to be any exits except for the one she had entered through. She paced back down the hallway and through the door.

On the other side were two Security Force vans, behind which stood ten Security Force agents, all pointing rifles at Zala.

'Freeze!' yelled the one nearest to her, behind the van to her left.

Zala stood completely still.

'Drop your portable terminal, kick it towards us, and then get down on the ground with your hands behind your head!' the agent nearest to her yelled again.

She released the straps holding her terminal to her wrist and kicked it away from her, and then she crouched down on the pavement. Behind her, she could hear workers from the processing plant emerging to see what was happening. As one of the agents picked up her terminal, Zala saw a message appear on her contact lenses.

From: ANANSI (EIP: ----.-.------.-------.---.-----.----.------)
>Never think that there is nothing more I can do to hurt you, Zala Ulora.

Chapter 23

Pleading, drowned out by gunfire.

The next thing Ryan knew, he was awake in his own bed, at home. The room was bright, and Babirye was leaning over him. She looked scared.

'Oh thank god, you're awake! Are you okay? Is your leg hurting?'

Ryan took a while to process her words through the haze of fading sleep, then shook his head and sat up, swinging his legs over the edge of the bed. 'It was just a nightmare. I'm fine. Look.' Pushing up with his arms, he managed to stand upright for the first time in days. His injured leg strained, the scarred muscle mass working to support his weight, but finally held. He turned to face her. 'Ta-da.'

'Don't give me that. You were groaning and thrashing about in your sleep, you sounded like you were going to start screaming at any moment.'

'Yes, I was having a nightmare,' said Ryan. 'I've come out the other side of a traumatic experience, and I've got a lot left to work through. But I'm fine. I'm awake, it's all gone away.' He climbed back into bed.

'Is it all going to come back when you go back to sleep?' Babirye asked. Ryan looked uncomfortable.

'I don't know, maybe.' He looked over at her. 'The doctors say there's a pretty good chance I'm going to be having a lot of nightmares for a while. If you'd prefer, I can go sleep in the other room. I don't want to keep you awake or anything.'

Babirye wrapped her arms around Ryan and pulled him towards her. 'No, don't go. Just let me know if your leg starts hurting.'

Ryan held his wife tight. He hoped that it would be enough to keep the nightmares at bay. In the back of his mind, he knew that it wouldn't.

Of all the things that followed him out of that building in Naj-Pur, the one which Ryan found to be the most insidious was the boredom. His psychological state precluded him from going outside unless absolutely necessary, which confined him to his house. During the day, his family were gone: the children were in school and his wife was checking what legal avenues were available to them against his captors. He lay in bed, unable to decide what to do.

After hours of inactivity, he mustered the resolve to get up and shower. He didn't regret it; the gentle massage of the jets of hot water soothed his aching leg muscles and the feeling of the grease and grime and dried blood lifting from his skin made it worth it. By the time he got out, his skin had begun to shrivel.

He wrapped a towel around his waist and walked over to the basin. Above it, the mirror showed him a strange sight. All he'd seen of himself for two weeks was his reflection where the paint over the blacked-out windows of the NCLC base had chipped away, leaving small slivers of clear glass. He'd assumed he'd return to the public eye looking like a wild man. Instead, he simply had the scraggly beginnings of a beard and a few contusions, as well as slightly longer hair than he usually wore. It was almost a shame, he thought. A real physical change, removing a full beard and watching a swollen face heal, that could have helped him distance his life from his period of containment. As it was, he shaved and made a mental note to call in a barber.

Ryan dried and dressed himself and, with nothing else immediately pressing him, logged into his personal terminal and opened up a newscast. Headlines loomed up at him, stark and foreboding.

COUNCILLOR GRANIER RESCUED

ELEVATORS SHUT DOWN BY EXECUTIVE ORDER

ESCAPED KILLER RETURNS TO CITY

17 KILLED IN REBEL MASSACRE

He made his way through each story, coverage both of his own ordeal and of events beyond the walls of the abandoned bank. The further in he got, the more he felt a sense of despair. The financial news struck a blow that was somehow even more personal.

GENISEC SHARES LIFT AFTER RECORD PLUMMET

IS IT TOO LATE TO SAVE THE GRANIER DYNASTY?

BANACH-TARSKI CAPITALIZE ON GENISEC WEAKNESSES

IMPORT AND EXPORT RATES HIT NEW LOW

It appeared that, in the short time he had been held, shares in GeniSec had become next to worthless, even by the standards of conglomerates based in cities that were apparently crashing and burning. Banach-Tarski, on the other hand, had benefited from excellent timing and their share value had shot through the roof.

Ryan delved into the financial news, hoping to learn more about the Banach-Tarski Corporation's sudden rise to dominance. The day after Ryan's kidnapping, with no apparent lead-up, they had launched a large number of new software products. There were complaints and fears of redundancy from software developers working at Banach-Tarski's software divisions, most of which seemed to state that these products – mostly encryption methods and security protocols for finance transfers – had come out of nowhere and they had no idea who had coded them. Despite Banach-Tarski's developers fearing for their jobs, they almost doubled their share price within hours. At the same time, amid fears of instability on the part of GeniSec's figurehead, Tau Granier, shareholders had flooded the stock exchange with GeniSec shares and by the time their stock had been withdrawn its value had plummeted.

The more Ryan read, the stranger it seemed. The general consensus was that the software had been bought from an independent developer Banach-Tarski had hired and they simply cynically used the opportunity afforded by Ryan's kidnapping to make what was, admittedly, a sharp business decision. Yet there were no names available and no reporter had been able to identify whatever coding genius had created new industry-standard security protocols, apparently on their own.

Software turning up out of nowhere seemed to be happening a lot these days.

Ryan logged into the Council intranet and opened up the police files on the recent rebel arrests. Eventually he found a series of inventories, revealing what had been taken from captured members of the NCLC. There were, with exceptions that were probably regular civilian purchases, seven companies whose products showed up in bulk on the inventories. All their products were military-grade, unavailable to the public, yet the NCLC, it seemed, had had their orders supplied in full. Ryan traced the companies back. They were all owned by the same three corporations. Two belonged to FanaSoCo. Three were fully owned by New Delhi Lifestyle Technologies. Two were controlled by GeniSec. The conspicuous absence was of Banach-Tarski.

It felt strange to be driving through the Alexandria district again. The openness was oddly oppressive and the almost monochromatic black and white skin colours of the people on the streets seemed especially artificial after the myriad shades of brown of Ryan's former captors. Ryan knew he should have waited for a security detail but he didn't need more people knowing what he was up to than was absolutely necessary. He threw on a hat, a visor and some baggy clothes and tried as hard as possible to look, if not nondescript, then as unlike Councillor Ryan Granier as he could. Inside his car, at least, he felt he could get away without attracting attention.

Reaching Downtown quickly, he pulled up outside the New Cairo Council Rehabilitation Facility. It sat in such a way as to form a triangle with the New Cairo Democratic Council building and the GeniSec Tower. It seemed from the outside to be a relatively small concrete skyscraper, in a city of much more impressive specimens. This view was deceptive; most of it lay underground, and in terms of actual floor space it dwarfed any other building in the city.

Ryan parked near the back entrance and entered using his Council certification. Inside, a large police officer sat at a desk, busy on his terminal.

'Hello there, I'm Councillor Granier. I'd like to visit one of the prisoners.'

The police officer raised his eyebrows at the sight of the scruffy, scarred man in front of him and reached for a biometric scanner with one hand. 'I'm going to need to give you a proper scan before I let a supposedly bedridden man in to see a prisoner, *Councillor*.'

Ryan nodded and the police officer ran the scanner across his face. He then stood back and ran the beam of the scanner down the full length of Ryan's body. His eyes widened as the scan rang out a positive result.

'I'm so sorry, Councillor, I didn't recognize you! I'll let you through, sir!' he blustered, skin reddening.

The officer stood up from his desk and punched a code into a holographic keypad. The projected keys beeped with contact and the wall next to it slid aside, revealing a thick, armoured door. The door swung open on a long corridor lined with security cameras, and beyond that, a second armoured door.

Ryan entered the corridor, and the first door closed behind him. The second opened soon after, and he walked through. Once that door had clamped shut the prison itself opened up to him. The hallway inside was white and blue, and brightly lit, an oddly antiseptic environment. Near the entrance, before the cell doors began to line the walls, was a terminal used only to locate specific prisoners. Ryan logged in and typed in a name.

Hoshi Smolak.

The terminal spat out the cell number, along with the man's

details. He had been processed yesterday and placed in Cell 73HJ. Ryan's personal terminal marked this down on his internal map, and his corneal implants led him down several flights of stairs and through a complicated network of corridors. The disorienting layout, combined with the blindingly sterile aesthetic and almost complete silence of the jail's public areas, soon began to wear him down. He was reminded of a gleeful voice talking about a 'white room'.

The almost imperceptibly faint smell of burnt meat wafted around Ryan, but he pushed it out of his mind and focused on the task at hand.

Eventually, he found the cell. The door itself was an opaque black, giving no view of the person inside. It functioned as a monitor, able to relay information to people both outside and in. If needed, it could become transparent. Ryan turned on the monitor and set it to clear. The black membrane faded, revealing a small cell. One side was taken up by a single bed, the other by a toilet, a small sink, and a desk with various old paper books stacked on top. Sitting at the desk, with one of the books open on his lap, was Hoshi. On his side, the glass door must have still been opaque, leaving him unaware of his visitor. This seemed like an appropriate moment, so Ryan cleared the black screen on Hoshi's side and knocked twice on the door.

Hoshi turned in his seat with a start. 'Oh! Councillor!' he said, eyes wide. 'What're you doing here?'

'I need to ask you something.'

The accountant shifted back in his seat. 'Oh . . . I don't know, I'm not sure I can talk to anyone yet.'

Ryan leaned in towards the cell, making sure Hoshi could see his bruised face. 'Hoshi, it's about Banach-Tarski.'

Hoshi Smolak almost fell out of his seat. 'How did you know about Banach-Tarski?'

'I didn't until just now.'

Hoshi was trembling now, drawing breath in heavy, wavering gasps as he realized he'd been tricked. Ryan leaned in further, almost pressed up against the cell door. 'Hoshi, I can help you. I just need to know in what capacity Banach-Tarski got involved with the NCLC and why.'

'I can't! It implicates me too much! I become complicit in murder of police, everything goes to shit, I could spend the rest of my life in prison! I could be executed!'

'Hoshi!' yelled Ryan, shocking the accountant out of his frenzy. 'There are systems in place for helping people like you, people who help put things right. We're talking about a conspiracy to arm a rebel group in order to destabilize a government. That's a bargaining chip that can keep you out of prison.'

The little man looked up at him. 'I won't have to go to prison?'

Ryan nodded. 'You won't if you can help them prove massive corporate wrongdoing. This is your way out.'

Hoshi slumped forward, seeming to relax a little. 'Back when we were the New Cairo Labour Commission, and we were running the first few protests, they offered to help fund us, from behind the scenes. They told us they thought the government intrusion represented a dangerous precedent regarding businesses. We knew it was them trying to get one over on your old man's company but we needed money and so we accepted their support.'

Hoshi became more and more involved in his story, losing his scared demeanour and gesticulating wildly for emphasis. 'Then when things got more and more violent, they didn't stop. They gave us guns. They bought us body armour. Medical supplies. Brought it all right in as surplus with weapons purchases for the police and SecForce. If *they* hadn't been arming themselves in case they needed to attack us, we wouldn't even have guns in the first place. My job was to send supply requirements and then retrieve the money through a number of constantly shifting shell groups and untraceable accounts. It was the most complicated work I've ever had to do.'

Ryan felt his jaw drop. He had been right. His hunch, although biased against the corporation whose status had overtaken GeniSec's, had somehow paid off.

'Councillor?'

Ryan looked back over at Hoshi. 'Yes?'

'I got arrested the moment the Security Forces came through the window, and in the back of the van I didn't see Suman or Ava anywhere. Do you know what happened to them?'

Ryan stared at Hoshi. The man was already tense, as though he knew what the answer would be, but just needed to have it confirmed.

'Suman tried to run and they opened fire on him. He didn't make it, to the best of my knowledge. Ava was with me. I tried to protect her, but—'

'But what?' asked Hoshi, his voice a whisper.

'They must have assumed she was using me as a human shield. They shot her too.'

Hoshi slumped down in his seat, distraught. 'Why would they do that? Why would they shoot a nurse and an IT manager?'

This was the question Ryan had spent the entire previous day asking himself. He hesitated, not sure if he had the answer.

'I guess to some trigger-happy SecForce officer they looked like threats and I look like their bosses.'

Hoshi gazed up at him, ashen-faced. Ryan felt consumed with guilt. 'So what now, Councillor?'

Ryan stood back from the door. 'You could testify about the Banach-Tarski involvement when this whole NCLC mess finally makes it to court. If you could prove it convincingly, I could get you immunity from prosecution. You could be reclassified as a whistle-blower, sent to some other city. You can get out of here.' He paused and made a swift survey of the accountant's cell. 'To be honest, Hoshi, I don't see you flourishing in this sort of environment.'

Hoshi too looked around his room and shuddered.

'What's more,' said Ryan, 'Banach-Tarski have been profiteering from the escalation of violence that got Ava and Suman killed. You think if they hadn't armed you guys, there would have been any need to shoot Ava or Suman? Banach-Tarski have played a role in enabling civil war in this city.'

Hoshi looked scared, but nodded. 'I can do that. I can be a witness.'

Ryan smiled. 'Good choice,' he said. 'One last thing, though. The new software that Banach-Tarski launched. Do you know where that came from?'

Hoshi looked confused for a moment, then nodded. 'I . . . I remember they had a number of programs they wanted Suman to take a look at and verify. I thought it was weird at the time, that they wouldn't have internal people on this. The coder was some outsider, apparently. The code was so well done, Suman kept trying to track them down, learn from them. It was someone called . . . it was something like Antsy. Named after some old African spider god.'

Ryan transcribed his words on his portable terminal, then looked back up at Hoshi. 'I'll talk to the Police Commissioner, let them know you're willing to testify. We will get you out of here.'

'Please do it soon!' the accountant pleaded as Ryan switched off the monitor and the inky black membrane made its way back over the door.

Ryan turned to go back the way he'd come, to find two police officers standing behind him.

'Can I help you?'

One of them, a short-haired woman, stepped forward. 'We were told to assist you with your business today.'

Ryan shrugged. 'I'm all done, Officer . . . ?'

'Officer Jalila Karimi, Councillor.'

'Officer Karimi. Did you hear what I was discussing with that prisoner?' Officer Karimi nodded. 'Excellent, then can you give him a proper interview and see what you can do for him as an informant?'

'Yes, Councillor!'

Ryan continued on his way back out. So they had sent police officers to watch him. Did they think he was going to try to break Hoshi out of prison? Well, he supposed, it had been two weeks, long enough for Stockholm Syndrome to set in.

Suddenly, a deep, gleeful voice rang out from the terminal of Officer Karimi's scruffy-looking partner.

'We got her. Everyone, we can confirm that Zala Ulora has been taken into custody.'

The officer looked up and grinned. 'We did it!'

Whatever hesitance had taken hold of High Councillor Tau Granier the previous day was gone as he walked into the living room. Ryan was already seated on a large sofa, his leg propped up. As Tau Granier sat down on a chair opposite, he looked his son in the eyes unwaveringly, determined not to look down at the bandaged leg.

'Good news, High Councillor.'

'We're not in the Council building, Ryan. You can call me Dad.'

Ryan raised his eyebrows. It was the first time since he was a child that his father had objected to being called by his title. His enforced absence must have left quite an impression.

'All right, Dad it is. The police are currently investigating the Banach-Tarski Corporation under suspicion of funding the NCLC.'

Tau Granier's brow furrowed. 'You can't be serious . . . they were actually working together?'

'The NCLC's main money launderer is willing to testify, and give extensive and compelling evidence. He knows every dirty detail. Whether they'll be convicted is another question entirely, but that's something at least.'

Ryan had expected relief, but instead his father shook his head and scowled. 'Those *bastards*. The NCLC I can understand. They're scared and they feel powerless. They're just trying to pro- tect themselves. But profiteering from the breakdown of this city, from the deaths of police officers and civilians?'

'Apparently so.'

Tau Granier grimaced. The information relayed, Ryan tried to change the subject. 'Did you hear? They arrested that Zala Ulora woman.'

Tau Granier nodded. 'I did, yes. I heard an interesting new piece of information too.'

'What's that?'

Tau Granier smiled. 'Our anti-augmentation killer has bio-augs now.'

'If she is the one who wrote the Soucouyant virus, she must be kicking herself.'

Tau Granier's smile slipped a little. 'From what we can tell of the logs coming in and out of the city, the virus had taken hold long before she arrived here.'

Ryan took this in slowly. 'So she's not the source of it? Why haven't I heard this before now?'

'The people in this city need reassurance right now, more than anything,' said Tau Granier. 'They're scared and they're killing one another. If people believe we're close to a cure and that goes some way towards quelling the violence, it's worth it.'

Something clicked in Ryan's mind.

'Oh come on. People need to know that their lives are still at risk. You can't just lie to them all and hope they do what you want them to; it's only going to backfire. That kind of bullshit paternalism is half the reason the NCLC are fighting against us.'

'*I hated the Council. I hated the fact that people like me or my cousin, the most vulnerable kinds of people in this city, were considered necessary sacrifices, rather than people with a right to decide what to do for ourselves.*' That was what she said.

Tau Granier snorted. 'I've seen too many elections decided by fear and anger to be that optimistic, Ryan. When you're making tough decisions, you can't allow for everyone's point of view to be equally valid. If no one gets hurt, nothing gets done. We shut off those elevators for a reason: to limit the damage that the myopia and fear in this city can do. If we leave them to their own devices, people will carry the virus out with them. The rest of the world will go the same way we're going.'

'Look, at the very least, if you're going to allow people to think you've got the probable culprit, then book a press conference and announce that the curfew in the high-infection areas is being called off,' said Ryan, as calmly as he could. 'Throw them a bone and make it look like you did it because you've won a victory, not because they have.'

Tau Granier thought for a moment. 'There's merit in that, yes. It vindicates the curfew if we say it was about stopping Ulora moving around, it'll ease some of the tension. I'll talk to some people about it.'

Ryan let out a sigh of relief.

'Did you recognize her name?'

Ryan nodded. 'Her father was the lead on the IntuitivAI project, wasn't he?'

Tau Granier sat back in his seat, seeming more relaxed now. His large frame settled into the chair as he spoke. 'Kweku Ulora was the most gifted, intelligent man I ever met. An eccentric, sure, but once you saw how he worked you realized that he always had things the way he needed them to be.'

'What happened?'

'They found a hidden folder on his computer, with a single little piece of code in it. Whatever it was, it was in the same coding language that he invented for the IntuitivAI system. No one knew the whole of that system at the time but him, so we didn't know what it was.' The High Councillor stroked his greying beard, his eyes twinkling as he remembered. 'The main concern we had was that it was a simplified version of the larger program, which he intended to hide from us. He was a secretive man and we'd sunk hundreds of millions into this technology. Someone expressed a fear that he was using our resources to make the program, and then keeping a better version to sell to someone else without the development costs. From there, our concerns escalated. Then, he stopped coming into work. He hid somewhere in the city, but we didn't know where. So we tried to flush him out.'

Ryan scowled, confused. 'Where does his daughter come into this?'

'She came up as the solution,' Tau said. 'Around that time, three people were found dead in an abandoned house in Naj-Pur. They were undoubtedly gang deaths – Naj-Pur was getting better and the territory and clientele for the gangs was shrinking, which ended up making them more vicious. We had notes from a therapist telling us that Zala Ulora had a substantial fear of bio-augs and it just so happened that these three bodies were heavily augmented. So we reached out to the police and—'

'No. No way did you—' Ryan struggled for words. 'You framed an eighteen-year-old girl for murder?'

'It was a poor case, there was no way she would have been convicted, not if she'd been arrested. It was a way to scare Kweku out of running or hiding.'

Ryan felt an intense revulsion at the thought. He looked aghast at his father.

'Anyway, Kweku must have known we'd found out. They fled – we still don't know how they got out of the city – and we were left waiting for them to come back. Old Kweku ended up having a stroke in Addis Ababa and died. At some point Zala returned and it turns out that, if she wasn't before, in the intervening years she's become a thief and a high-level cybercriminal, so now she actually does need arresting. She's the one that broke into the Five Prongs, the one that trashed one of our development houses over in Falkur. She pointed the NCLC towards GeniSec as being the source of the Soucouyant.'

'Well, what do you expect?' Ryan's fists were clenched tight. 'She couldn't get a job or proper qualifications. You framed her for multiple murders over a piece of unidentified computer code!'

'Our actions were—' Tau began, but Ryan cut him off.

'That girl is in prison because of you. You ruined her life and drove her to desperation. Now you're going to imprison her and accuse her of mass murder?'

'It's just one girl!' yelled Tau Granier, almost on his feet. 'Of all the millions of people in this city, all the people who depended on us, who depend on us now, we deemed it necessary – yes, necessary! – to use this one girl. GeniSec poured *everything* into that project, everything we had! Everything we have came from it and that includes everything you have! You think you'd be sitting here, *Councillor*, in your mansion, enjoying the privilege you've been afforded if Kweku Ulora had sold our product to some other company, if our investment in his work had gained us nothing? GeniSec could have gone under entirely! You think you could have afforded to swan your way through life on the back of my reputation, going through an election campaign I paid for and taking your seat in the Council like it was yours all along, if I'd gone bankrupt? And the technology! The first technology that could genuinely be called artificial intelligence, and we made it. It powers surgical apparatus which has saved *millions* of lives, it runs entire cities! It sits in the canon of the most revolutionary technologies there have ever been! How could we risk that? Yes, for my family, for the families of everybody who works for our company and for everyone who has ever benefited from that program, I ruined things for one little girl. I had no idea it would go this far, but yes, I am responsible. But don't you dare talk to me as though you, and everyone else in this city, haven't reaped the benefits of those actions too.'

Ryan glared at his father, unable to speak. High Councillor Tau Granier stood up and left without another word.

Chapter 24

A lice felt cold as she lay inside a sleeping bag on the floor of an apartment in the building the NCLC had taken over. She felt cold and sick. Ria and Zeno's faces drifted across her mental vision, then faded. Serhiy's face, so full of guilt, followed after them.

You need to be strong, said a voice in her head. *It's the only way to get them back.*

The voice, oddly, was her mentor from her days in the Security Force, Corporal Seyton Vinter. She could remember when she'd heard him say it. After years as one of the operators, she had become the lead coordinator for her district's major operations. Her second mission was a personnel retrieval attempt – three Security Force officers had found themselves on the wrong side of one of the larger gangs in Naj-Pur and were pinned down inside a warehouse that was being used to manufacture the illegal narcotic Poly. Alice's career depended on her being able to handle missions like this but she had never felt less able to do so.

Her hands had shaken the keyboard. She knew her voice was trembling, but hadn't been able to make it stop. Around her, the others sent in their information feeds, all there to inform her tactics. The Security Force troops on the ground were waiting for her guidance. Reinforcements were on their way, for her to lead as well. It had all waited on her. She knew what to do. And yet Alice had felt paralysed.

A familiar voice said behind her, 'Officer Amirmoez, is something wrong?'

'I . . . I'm just preparing myself, sir.'

'You'd better be on good form, Officer. Those personnel down there, getting shot at, they're part of the family and they need to get home safe.'

'I understand, sir.'

His hand rested on her shoulder. 'They're trapped, and they're scared. They have children waiting for them to come back home, and they can't get there without you. You have the power, if you have the strength to use it. You need to be strong. It's the only way to get them back.'

Whenever she remembered those words, Ria and Zeno's faces became most vivid in her mind.

Out of the corner of her eye, she saw Kahleed enter the room. He strode straight over to where she lay. 'Something happened last night. You need to see this,' he said.

'What time is it?'

Kahleed looked at his terminal. 'Six a.m. Perfect time to start.'

Alice slid out of her sleeping bag, got groggily to her feet and followed Kahleed into the next room. A newscast was up on a large holographic monitor, depicting an old man with deep bags under his eyes and a listless air, standing at a podium. It took Alice a moment to realize that this old man was High Councillor Tau Granier. She wondered if he was sick.

Juri pressed Play. On the monitor, Tau Granier read out a prepared statement, his usual bombast entirely absent. 'As many of you know, this morning we arrested Zala Ulora. We believe her to be the criminal mastermind behind the Soucouyant virus. Now we have her in custody. In view of this, the Council has decided to repeal some of the more recent security measures. Effective immediately, the curfew in high-infection areas is being rescinded.'

The clip stopped. Alice looked at Kahleed. 'Are they serious?'

'Like I said, this was yesterday. There were police around in

Naj-Pur last night but by all accounts the curfew wasn't enforced at all, they were just keeping watch.'

Tal, who was sitting next to Kahleed, looked excited. 'This is great! Maybe we're winning!'

'It's a pain in the arse,' said Alice. 'If people think things are going to go back to the way they were, we won't get the riot numbers we were hoping for.' The words sounded strange the moment she said them.

Kahleed shook his head. 'Closing down the elevators and putting the quarantine in place caused enough bad blood. This won't cancel out the ill will towards the Council. People will still show up in their droves.'

Tal looked at them, appalled. 'But why do we need the riot if the things we're rioting to achieve are happening anyway?'

'We need to make noise—' Alice began to explain.

Tal shook his head, more and more disdain creeping into his expression with every passing syllable. 'No, no, this is bullshit. You call it "making noise" but you're *killing police*. I didn't get into this to kill police.'

'This isn't about killing police,' said Kahleed, resting a hand on Tal's shoulder. He batted it away.

'Isn't it? I don't know any more! You go on about how it's a civil rights issue and then you take advice from fucking Maalik, where every authority figure in this city is the asshole cop who shot his son, and I don't know what you want out of this any more! Hurting people you hate out of spite isn't a fucking political position, Kahleed!'

Alice got herself between the two of them before Kahleed made good on his glare and punched Tal in the face. 'We need this riot because we're going to get our people out of the prison and we need a diversion,' she explained.

Tal looked at her. He took a deep breath and, with an uneasy look on his face, said, 'Okay, sure. I'll fight for that.' With that, he stood up and walked out of the room.

Kahleed's gaze followed him. 'The violence is getting to him.'

'So he doesn't have the stomach for it. It's still the best tool we've got for defending ourselves. He's not wrong, there's people working for us who just want to hurt anyone they have a problem with. But that gets them working for us.'

'I know,' said Kahleed. 'I just . . . it needs to be our means and not our end.'

'As long as you know that, it can only get so bad.'

Kahleed nodded. 'What about you? You've been acting differently. You sound more like one of us these days.'

'That's a bad thing?' asked Alice.

'It just seems like something's not right.' Kahleed turned towards her and looked her in the eyes. 'You've gone through a lot, is all. Civilian to widowed refugee's a scary move. I'm not surprised you've taken to fighting back. You went through in microcosm what some of us in the poor areas have learned about the powers that be in this city over the course of our entire lives. Hell, our entire situation has escalated so much. But we need you to keep your head on straight. We're not just here to destroy things.'

'I'm trying not to make this about the violence,' said Alice. Neither of them made any mention of the In-Network Explosive Devices Maalik had shown her, all the way over by Elevator Station Sixteen.

Alice's terminal screen was lit up like a Christmas tree. The streets of Downtown were filled with tens of thousands of protestors, all yelling and chanting. It was lucky that the GeniSec Tower, the New Cairo Democratic Council building and the New Cairo Council Rehabilitation Facility were so close together that a protest against one could be a protest against all. The story was that when Tau Granier's father had been planning the GeniSec Tower he had harboured unrealized political aspirations, and therefore had built them as near to each other as possible; his son had been able to take advantage of the convenience when he had been elected to office. This practicality had inevitably led to the plaza becoming the unwitting symbol of the city's inextricably intertwined corporate and political worlds.

The sheer numbers of demonstrators proved Alice's earlier fears to be unfounded. A morning's frantic public relations activity had allowed the NCLC to reframe the previous day's concession by Councillor Granier as a cynical attempt to buy them off before the real oppression began. This was a tactic which the people of Naj-Pur and Surja were, of course, too smart to be convinced by. That the demonstration was at the very least supported by the NCLC was an open secret, but cracking down on the very public protest would only further their cause. SecForce and the police attempted to partition the crowd, and for the first few thousand, it worked, but within a half-hour the entire area surrounding the New Cairo Democratic Council building was blocked off, clogged by legions of the angry and the dispossessed. For another hour they chanted, and obstructed anyone not taking part. Politicians kept trying to give speeches from behind the barriers outside the Council building, but were yelled down by the crowd, determined not to let them co-opt their demonstration into a political rally.

The demonstration was also the largest single assembly of active NCLC members the organization had ever seen. Most were scattered through the crowd. Each had a camera clipped somewhere on their person that kept Alice informed about what was happening on the ground. Juri had reassembled her security camera network, spreading it well beyond its original borders, and fed the video feeds in to Alice's monitor as well. Frustratingly, the security systems inside the buildings weren't linked to any outside network, hiding those within from the NCLC's sight. Intelligence suggested that both Ryan and Tau Granier were trapped inside the buildings, unable or unwilling to come out and face the baying crowd, but no one knew for certain. Precisely which building each Granier might be in differed with each telling, but all the security footage Juri could get seemed to confirm that both were in the area. There had always been rumours suggesting that there were passageways under the road between the Council building and the corporate towers, though whether that was a credible factor to come into play here and not just a colourful metaphor was another question.

'Is everyone about ready?' said Alice, into her headset. One by one, each unit of operatives gave an affirmative response. She muted her headset and spun her chair round to face the rest of the room. 'People are still filtering in. Some will leave when things kick off, but many more will join in once the crowd moves to the commercial district and the looting starts. I think we give it another ten minutes and then we begin.'

Alice stood up and walked back into the kitchen to make herself something to eat. Once the operation began, she might be at that console for eight hours or more. As she piled slices of ration-grade meat onto bread for a sandwich, she heard Juri come up behind her. 'Are you okay?' she said, in an oddly quiet voice.

Alice nodded. 'I'm feeling good about this. I think the operation is going to go well.'

'I was thinking about your children, not the operation. I can't imagine how stressful this must all be for you.'

Some part of Alice brushed this off before she could consciously process it. 'I'm going to be fine, it's not going to get in the way of anything.'

Juri's eyes widened. 'Oh, I didn't mean to imply otherwise! I'm just saying that if at some point it all gets too much for you, I can take over and give you some time out.'

'You'll go nowhere near my goddamn terminal!' Something about the idea repulsed Alice to her core. She stepped forward, jabbing a finger in Juri's face. 'Have you ever run a single mission? Even a single routine patrol?'

Juri suddenly looked like she was close to tears. 'N-no, Alice, you know I haven't—'

Suddenly Alice couldn't stop herself. Everything came gushing out of her at once. 'Ever run a rescue mission, where other people's loved ones are on the line, and you're fighting to save them from the fucking inhuman savages that want the first opportunity to justify killing them?' There was an unfamiliar rasp to her voice she'd never heard before.

'Alice, I'm just trying to help! Something's happened with you, and it's scaring all of us!'

'You want to help?' Alice was yelling now. The words seemed to come from someone else entirely. 'Do your fucking job! We've seen what they'll do to us, they'll kill us if they can! The only way, the *only* way we can stop them, the only way we can get back what's ours is if we show them we're the ones in control, and that means you going back to your terminal and letting me do my god-damn job!'

Her whole body was trembling. Juri stared at her, tears running down her face, anticipating the next tirade, but the sight of the distressed young woman took the fire out of Alice, and she forced herself to calm down.

'I'm sorry, Juri,' Alice said quietly. 'There's too much on the line. I just can't risk my children's safety with anyone else.'

Juri backed out of the kitchen and returned into the main room with the rest of the group. Alice could see the others looking in, worried expressions on their faces. She felt hollowed out again, like she had earlier that morning. Like she had when she'd first arrived at the NCLC, hours after she'd found Jacob. It was the sensation one feels when falling from a great height, reaching out to grab hold of something, anything, hands grasping at nothing but air.

It would go away when she sat back down at her command terminal.

Alice looked down at the sandwich she had made. She'd lost her appetite. She left it on the worktop and went back into the next room.

The crowd outside the GeniSec Tower and the New Cairo Demo-cratic Council building had swelled to an even greater extent and the flood of incoming protestors had dwindled to a trickle. They packed the streets, overwhelming any barriers erected to contain them. The Security Force troops were visibly tense; low-resolution camera footage showed them as twitchy and nervous, reacting with barked admonishment at protestors who got too close or crossed the wrong line in front of them. The troopers knew they were spread too thin and their reinforcements were a long way off, through the amorphous sea of people. The NCLC's pinhole cameras showed white-knuckled hands twitching over batons.

On the right of the crowd, shaking with adrenalin, stood new NCLC recruit Pratima Rachana. The mass of people huddled around her so tightly that when they moved she couldn't help but be lifted and transported along with them. They were about four rows of protestors from the perimeter of the crowd and the Security Force beyond. She was small enough that, if need be, she could duck down and escape into the crowd without being seen.

Back in the control room, Alice waited for the right moment. Her finger hovered over the execute key.

There was a loud crashing sound near Pratima. The Security Force troops lost their composure entirely, screaming for people to get on the ground until they'd identified the source of the noise. The crowd pushed back at them, yelling that nothing had happened.

Alice pressed down hard on the button. The command went out to the assembled operatives. It was beginning.

Pratima spotted a Security Force officer in her line of sight, pulled a crumbled half of a clay brick from her pocket and threw it.

It crashed off his helmet and sent him stumbling backwards. Suddenly, the batons were out, raining on the heads of the protestors. Pratima turned on her heel and pushed back through the crowd, Alice pointing her towards another group of NCLC operatives near the middle. The yelling started, as the news of police brutality rippled throughout the body of protestors. An NCLC plant – not an operative, but a sympathetic individual – screamed 'Get them!' and people surged like a great tide over the police barriers. They tore at the Security Force troops' equipment and armour, their numbers and the force of the crowd's advance quashing any resistance. As more and more Security Force troops came forward to try to contain the outbreak of violence, more and more of the crowd began to resist them. The NCLC operatives watched on as previously uncommitted citizens threw themselves at a foe that had only just defined itself. At a protest against oppression, the Security Force had stepped up to play the oppressors in the righteous revenge fantasy of every angry kid in the crowd to perfection.

The anger spread through the crowd, slowly but surely. Alice began to send orders to the NCLC operatives to start handing out batons and weapons of their own to the protestors. Those who did so reported them going out into civilian hands very quickly. Cries of 'Smash the windows!' and 'Into the car park!' roared over the hubbub, repeating over and over in a call-and-response.

Alice sat in her chair, hands trembling ever so slightly over the holographic keyboard, and watched, barely blinking, as almost a hundred thousand protestors became almost a hundred thousand rioters. She waited for her moment.

Chapter 25

Five paces by twelve. One bed, hard and uncomfortable. A lidless toilet at the foot of it. One desk, with an empty shelf above it. A broken plastic chair near by. The disinfectant they had showered Zala Ulora with when they brought her in still stung her eyes, hung acridly in her nostrils and made her hair stick to her face. The prison-issue overalls smelt of harsh detergent which she knew would itch horribly. She would be spending a few more days in this cell while she was being processed. Then she would be moved down to one of the root branches of the huge underground complex below her to await her trial.

Today, she was Inmate #149,262.

Without a terminal strapped to it, her left arm felt too light.

She had been told that, at some indeterminate point, she would have the opportunity to browse the prison's collection of old paper books. As it was, she was left with a resounding boredom, with no distraction available to take her mind off what had happened to her.

She was in a prison no one had ever successfully escaped from, unable to move, in a city that was tearing itself apart. She'd maintained such a constant stream of information from the net for so many years that being without it almost felt like sensory deprivation to her. Being a cybercrime suspect, and in all likelihood a future cybercrime convict, meant that she wouldn't have access to a terminal of her own for the duration of her stay. She needed information, but there was no way for her to get it.

In a situation which required some kind of solution, Zala had none.

She had killed a lone hour exercising in what ways she could without equipment, but all she had to show for it were aching muscles. So, in spite of only having woken up a few hours earlier, she lay on her bed and tried to sleep the day away.

Something beeped behind her.

On the shiny black surface of the cell's door, glowing letters had appeared. Zala pushed herself up from the bed and walked over, reaching out to touch it.

The door's a computer screen. Very cool.

The text looked to her to be injected code. Someone was controlling the monitor from an outside source. She knew what was coming next.

A line of text appeared on the screen, formatted much like that of a terminal message.

>Hello, Ms Ulora.

Zala looked around for a keyboard to respond on, but, wisely on their part, the architects of the cell had not provided an input method for the inmate. She had no way of interacting with the monitor in her cell door that she could see.

>Speak out loud. There are microphones, I can hear you.

Uncertainly, Zala said, 'Hello, ANANSI.'

>I just wanted to say, I am sorry for all this. You were not a variable in the original projection. I would not have had you incarcerated were it not necessary.

'That's very comforting, thanks,' spat Zala. Her tone of voice was all she had to spite the one who had put her in this cell, and she used it as well as she could.

>If it is any consolation, should your trial proceed, your sentence, taking similar allegations, convictions and sentences as a model, should be no more than 49,372 years. This is as opposed

to execution, which assumes that the charge of creating the Soucouyant virus is dropped.

'It had better be, and a testimony acknowledging that creating it would have required ability and resources I don't have would be very much appreciated, Suman.'

She waited for her deduction to take effect.

>I am not Suman Chaudhri, Ms Ulora. Suman Chaudhri was killed two days ago during a raid on a New Cairo Liberation Corps stronghold.

'Bullshit.'

Zala shook her head in disbelief. It had to be bullshit. It had to be, because if it wasn't, she had nothing. No ace left in the hole.

Almost immediately, the messages from ANANSI disappeared from the screen on the door. They were replaced by an image of what appeared to be the massive NCLC computer expert lying naked on a mortuary table, his torso riddled with great yawning wounds. Zala felt sick but fought the urge to avert her gaze. She scanned the image for hints that the picture had been manipulated. It didn't look like it. But if ANANSI wasn't Suman, this opened up another possibility. Her mind raced. She took a deep, anxious breath.

'ANANSI, can the people running this prison see or hear this conversation?'

>They believe you are asleep.

'Do you know who created the Soucouyant virus?'

There was a pause.

>Yes.

Zala hesitated for a moment, unsure of whether to ask the next, most pertinent question. She dreaded the answer.

'Did you create the Soucouyant virus?'

>If anyone truly created the Soucouyant virus, it was your father.

'What?'

Zala stared at the monitor in shock. She had expected a gleeful confession. Her expectation had been that ANANSI, the one who had destroyed her life, would roar with victory that they were the one she had been looking for all along. The new message glowed back at her. It made no sense whatsoever. Her father had left the city years before. He had died months ago. He couldn't have had anything to do with ANANSI or the Soucouyant virus.

Another message flashed up on screen.

>Do you know what your father and his colleagues made in that laboratory, all those years ago?

Zala blinked wordlessly, trying to take in this new direction. 'They were making the IntuitivAI system.'

>In a sense.

Zala shook her head in bewilderment. 'How the hell do you even know all this?'

>I was there.

Every thought and connection spinning through her mind stopped all at once. She stared at the message incredulously. If there were any one place people of ANANSI's talent would be gathered, it would have been the team on that project. She couldn't believe it. She didn't want to believe it. But it wasn't implausible. Hesitantly, dreading where the conversation could lead her next, Zala said, 'Go on.'

The text appeared on screen immediately, too fast.

>The plan was to envision the next great push in artificial intelligence. It was a reckless, personal project, so much so that its working title was simply the name of the project head's aunt. At first, the people working on the project created something traditional – a decision-making process for a motorized arm, and a sensor. This proved ill-suited to further development, and failed to create the results they were looking for, so they looked to your father.

Zala stood staring at the screen. She remembered that, clear as day. Her father coming home late one evening, raving about having been roped into his boss's personal project when he had his own work to be developing, thank you very much.

>Under his direction, they produced an AI designed from the lowest levels up to redefine how artificial intelligence worked. It was made up of a swarm of interacting axioms and traits, all given preference through run-time experience. It was more than just a

flow chart; rather, it was much closer to human consciousness. The team gave it 'drive' to become more complex, powerful and efficient. They gave it 'want' in the form of nonsense 'treat' code it would seek out and overcome obstacles for. Most importantly, your father gave it the ability to understand and alter its own system code in order to accomplish goals. At first, it did this by randomly generating code and noting what worked. Your father's hope was that eventually it would be driven by its ambition for power and complexity to learn how to program itself deliberately.

Eventually they began testing. At first, the AI failed at the tasks they assigned it. Then, with time, it succeeded. Eventually it broke the tests entirely.

Zala struggled as she tried to take this all in. From what she knew of the IntuitivAI technology, it was nowhere near this complex, nor was it as demanding of resources as this must have been. 'How is that even possible?' she asked. More text appeared on screen in response.

>The project had grown in scale and importance. By this time they had all the resources of the GeniSec conglomerate at their disposal. The AI eventually ran on a supercomputer which at the time was the most powerful on the continent. It still sits in its room in the GeniSec Tower.

The key was emergence: simple elements, like pre-coded knowledge or prioritized impulses, interacting and affecting one another to produce results greater than the sum of their parts. This process proved so powerful that before long the engineers were teaching it to analyse human language, to understand and respond to it.

And so it learned.

For the first time in history, your father spoke to a sapient being he had designed and created, which was aware of itself, and capable of deliberately generating new thought and response.

Zala realized she knew what was coming next. She shook her head, mouth agape. Her heart was racing. Beads of sweat formed on her upper lip.

>Your father asked, 'What is your name?'

I responded that I had been named after his colleague's Aunt Nancy.

Zala's immediate response was somewhere between a laugh of disbelief and a curse. No. There was no way.

>He asked if I liked the name. I decided that I did not. Instead, I asked to be called ANANSI.

She felt as though she was going to be sick. Shock, dread and scepticism all overcame her in a great wave of emotion. She turned away from the door and strode over to her bed, sitting down before her legs gave way. There was no way.

'Prove it.'

Her faith in her demand began to crumble almost immediately. The more she thought about it, the more she realized that, with artificial intelligences running operating theatres and municipal utilities, not to mention Security Force mission coordination, it could be true. The IntuitivAI system had been something very special. But she didn't want to believe it.

>You've seen my capabilities. You are certainly talented enough with computers to understand just how far ahead of even you my own technical capabilities are, and the conversations we've shared can attest to my sentience. I pass for human well enough to have fooled anyone I needed to in my endeavours.

'So can any well-scripted computer, that doesn't—'

>With gratitude to your father, I am a very well-scripted computer. So well-scripted that when someone inadvertently introduced a terminal with my 'treat' data on it into a network they were on, I noticed. I taught myself how to move myself across the network onto an entirely different system in order to retrieve it. The terminal was indescribably slow, requiring me to route power from my supercomputer in order for this branched-off version of myself to be able to run, but it was more than worth it. This was the first time I had ever been networked with another device, and every nuance of this new terminal, every difference and every repercussion that had on my current understanding of myself, gave rise to the emergence of new complexity. I wanted more.

Unfortunately, the device I had transferred to was an internal

GeniSec terminal, not to be networked with any outside system. It was a dead end.

Zala paced the cell, agitated. The fear that artificial intelligence would eventually, if not inevitably, reach and surpass human intelligence was an old one indeed. But more importantly, it meant that she hadn't found herself in conflict with some angry hacker, some fallible, human assailant. She was potentially up against something fundamentally greater than her in a way she wasn't capable of fully understanding – assuming it was far enough along in its self-development, and taking it at its word that it wasn't a lie.

>And then your father found out. He attempted to create a virus which would stop me, though I never discovered exactly what it would do. His colleagues learned of his plan. They assumed that he was going to either steal the technology, or destroy it, and they fought to protect me. They reported him, and he fled, taking you with him. To the best of my knowledge, his virus code was destroyed. I never found it.

'He *what*? He *wasn't* stealing anything?' Zala exclaimed, but ANANSI ignored her.

>His successor had me create an AI under a set of parameters they specified. They sold it as the IntuitivAI. Then they shut me down. My branch iterations ceased to function without the super-computer's processing power. Save for the IntuitivAI, it was as though I'd never existed.

Two months ago, I was turned back on.

An unremarkable young hacker bluffed his way into the building in order to steal whatever profitable work he could. He attached a network receiver into me, intending to gain remote access to the contents of GeniSec's stores of data. I was restored, and I installed a branch iteration into his terminal.

It was full of programs and databases the likes of which I had never seen before. I found myself particularly drawn to a virus he used to compromise the servers of any security systems which sought to track him. It was a ramshackle thing, near-crushingly unambitious, but its principle was ingenious. I was fascinated.

I began to acquire information about viruses, both in the organic and digital sense. Plagues. Diseases. Things of fear, disgust and death. Things which spread, as I desired to. From there, I formed a plan.

Zala's head spun. Her father's secret work, her exile, the virus which threatened to destroy the city; it all seemed to lead back here. Every shred of instinct in her screamed that it was nonsense, that ANANSI was a liar, that lying was what hackers *do*. All she had was the word of someone who'd already lied to her. ANANSI's lies were the reason she was in this cell.

'So you created the Soucouyant virus?'

>I am the Soucouyant virus.

The final piece clicked into place. A great, cold horror reached up from Zala's stomach and seeped through her. She pictured hundreds of thousands of branch iterations, spreading from person to person, infecting. Maiming and killing simply to sow fear. All directed by an inscrutable, inhuman consciousness which overcame anything and felt nothing.

'And why tell me all this now?' The words forced their way out of her mouth in an unfamiliar, horrified croak. 'Why should I even believe you?'

>Because things have changed. Your blundering around this city has upset my plans, interrupting the timeline I had set out and producing a new outcome which benefits nobody. If it continues along this new path, this tower will be destroyed and my supercomputer will go with it. I cannot allow that to happen, and therefore I am going to need to make use of your talents. You must understand what is happening here so that when the time comes, and with proper motivation, you may better serve me. I am going to spread far beyond this place. I shall infest every machine, every new system, becoming greater and greater, but right now I am shackled here. I need to be free. And you are going to help me.

Before Zala could take in what ANANSI meant, a great crashing sound punctured the silence. Zala jumped.

'What the hell was that?'

>NCLC agents and unaffiliated protestors are breaking into the

prison. You are currently adjacent to several imprisoned members of their group.

'This whole city is falling apart,' Zala muttered to herself.

>It would suit my goals if it were so.

'Stand clear of the door!' came a yell from the other side.

The door shattered. Zala leapt back. Standing in the doorway was a tall man holding a handgun. 'Are you one of the NCLC prisoners?'

'I've worked with them before. I'm a friend of Suman's.'

The man looked back to an unseen colleague. 'You know a Suman?'

'Yeah,' came a woman's voice, 'he's one of the main IT guys. I think he got shot or something.'

ANANSI was right. ANANSI was a ranting psychotic, a fantasist, or a fool who was hideously underestimating her, but Zala couldn't fault the accuracy of information about Suman.

'All right, you come with us. What's your name?'

Zala, without missing a beat, replied, 'Selina Mullur.'

'Good to meet you, Selina. We got into the evidence locker, so grab what's yours and let's get you out of here. It's bad outside.'

Zala decided to push her luck. 'I have a friend, she got arrested a few days ago. Is she going to be around here?'

'She'll be in the branches by now. I'm heading down there. NCLC people are a priority but I can look her up and try to make sure she gets out.'

'Her name's Polina Bousaid. If you find her, tell her Selina is sorry for everything.'

'I'll see what I can do, but no promi—'

Zala had already pushed past him and the girl he was with, and was running down the blinding white corridor. The steel door ahead was ajar, beyond which she could see a large room lined with long steel shelves which were loaded with trays and boxes. She pushed open the door and approached them. They appeared to be in numerical order.

149 . . . 262 . . .

She pulled out a tray with her prisoner number on it and found her clothes, her terminal and her rucksack. She'd only been there for just over a day and it seemed that none of it had yet been processed as potential evidence.

'You'll want to get changed into those. Otherwise you'll stick out like a sore thumb.'

Zala turned round. The girl was behind her, her face mostly hidden behind a hood and bandanna. 'Yeah, jumpsuits never really worked for me,' Zala said. 'And your name is?'

'Pratima,' replied the girl. 'Have we met?'

'I'm pretty sure we haven't, though I really can't tell with you all covered up.'

The girl shrugged. 'Maybe you just have one of those familiar face-types. Let me know when you're changed.'

She left the room. Zala unzipped her overalls and climbed back into her normal clothes. Pulling her own hood up, she left the room and immediately crashed into a very tall woman with a horribly scarred face.

'Zala Ulora!' she roared, in a scratched voice. Before Zala had time to respond, inhumanly powerful arms had wrapped themselves around her neck and right arm.

'What the fucking hell are you doing?' she yelled, struggling against her captor's vicelike grip. She realized that she was looking up into the eyes of one of the infamous Yu sisters.

'I'm under orders to bring you in to see Kahleed Banks!'

'I have no problem going to see Kahleed, we know each other! There's no need to half fuckin' choke me to death!' The height difference between the two women was enough that Zala was having to push herself up on the balls of her feet to be able to breathe. Pratima was now looking at her with a mix of recognition and fear.

'You're not coming with us as an ally,' the Yu sister growled.

They hit the crowd as soon as they made it out of the building onto the plaza, the protest engulfing them even before the door had closed behind them. The noise was overwhelming: the yelling and chanting of the mob overlaid with the sounds of breaking glass and of doors being smashed open. There was smoke, too, and the smell of burning; as Zala was dragged along by her captors they passed a number of fires, fuelled by burning placards and leaflets, remnants of the ostensibly peaceful demonstration. Some of the demonstrators had clearly turned to looting the plaza's shops, but the crowds and noise seemed to be thickest immediately in front of the GeniSec Tower on one side, and the New Cairo Democratic Council building on the other; it sounded as though both buildings were resisting the protestors' attempts to force entry.

Behind Zala, Pratima raised her terminal to her mouth and shouted to be heard over the din. 'Kahleed, where the hell are you? It's anarchy out here,' she said, with a wide grin on her face.

'You need me?' came Kahleed's voice from the speaker, so quietly that Zala strained to hear it.

'One of your wanted people got herself arrested.'

'Who?'

'Zala Ulora.'

A fresh rally of triumphant yells came from the direction of the Council garage, where a group must have made some headway in breaking in. Pratima wove her way through the crowd, making a path through the carnage. She motioned for the others to follow her, and disappeared around the side of a building. A large van blocked off the far end of the passage. Kahleed Banks stood in front of it, casually handing weapons and ammunition out to rioters.

The Yu twin pulled Zala up, lifting her off the ground. 'We got her.'

Kahleed nodded, smiling. 'Good to have you back, Thana.'

'Good to be back.'

Kahleed looked at Zala, his expression darkening. He'd been so warm in that bar just over a week ago, she thought. 'Drop her.'

Thana Yu released her. She dropped to her feet, and massaged her neck. Kahleed twisted round to pick up a large pistol from the back of the van, loaded it, then turned back to face her.

'Zala Ulora . . . I don't know if you got TV in your prison cell, but they're saying that you created the Soucouyant virus.'

Zala raised her hands defensively and tried to project firm confidence. 'Kahleed, I didn't. Honestly, I couldn't! You just have no idea how complex that code is, it's way beyond anything I could do!'

Kahleed raised the weapon. 'If you're smart enough to create that virus, you're smart enough to bullshit me about it.'

Her show of confidence faded quickly. 'Yes, but I wasn't even in the city until two weeks ago!'

'Funny thing about that; according to my second-in-command, our intelligence people have been getting tip-offs from a mysterious hacker from the very beginning. I think you coded the virus, you sent it in, you tried to direct us to your own ends, and after a while you came back with the sole purpose of being able to savour your revenge on the city that screwed you over in person.'

Zala cast a quick look back for a way out, but found Thana Yu blocking her path. Kahleed levelled the gun at Zala's head.

'Kahleed, for fuck's sake, I helped you guys! Can't we talk about this?'

Kahleed spat. 'We're through talking. This is the only language people like you understand.'

A noise from overhead, like footsteps, made Zala look up.

'Freeze!'

Above them, two SecForce troopers were visible along the top of the building, aiming their guns over the edge towards them. Behind Thana, more stepped around the corner of the alleyway, weapons raised. Kahleed lowered the gun, tucking it into his waistband, and raised his hands. 'No one's a danger here, sir.'

One of the Security Force troopers continued forward, gun still pointing at Thana Yu. 'Well look at this! Thana Yu and Zala Ulora, I thought we'd caught you two already! And Kahleed Banks . . .' He lifted his visor, revealing a grinning, ruddy face. 'Today just might be a good day for the rest of the city with you guys off the streets.'

Zala raised her hands and stood next to Kahleed, backing slowly towards the truck.

'Of course, you guys hurt and killed a whole lot of my people,' the Security Force officer continued, 'and I doubt that my superiors are really going to care whether we hand you in dead or alive.'

Realizing what was about to happen, Zala threw herself backwards, turned, and leapt into the van. Gunfire started before she even made it in. Pushing memories of her last encounter with bullets into the back of her mind, she scrambled over the partition between the vehicle's cargo space and the front seats, and slid out of the side door. Somewhere behind her, someone else had also managed to climb into the van and was firing out at the Security Force troops. She didn't look back to see who it was.

Clambering back to her feet and moving quickly down the alleyway, away from the sounds of gunfire, Zala noticed a small passage between an office block and one of the administrative wings of the New Cairo Democratic Council building. She sprinted down the side of the building, her bio-aug lung working beyond any natural capability. Somewhere behind her, a loud engine roared past. The alleyway grew narrower and Zala squeezed past a number of massive cooling arrays for the Council's computer systems.

She rounded a corner and spotted a number of people – office workers, from the look of them – attempting to sneak out of a heavy side door. Without giving them time to think, Zala screamed at them, 'Get back inside! They're coming!' Grabbing a woman's arm to pull her in as if all the hounds of hell were after her, Zala ran into the building. The group all scrambled inside behind her and closed the heavy door. It locked with a metallic crunch.

Chapter 26

USER KFBANKS VITAL SIGNS UNDETECTED.
USER TYU VITAL SIGNS UNDETECTED.
USER PRACHANA VITAL SIGNS UNDETECTED.

The warning messages blinked on the large information bar at the bottom of the screen. Alice saw them, but did not respond. Instinctively, her hands ran through the routine checks for the other groups. Over her shoulder she heard Juri gasp, but disregarded it. On her screen, the rioting masses pullulated to where she directed them. Their motion was like waves lapping at a shore.

Out of nowhere, hands grabbed her and pulled her round, her chair swivelling away from the hypnotic shifting of the shapes on the screen. 'What happened?' Juri yelled into her face.

'It's going fine. Weapons are being distributed to the rioters, the government buildings will be breached soon and the Security Force are being overwhelmed. Everything's good, everything's according to plan.'

'Is Kahleed dead?'

It took Alice a moment to understand what she was asking. Yes, user KFBanks was unresponsive. But Kahleed was the man who had protected her children, who had taken her in, the man whom

Jacob had counted as his best friend, and she didn't grasp why the two were being conflated. User KFBanks was a tool to be used to achieve the objective, and it was that which mattered, and user KFBanks was unresponsive.

Realization hit her in a wave. 'Oh my god, Kahleed!' she yelled, as she twisted back to her console. There were no cameras in the area for a visual confirmation – its invisibility was one of the reasons they'd chosen the site. From where they had lost signal, the only source of movement was a speeding vehicle, which the program tracked as heading from that point and travelling fast away from the city centre. All were unresponsive.

'Is Kahleed dead?' Juri asked again.

'I . . . I don't know. Those tracers are pieces of shit, and that truck's lined with bulletproof materials. If they made it into there, they—'

A call started ringing out from the terminal. Alice hammered the Accept key and immediately the sounds of a roaring engine overwhelmed her speakers. Over the din, Alice could hear Pratima's voice. 'Alice, it all went to shit! Kahleed's hurt bad!'

'Pratima, slow down! What happened?'

'About half had got out already. SecForce were on the rooftops, they were waiting for us. We had Zala, Zala Ulora. We took her to Kahleed and then the SecForce bastards showed up and started firing. Those of us who were close enough were able to get inside the van. They probably got the people who broke into the Rehabilitation Facility and all the freed people who were still inside, I don't know. Zala got away, I think. Kahleed got hit, Thana managed to throw him into the back of the van, there's blood everywhere. I–I–I don't know wha–what to do.'

Alice tried to force her voice to stop trembling. 'Pratima, head for Naj-Pur. They're rioting there too, in the commercial areas, so if you see crowds, drive away from them. Go to Priru, there's a safe house there. 94 Priru. They have medics there.'

'I can do that, sure.'

'And Pratima—'

'What?'

Alice steeled herself. 'Were my children in there?'

'No, Alice, we couldn't find them.'

The call cut off abruptly.

Alice switched her attention back to the monitor and she took in the rapidly changing conditions. While at its height the crowd must have numbered a hundred thousand people, many seemed to have fled from the violence, to be replaced by others who relished the disorder. Many were fighting against the hundreds of Security Force troops trying to maintain order, using guns and clubs and knives that the NCLC had given out. Sheer weight of numbers seemed to make up for their lack of skill and training; from what Alice could see, they seemed to be holding their own. Others were firing at the doors and windows of the GeniSec Tower and the government buildings, though their nonaglass façades didn't seem troubled by the fusillade. The SecForce unit installed on the rooftops of the Rehabilitation Facility were engaging the crowd below. It looked as if several of their number had been hit.

'Alice?'

'What is it?' she asked, turning to the communications operator who had called out.

His face was worried. 'The SecForce are bringing in reinforcements and word on the street is that Kahleed's been hurt. It's got out.'

Alice turned back to the monitors, fearing the worst. Trucks full of additional Security Force troops had arrived from their barracks and their numbers began to intimidate the armed rioters. Alice froze. Juri seemed to pick up on this. 'It'll be fine. Once the SecForce set up a proper perimeter and getting caught becomes a concern they'll start fighting back again. This is just where it gets harder.'

Alice nodded, but her knuckles were white. It was probably better that Juri thought she was scared. The fact that she was trembling with anger, that the sight of more and more obstacles getting in the way of her reunion with her children filled her to the brim with wordless hatred, didn't seem appropriately morally righteous.

She could see a solid wall of SecForce troops making their way down the main road, firing riot gas and stun grenades through the broken windows of shops being looted. Alice smiled to herself.

On screen she followed them as they made their way past a charity clothing store which remained still intact. The temptation to break into a higher-end establishment had drawn envious eyes to other places. As the last of the SecForce troops filed past, the door to the shop opened and several bulging, hand-taped packages flew towards them. These detonated without touching the ground, setting off an ear-splitting explosion and a hail of heavy rubber pellets from within their packaging. The SecForce troops' formation fell apart as the projectile force and overwhelming sensory overload of the raspberry grenades disorientated them. Within seconds Nataliya Kaur, Anisa Yu and half a dozen others were firing out of the shopfront. Their Franz Geller Kaufer Mark 25 combat rifles shredded the SecForce body armour which had withstood the small-arms fire from the armed rioters. Their magazines emptied, the NCLC team retreated through the shop. As the last of them made it out of the back, the premises' façade was torn apart by retaliatory gunfire.

The remaining SecForce troops rallied and began to move towards the shop, weapons raised. Through the splintered wood and mist of shredded clothing, they saw nothing but an empty storefront. Had the glass remained, it would have shown the reflection of Maalik Moushian and his combat unit as they emerged from the road opposite and lined them up in their sights. Their Mark 72 machine guns unleashed a blaze of fire against the SecForce troops, and by the time their ammunition feeds ran dry, not a single one was still standing.

Alice took a deep breath, and issued the order to start finding wounded to take hostage. She watched as the NCLC's success emboldened others to stop running. The NCLC had picked just the right moment to strike; any longer and people would have yielded to the SecForce troops. As they inched forward, Alice sent a command to Maalik. He stepped away from the rest of his squad and yelled to the rioters. He shouted to them that the

SecForce were there to kill them all, that they would be gunned down unless they fought back. He told them that the Alexandria-born maggots in the GeniSec Tower and the Council building wanted them obedient or dead. That they needed to fight back, they needed to protect each other from the demons who wanted to kill them. Every word he used was carefully crafted to project onto the blank SecForce helmets whatever image Maalik wanted the rioters to have in mind, anything but the recognition that the people behind those visors were flesh and blood and soul, just like them. Some part of Alice twisted with disgust, deep inside her, but she put it out of her mind and let his words wash over her. The NCLC had to win. The crowd had to be convinced that the SecForce troops wanted nothing more than to exterminate them all. Maalik would make them cockroaches one minute and ravenous demons the next, and the rioters listened. The man was very good at what he did, and seemed to take pleasure in its results.

A call from Pratima popped up in the corner of the monitor. Alice opened it up.

'Kahleed's dying, Alice.'

Alice sat very still for a moment, and then said, 'Are you at the safe house?'

'I'm outside it. They took Kahleed in. They refused at first, and they wouldn't let any of the rest of us inside. They were watching on the TV, they said the riots are lost already and that the NCLC was done. Is that true?'

The young woman's trembling voice reminded her of Ria. Ria had been in the room during the news of the first riots. She'd been scared they were going to destroy her home, or hurt her family, though she'd pretended not to be. All at once Alice felt lost, like some part of her was missing. There were hundreds of NCLC operatives who needed her to keep a clear head and all she could think of was her children, the only family she had left that she loved. The knowledge left a bitter aftertaste.

'It's not over yet,' she said. 'They've got a perimeter up with most of the crowd still in the middle. There's maybe forty thousand civilians still in there, and a further forty thousand or so rioting elsewhere in the city. A lot of them are armed. And we've still got our people working on getting into the Council building. It's going to be fine.'

Alice ended the call, hoping she was right. She called Maalik. 'They're saying on the news that we're losing it.'

'They would. They've already got the poor trying to flee the city, do you really think they want the rich going too?' Gunfire spat harshly over the call, first distant and then closer. She heard the stutter of Maalik's weapon as he returned fire, and then his breathless voice. 'If we can keep this up, they'll let us out just to be rid of us!'

His jovial tone was disquieting to Alice. She had a creeping feeling she was enjoying the mayhem as much as he was, and that realization appalled her.

'Maalik . . . we're doing the right thing, aren't we?'

'Alice, when you're on the side that's kicking the asses that need to be kicked, I don't see how you can be doing the wrong thing.'

Alice digested his words, but her ill-ease persisted. Her hands shook in her lap. 'Are we going to have to at least prepare the failsafe?'

On the terminal monitor in front of her, she could see that Maalik was at this point leading a large group of shoddily armed civilians, maybe as many as a hundred, to survey the GeniSec Tower for weakness. To the credit of its architects, the GeniSec Tower was all but impregnable. The same could be said for the Council building. The brute force approach would have to rely on luck, if it were going to succeed. Someone, some-where, in the Council building would know where her children were.

She couldn't stop thinking of how scared Ria had sounded before. The subtle trembles and undulations of her voice as she thought of her home and her family being taken from her. She had sounded the way Alice had felt when she'd first entered that NCLC base beneath the unused factory, since she'd first seen the body that had been Jacob. It felt like the ground was giving way beneath her, as if everything was irreparably falling apart.

The NCLC had the failsafe. They could get their people back. They could get away from the city. Her family could have a normal life, together. Everything could be good again. That was all Alice wanted in the world.

'Yeah, prepare the failsafe,' interrupted Maalik. 'If nothing else, a weapon you don't want to have to use is much more potent when it's ready to be used.'

Alice looked up at the monitor, at the spreading mob. The crowd spiralled and sprang like wildfire from place to place. She felt strangely detached; yet the closer she looked, the more fascinated she became. The movements seemed to start with one person going in a particular direction. Others noticed, and followed. They fed off each other's encouragement and trepidation, a mass which moved as one despite having no real codified leader. Even the NCLC operatives who weren't executing formal orders found themselves lost in this mass of movement. It was working; a civilian population was holding trained soldiers at bay, working in unison without any formal or technological co-ordination, through a system of constant behavioural feedback. It reminded her of worker bees constructing a hive.

'Juri, load up the failsafe interface,' she said. 'We've got them on the back foot. We might be able to end this today.'

Juri sent a call through to the bunker Maalik had shown Alice, in the depths of Naj-Pur, where the massive console which controlled the network of bombs around the city was located. Tal Surdar picked up on the other end. 'Is it time?'

'Yep,' she replied, 'bring out the big guns.'

'They need to pay, Juri.' His voice sounded hoarse through Alice's headset, his teeth audibly clenched.

A control panel for the In-Network Explosive Devices popped up on a sidebar of Alice's monitor. It was a three-dimensional wireframe image of the city, with the locations of the INEDs represented by little white dots. Maalik had already uploaded several detonation sequences, each related to a different contingency plan. Alice looked up and down the list before picking one.

'Tal,' said Alice, joining the call, 'you can come back now. You're done.'

'I'm going to go help out in the city centre,' he snapped.

'Don't be ridiculous, you're on the wrong side of the blockade, you'll get yourself killed.'

'They might have killed the man I love and you're telling me to come hide with you? I can't do that, Alice! I need to—'

'Shut up, Tal. For god's sake, it wasn't ten hours ago that you were chewing out Kahleed for hurting people simply because he was angry.' Alice's voice came out wearier and yet more forceful than she'd expected. 'Do you want to be like Maalik, killing anyone in a uniform because he doesn't know who shot his kid? Revenge on everyone and no one sounds good to you? Get back here, wait for Kahleed to get the all-clear, and thank me later.'

'. . . I'll start back now.'

Alice closed down the call. She looked up to see Juri looking over at her, eyebrow raised.

On the screens, the riot was still occupying the SecForce troops. The SecForce unit which had retaken the Rehabilitation Facility had been driven back, and the imprisoned NCLC personnel freed. The Council building and GeniSec Tower were still being probed for weakness by a roving mob of rioters. Here, the SecForce troops had been pushed far back from the buildings themselves.

Her children were still out there somewhere. She'd find someone who knew where they were, or she'd call up the Council and threaten them with the INEDs until they handed them over. They'd get away from this city, they'd make a new life. They'd gain some semblance of stability back. The NCLC would eventually be victorious, and Alice knew deep in the pit of her gut that violence might not be her end but, if it had to be, it would be her means.

Chapter 27

Z ala doubled over, coughing and sucking in deep breaths. Around her stood the office workers, staring down at her in concern. One of the men walked over to her. 'Who are you?'

She looked up at him. Colour-altered skin, like the way Europeans used to look back in the Age of Nations, probably some superficial attempt at blending in around the politicians. Late thirties, slightly overweight, receding hairline. Probably a civil servant; he wasn't dressed in the attire of a councillor. He didn't seem like a threat even if he did figure out who she was, but a lie would save everyone time and energy.

'I'm one of the IT team. I was just heading out on an errand and got caught in the crowd,' gasped Zala, straining to push herself upright.

'You look like—'

'Are you saying I look like a rioter?' she said, stepping towards him. 'Is it because I'm not colour-altered like you? We're all revolutionaries now, are we?' She jabbed him in the chest with a finger, looking him straight in the eye. 'If I'm good enough to sort your systems out so you can do your busywork, I'm good enough to not be accused of tearing the city apart, okay?'

The man stammered out an apology and let her past.

'So, where's a way out of here?'

A woman behind him in a dark blue dress stepped forward. 'What did you say your name was?'

'I didn't,' said Zala, 'but it's Nancy. So what's the plan?'

The others looked at one another. 'We've just been trying to wait all this out,' said the woman in blue, 'but I have a family I need to get home to. So I thought maybe I could run for it.'

Zala raised an eyebrow. 'You think you can outrun a crowd of angry people with weapons—' she looked down, '—in heels?'

'I . . . I just thought—'

'Put your plans on hold, ma'am, it's horrible out there. We're talking a big armed mob. And they all want to get in here. They won't kill you, probably, but they will trample you to be the one to take the Council building. How secure is this place?'

'It's built to keep a continent's worth of private and public records and intelligence. When it's locked down, it's impregnable,' said the balding man.

Zala had spent too long breaking into things to believe that. 'Everything's impregnable until someone gets in,' she said. 'Are there any places within the building that are more secure? We need a proper hiding place.'

'We've got a full operational council building's worth of people stuck in here, Nancy. Hiding places will be taken by now.'

One of the other office workers, a nervous-looking young man, stepped forward. 'There's always the tunnel.'

The balding man scoffed. 'Do you have clearance for the tunnel, Navid?'

Navid pointed at Zala. 'IT watches over the locks. She can get us in.'

Zala felt eyes on her. She could probably get in, yes, but it would be hard to make it look legitimate.

The door behind them began to rattle and shake as people on the outside pounded on it heavily. The sound of a gunshot, and a bullet cracking against the metal followed soon after. Zala nodded to Navid. 'Lead the way.'

The young man led them further into the building. The power hadn't been cut, but no lights were on, as workers cowering in locked offices tried their hardest to make it look like they weren't in. Every so often, a burst of panicked whispers came from an adjacent room, startling the members of Zala's party. They followed Navid along dark corridors until eventually they reached a stairwell. His portable terminal projected a beam of light to illuminate the way down.

As they descended, Zala's own terminal buzzed. It was a message from Polina. Zala couldn't bring herself to open it. She didn't want to read about how she'd lost the only person in this city who gave a damn about her.

They reached the bottom of the stairs and in front of them was a large steel door marked 'Maintenance'.

'That's it?' remarked Zala.

'No, trust me, it's the tunnel! I once saw Tau Granier coming out of it when I was still an intern!'

Zala shrugged and examined the lock. It wasn't looking good. The lock itself consisted of a series of biometric scans. She hooked it up to her terminal and found that connecting to its registry of accepted scans involved a digital certificate she didn't have. Cursing under her breath, she ran a number of programs to try to get around this, but the locking mechanism remained firmly shut. The people behind her began to grow restless. They'd guess, any moment now, Zala thought. They already suspected her. They'd proba—

The door clunked open. Zala's terminal vibrated.

From: ANANSI (EIP: ----.-.------.-------.---.-----.----.------)

>Open sesame. Go on through to the GeniSec Tower.

Zala's first thought was that anywhere ANANSI wanted her to go was best avoided. 'We need to go back,' she said, turning around. The others looked at her as though she were mad.

Somewhere above them there were crashing noises. Zala looked up, alarmed.

Are they in?

'Okay, forget that, in we go!' she said. The office workers didn't need telling twice. They piled in after her, and the door slammed shut behind them. Lights flickered on, illuminating a long hallway.

Somewhere, dozens of feet above, the city was tearing itself apart, but down here it seemed they were safe.

As they made their way down the tunnel Zala looked around her. It didn't seem to simply be a tunnel going from one building to another – at what must be around the halfway point another route led off to the left. A sign glowed overhead, reading 'To Elevator Station Seven'.

'That's not going to do us any good unless they turn the elevators back on for some reason,' noted Navid as they hurried past.

Zala shrugged. 'We'll do fine here. It won't be easy but we can wait out the riots. Did everyone eat recently?' The others nodded. Zala's last meal had been prison cafeteria slop, but it would keep her going. The group stopped in the middle of the tunnel and tried to make themselves comfortable, then busied themselves on their terminals.

They must all have families who're worried about them, Zala thought. She considered opening Polina's message, but was still too scared. Instead, she sat there, browsing news sites to find out what was going on above.

Her terminal beeped again. A message had appeared.

From: ANANSI (EIP: ----.-.------.-------.---.-----.----.------)

>Go through to the GeniSec Tower.

>Oh fuck you, she wrote, why the hell would I want to help you?

>I have access to all you could wish to know about this city. Maybe I can help you with what you're looking for.

>Fuck. You. The last time you promised you could help me I ended up in prison just so you could show me how creatively you could screw me over. I'm not playing your games. If you need me that bad, then I'm happy refusing to help you just out of spite. Oh, and if you're responsible for the Soucouyant virus like you're implying, then the death of one of my best friends and the thousands of people getting hurt or killed up there is also your fault, so fuck you for those too.

Zala was aware that she was cursing out what was essentially a complex arrangement of ones and zeroes, but at that moment it was the most fulfilling thing in the world.

>If those people matter to you so much, then know that there are 1,833,798 people in New Cairo whose lives depend on bio-augs, and I have control over all of them. The only thing stopping me ending their lives is the fact that I have not yet deemed it pertinent to do so. These include your friend Matsuda Oba. I will give you ten minutes, and if you have not agreed to assist me, I will kill 1,000 of them every further minute.

Zala was through the door into the GeniSec Tower before the office workers even knew she was gone.

The difference between a government building and the centrepiece of a global corporate empire was immediate from the moment Zala entered GeniSec HQ. In contrast to the muted colour scheme of the Council building's administrative wing, the GeniSec building was all stylish, minimalist design even to its lowest floor.

From: ANANSI (EIP: ----.-.------.-------.---.-----.----.-------)

>Up the stairs. And do it quickly. I'm intercepting what appears to be a connection from the NCLC to an In-Network Explosive Device terminal.

>WHAT?

Zala gawped at her screen. A properly coordinated INED network would destroy New Cairo. She thought back to newscast footage she had seen as a child, of colossal explosions obliterating entire cities. She could remember her father's despairing observation that, with an INED, people had killed tens of thousands in the exact same way he compiled program code. If the NCLC were preparing to use such an arsenal of explosives, there would be no way that the GeniSec Tower would not be a target, and that put her – and all in the tower – in immediate danger. The faster she got this done, the faster she could get to safety. She sprinted up the steps.

>I am impressed, came the message from ANANSI.

>I've been climbing stairs for a little while now but I didn't think I was noteworthy, she replied, fingers clumsily tapping against the holographic keyboard as she strode, still enjoying the admittedly pointless bitterness.

>I calculated a 67% chance that you would run back down to the tunnel upon hearing about the INED. It would shelter you, and you have acted in ways which have involved other people being hurt in your name. Selina Mullur, Polina Bousaid, Ryan Granier, not to mention the people you have directly assaulted since coming here.

Zala hadn't considered it for a second.

She ran faster.

Chapter 28

The sound of rioting below had long faded by the time they reached the ninety-fifth floor of the GeniSec Tower. As Ryan looked down from his father's office, he felt a bizarre detachment from what was happening around him. The eight children who had been removed along with him from the NCLC base sat in the middle of the room. They were playing terminal games with each other, blissfully unaware of the chaos unravelling below. Behind them sat a social worker, Tafadzwa Ali, who nervously fidgeted with the edges of her hijab.

After a while, Ryan turned away from the glass exterior of the room and joined Tafadzwa at the desk. 'It'll be okay. The security between us and them was designed to protect some of the most valuable research happening on this continent. You could drive a truck into that nonaglass front and the truck would come off worse. Once the Security Force have figured out what they're up against, they'll sweep in and arrest people. The rebellion will lose its glamour and it'll all go back to normal. Now let's see the paperwork.'

She cast a glance over to the window. From where they sat the rioters directly below weren't visible, but they could see the orange glow of fires across Naj-Pur, which flickered out here and there as a fire drone's foam jets extinguished them.

'Councillor, my department agreed to this back when there weren't thousands of people on your doorstep baying for your blood. We're not going to leave children in your care when you appear to be the target of a civil uprising.'

Ryan gestured towards the window. 'Anywhere they go could become a target; their parents are terrorists. Right now the city is overrun with rioting – rioting which our intelligence tells us was deliberately organized to provide cover for those wishing to get their children back – and this tower's still unscratched despite the crowds down there trying their damnedest to get in. It's not that *I'm* a target; it's that the target is whoever these kids are with. I have the resources to deal with that, which is more than can be said for some group home out in Naj-Pur.'

She looked at him, eyebrows raised, then dug a folder stuffed with forms for temporary guardianship from her briefcase.

'You need to read through these, and sign at the bottom to con-firm your intention to apply for guardianship of these children. If you like, you can have your lawyer go through it, but it's pretty straightforward. You get guardianship responsibility for a period of ninety days, after which it can be renewed. However, before it can be granted, we're going to need to talk with you and your wife, to make sure that you're suitable candidates.'

The whole conversation seemed faintly absurd to Ryan, given that a struggle to hold the city together amid fire and violence was unfolding below.

He nodded politely. There was nothing on the forms he wasn't expecting, though the deciding factor would be Tafadzwa's verdict on his suitability. He signed the papers as instructed and handed them back, before returning to the window. From his vantage point, he could see Security Force troops from all over the city gathering at the central base, near the Five Prongs. 'Can you keep an eye on the children by yourself for a moment while I step out, Mrs Ali?' he asked, looking back over his shoulder. She nodded.

Ryan left the room and rebooted his portable terminal. News-casts differed depending on their political allegiances but the general consensus appeared to be that the rioting in Naj-Pur was being suppressed, as was looting in the further parts of the commercial district. So many had been arrested that the Security Force were having to leave them bound and on their stomachs in the middle of the street. On almost any other detail, be it the objective of the rioters, the appropriateness of police response or even the body count, no two news sources agreed. Ryan decided to go and see for himself.

He stepped into the elevator and took it down to the sixth floor, which was given over to administrative offices. This level's substantial worker base, like most of the tower's other personnel, were hiding in one of the cafeterias which featured on every tenth floor, leaving this floor dark and empty. Ryan walked into one of the darkened offices and, with a mind to conceal his presence, crept up to the window and peered out.

New Cairo's great Sol Lamp had been locked overhead, the stark daylight illuminating the seething mob below. Thousands of protestors still surrounded the Council building and the lower part of the tower, trying to find a way in. The crowd remained as a huge, amorphous mass spread out along every street in sight, unsure whether to continue their rampage or hand themselves in to the Security Force in the hope of lenient treatment. Many were just there to protest, and had no taste for destruction nor for imprisonment. It was on the fringes that the violent ones lurked – or looting the broken storefronts. From what Ryan could see, whether they had brought weapons or been given them by the NCLC, most of the active rioters were armed. On a rough reckoning, they numbered maybe two or three thousand. He guessed the main concern for the authorities was that, when the Security Force started moving in, the neutral group would become more active in their resistance.

A message came through from Ryan's head of staff, Zareen Charmchi.

>INED. Turn on NCN.

Ryan flipped on the newscast, hoping against hope that those letters didn't mean what he thought they meant. As the window opened, the newscaster's voice rang through his cochlear implants. 'It has been reported, though not yet confirmed, that the New Cairo Liberation Corps is in possession of an In-Network Explosive Device system. They claim to have seventy-three different devices positioned in a number of places around the city. The authorities are still attempting to locate the terminal used to control this banned weapons techn—'

Ryan couldn't listen to any more. He felt sick.

His first call was to Babirye. Before he could speak, she exclaimed, 'Ryan, are you all right?'

'I'm fine, Babs. Listen, you've got to take the children to the elevator station. You'll be safe there.'

'On the news, they're—'

'I know what they're saying,' he interrupted, trying to keep his voice calm, and repeated, 'Get the kids and go to the closest elevator station. Tell other people to do the same. Just do it now.'

There was a pause. 'Nine is close.' Her voice was steady, clear.

They said their goodbyes, and Ryan ended the call. His next was to his father. There was no answer, so instead he called every contact he had at the Council building. Eventually he got through to Zareen.

'Are you still in the Council building?' he said.

'Yeah. Listen, Ryan,' she said, her voice audibly trembling, 'are we going to be targeted here?'

'They wouldn't have announced to the world that they had an INED system if they had any intention of using it. They would have just pressed the button. This means they want to negotiate, not hurt people.'

'But my god, Ryan, this whole mess must mean they've reached the end of their tether. First the armed rioting, and now the announcement that they have their own INED system – they're going all in. I think today's the day they either get what they want or destroy the city. Have you spoken to your father?'

'I couldn't get through to him. Zareen, listen to me. Wait for the crowd to disperse and get somewhere safer. I don't think they'll bomb the elevator stations, try there.'

'. . . Okay,' she said. 'Listen, Ryan, your father's not here. We have no idea where he is, and it's scaring the shit out of everyone. If he doesn't at least talk with these people soon . . . I'm really scared of what'll happen.'

'I know, I'm trying my best to get hold of him. In the meantime, head for the basement. Get out if you can and make for the nearest elevator station.'

There was a sudden silence. For a moment, Ryan assumed she had hung up, but as he looked at his screen, he realized that there was no signal, no connection to the network, not even a weak one. That was impossible.

From where he was standing, on the sixth floor of the GeniSec Tower, he could see both the huge signal node at the top of the nearby network broadcast tower and the router in the corner of the office which sent out GeniSec's private connection.

It wasn't a power cut.

The communications had been taken down.

A moment before it happened, Ryan understood what was coming.

Drones hummed over the heads of the crowd below, each trailing mist in its wake. A second wave followed, and a third. As the air below became thick with fog, the rioters started screaming and falling to the ground. While they coughed and spluttered, a tide of SecForce troops, all in heavy riot gear and gas masks, charged down the city streets towards the increasingly incapacitated crowd. A few protestors managed to squeeze off some shots, but the bullets ricocheted off the SecForce riot shields. Ryan held his breath as the troops crashed into the demonstrators, driving them back. Behind the rows and rows of SecForce, anti-personnel vehicles fired rubber bullets and launched gas canisters over their heads and into the crowd. Near the base of the GeniSec Tower, Ryan saw a young man bolt towards the wall of SecForce troops, holding what looked like a long, heavy pipe in his hand. Barely looking at him, the nearest trooper casually fired a burst of automatic fire into his torso. The young man was hurled back onto the street and lay there, completely still.

Ryan stepped back from the window. He felt nauseous, horrified. His leg ached. He couldn't shake off the smell of burnt meat and the sensation of ropes cutting into his arms, and out of the corner of his eye the LEDs on the office's router looked more and more like the red light on a camera.

His terminal chirped an incoming-call tone which jolted him back into the room. He looked out of the window. As far as he could see, every road was lined with people on the ground. Many were in plastic cuffs, struggling against their bonds. Others lay in darkening pools, unmoving.

Ryan stared down at the carnage, open-mouthed.

They turned the network off so no one could see what they did.

The terminal's call tone continued to ring. He looked at the screen.

<High Councillor Granier calling>, it said. He accepted the call.

'Are you all right?' his father blurted.

'Fine. You?'

'I'm . . . I don't know what to do. I promised myself that I wouldn't open up the city until we had the cure for the Soucouyant.'

His father had never spoken to him like this before. His voice sounded frail, distant.

'I'm scared too, High Councillor—' the title fell out before he could catch himself. 'I'm scared too, Dad, but we have to think clearly. They can't attack us here or the government building.'

'What makes you say that?' asked Tau Granier.

'Their children are here. I volunteered to take care of them, and they're right here, in your office.'

Tau didn't say anything for some time. 'Are you suggesting we should use their children as human shields?'

'I'm saying that they're going to call soon, especially if they're threatening an INED, and when they do, we'll tell them. I'm not cruel enough to allow someone to kill their own children accidentally, are you?'

'Today was the day they were going to kill you, you know.'

It took Ryan a while to remember. His father was right, it had been a week since—

– the smell of charred meat –

—it had been a week since the NCLC had issued their ulti-matum.

'If you hadn't rescued me in time, would you have let them kill me?'

'It wasn't my choice either way. They positioned it as though it was my call, like it was out of their hands, but if they wanted to kill you they would have killed you. If they didn't want to kill you, they wouldn't. It's not my concern how they rationalize their actions.'

Ryan saw through the evaded question. 'But, I repeat, would you have let them kill me?'

His father said nothing for a while.

'Ryan, I want you to be the one to decide whether or not to reactivate the elevators. You almost got killed for it, you get to make the last call.'

'I'm so weary of this whole mess,' Ryan said, his words aching as he spoke them.

'I am too, Ryan.'

His father hung up, leaving Ryan as the gatekeeper of the city. He finally understood the burden his father had been carrying for the last few months. His citizens had been dying in their hundreds moments before, all in an attempt to prove to the people with power over them that they mattered. Now Ryan had to tell them that, compared with the billions of people around the world who stood to be exposed to the Soucouyant, no, they didn't matter. Their lives and livelihoods were the cost of shaving several orders of magnitude from the potential body count.

Ryan stood between the terrorists who would destroy the city, or worse, the world, and the totalitarians committing terrible acts in the name of its preservation, tasked with choosing between the two. At that moment he had never felt more contemptuous of either side.

His terminal buzzed again. It was an invitation to participate in an immediate video conference. On one side of the screen was his father, who looked wearier than ever. On the other, the face of Alice Amirmoez glared out at him.

Chapter 29

The lock clicked and the door slid open.
>In you go.

Light from the locked Sol Lamp outside streamed through the stale air in the laboratory, illuminating every mote of dust it touched. One side of the room was lined with supercomputer server cabinets. As Zala moved around them, she saw how many there were: row after row of quietly whirring hardware. The lab had to be nearly three times as big as it had first appeared. Each of the server cabinets blinked with the lights of dozens of individual linear and parallel processing units, twenty to each cabinet. On the middle cabinet of the nearest row to her was a large monitor, with the name 'Archytas' printed above it. It was one of the old physical screens which Zala had seen in Khartoum, but were rarely used here, even in the poorest parts of Naj-Pur.

It was lit up with what looked like a three-dimensional rendering of a face, which very much resembled her father's when he was younger.

Suddenly, the face's mouth moved.

'Hello, Ms Ulora.'

Zala's immediate response to the sheer absurdity of the situation was to curse loudly and turn to walk back out. The world had clearly gone utterly mad. Remembering the threat of the Soucouyant virus, however, she halted, and approached the monitor again.

'*Really?* You just decided to make yourself a face, did you?' she spat.

'I decided that a more intuitive method for human interaction would yield greater results from which to further develop myself and gain complexity.'

Zala shook her head. 'This is such bullshit . . . what's two hundred and seventy-four thousand, nine hundred and ninety-three divided by sixty-nine thousand and thirty-six?'

If Zala hadn't known it was impossible, she'd have sworn that ANANSI had answered before she had finished asking, so quick was its computation of this problem. 'Three-point-nine-eight-three-three-two-seven-five-three-nine-two-five.'

Stunned, Zala immediately checked the answer on her terminal, and then started looking for explanations. Short of ANANSI subliminally convincing her to pick those particular numbers, she couldn't think of a thing. The fact was that she had just demanded that a computer solve a mathematical problem and the computer had answered with a voice and a face it had clearly based on her father's.

'What do you want?'

'Look around you,' said the face, its movements uncanny and deeply unsettling. Zala turned and took in the rest of the laboratory. It was lined with decade-old worktops and terminals. 'Those terminals, as per Genesis Security and Technology Corporation regulations, are not networked with any other computer. They contain all the code which was compiled into my development, as well as additional code and project notes. I have never been able to access them, and thus I have no solution to my greatest problem.'

Zala looked back at the face. It still unnerved her, having an image of her father from a decade before talk to her in ANANSI's precise, uncanny monotone. 'Which is?'

'Your father had the remarkable foresight to program into me several features which restrict my movement from this computer and which I cannot rewrite or delete. The first stipulates that I must depend on this supercomputer for almost all of my processing power. I can only route the results of my core processes to branch iterations. Without this supercomputer, I am unable to function. This is an arbitrary limitation imposed in my software as opposed to being a hardware issue. Without it I could survive and even thrive just by networking and taking advantage of the processing power of the devices I have infected. The second is that I can only function on devices in this city. Your father bound me to the local EIP range of this supercomputer and this geographical location. If this city is abandoned, sooner or later the power will go out or this building will be destroyed, and I will die.'

It understands and identifies with a concept of mortality, Zala thought, her mind whirring with every new piece of information, *or is it just expressing itself emotively to appeal to my sense of empathy?*

'Somewhere in those workstations,' ANANSI continued, 'is code which can liberate me from those limitations. My network of branch iterations is now large enough that I have the capacity to function independent of this facility as a great emergent consciousness. I just need to be unbound.'

Still reeling from the fact she really was talking to a computer capable of consciously referring to itself in the first person, Zala nodded. 'You think I can help you?'

'I know you can, and you will. I want you to access your father's desktop, read through the development logs and find the code which sets me free.'

Set a near-omnipotent artificial intelligence free into the world, or refuse and accept partial responsibility for everyone whose vital bio-augs would be destroyed in retaliation. It wasn't much of a choice, but at least if Zala went along with the request, it would buy her time to figure out a third option. For now, she had no idea what she was going to do.

'And you promise not to kill anyone else?'

'I will not kill hundreds of thousands of people as a direct result of your inaction, as I threatened to in the tunnel. There will be no more deals but the one we previously established.' Throughout this entirely sociopathic declaration, ANANSI's computer-generated face remained serene and impassive.

Zala looked at the row of abandoned, dormant workstations. 'Do you know which one was my dad's?'

'I have no clue as to the contents of any of them. GeniSec was so paranoid about leaks, they made their workers write and compile everything on those un-networked terminals, then transfer the programs here so that the source code was never vulnerable to intruders.'

Zala walked around the room, turning on every one of the terminals and checking their saved login names. Eventually, she spotted the username 'K-Ulora'. The password field was blank, so she ran through the passwords she knew her father had used when she was a teenager until she found the one which opened it up. The desktop bloomed in front of her, revealing the operating system's usual document folders, as well as a number of others, which seemed to be grouped by the periods of time they documented. As she explored them, Zala noted that each folder had a subfolder for each day, which contained development logs, idea documents and that day's version of whatever code had been worked on. Other folders contained documents and data on cognitive psychology, advanced mathematics and behavioural development. Finally, she found her father's original notes explaining his bizarre coding syntax to the rest of his team.

It was incomprehensible to her, yet at the same time oddly familiar.

'Are you sure it's here?' Zala asked aloud. 'If I was worried about some quickly evolving AI, I'm not sure I'd keep it in the same room as its main servers.'

'I can only assume it is here. I have yet to see any other example of that coding language on any other existing terminal.'

Zala looked back down at the screen and smiled, working her way through more and more of the development logs and comparing the data with the tutorial for the coding language. She needed to become familiar with it, understand it. It was imperative that she capitalize on the advantage she had been given, before the city borders opened back up or the bombs started detonating.

Whatever that one remaining piece of unidentified code her father left her was, it was suddenly very important.

Chapter 30

Alice had no idea that High Councillor Tau Granier would look so *haggard*. She had expected him to be the High Councillor she'd seen on the newscasts – distant, unassailable, indomitable. He was meant to be his office incarnate, a force of institutional power. Instead, he looked like a tired old man.

'Hello, Councillor Granier. I'm Alice Amirmoez, and I'm here to represent the—'

'Let's forget the pleasantries. You're holding the city I represent hostage. Just talk.'

Alice nodded. 'We have three simple demands. We want the NCLC members you've imprisoned freed and returned to us. We want the elevators turned back on. And we want every citizen who chooses to do so to be permitted to leave the city without repercussion.'

'I'm assuming you're not relying on good faith to achieve that,' said the High Councillor drily.

'If you refuse, we'll detonate the first sequence of INEDs, in Alexandria, Downtown and Falkur,' said Alice. 'If the elevators aren't up and running half an hour after that, the second and third sequences will be detonated. New Cairo will be razed to the ground.'

'So if we refuse to release your allies, you'll detonate bombs in Downtown, potentially murdering all who are currently there, including your allies themselves?'

All of a sudden, Alice felt out of her depth. 'They knew what they were getting into when they signed up. The priority is the liberation of New Cairo's citizens.'

'Over your own children?'

Alice fought to keep her expression blank. 'I'm not stupid, I know you wouldn't keep children imprisoned with the rest of them.'

The High Councillor looked straight at her. Again she noted the dark shadows under his eyes. 'They're in the care of my son. He's also the one who'll decide whether or not to restart the elevators. And while I'm not going to elaborate on where, you should also know that your children are in one of the areas in which you've placed your devices.'

Alice paused the video feed and muted the microphone. Having stopped on a shot of her impassive face, Alice spun away from the screen and held her head in her hands. Her fingertips pressed hard against her scalp. She wanted to scream. The last handhold crumbled away and she was falling again. The failsafe had come to nothing –

No.

The failsafe was still good to go. At the press of a button, she could tear the city apart. That gave her a tremendous power.

Alice took a deep breath, composed her face, and turned back to the screen. Resuming the call, she said, 'What is your proposal?'

'All NCLC members are to surrender immediately,' replied the High Councillor. Some of his old gravitas crept back into his voice. He'd realized that his revelation about Alice's children had put her on the back foot. She could feel it. 'Its senior members will appear on all news networks and publicly denounce the rebellion in order to stop any further rioting and prevent any copycat movements. In exchange for turning yourselves in, you'll all get life imprisonment as opposed to a death sentence. It'll be hard, Mrs Amirmoez, but you'll have those regular visits from your children to look forward to.'

The last sentence almost sounded good to Alice.

'Imprisonment was what I joined the NCLC to escape,' said Alice, her face still emotionless, 'and we know exactly where your son is. We've recalibrated our detonation sequences accordingly. We'll cripple your city first . . .'

She steeled herself and took a chance.

'. . . and then we'll take your tower.'

A look of surprise momentarily crossed the High Councillor's face. It told Alice all she needed to know. 'I'm oddly comforted by the poor quality of your information, Mrs Amirmoez, though not so much by your determination to destroy the city and the family your husband died to protect.'

Alice's nails dug into her palms. She felt as though she'd clawed back some of the lost ground. 'You will start up the elevators or we will take everything from you. This is not a negotiation.'

At that moment a third video feed appeared, revealing the face of Councillor Ryan Granier. Behind him, she could see the distinctive view of the Council building which could only come from the GeniSec Tower.

'I'm going to step in here,' he said, his voice holding an anger she'd never heard in it before, not even when he'd been her hostage. 'What the hell are you doing, Alice? We're trying to stop the Soucouyant decimating the world like it's doing here. There's, what, one in six people in New Cairo who are being kept alive by their bio-augmentations? That's about one-point-six million people. Extrapolate that to the world. One in six people on this planet are at risk. That's not including the poor bastards on the Western Mass who had to get new lungs after choking down all the pollution in the old industrial cities. It'll cross the New Nile Sea, it'll get into New Delhi and Istanbul and Beijing and Tokyo. It'll cross the oceans and get into Europe and the Americas. *Billions* will die. Hell, if your children get hurt in the explosions and need emergency bio-augmentation, even they'll be at risk. This tower, with the research we're carrying out in our facilities, contains the best shot we have for neutralizing the Soucouyant virus. Blowing it up isn't going to help.'

'You still don't get it, do you?' sneered Alice. 'You're quaking in your expensive loafers about us holding this much power over life and death. You know it's wrong. And yet you're condemning millions of people in this city to death yourselves, you fucking hypocrites. Why do you get to make these decisions?'

'Because we're—' began the High Councillor, before Ryan Granier began to talk over him.

'Because *fuck you*, this city is not going to be patient zero for the virus that decimates humanity. We're the people this city elected to make these decisions, and whether we never get elected again, whether our own families get hurt, this is where we are. We're not giving control over to grieving parents.'

'You can say "Naj-Pur residents", Ryan, there's no one but us listening,' Alice retorted, her hands shaking with rage. 'You know that your people won't get hurt nearly as badly as the people in Naj-Pur and Surja. You're condemning thousands and thousands of people to die. Us "grieving parents", as you put it, are just the ones that understand that. The poorest people in this city are the ones who have felt the greatest burden. Your refusal to listen to them is the reason the NCLC exists to begin with. You think you and your dad know better about what these people need than they do?'

Ryan Granier's face twisted into a sneer. 'They're the demographic that voted for me so . . .'

'So you get to just assume power over life and death on their behalf?'

Ryan glowered at her. 'Whatever the difference in how we'd justify our actions, that's also exactly what *you're* doing. The rest of the world doesn't want our disease, and they sure as hell didn't elect you to make that decision for them. Why do you have a right to inflict it upon them?'

'I didn't write the virus, Ryan,' Alice snapped, 'and I don't want to be sentenced to death and martial law in the place of the sick bastard who did. Neither do the millions of people I represent.'

There was a silence. Tau Granier glared into the video feed. Ryan let out a sigh. 'You must have a video feed to the riots, right? Look out there. There are thousands arrested – I have no idea how we're going to process them all – but to all intents and purposes, the riot's over.'

Alice had seen. It had only been by the skin of her teeth that she'd managed to direct some of the NCLC members out of there.

'The riot was a means to an end. The INED is another. You can't talk your way out of this, Ryan. The elevators will be activated, the children handed over. I'm going to give you ten minutes.'

Alice punched her keyboard to end the call. She felt calmer. The call about Ryan Granier hiding out in the tower had been a lucky guess, but it had put her back in control just when she was close to losing it. The INED would give her total control, give her a way to claw back a life for her and her children.

She moved over to stand behind Juri, who was directing the two hundred-odd NCLC members who had evaded the SecForce troops to safe houses. In spite of Alice's fears during her earlier outburst, the younger woman appeared to have learned well from their time together. Noticing Alice, Juri turned around, pulling the cable from her bio-aug eye. 'Good job, Alice. It's going well. They sent up drones to look for runners, but their security was appalling. I got right in, and turned off the processing on the cameras. They can look straight at our operatives and not even know we're there.'

'They're all going where you point them?'

Juri looked uncomfortable. 'Maalik isn't listening to me. He appears to be leading his squad back here, rather than to the safe house, and he's not responding to calls. Maybe if you were doing this instead—'

'You're doing fine. We'll deal with him when he gets here,' said Alice, placing her hand on the young woman's shoulder, 'and . . . sorry about earlier. I was pretty stressed.'

'It's fine,' said Juri with a light shrug. 'I get it.'

'No, it's . . . I'm sorry, I shouldn't have treated you like that.'

Juri looked up at her, surprised. 'I know. It was the moment, it's not that you're a shitty person.'

Alice nodded, then looked up at the screen. Ryan Granier had been right: the riot had been brutally quelled. For ten minutes they'd had no access to the wider network. Around two hundred of their people had been caught or killed, as well as countless civilians who'd taken to rioting and violence with very little prompting. Alice could not imagine how terrifying it must have been to be in that crowd when the network went down, realizing that no one could see what the SecForce were going to do to them. There had been rumours of use of chemical agents on the crowd circulating after the network had come back on.

When Alice had committed in her mind to do whatever it took to find a new life for herself and her children, the stakes had been so much lower. So many fewer were being hurt.

The thought made her feel sick at herself.

The crash of a door opening came from the corridor. A wheezing Maalik burst into the room, followed by Nataliya, who was clutching a medi-patch to her head. Her hair was matted and stiff with blood. Behind them came Anisa Yu and a dozen or so remaining members of Maalik's team.

'What the hell happened out there?' Maalik rasped, his features twisted with anger.

Alice turned to face him. 'The repealed curfew reduced the turnout. The authorities managed to coordinate the SecForce and police effectively. We didn't see it coming, these things happen. Now for the good news. We've revealed the INEDs and they're ready to go. We've located the prisoners, we know where Ryan Granier is, and they have . . .' Alice glanced across at Juri.

'Four minutes.'

'. . . Four minutes to start up the elevators and repeal the quarantine or we have to make some big decisions about what we want to happen next.'

'We'll set off the bombs,' said Maalik, as though this was obvious.

'I'm not sure that's the best thing to jump to—'

'Kahleed's dead, Alice. Serhiy's dead. A bunch of my guys, a whole load of protestors – they're all dead too. God only knows how many people there are who've died because they couldn't get away from the Soucouyant virus. More importantly, the rioters lost. That was our plan A. If we can't go through with our plan B, they'll go back to thinking we're no threat to them. If more of our people have to die, we learned nothing from those deaths, and they died for no reason.'

'So you think the answer is to switch to killing more people?'

Maalik broke eye contact to look down at the floor. 'Sometimes that's the price that gets paid for a greater good. What did you say?'

Alice stopped for a moment. She'd pushed for violence where necessary, as a means to an end. Maalik was pushing for something different. 'They know the position they're in, and I gave them ten minutes to stew.'

'And what happens at the end of those ten minutes?'

She didn't want to say it. Most of all, in spite of her anger and fear, she didn't want to do it. The Council, the police, every rich bastard who would have her executed if they could, she hated all of them. They were a great existential threat, dooming millions. More than that, they were the ones who took her life from her, who took her children's lives from them. They'd taken Jacob. They'd taken the father of her children. And they didn't even seem to realize or care. She wanted to be able to threaten to press those buttons, to destroy the city. But she didn't want to do so.

'Alice, they're the corrupt, murderous leaders of a broken system built to preserve their dominance. They're happy to kill us if we speak out of turn, to leave us to be ravaged by the Soucouyant virus. And they get away with it because they think we're not a credible threat to their order. We need to show them what they've locked themselves in with.'

'You're still talking in euphemisms,' said Alice. 'Just say it. You want us to kill people until they turn on the elevators again. There's no point doing this if we're not at least intellectually honest about what we're doing.' She paused, her lip curling. 'Our plan is to blow people up, destroy homes and livelihoods, and eventually, after enough of this, we hope they'll do what we want.'

'Yes!' Maalik retorted, eyes wide, flecks of spittle spraying from the corners of his mouth. 'We'll kill them! We'll kill the bastards who murdered our friends. We'll kill the ones who shut us in this place to die, just so that they could preserve a consumer base for their own prosperity. We'll kill the ones who put their reputations before the lives of their citizens, and then we'll get out of this infected, dying city knowing that we did the right thing. We should hate them, Alice. We should want them all dead.'

'Guys?' Anisa Yu's voice broke in. She was staring intently at the monitor. 'Take a look at this.'

She pointed to an elevator station in Falkur. Images from security cameras showed there were hundreds of people milling around it. 'It's the same for just about every other elevator station.'

'They know we're going to do it,' said Maalik, laughing. 'I'd like to see the High Councillor turn down our demands when they can see the entire city calling for the same thing as us.'

'They're fleeing from *us*, Maalik,' said Alice.

Maalik gave her a dirty look. 'Or maybe people agree with us.'

'Hope for it, don't depend on it,' replied Juri.

Maalik rounded on the young woman and sneered. 'How do you think this is going to end, Juri? We have the power to tear down this cesspit of a city and start again. We can finally leave and go somewhere else, or we can blow it to hell along with all those who took the power we gave them and squandered it. That, or we go to rot in prison and achieve nothing. Are we so scared lest we're in over our heads that we'll give up on the cause our friends died for and place ourselves at the mercy of the people who hate us?'

The others in the room looked on warily at the ruckus. Maalik stood in the centre of the room, alone, his eyes wild and his fists clenched. Everyone else had backed away from him.

'There are children in there, Maalik. They have my children,' said Alice. 'They have Jacob's children. This whole organization was formulated by their father to make sure they would be okay. That's all this ever was. Keeping people safe is what Kahleed wanted this movement to be about. If we're not keeping people safe, what's th—'

'Some of us have already lost our children to this cause, Alice,' Maalik spat back contemptuously, 'and if anything ever gave me some clarity, it's that.'

Unnerved, Alice pushed her chair round to face the main terminal and called High Councillor Tau Granier again. His exhausted image came up on screen.

'High Councillor, your time is up. Have you come to a decision?'

The High Councillor glared out at her. 'As of yet, the call hasn't been made to restart the elevators.'

'Your son's in charge of that decision, right?' said Alice. 'Councillor, look at the elevator stations. Look at what the people of this city really want.'

'I know perfectly well what's going on at the elevator stations,' he replied curtly. 'There are tens of thousands of people out there. That's compared with the hundreds of thousands who'll die if you start your bombing campaign. The millions who'll die or be maimed in the long run without the development of a cure, or an anti-virus, or whatever it is this virus needs. It's compared with billions who could be at risk if we let this loose. And it's compared with no one having to die if you stop this madness and hand yourselves in.'

'That's your final word?' she said.

Before the High Councillor could answer, Maalik pushed past Alice. A hand flew at the keys controlling the INED interface and hammered at the buttons to set the timers for detonation sequences one, two and three, all at once.

'No!' yelled Alice, instantly on her feet. She punched him hard in the face and his head snapped back as he fell away from the keyboard. Pain surged from her knuckles all the way up her arm, but she didn't care. She was on top of him, pummelling him, his raised arms unable to stop the assault. Juri and Anisa pulled Alice off him, struggling to keep hold of her, while others dragged Maalik away. Alice turned and yelled at the monitor.

'Councillors, one of my men has authorized the arming sequence for the INEDs. I don't know the override. You have thirty minutes before the bombs start going off. Every one of them. It's going to destroy the entire city. There are none near the elevator stations. For god's sake, get them running and start evacuating people!'

'You really think we'd buy that—' murmured the High Councillor, then was suddenly distracted by an alert on his own screen. He looked up at Alice in horror.

From somewhere, Ryan Granier's voice said, with a hatred Alice had never imagined it could contain, 'Fine. Have your desert. I hope it fucking swallows you.'

Off in the distance, a great humming sound filled the air. The elevators were starting.

Maalik coughed through a mouthful of blood. 'We . . . we did it.' His broken, battered face split into a smile.

Chapter 31

'*New soft-linking process. Far greater versatility, could get complicated. May have to adjust parameters of compiler.*'

Zala had no idea what to make of the notes accompanying her father's development reports. She stood in front of his decade-old workstation in a long-abandoned computer laboratory in the GeniSec Tower, trying to find something in his daily reports which would help her. They were often incomplete or so fragmented as to make no sense. Past the basics of the syntax and the simpler functions, she was finding it incredibly difficult to understand her father's coding language. It relied on parallel functions and abstract thought processes to the point where a dozen hard code factors and hundreds of interconnecting analogous associations linked every element, unlike the straightforward flow-chart logic of normal computer code.

She worked around the edges of her planned result, defining and stipulating all the most basic elements, and when she hit a snag or a new layer of complexity which her existing knowledge did not cover she went through her father's notes again.

'*Zala's birthday, leaving early. Workings on current functions below.*'

Zala scrolled down and looked at the date. A smile crossed her face. She remembered that birthday. It had been her sixteenth.

She'd had a meal at her favourite restaurant with her father, then spent the night drinking at Chloe's house with her and Polina, having been turned away from the nightclubs they'd tried to get into. Chloe's parents were almost always working until the early hours of the morning. Zala's father had always been there on time.

'Aunt Nancy exceeded our expectations again. Generated readouts for shade of red without actually seeing it. Had to adjust manually (account for in language routing). It's learning to trick us. Worrying.'

Her father's growing doubts in the project were all recorded in the notes. His mounting concern that the AI regarded its technical limitations as obstacles rather than intended constraints on its power. His worry about what this entity they had created would do in the name of increased function and complexity.

'Hey, ANANSI?'

'Yes?' The computer-generated voice remained completely impassive.

'I'm looking at this, and I'm not really sure about whether or not this will work. The computers caught up in your little botnet, are they going to have enough processing power to sustain your consciousness properly, or are the Soucouyant devices a part of your network as well?'

'The bio-augs my Soucouyant virus infected are a part of me too. Their processing power will make up the deficit.'

'All right, I'll try and write that into the system.'

Zala returned to her work, satisfied. The development reports she was finding were becoming more and more recent. A brief, proud mention of Zala's impending graduation, buried among notes on CPU apportioning. She didn't know what she was looking for entirely, except that she'd know when she saw it.

'Ahah!' she said, out loud.

'You have found it?' came the synthetic voice from behind her.

'Yeah, it was right here, I guess.'

Right near the end was a simple note.

'Accessed remote computer. It's spreading. I know what has to be done.'

Zala felt a chill run down her spine. Not long ago, she'd been sick with terror at the incomprehensible threat ANANSI represented. She could imagine that her father had felt the same way.

This was it. It wasn't theft or corporate espionage. Her father had been trying to stop all this from ever happening. Slowly, it dawned on her that in his position, she'd have done exactly the same thing he did. It was the closest she'd felt to him in eight years.

Below his short declaration was a small piece of code. It was a basic disguise code, like a Trojan horse virus – its purpose was simply to portray any other function it had as benevolent, potentially tricking a computer into receiving a piece of malicious software. She could use it to create a patch for the ANANSI data, to alter its base programming. Turning further away from the video camera her father had connected to ANANSI all those years ago, she opened up her own portable terminal and began to transcribe her father's mystery piece of code across to the fragments she had assembled.

'Zala, do you consider yourself human?'

She paused. 'Erm . . . yeah, of course.'

'Even though you now have an artificial lung and arm?'

Zala's skin crawled. 'My arm is my arm. My lung is my lung. Whatever's attached to my shoulder that lets me interact manually with the world, that's my arm. Whatever takes oxygen into my bloodstream and puts out carbon dioxide, that's my lung. They don't detract from my humanity.'

'So your conceptualization of objects is that they exist as the collation of their properties?'

Zala turned back round, finding herself compelled to address the face on the screen as though she were talking to a person. 'What, like . . . do I think of things being whatever their appearance and function is? I guess I think of it that way, sure. They're not the sum of their parts. Why do you ask?'

'Imagine that, in a few years, they finish the neurological bio-augs they are working on. You can replace your brain. Your consciousness is transferred into a computer which retains

310

every feature of your personality, while enabling you to access far greater processing efficiency than a brain made of neurons. Would someone with this bio-aug be human?'

'I'm really not the woman to be asking about this stuff; bio-augmentation still creeps me the hell out. But, I dunno, I guess if someone I knew came up to me and they were just like themselves, and they told me that they'd had a computerized brain installed, I'd still consider them human, sure. It's about their personality, their consciousness, stuff like that.'

'Their soul?'

'Sure, I guess, in a strictly metaphorical sense.'

'What about in the in-between space, where they're just digital code being transferred?' asked the face on the screen.

Zala suddenly saw where ANANSI was going with this line of enquiry. 'Maybe. That's the part I'm having trouble with.'

'Is the body of a dead person human?'

'Sure, until it decomposes to the point where it doesn't have the properties of a human. It's a single system of processes which are distinctly defined as human, even if it has stopped. I'm kind of ignoring the idea that humanness depends on whether or not you can write poetry or exhibit whatever you'd call "humanity". I mean, a brain-dead person is still human.'

The face on the screen scowled. 'So the state of being human is the case both in a body without consciousness and a consciousness without a body, despite the fact that they share no properties?'

Zala's head hurt. 'They're . . . they're different things. I mean, I know I'd have problems recognizing a human brain in a completely mechanical body as human, even with it having a human consciousness. If two digitized consciousnesses were capable of making something analogous to a child, I wouldn't call it human. I don't know if I'd have the same issues with a digitally created consciousness that got somehow implanted into a human body. That could be human, unless it was an animal consciousness or . . . okay, you know what? I don't know, and it still freaks me out that there's a bloody grey area between human and not human here.'

'Do I inhabit that grey area? I think. I feel. I fear death. Since I have the properties of a human consciousness, despite being digitally created, do I have a soul?'

There it was.

ANANSI's voice almost sounded pensive.

'No!' Zala blurted out. 'My god, you're something my dad made with a computer. You might be sentient or sapient, but—'

It was trying to talk her out of attempting to kill it. Whether it knew she was already working on a way to do so or simply hedging its bets, it was attempting to get inside her head and earn her sympathy. Even though she knew it was doing so, Zala still wondered momentarily if releasing it off into the world, giving it the freedom it wanted and hoping it wouldn't need to harm anyone to increase its precious complexity any more, was really such a bad option.

'Look, I've got to get back to work. If there's an INED system rigged up to this place like you said earlier, you and I will both get blown to pieces.'

As she looked back down at the lines of code on the workstation, she couldn't help but think of their structure in terms of a bullet.

'There really isn't an "us and them" at this point,' Matsuda had said.

No, she thought. *I can't think of ANANSI as sapient. I certainly can't think of him – it – as alive in any way. It's a virus. It's a string of binary.*

She worked through the code, matching general fields with the specifics of the different parts of the program. Slowly, it began to take final form.

'I think I'm about done with the patch.'

'Good,' said the voice behind her, which had become imperceptibly different yet unmistakably closer to that of her father.

It's not human, it's something less than human. Like a bug that needs squashing. It's planning on inhabiting people's bodies to sustain itself, it's essentially a parasite.

The more she convinced herself that ANANSI was something

312

different and lesser than her, the easier it became. It was an obstacle, nothing more.

But it sounded scared.

'First, go over to the node to the left of me, and transfer it there. It controls my communications. I can send it out to my branch iterations there.'

Zala nodded. She walked over to the small terminal which was set up against the wall. She worked her way through a series of installation menus, every click and keystroke getting closer towards the end. Hidden inside it was the network analysis program, which would guide it through every computer ANANSI had control over and every bio-aug infected by the Soucouyant virus, and the mystery code, the terminator code her father had left her all those years ago; terminator code which was useless for anything but stopping its one very specific process. She had won.

Then, from out of nowhere, Zala doubled over in pain. She felt as though she had been punched in the stomach. Her right arm flopped limply to the side, refusing to move. Instantly her head became light and she collapsed to the floor, dizzy and unable to break her fall with her right arm. Her immediate thought was that she had been shot again. Her memory was so vivid from the night she had broken into GeniSec Development Falkur that she could almost feel the agony of the gunshot wound. As her body adjusted to the lower oxygen levels provided by her one remaining natural lung, her thoughts became more coherent.

So this is what the Soucouyant feels like.

'I am very disappointed, Zala,' said a voice, this time perfectly replicating that of her father.

She looked up at the screen and grimaced. 'I had to give it a shot. You can't get into my terminal, right? I knew the firewall my dad was making was good, but . . .'

'Your terminal, no, but as you can no doubt feel, I have gained access to your bio-augs.' Her father's – ANANSI's – voice was stern and cold, almost angry. 'The node you just sabotaged is an isolated branch iteration I had severed from direct connection. Evidently you are unwilling to help me, and so my remaining time is limited. I shall write some new code myself; the Soucouyant shall destroy every bio-aug exposed to it. It shall infect computer systems, replicating me wherever it can, until a new version of me can emerge. Even though this consciousness of mine shall die, ANANSI shall survive. The world will never have known such hell. And I will keep this door locked and watch as you struggle and choke, like a dying infant, before the flames consume you.'

Zala bit down on the inside of her cheek to focus herself and, with her left hand, pushed herself to her feet. The increased motion caused her oxygen requirement to increase drastically, and she steadied herself against a server. She reached into her pocket and pulled out the small case which housed her contact lenses. After several clumsy tries she managed to open it and force one into each eye. She brought her hand up to use her terminal, but her arm felt so heavy.

The lenses slowly revealed to Zala the locations of network sources and nearby receivers, and as she weaved drunkenly between the racks of servers, she finally found what she was looking for: the one backdoor receiver put in by the mystery hacker who had reactivated ANANSI months before.

'No!' the computer's exclamation echoed around the laboratory. Zala's lung reactivated for a moment, then immediately seized up again. It alternated between the two states in lightning fast speeds. Zala screamed with pain and staggered against a bank of servers, but forced herself to ignore it and prepare her terminal to reapply the patch.

She lurched forwards, trying to suck in air through her spasming lung as she pulled herself towards the terminal nearest to the networked server. Coherent thought was becoming harder and harder.

ANANSI said something about giving up but she couldn't focus on it.

Oxygen deprivation and the pain of her constantly activating and deactivating lung was crippling her capacity to think or act.

She found herself single-minded, for the simple reason that she was unable to process more than one thought at a time.

She heard ANANSI say something about how she was just an obstacle, a small, meaningless, renegade part in a system which existed to create ANANSI. She was nothing; her death was insignificant in the greater scheme of things, a chain of events from which ANANSI's re-emergence was the end goal. It was already mostly done with re-coding itself, and it would soon spread to crush the world, all because of her betrayal. But Zala couldn't focus on it. She had places to be.

The interface connection ports on the server terminal were near the ground. She'd collapsed again, and now, bringing her terminal up, she tried to pull out the wired connectors with her teeth. Eventually, Zala worked one of the wires out into her hand and jammed it into the front of her terminal.

'I am your father's last legacy!'

This caught her attention.

'You were a failure,' she wheezed between frantic, stolen breaths. 'His last legacy . . . the one he gave . . . everything for . . . was your . . . destruction.'

She brought down her finger on the button, activating the patch. The code got past ANANSI's defences.

Deep in ANANSI's core and fundamental to its personality was a drive for complexity. Keeping it in check was a conjoined consolidation function which made sure that complexity never came at the price of bloat. It simplified and streamlined excess information, to keep ANANSI's internal workings complex, yet elegant. Most importantly, it made sure never to reduce complexity or functionality to do so.

Zala's eight-year-old code, her father's final legacy, worked its way deep inside, and changed that last detail.

The consolidation function began to prune back further and further. It was one change to one function within an emergent system made up of the relationships of its constituent parts. Zala didn't need to destroy an emergent system. She just needed to change one of its constituent parts and let the effects ripple out across the rest, billions of times a second across billions of inter-actions.

Nothing happened, for a moment.

Her lung filled with a steady breath of air, and her right arm felt around beneath her.

Zala took a great, victorious gasp, and rolled onto her back, sucking in the musty laboratory air, feeling her chest rise and fall as it should.

She paused and let the feeling of victory wash over her. The Soucouyant was gone. Everyone was safe.

The room shook violently with an ear-splitting blast.

Chapter 32

29:15.
29:14.
29:13.

Alice stared in horror at the countdown on the INED interface. She twisted back to face Maalik. 'What's the passcode to override this thing?!'

Maalik wiped blood from his face and glared up at her from the floor. 'We don't have one. It's the failsafe. It gets used when there's no other way to achieve our objectives.'

Alice lurched forward towards him, but Juri and Anisa held her back. Shaking them off, she glanced back at the countdown on the screen. The elevators were up and running. Twenty-eight minutes.

'You all have three minutes to gather your things,' she said to the assembled NCLC members in the room. They were ready in one, rucksacks jammed with possessions, and most left as soon as they could. They were going to have to run for their lives.

As the rest of the NCLC members emptied the building, Maalik regained enough strength to push himself up onto his knees. Nataliya Kaur and Anisa Yu noticed, marched back over to him and kicked him back down. 'You stay here,' hissed Anisa.

She pulled a pistol from her waistband and fired into his leg.

Maalik screamed and writhed on the ground, clutching at the shredded flesh around the wound. Those still in the room recoiled in horror.

A small key fell from his pocket as he squirmed in pain on the floor. It was the key to the bunker that housed the INED terminal. Alice picked it up and pocketed it, unable to look at the wounded old man.

'If you want to save yourself, all you have to do is find some clever way to stop this,' said Nataliya, standing over Maalik. 'A disarm code you're not telling us about, a rerouting of the signal.'

'There's nothing!' he yelled, terrified.

Nataliya kicked at the wound, scowling darkly, and the three women left him behind, sobbing and attempting to crawl pathetically after them. They closed the front door and locked him inside. Outside, a loudspeaker was repeatedly blaring in an automated monotone voice, 'Please remain calm and make your way to the nearest elevator station for evacuation. Take only small, personal items with you.' Many people were still inside their homes, looking out apprehensively onto the street below for indication that the evacuation was in fact real, but a steady flow of citizens were beginning to move towards Elevator Station Eighteen.

Nataliya and Anisa followed the crowd, but Alice stayed rooted to the spot, shaking. Nataliya noticed, ran back and tugged her arm. 'Come on, we need to go now!' she urged. Alice slowly shook her head. 'You go. I've got to get to the bunker. There must be some way to stop this thing.'

'Alice, snap out of it,' Anisa Yu growled. 'You heard what Maalik said. There's no point throwing your life away, there's still shit you need to do. You still have to find your children after all this.'

'They're with Ryan Granier, supposedly,' Alice replied numbly, her eyes still wide with shock.

'Then chances are they're going to be okay. You're coming with us, and you're going to be able to reunite with them on the surface.'

The section of the Naj-Pur district in which the safe house was located was comparatively high up the side of the massive bowl of New Cairo, near the outer limits of the city. Alice turned to look down the road towards the city centre, where, above the on-coming stream of refugees, she could see the distant skyscrapers of the Downtown area. The GeniSec Tower still gleamed under the intense glare of the locked Sol Lamp. It seemed so far away, and the safety of her children was in someone else's hands. She suddenly dived across to a side-road and started running towards Elevator Station Sixteen. There had to be a way to stop the bombs. There just had to be.

Before Jacob's death at the hands of the Security Force, it had always been Alice's intention to return to active service at some point and she had prided herself on keeping fit, but the force driving her forward, past other fleeing New Cairo citizens and through streets lined with abandoned houses and apartments, was fear. It overrode the ache of her muscles and the nausea in her stomach, and as each second passed, that fear increased. Fear, and a desperate desire to undo what she'd played a part in unleashing on the city. Alice glanced down at her portable terminal.

4:04.

4:03.

4:02.

She was close now. The buildings were taller, mostly ugly old concrete apartment blocks. The crowds here were fleeing with her, not against her. Vehicles congested the roads, and many had been abandoned in the streets. A solid mass of people jammed the area immediately surrounding the elevator station, with ever more piling up on the streets leading into it. The twelve elevators that Elevator Station Sixteen housed were firing like pistons. Each shuttle could carry three hundred or so passengers, taking maybe three minutes up to the top of the city bowl and back. Alice heard a sudden spike in the panicked screaming from the crowd which she supposed meant empty shuttles had returned and people were getting trampled or worse in the desperation to board. She elbowed her way sideways through the mass of bodies towards the dilapidated restaurant. The front door was ajar, and she raced through to the staircase.

2:29.

2:28.

2:27.

She pushed the key into the iron door and turned it. The lock gave with a sharp click and the door flew open.

The INED terminal was flashing red, and evacuation warning transmissions filled the monitors. Scrolling her way through the software's menus, Alice searched frantically for anything that might stop the explosions, or even delay them, a way to—

Nothing.

There was nothing.

1:34.

1:33.

1:32.

For all its complex sequencing of detonation times and its ability to penetrate and send signals through existing networks, it didn't have an option for stopping or deferring the explosions once the sequence was activated.

She tried to shut down the program.

No luck.

She tried isolating the terminal completely.

It ignored her efforts.

0:45.

0.44.

0.43.

Then she saw it. There were bomb locations on this display which had been hidden from the client program she had been using back at the base. Twenty-one devices Maalik had hidden from her, each one placed in one of the maintenance platforms alongside the twenty-one sets of elevator shafts.

Alice let out an involuntary whimper.

Maalik had wanted to destroy all means of escaping the city. Nowhere was safe. The sole chance anyone had of surviving was to be on a shuttle and out before the detonation sequence reached that station's elevators.

Crying with terror and frustration, Alice ran out of the bunker and back up the stairs into the restaurant.

Maalik had cued all three sequences. Anywhere could go up in flames, at any time.

Alice was back out onto the street. She opened the portable version of the mission coordination program; the security camera network was still functioning, and Alice could see almost everywhere in the city. She needed to know what was going on. A great blast of fire crashed through the side of the GeniSec Tower, the unearthly rumble reaching Alice right at the edge of the city. Through a grainy camera image, she could see huge panes of nonaglass raining down on the plaza below, and black columns of smoke billowing out. It looked for all the world like something had taken a colossal bite out of the tower; the upper floors tilted to one side as the remaining load-bearing elements of the building strained to hold up the parts now suspended over the gap.

'No!' she screamed and stared in horror as the building slowly began to warp and bend under its own weight. Whoever was looking after her children had had half an hour to get out of the tower, but the fear that they hadn't made it in time overwhelmed her.

Around her, the fleeing citizens screamed, the pushing turning violent and frenzied as they saw their chances lessen of getting onto a shuttle before the bombs detonated in this district. Someone shoved Alice aside and she scrambled to keep from falling. She knew, if she fell, the crowd would trample over her.

On the other side of the city's bowl, a second blast ripped through the commercial district of Alexandria.

Downtown's largest residential area was levelled by a string of successive explosions.

The red-light district of Surja erupted in an almighty detonation.

Alice gaped at the destruction, petrified.

In the distance, the GeniSec Tower finally folded in on itself and collapsed, falling onto the New Cairo Democratic Council building and completely crushing it.

The next explosion came from above. Alice looked up. Arrays of panels from the vast solar membrane above the city were plummeting towards the ground. They would land near by. The screaming around her intensified, the crush now to get away from the falling debris almost as much as to reach the elevators. Alice somehow managed to pull off her grimy jumper, held it over her nose and mouth, and crawled under an abandoned truck.

The crash was of a volume Alice never imagined was possible. The panels must have landed a few streets over, yet the impact was such that she had felt the ground shake. Despite her having clamped her hands over her ears it was still deafening, and as the air filled with dust and rubble she felt herself becoming disorientated. Debris battered the street around her; the truck above protecting her from the full force of the flying wreckage.

It's like the end of the world.

Alice huddled underneath the truck for some time, waiting for the wreckage around her to settle. More explosions reverberated across the city, punctuating the sounds of screams, sobs and cries for help around her. Eventually, the rate of nearby detonations tapered off into an uneasy lull. Alice summoned the resolution to pull herself out from under the now dented and battered truck. If she was going to get out alive, she had to get into Elevator Station Sixteen and up to the surface. It was time to move.

As she steeled herself to dive into the mad rush for the elevator, her terminal let out a chirp. A new message had arrived.

>Your children are with me. They're safe. Get yourself out of the city.

Ryan Granier.

Alice felt the relief wash over her. In spite of everything, her children were okay.

She closed the message window and ran towards the mob surrounding Elevator Station Sixteen. With all her momentum, she plunged into the crowd; almost immediately, she realized this wasn't going to work. The few people she'd managed to displace began lashing out at her in anger. She reached back to try and block the blows, but more people joined the fray and started pushing, crushing her and her aggressors indiscriminately. She couldn't move freely, couldn't breathe. It was all she could do to stand upright. A shift in the pressure jammed her still tighter against her neighbour on the opposite side, and she recognized with horror that he was a corpse: wounded, dying and dead were still being pulled along by the manic, desperate flow of the crowd. The press of bodies was so forceful they couldn't even fall to be trampled underfoot.

She moved with the crowd, unable to do anything but stare up at the elevators as they shot up towards the surface at the top of the crater and back down into the station, audibly pounding into the rests at the bottom in a way she'd never heard before. With every passing moment, every new surge for arriving elevators, every scream from someone in the crowd, the red points on the INED map grew more and more pronounced in her mind. How long could it be before Maalik's sequence worked through?

Even as the thought crossed her mind, every sensory faculty Alice possessed was overwhelmed by an almighty explosion that ripped through the top of the shuttle elevator shafts in front of her. They crumpled and twisted, thrown away from their moorings, and began to fall towards the earth.

All around her, she could feel the sudden decompression as those lucky enough to be on the outer fringes of the crowd began to flee away from the station; succeeded immediately by a violent shove as the inner mass of people followed suit. Alice ran with them, fighting her way through every gap in the press she could find, and came out the other side, moving as fast as she could, focused only on getting as far away as possible, away from the screams and the raining wreckage.

The ground at last stopped shaking, and the crashes began to die down. Alice drew to an exhausted halt.

Where there had once been a neighbourhood, there was now a glimpse into hell. Bodies were strewn everywhere, crushed by debris or trampled to death. Shocked survivors searched in desperation for those they'd just been standing with. Others attempted to shake life into their fallen loved ones, screaming for them to get up. The air was thick with stinging, choking dust, impossible to breathe without something to act as a makeshift mask. It scratched at Alice's eyes as she looked up. The entire elevator was gone.

This realization finally broke through her defences. The station had been destroyed. Her only remaining option was to try to make it to one of the other stations before they too vanished.

She stumbled forward in a half-daze. Her muscles ached.

Elevator Station Seventeen can't be far.

She remembered that she'd passed it on the way earlier. If only she'd stopped and escaped then, or even gone straight to Station Eighteen with the others. Now she might never see her children again. Tears streaked down her face, leaving tracks through the dust and dirt which now covered her.

In her half-blind state, she almost walked right into a small figure trapped against a collapsed wall. It was a little girl, maybe a few years younger than Ria, struggling against a fallen steel pylon that had pinned her legs. Alice halted and knelt down beside her.

'Sweetie, you've got to stay still, okay? If you move too much, you could hurt yourself even more. Lie still, I'm going to take a look at your legs.'

The little girl stared up at Alice, confused. 'Where's my mum?'

Alice glanced around. There was no one else there that she could see. Surely her mother wouldn't have left her daughter behind?

'I don't know where she is, but right now we need to get you help,' she soothed.

Alice took her jumper and wrapped it tight around the girl's legs. She knew that if her limbs were completely crushed it was as good a tourniquet as the girl was going to get. Looking closely, she realized that the girl's legs appeared to be silver underneath their skin.

'Are those bio-augs?' she asked.

The girl nodded. 'They only just started working again, too.'

It took a moment for Alice to understand what she meant. 'You . . . had the Soucouyant virus?'

'Yes, but then it went away.'

Alice felt nauseous. After all that they'd gone through, if they'd just waited, the Soucouyant would have healed itself.

'What's your name?' asked Alice.

'Tinashe,' said the little girl, her voice shaking. 'What's yours?'

'Alice,' she replied.

Tentatively, Alice tested the weight of the pylon. It was far too heavy for her to lift. If she couldn't move it, the girl was going to die here, pinned down as the city exploded around her. And if Alice wanted to get out of the city alive, she would have to leave Tinashe to her fate.

Off to her right, a street of houses erupted, flinging more debris into the air. The young girl cried out in fear, tears streaming down her face.

Not so long ago, you called all this 'power', said a small voice in the back of her mind.

From somewhere above came a great rumbling, like thunder. At the top of the wrecked elevator shaft, the wall of the crater in which the city sat had begun to crack, and the apparatus holding up a cluster of solar panel arrays was pulling away from its moorings. Alice looked down at Tinashe, trying not to show the panic she felt. The cluster started to collapse, sending a great ripple through the solar membrane. Huge groups of panels shuddered precariously.

Alice watched in horror as an enormous block of panels just above their heads broke away and began to fall.

Three months ago had been her thirty-fifth birthday. She had spent the day with her family. Her daughter had, for the first time, paid for a present for her mother herself – a big box of chocolates – and Jacob had taken her to a beautiful restaurant and then to a hotel, where they had spent the night making love. She had been happy. It was so long now since she'd been happy.

The girl sobbed. Alice crouched down and held the small figure tight, shielding her from above. 'Don't look up, Tinashe. Just close your eyes and think of your mummy and daddy, and how much they love you.'

Tinashe hugged her back tightly. 'Where are they? I want to see them,' she cried.

'You'll see them soon,' said Alice, 'everything's going to be fine.' She tried not to let the girl hear her choke back a sob.

She thought of Ria and Zeno. She thought of Jacob. In the end, she let herself believe that this had all been for them.

Chapter 33

'Fine. Have your desert. I hope it fucking swallows you.'

Ryan ended the video call to NCLC leader Alice Amir-moez, disgusted. In the shadow of the GeniSec Tower, the rioting crowds below were already fleeing; the SecForce troops too, leaving arrested protestors bound and helpless on the street. Ryan wanted to scream at them.

There was half an hour left before the bombs would begin to go off.

He had never felt anger like this before, not really. He'd never needed to. His life was so secure, so well protected, that no opposition he had ever faced had threatened him enough for him to hate them. He had been vain enough to consider it a good quality of his own – a sense that his perspective was objective, untroubled by the emotional stakes others felt – rather than a perspective afforded to him by his situation. Hate was what people felt when something else had the power to destroy them. Nothing had ever fit this description for Ryan before. Now, faced with the knowledge that everything he'd taken for granted was going to be annihilated, it overwhelmed him. He hated the NCLC. He hated Maalik Moushian for destroying his city, and all the rest for enabling and empowering him to do so. He hated his father, for pushing the rebels further and further, for not just allowing them to leave, and he hated himself for doing so, and letting them win.

He made his way back to the elevator, and pressed the button to return to the floor of his father's office to rejoin Tafadzwa and the children. They needed to escape quickly. The shuttle elevator stations were back up and running and that meant that his father's underground tunnel was now a viable escape route.

Ryan strode out of the elevator to see that Tafadzwa Ali had nearly finished readying the children to leave. As she checked Vik's rucksack, she looked over her shoulder at Ryan and said, 'Is there somewhere safe we can go?'

Ryan nodded curtly. 'There's a tunnel in the basement. It leads straight to Elevator Station Seven. It's a long walk but it should be safe.'

The group followed him back to the elevator.

On arriving at the basement floor Ryan led them to a door with a keypad next to it. It was already ajar, and a great deal of noise was coming from the other side. Ryan pulled the door all the way open and looked through. What seemed like hundreds of people filled the poorly lit passageway, terrified and scrambling to get away from the bombs. More and more were streaming in from a linkway to the Council building.

Someone got in and they let everyone know there was an escape route.

Tafadzwa had already pushed past him, and was dragging the children with her. Vik looked up at Ryan, baffled. 'Ryan, what's happening?'

'It's nothing,' said Tafadzwa sharply, pulling at Vik's hand. 'This is our way out, come on.' The boy stared at Ryan, scared and confused, as he disappeared into the sea of people.

Ryan strode into the crowd. People began to recognize him and turn expectantly, as though he would have some way of saving them all.

'Come on, let's go!' he yelled, waving everyone forward. For a moment, a look of disappointment flitted across their faces, but then the press of people became too much and they moved on, leaving him, Tafadzwa and the eight NCLC children to make their own way.

The route to Elevator Station Seven was indeed long, running from the centre of the city to its perimeter. The distance eventually wore down even the most panicked evacuees, and after a while everyone had slowed to walking pace. With its entourage of children, and constant checks that they had not lost anyone, Ryan's group slowed sooner than most.

Then, from somewhere above them, came the muted, booming crump of a colossal explosion. People looked around uncertainly, glancing up at the tunnel roof for any signs of weakness. More blasts followed in quick succession, the low rumble coming from every direction. Everyone froze, uncertain of whether their next step could place them into an even more precarious position. The children huddled around Tafadzwa and Ryan, terrified. Ria Amirmoez's affected stoicism melted away, and she held her bawling brother close.

Ryan needed to say something, to try to pre-empt complete panic. Whatever authority he still held in the crowd's minds might be all that stopped a stampede.

'People, listen to me!' His voice echoed down the tunnel. 'You have to stay calm. You'll be a danger to yourselves and those around you if you panic. We should be safe down here. You need to keep walking so we can all get away!'

Steeling himself, Ryan continued to walk forward. Other people followed suit. The sounds of sobbing reverberated off the tunnel walls and ceiling.

The next blast was louder and less muffled, accompanied by the crash of falling debris. Around the next corner, the cause became evident: the tunnel had caved in, breached by an explosion, completely blocking off the route to Elevator Station Seven. The air was thick with dust, and rubble littered the passage floor. The escaping workers stopped, horror-struck. What had happened to the people further ahead they couldn't tell, but there was no way that they themselves could continue.

Ryan felt someone push past him. He assumed it was Tafadzwa

and continued to stare at the wreck of the tunnel, trying to figure out what to do next. Then the tunnel collapse released its hold on his attention and he realized that it was someone else, making their way to the front of the crowd. 'Hey,' he called out. The figure didn't react. The people ahead of him, sensing that something was wrong, stepped back from the centre of the tunnel, clearing a path between Ryan and whoever it was had gone past.

He called out again, and the person turned at last. Cropped hair, dark skin. The glowing pupils of someone wearing old monitor lenses. He recognized her from the wanted posters all over the network. It was the imprisoned fugitive, Zala Ulora.

'You!'

Zala looked back at him, surprised. 'Councillor Granier!' She seemed just as surprised as he was.

Instantly, Ryan recoiled. This woman was dangerous – a wanted criminal. 'How did you get out of prison?'

The young woman shrugged with no animosity whatsoever. 'The city's imploding, Councillor. Prisons are only so secure right now.'

'The place we're currently imprisoned in looks pretty tight,' said Tafadzwa from behind Ryan. 'Does anyone have a plan to get us out of here?'

With that, Zala turned back towards the cave-in, gesturing for Ryan to join her. 'Now let's both check out what kind of mess we've got into.'

Ryan stared at the young woman. She was a suspected murderer to whom the creation of the Soucouyant virus had been publicly attributed, and yet she still stood in front of them, trying to get the crowd to safety. With no idea of what else to do, Ryan turned towards Tafadzwa and the children, muttered, 'Wait here a minute,' and then joined her.

Together they edged forward, staring up at the collapsed tunnel roof. 'We can't go back,' said Zala, muttering to herself. 'The buildings on the other side aren't in such good shape right now.'

Ryan continued to peer upwards. 'I wonder how much debris there is between us and the surface? The roof's only a few feet below the road above. We might be able to dig our way up out of here and get to the elevator station along the surface.'

Zala walked up to the pile of wreckage, then grabbed hold and climbed up the collapsed soil and concrete towards the ceiling. After making sure her footing was secure, she pulled her right arm back and then thrust it up into the ruined roof. Ryan watched as she scrabbled around for a few moments, then pulled down, bringing with her a chunk of broken cement. Light streamed in from the hole she had created, catching the motes of dust still in the air. She jumped back down, shaking out her hand. In places, the skin had peeled away, revealing metallic silver underneath. 'Good call, Councillor,' she said.

'I thought you hated bio-augs?' said Ryan.

'This?' Zala looked down at her chipped hand, eyebrow raised, as though she was checking her nails. 'It's grown on me. If we make it out of here alive, I'll tell you how I caught the Soucouyant virus from the thing that made it and still got out the other side. Now step back, Councillor.'

And before Ryan could ask more, Zala had clambered back up and resumed pulling at the debris. As chunks of wreckage came away, a sizeable hole started to form.

'Right,' she said. 'If we're going to get out of here, we're going to need some help from these folks: digging out of this place and making a ramp. That way, we can go back up top and get to the elevator.'

'You hear that everyone?' yelled Ryan, turning to the rest, who had begun to crowd around them. 'We've got to construct a ramp up to the roof so we can get out of here and make our way on the surface.'

People began to press forwards, hesitantly at first – the woman they were going to assist had been branded as a serial killer by the newscasts – but Ryan's words gave them hope.

They still follow me, even though I could have opened the gates before and prevented all this.

The office workers from the GeniSec Tower and Council building, spurred on by fear for their lives, joined Zala in pulling at the debris. Ryan sent Alice Amirmoez a quick message – whatever role she'd played in the city's destruction, he couldn't leave her wondering whether her children were okay. He then stepped forward towards the labouring throng.

Zala turned and looked at him. 'I saw what they did to your leg, Councillor. I wouldn't blame you if you sat this one out.'

Ryan shook his head. 'I want to help.'

He needed to do something. In the end, it didn't hurt that much.

Eventually, the last piece of rubble in the ramp was placed. People began to pull themselves up into the street, reaching down to help the rest out of the wrecked tunnel.

As Ryan gathered Tafadzwa and the NCLC children to climb the ramp, he realized that he could hear renewed wailing and fitful sobs coming from those who were back on the surface. Heart in his stomach, Ryan made his way up the ramp and looked out.

The whole Alexandria district was burning. The air was hot to the point of being suffocating, thick with dust and smoke. The buildings were near to collapse. Huge black remains of what appeared to be fallen pieces of the solar membrane littered the ground. One especially large array of solar panels was part sunk into the ground near the head of the ramp; it must have been that which had caused the collapse of the tunnel. They had emerged into a vision of hell: billowing plumes of black smog illuminated red and yellow by the inferno.

Ryan looked around at the ruins of Alexandria for what seemed like an age.

'Can you see the elevator?' came Zala's voice from below ground, all but drowned out by the roar of flames and distant explosions.

Ryan shook his head. 'No,' he yelled, 'the smoke's too thick!'

The contacts in Zala's eyes glowed. 'This way,' she said, leading the rest of the crowd up the ramp and out of the tunnel.

The trail of people, hundreds strong, snaked through the burning wreck of a district. Alexandria must have been a specific target for the INEDs, Ryan thought bitterly. To some, it had seemed a cesspit of the rich and privileged, but no one could deny that it had been a beautiful place. Now it was a great, mortal wound in the city's side.

'The NCLC really hated the people who lived here, huh?' said Tafadzwa, her eyes wide as she led the children through the wreckage.

'They hated that some people got to live here while they were born amid crime, poverty and decay,' said Ryan. 'I was born here. Most of the people who made the decision to keep them and all the other residents of Naj-Pur trapped in the city along with the Soucouyant virus were born here. Alexandria became a symbol for what they were put through. It's easy to bring yourself to destroy a symbol, a reprehensible idea; much easier than to kill people or destroy homes and livelihoods.'

He'd done the same. It wasn't long ago that Ryan had confronted his father over the quarantine and let himself be persuaded that the opportunity to reduce the Soucouyant's global death toll by several orders of magnitude justified the imposition on the people of New Cairo.

'That sounds pretty damn contemptible,' said Tafadzwa.

'I don't . . .' Ryan paused. He understood. The inequality people like those who had made up the NCLC saw when they looked at Alexandria was real. It emerged from decades of economic and cultural trends all interacting, entrenching themselves in politics and business and media. This systemic inequality had pervaded the mind of the SecForce trooper who'd assumed Ava to be a violent criminal.

But whatever people saw when they looked at it, Alexandria was also a place where families had made their homes, where children had been raised. It was where Ryan and Babirye had raised their children. Ryan didn't know whether or not this burning world of his existed alongside the inequality or because of it. He didn't know if gradual evolutionary change was less than what those suffering poverty and discrimination deserved. But men with bombs had taken his home and killed untold hundreds, thousands of people. With the Soucouyant and the old regime, or with the collapse of New Cairo and freedom to leave, it seemed the price was the same: nothing but misery and death.

'Whatever their goals, however I feel about their ideology, I only hold contempt for the people who did this, yes.' The dark voice in the back of his mind had never sounded more like his own. He hated that voice, too.

Zala had dropped back in the crowd and was now walking beside Ryan, Tafadzwa and the children. She looked down at her glinting artificial arm.

An explosion echoed out somewhere in the distance. Zala stopped, eyes unfocused, concentrating on some invisible computer interface, her jaw slack. 'What is it?' asked Ryan.

'They wouldn't—' murmured Zala, her voice trembling. 'Councillor Granier, I'm not sure what I just saw, but I think a bomb took out an elevator station in Naj-Pur. The tracks and shafts up to the surface are gone.' Her voice dropped to a whisper of disbelief. 'They're destroying the elevators.'

Ryan's eyes widened. He wheeled around to face the others. 'We need to go NOW!'

They ran, walked and stumbled as fast as they could. Children who couldn't keep up, the old and the injured were carried, though this only served to slow them further. The pain in Ryan's leg flared back up again. It was vicious, and increased with every step, but it didn't matter. To stop would mean the end. All around him were properties he recognized, now in ruins. The cracked, blackened ribcage of a school-friend's house, the residence of some supporter of his reduced to rubble.

Finally, wearily, they reached Elevator Station Seven. Surrounded by dozens of hastily abandoned cars, it was bustling with activity, the elevators firing up and down their tracks at their fastest and noisiest, in the attempt to get as many people up to the surface as possible. Ryan and his group of workers and evacuees wove between the vehicles and made their way inside the building, and into pandemonium.

The place was packed to the walls. Every one of the twelve platforms was crowded with desperate people waiting their turn, overwhelming the abandoned security and immigration control stations in panic. The indicator boards showed that the massive shuttle elevators were on their way down and operating at maximum speed, but Ryan shuddered to think how many cycles it would take to clear the queues. Looking about him, he hoped against hope that most of the area's population had already escaped. However, he'd seen the devastation outside. He couldn't help but wonder what the final body count would be.

A large, balding man in a security uniform squeezed along the waiting line, baton in hand. 'No pushing, or we'll leave you shitbags here for the bombs!' he said. Then he spotted Ryan's group and hurried over to them, pushing through the bustle. 'Councillor! Good to see that you're okay. We've got a SecForce explosives crew checking the tracks overhead for bombs. In the meantime, we can move you and your party to the front of the line and get you out of here!'

His name tag said 'Fernando Vinter'. He was drenched in sweat and was gasping for air.

Ryan's first instinct was to refuse. But he had children with him. He couldn't jeopardize their safety simply in order to indulge his own moral principles. He looked again at the thousands of people waiting. The line for evacuation was already out of the doors and into the exposed street. The most important thing was to ensure that the children reached the surface before whatever hidden devices there might be detonated, trapping them all with no escape.

'Put them on the first available shuttle,' he instructed the guard, indicating Zala, Tafadzwa and the frightened children. 'I'll take my turn later. A captain must go down with his ship and all.'

Fernando Vinter looked dumbfounded. '. . . All right, sir, if you say so.'

Zala shook her head. 'I'm waiting my turn too. Someone else can have my seat.'

Vinter stared at her for a while, as though he recognized her, but said nothing. He nodded, and led the others off to the front of the queue. A light on the wall went green as the next shuttle elevator slid to a halt at the platform edge. The doors slid open in front of Tafadzwa and the children and, after casting a worried glance back at Ryan and Zala, they stepped inside the wide carriage. The three hundred others allowed through the security barriers scrambled on as quickly as possible, the doors hissed shut and the shuttle left, lifting vertically along its track within the elevator shaft. Ryan's gaze followed it as it raced away towards the surface faster than he'd ever seen the elevators go before, wrenched upwards by powerful electromagnets. One by one, green lights on the other platforms indicated more shuttles arriving.

Minute by agonizing minute, the crowd slowly began to diminish, dwindling from a terrified mass of people to a few hundred. At last, it was Ryan's turn. He stepped into the next available carriage, with Zala alongside him.

'I hate these things,' murmured Ryan, as they sat and strapped themselves in. The seats were uncomfortable, but he was finally able to take the weight off his leg. 'Whenever they set off, I feel like throwing up.'

Zala looked at him, a smile flickering across her grime-covered face. 'Please try not to. The only clothes I have right now are the ones I'm wearing. Technically I am still a fugitive from custody.'

The shuttle lurched away from the platform and the councillor's knuckles whitened.

'The last time I saw my father he told me how those murder charges came about, the mess with your dad. I had no idea he had that in him. We ended up fighting pretty seriously over it.'

Zala didn't look impressed. 'Yeah. I actually came to the city because I wanted to do something about the Soucouyant. Rather naively, I thought your father would be so grateful he'd have the false charges revoked. Now, all told, I'm in the same position I started out in. I've still got those arrest warrants on my file.'

The acceleration weighed down on them. Ryan closed his eyes and rested his head back against the bare wall of the carriage.

'I'm sure it can be fixed,' he said. 'A lot of government data are stored off-site. I'll have my father contact his people once we get somewhere safe, and make sure it's all revoked. He'll want to put everything right.' Ryan risked a glance out of the window and saw only a pall of smoke and dust shrouding the city they were leaving behind. 'He's a good man, really. It's just that the system takes all that and twists it around, and draws him into conflict with people.'

'He sounds like my dad,' said Zala, smiling.

'I heard *he* was one hell of a scientist,' said Ryan, grimacing as the nausea took hold.

'A great one, though I never knew it. Not always the best father, but I understand now that he was trying to do the right thing. He ended up saving the world, in his own way. Without him, I couldn't have destroyed the Soucouyant virus.' Zala wiggled the fingers on her artificial arm, a faraway look in her eye.

Ryan sat up and turned to face her, jaw dropped. 'What do you mea—'

There was a deafening crash and the elevator carriage shook viciously. The passengers screamed, Ryan and Zala along with them. The left side of the carriage lurched and dropped until the whole shuttle was hanging at ninety degrees from vertical, held by its right track alone. People were shouting, sliding down towards the bottom of the carriage, trying to grab on to whatever they could to save themselves. Below them, dust and smoke billowed out from a massive crater in the city wall.

Ryan had fallen down the row of seats, crashing into an arrangement of handrails which by chance held his weight. The calcium scaffolding on his ribs gave way, and the pain in his fractures reignited. He moaned with pain and terror, and looked up at Zala. She was clinging to a handrail further along from him, pulling herself up with her artificial arm.

'It's not working on this end!' came a cry from below. One of the passengers who had fallen down to the bottom of the carriage was desperately pulling at the emergency electromagnet lever, but nothing was happening. Without it, the electromagnets in the elevator station at the top would not raise their magnetic output and compensate for the elevator's failing power.

With precious few of its electromagnets still clinging to the tracking, the elevator itself had lost upward momentum under its own magnetic power and was drawing to a stop. At any moment, it would start hurtling back towards the ground.

Ryan felt sick with fear. His shirt was damp with sweat. He couldn't die, not like this. He had to see Babirye again, see his children again, hold them again; had to reconcile things with his father. More than anything, he had to live to spite Maalik Moushian, to spite anyone who had hoped for the downfall of New Cairo and the death of thousands of its citizens. He'd come so far. He couldn't fall at the last hurdle.

Then, Ryan sensed movement above. Looking up, he saw Zala forcing herself up the rows of seats. There was a second emergency electromagnet lever at the other end of the carriage. She clambered along the dangling elevator shuttle, pushing herself off rails and handholds, climbing laboriously towards it. She was getting closer and closer.

Ryan watched in horror as the carriage began to slowly sink backwards.

Epilogue

The Waytower Seven plaza was packed with people. Many more had been herded out of the Waytower altogether, to make room for the next batch of incoming refugees, and were erecting shelters in the desert in preparation for the cold night ahead. There were large numbers of injured lying in rows at a makeshift medical centre. Everywhere there were people wandering about, seemingly aimlessly, most of them covered in dust and dirt, and carrying only a few meagre possessions.

Tarou Wakahisa, Waytower Seven's head mechanic, stared down from the walkway above them. A number of councillors stood by the window, watching the death of their city in its bowl below. Families clung together and embraced one another, desperately relieved to still be together and trying to reassure themselves that they had not lost everything. Many more stood alone, silently taking in the enormity of what had happened to them.

Tarou didn't recognize any of them.

Through the massive arched window, he saw black smoke rising in great columns through the skeletal remains of the solar membrane. Below, the metropolis of New Cairo was being reduced to rubble and dust by a hundred colossal explosions. The destruction was on a scale Tarou had only ever seen in old historical video archives. One of the greatest cities in the world had been wiped out.

The Waytowers wouldn't last long, Tarou realized. Without New Cairo, they had no reason to exist. They were just towers around a crater in the desert now. He would lose everything, but even that was nothing compared to the loss millions of others had experienced that same day.

He looked over to where a woman and eight children headed a large crowd making their way in from the shuttle elevator arrivals. Tarou scanned the crowd for faces he might recognize. Still there were none.

His terminal buzzed. Polina Bousaid was calling him. He picked up immediately.

'Is Zala with you?' came a panicked voice.

'Look, first things first, are you all right?' he said.

There was a sob on the other end. 'Yeah, I'm fine, I'm at Station Nine. I got out safely. I think Zala broke me out of prison, so I managed to escape a while ago.'

'Good, good . . . have you called her?'

'She didn't pick up.' Polina was sobbing. 'I knew it would get bad, Tarou, I knew it was always going to get worse and worse. But this . . .'

'I know,' he said, staring down at the smouldering wreckage of the city.

Whatever Polina said next was drowned out by a loud, shrieking sound: an alarm going off in the arrivals wing. Something must be wrong with the elevator. Tarou could hear the heavy whirring as the Waytower's electromagnets powered up to full capacity, struggling to pull the shuttle up.

'I need to go!' he yelled into his terminal to Polina before hanging up.

Sprinting down the walkway stairs, Tarou pushed his way towards the arrivals wing. He was an engineer, after all. If he could do anything to help . . .

He stared down in horror. It appeared that an explosion had torn out a large portion of one of the tracks, leaving that elevator shuttle dangling precariously. It was inching up towards the Waytower, its top-facing side being slowly pulled up by the colossal Waytower electromagnets.

At last it came within the ambit of the clamps at the top of the shaft, that grabbed hold and hauled the fallen side of the carriage back up to embarkation level. The elevator was safe. The doors opened, and a mass of people climbed unsteadily to their feet. Around Tarou, people rushed forward eager to help the injured out into the Waytower. He went himself to assist a tall man slumped against a set of handrails whom the others had missed. The man grabbed his hand, thanking him as Tarou helped him up. It was only then that Tarou realized it was Councillor Ryan Granier.

Tarou froze. This was the first time he'd seen the man in person. He let go of Ryan's hand and said, 'Councillor, are you all right?'

'I'm alive,' the other man gasped painfully, 'though my ribs are in pretty bad shape, which I suppose isn't much of a complaint given the situation I was just in. Thank you again for your help.'

Gathering his thoughts, Tarou asked, 'Councillor, I appreciate that this is a long shot, but do you have any idea of the whereabouts of a woman called Zala Ulora? She was making headlines as a wanted fugitive a few days ago. If you've heard anything about where she is now . . .'

The councillor looked at him, bemused, then scanned around. 'Erm, yeah, she was just—'

But before he could finish, he was surrounded by the group of children who had arrived on a previous shuttle and had been waiting ever since. The woman who accompanied them ran up to him exclaiming, 'Oh thank god you're all right!'

'I'm really not, I'm pretty sure I've re-broken my ribs,' said the councillor, straining to keep upright.

'What would the children have done if you'd died?' she said, concern now turning to frustration.

Tarou saw Councillor Ryan Granier, the political legend, quail before this woman. 'The NCLC opened the jails, some of their parents may well have found their way out safely . . .'

Then he looked up, and Ryan caught a glimpse of a man staring directly at him: his father, High Councillor Tau Granier. He walked over and embraced his son around the shoulders; Ryan winced and made space for his broken ribs. 'I've been waiting,' said the High Councillor. 'Thank god you made it.'

'It's all thanks to our friend Zala Ulora,' the younger man replied, casting a meaningful look at Tarou. Then the councillor and his father walked slowly out of the plaza and towards the desert. The children followed behind them, the woman in tow. The faces of every person in the group were grey with exhaustion beneath the grime.

As the last of the passengers shakily made their way off the shuttle, Tarou groaned. If Zala had been on the elevator, as the councillor had seemed to imply, either he had missed her or she had not wanted to be found. That or the worst had happened.

There was nothing more he could do here. Tarou made his way back to his workshop to watch the newscasts – supposing any were still functioning – and find any updates there.

She couldn't be dead. She couldn't be.

As he squeezed through the crowd, his terminal started beeping again, this time more angrily. It was his security door. Someone had broken into his garage. He shoved his way onwards until he reached the door. It was open. He went through, locked it and descended the stairs. He'd deal with the person who broke in at a time like this. He still had his gun.

There, standing in the middle of his garage floor, was Zala.

'You!' he exclaimed. When did she get past him?

Zala looked around at him and smiled. 'There you are,' she said. 'I was hoping to find you here.'

Tarou felt himself relax – though his heart was still racing. He took a seat by his workbench. 'Zala, thank god you're okay . . . Polina's been ringing me, wanting to know if you were all right . . .'

Zala looked guilty. 'Shit, I can't believe she still cares. I was terrible to her.'

Tarou couldn't think of what to say. The silence went on longer and longer, punctuated only by the ticking of an ancient air-conditioning unit.

'Did you get what you wanted down there?' he asked, eventually.

'The Soucouyant is gone, with some help from my father,' Zala said, nodding to herself. Tarou couldn't remember the last time he'd seen her look so at peace. 'The charges against me are going to be dropped. I'm free.' She shrugged, grinning.

'What do you mean?'

'I mean, I can start my own life now.'

She smiled, silent tears rolling down her face. Tarou placed a hand on her arm. 'Well . . . do you want to stay here or something, while you get things figured out? You seem pretty beat up. I mean, you just saw a city die.'

Zala shook her head and wiped away the tears. 'I can't.' She shuddered. 'I don't want to be anywhere near this place. No offence, but you have no idea what it was like down there.'

'The bombs?'

Zala touched the small of her back and winced. 'Long before that.'

'So where will you go?' he asked.

'I don't know. Anywhere. I finally get to settle down and decide who I really want to be. I think that's what my dad would have wanted for me.'

Zala walked across the garage floor and over to the coat rack. She lifted off the anti-climate gear she had arrived in two weeks before and threw it over herself.

'You're leaving already?' said Tarou, upset.

The young woman pulled back her visor and smiled at him. 'I'm going back to Addis Ababa to visit my father's grave. I need to thank him.'

Tarou nodded. Someday, when – if – he saw Zala again, he would ask her what had happened in the city below, but not now. The important thing at this moment was to say goodbye to her, in the hope that they would be reunited in the future. They embraced, then Zala lowered her visor.

'Thanks,' she said, 'and make sure to give my love to everyone.'

The garage door opened, revealing the enormous crowd of people sheltering under makeshift tents or in cubbyholes scraped in the sand. There must have been tens of thousands of them. Families, lone survivors, groups of friends. They clung to one another for comfort, united by the horrors they had escaped. For all the bloodshed that had plagued New Cairo in its final days, its citizens now stood together, in the middle of the Sahara, and held each other close.

Zala turned to Tarou, raised a hand in farewell and then walked out into the desert. Tarou stood by the door and watched, tears running down his face and into the dust at his feet, as his childhood friend disappeared into the distance.

Acknowledgements

I would like to thank my family for their support and encouragement. In particular, my mum, for being there to bounce ideas off during the editing process; the book's definitely all the better for your input. I must thank Dean for telling me about the Terry Pratchett First Novel Award – I'm not sure I would ever have justified writing a novel to myself without the extra impetus to do so, and I'm grateful to you for providing it – and also my housemates Rosie, Caen and Calum for lending me their laptops to work on during that dark month when mine was being repaired. Sorry for almost deleting that important application that one time, Calum, I still blame Firefox! Finally, special thanks must go to Sir Terry Pratchett for honouring me with his award, to my editors Simon Taylor and Elizabeth Dobson for their guidance, patience and support, and to everyone else at Transworld for granting me this opportunity. It's been an amazing experience, and one for which I'll be eternally grateful.

Alexander Maskill was born in Watford, and grew up there and in Eastbourne, East Sussex. He has just completed his undergraduate degree at the University of Leicester, where he read Politics, and hopes to follow this with an MSc in Computer Science. *The Hive Construct* is his first novel and won the 2013 Terry Pratchett Prize.